Delores Fossen, a *USA TODAY* bestselling author, has written over one hundred novels, with millions of copies of her books in print worldwide. She's received a *Booksellers'* Best Award and an *RT Reviewers' Choice* Best Book Award. She was also a finalist for a prestigious *RITA®* Award. You can contact the author through her website at www.deloresfossen.com

Cindi Myers is the author of more than fifty novels. When she's not plotting new romance plots, she enjoys skiing, gardening, cooking, crafting and daydreaming. A lover of small-town life, she lives with her husband and two spoiled dogs in the Colorado mountains.

PURSUED BY THE SHERIFF

DELORES FOSSEN

DISAPPEARANCE AT DAKOTA RIDGE

CINDI MYERS

MILLS & BOON

First Published in Great Britain 2021
by Mills & Boon, an imprint of HarperCollins*Publishers* Ltd
1 London Bridge Street, London, SE1 9GF

www.harpercollins.co.uk

HarperCollins*Publishers*
1st Floor, Watermarque Building,
Ringsend Road, Dublin 4, Ireland

Pursued by the Sheriff © 2021 Delores Fossen
Disappearance at Dakota Ridge © 2021 Cynthia Myers

ISBN:978-0-263-28364-8

1221

MIX
Paper from
responsible sources
FSC™ C007454

This book is produced from independently certified FSC™ paper to ensure responsible forest management.

For more information visit: www.harpercollins.co.uk/green

Printed and Bound in Spain using 100% Renewable electricity at CPI Black Print, Barcelona

PURSUED BY THE SHERIFF

DELORES FOSSEN

Chapter One

A jab of lightning sliced through the night sky, and Sheriff Jace Castillo caught a glimpse of the man he was chasing—just as the bullet from the guy's semiautomatic slammed into Jace's left shoulder.

The pain was instant and raw. A searing jolt of fire knifed through him, but Jace managed to scramble into a cluster of trees.

It was too dark for Jace to see the wound, but it was already throbbing. And bleeding. He was losing way too much blood. He could feel the warmth of it spreading across the front of his shirt and his sleeve.

Jace looked out into the curtain of rain, the fat drops dripping off the low-hanging tree branch that he was using for cover. He couldn't see the man who'd just shot him, but Jace knew he was still there. Detective Gideon Martell likely wouldn't just walk away from this. Or turn himself in.

Because Gideon was a dirty cop.

Jace had proof of that, and that was why he'd come to Gideon's rural house just outside of Culver Crossing—the town where Jace was the sheriff. He'd intended to arrest Gideon and take him to San Antonio, where Gideon was a decorated officer.

And where they'd been friends, once.

"You still alive, *Sheriff*?" Gideon called out. He said Jace's title as if he didn't have much respect for it. Of course, as Jace had recently learned, Gideon didn't have any respect for his own badge. "It was real stupid of you to come to my place without backup."

Yeah, it had been, but Jace had thought he could talk Gideon into surrendering. So much for that plan. Gideon had run. Jace had gone in pursuit. Now, he'd been shot, and they were deep in the woods, a little more than half mile from the road. Despite the darkness and the storm, Gideon had managed a good run so he could escape.

"You don't want to add murder to your sheet," Jace threw out there, and he moved as fast as he could, darting to the side.

Good thing, too, because Gideon sent a bullet toward the exact spot where Jace had just been. The storm obviously hadn't affected Gideon's hearing or vision, because he had managed to pinpoint Jace's location.

Wincing at the movement and listening for any sound that Gideon was coming closer, Jace took out his phone to call for backup. And he cursed. No signal. There were plenty of dead spots like that in rural Texas, but this was one dead spot that could be fatal for him. He wasn't sure he could make it all the way back to his truck. Especially since he was already starting to get dizzy from the pain and the blood loss.

"My guess is you're hurting pretty bad right now, huh?" Gideon called out.

Again, Jace heard the taunt in his tone and figured the detective was hoping he'd answer. Then Gideon could try to shoot him again, this time with a kill shot.

Too bad about that, on several levels.

It was bad enough that his former best friend wanted him dead, but it also meant he wouldn't be able to talk to Gideon, to try to get answers that he desperately needed.

Answers as to why Gideon had sullied his badge by stealing and then selling confiscated weapons and drugs.

Heaven knew how long Gideon had gotten away with his crimes, but he'd sold the illegal goods to the wrong man. One who'd not only reported it to Jace but had also given him the proof to back it up.

Dragging in a hard breath, Jace put away his phone and focused. He needed to turn this situation around. Needed to figure out Gideon's location so he could end this before he passed out and died here.

"What about Linnea?" Jace asked a split second before he moved again. As expected, Gideon fired a shot and, thankfully, missed this time. "Have you thought about what this will do to her?"

Silence. And Jace hoped it was a good strategy, to use Gideon's sister to make him rethink this. Gideon and Linnea were close, and it would tear out Linnea's heart to know what her brother had done.

"To hell with Linnea," Gideon snarled. "She's the one who ratted me out."

Everything inside Jace went still. He hadn't known that. And he wasn't even sure it was true. Jace certainly hadn't gotten any proof of his wrongdoing from Gideon's sister.

"As far as I'm concerned, Linnea can die right along with you," Gideon added in a snap.

Jace pushed aside those hard words, and he knew it was now or never. He darted out from cover, took aim at the sound of Gideon's voice and fired. Not once but three times. Jace heard the sound of a bullet ripping through flesh. Heard Gideon's sharp groan of pain.

Then he caught a glimpse of his former friend collapsing onto the ground.

Jace's stomach clenched over the thought that he'd likely just killed a man. But he worried even more over another possibility. That he *hadn't* killed Gideon. That Gideon could get up and finish him off.

Because he had no choice, Jace caught onto the tree, using it to anchor himself. The rough bark dug into his hands, but his grip stopped him from falling. For now anyway. Jace could feel himself losing it, though. Losing the battle to stay on his feet, or even to remain just conscious.

The dizziness came with a vengeance. So did the pain. Like hot pokers jabbing at him. Mercy, there was no way he could walk out of this.

He gulped in his breath, and even though he tried to keep holding on, he found himself unable to. He fell, his head smacking against a sharp rock. More pain, but he didn't have enough breath to do anything other than groan.

Jace saw another jab of lightning. Right before everything turned dark.

Chapter Two

With the shotgun gripped in her hand, Linnea Martell stood at the window and kept watch.

It was still storming, the rain and angry wind battering against the tin roof of the tiny log cabin, but it was now thankfully light enough that she could see the small clearing and the woods beyond it. Of course, even with daybreak she might not be able to see the danger before it was too late.

Heck, it could already be too late.

Forcing back that thought, Linnea glanced over her shoulder when she heard the moan. It wasn't a surprising sound. Jace had been doing a lot of moaning since she'd brought him here about six hours ago.

Even though she didn't have any lights on in the cabin and the bed was tucked at an angle deep into the corner, she could see that he was way too pale from the blood loss and the head injury. Also, even in sleep he was likely in pain from the makeshift nursing job she'd done on his shoulder.

She prayed she'd done the right thing.

It occurred to her that she'd never seen him in bed, much less weak and hurting. Linnea had known him since they were kids, and once they'd been as thick as thieves along with her brother, Gideon. She was betting there'd be no such *thickness* now. In fact, it was possible that Jace might want to arrest her for what she'd done.

He moaned again, turning his head from side to side, as if to ward off some nightmare. Or the pain he had to be feeling. His midnight-black hair brushed against the stark white pillowcase, and his forehead bunched up. Since he'd also been doing that a lot ever since he'd been in her cabin, Linnea figured he would just drift back off. His body needed the rest.

But his eyes opened.

Even though she couldn't see the color of them from where she stood, she knew they were a deep, smoky gray. Cop's eyes. But once they'd caused her heart to jitter in a different kind of way, when she'd had a crush on him. Maybe she still did, but it wasn't a crush she was feeling right now.

"Where am I?" Jace mumbled. Wincing and grunting, he tried to sit up, but Linnea hurried to him to ease him back down.

"Don't move," she warned him. "You'll start bleeding again."

He blinked, then stared at her. "Linnea?" It was enough of a question to make her think that his vision was blurry. But the blur was better than his being unconscious.

"Yes." She kept her voice soft and as reassuring as she could manage, which probably wasn't very effective, considering she was holding a shotgun.

And Jace noticed that, too.

His gaze drifted from her face to the gun and then around the cabin. Since the place was only about eight hundred square feet, there wasn't a lot of it to take in.

With his breath gusting, Jace stayed quiet several long moments, clearly trying to process everything, and then he cursed when he looked down at the bandage. Linnea had wrapped it around his chest, anchoring his arm to his side so that he couldn't move it too much while he'd been unconscious.

"Gideon," Jace muttered.

He groaned, squeezed his eyes shut a moment and cursed some more. It was like profanity stew, the words running together in a jumbled heap.

"Gideon's dirty," he finally managed to get out. "He's the one who shot me."

"Yes, I know," Linnea whispered.

She didn't hesitate with her response, but just admitting it out loud felt as if someone had clamped a fist around her heart. Sweet heaven, this hurt. It hurt more than anything she'd ever felt—including when her parents had died. Probably because that'd happened in a car accident. But what Gideon had done was on purpose.

"Gideon doctored chain-of-evidence records," Linnea continued a moment later. "He took guns and drugs from evidence stored at a San Antonio PD warehouse, and he sold them."

Jace went quiet again. Then he nodded. "*To hell with Linnea. She's the one who ratted me out.* That's what Gideon said to me right before he shot me." Something flickered through his eyes, and he tried to get up again. He managed to sit up even though he went sheet-white, and grimaced from the pain. "I shot him. I think I killed him."

Linnea glanced quickly out the window and then looked Jace straight in the eyes. "No, you didn't. I mean, yes, you shot him. At least I think you did. But he's not dead. I looked for his body, and I didn't find it."

That had caused her to feel a flood of relief.

And dread.

Gideon wasn't dead. Or at least he hadn't died in or near the spot where he'd likely been shot—which would have been fairly close to where she'd found Jace. That meant Gideon had managed to move, to get out of the area without leaving any trace of himself behind. But depending on his injury, he could have collapsed elsewhere. Or he could have escaped and gone on the run. Sadly, that last one was the best-case scenario for Jace and her.

She watched as Jace tried to process what she'd just told him, and the muscles in his jaw stirred against each other. "What happened? How'd I get here? And where the hell is Gideon?"

All reasonable questions for a man who'd been shot and then unconscious for hours. Since this wasn't going to be short and sweet, Linnea went back to the window to keep watch.

"I don't know where Gideon is," she said. "But he could be close by. That's why I've been keeping watch."

Jace glanced around again. "Where are we? Where is this place?"

"We're about ten miles from Culver Crossing. This cabin belonged to my grandparents, but I inherited it. I came here after I found out what Gideon had been doing."

It probably wasn't smart to come to a location that Gideon knew about, but she hadn't wanted to go to her house or her office, both of which were in Culver Crossing, and she hadn't had enough cash to go to a hotel in a nearby city. Linnea had been a cop's sister long enough to know that if she used her credit card, Gideon would be able to trace it.

And find her.

"Before I came here, I went to his house, confronted him, and…" Linnea had to stop, gather her breath and tamp down her heartbeat, which was starting to race. "He told me to mind my own business. He said that if I truly loved him, I'd forget what I'd learned about him."

"He threatened you," Jace concluded after several long moments.

There went that fist around her heart again. It tightened like a vise. "I think he would have, but before he could threaten or try to intimidate me, someone came to the door. A man. I don't know who he was, but while they were talking—arguing, really—I slipped out Gideon's back door, ran to my car, jumped in and drove off."

But she hadn't just left. Linnea had sped away, getting out of there as fast as she could. She'd caught a glimpse of her brother in her rearview mirror, and what she'd seen on his face had turned her blood to ice. There hadn't been a trace of the love that'd once been between them.

"Did Gideon follow you?" Jace asked. He was sounding more like a cop now, trying to get to the truth.

She shook her head. "But that probably would have been his next move if I hadn't turned onto a side road and hid between two buildings. Then I called his boss, Lieutenant Bryce Cannon, at San Antonio PD, and I told him everything. Lieutenant Cannon said they'd send someone out to pick up Gideon, so I came here. To hide out. To try to make some sense of why my brother had done this."

It'd been hours now, and she still hadn't made sense of it. Linnea knew there was the possibility that she never would.

"Why'd you go back to Gideon's?" he asked. "Because I'm guessing that's where you were when you found me."

She nodded. "I wasn't going to confront him, but I wanted to see if he was still there. Or try to figure out where he'd gone so I could tell his lieutenant. I knew as long as Gideon was out there, that someone could be hurt."

And she'd been right about that.

"Anyway, I walked through the woods from here to get to Gideon's house," she continued. "It's about a mile and a half away on the trails. I was still on one of those trails when I heard the shots being fired. I didn't know what was going on, but then I found you."

She'd been terrified that he was dead. Then, when she'd realized Jace was alive, her first priority had been to keep him alive.

"If Gideon's injuries aren't that serious, he'll come here," Linnea said.

"To finish us off," Jace added.

Linnea didn't want to believe Gideon would kill them. But her brother was desperate, and since he'd already tried to murder Jace, it wasn't a stretch to believe he'd try again.

Cursing again, Jace threw off the cover and managed to swing his legs off the bed. The sheet stayed over the lower half of his body, but his face became masked with a fine mist of sweat and pain.

"You really should lie down," she warned him. "It took some doing to get the bleeding to stop. You were lucky that the bullet went clean through." Though she doubted he was feeling particularly lucky at the moment.

Jace didn't lie down, but he didn't try to get up, either. His gaze skimmed his bare chest and his clothes that were draped over a chair at the foot of the bed.

"You were soaking wet when I got you here," she explained. "There's a washer and dryer, so I stripped off your clothes and dried them."

He glanced down at the sheet then and obviously didn't have any trouble figuring out that he was butt naked. Jace gave a soft grunt, as if to dismiss any qualms over that, and lightly touched his fingers to the lump and bruise on his forehead.

"You tended to me?" he asked. "You put this bandage on me?"

She nodded. "There was a medical book with the first aid kit in the storage cabinet. It didn't say how to treat a gunshot, but I followed the instructions on a deep puncture wound. I don't think I screwed it up, but there wasn't anything I could do about the head injury. For that, you need tests done at a hospital."

He mumbled what she thought might be a thank-you. "How'd I get here?"

Not easily, but Linnea gave him the condensed version. "After I found you shot, I came back here for the ATV that was in the shed." Thankfully, the shed had been big enough for her to put her car inside so that anyone coming near the cabin wouldn't immediately see it. "I managed to get you on the ATV, and I brought you here."

Again, Jace stayed quiet a moment, obviously trying to process what she'd told him. "We need to call for backup," he insisted.

Linnea knew he wasn't going to like this. "There's no signal out here, so the phones don't work. There isn't any internet, either, so I can't email anyone."

Jace groaned, shook his head, and she could see the frustration on his face that was no doubt on hers. The rest of what she had to tell him wouldn't help.

"The storm washed the road out, so we can't leave in my car. How far away are you parked?" she asked. Though it would be a challenge to get Jace anywhere right now—especially if Gideon was out there, waiting to gun them down.

He considered it a moment, repeated the headshake. "Not close enough. We can get out with the ATV."

Linnea had already given this plenty of thought. And dismissed using it. "It's still storming, and any movement could cause you to start bleeding again. I couldn't do stitches, so basically I've just bandaged you together with what I found in the first aid kit."

At least there'd been some antiseptic salve and even gauze to pack the wound, but everything she'd done was just a temporary fix.

"I'll be okay," he grunted. But when he tried to stand up, he groaned in pain and dropped back down onto the bed.

"There's ibuprofen," Linnea offered. She tipped her head to the bottle and the glass of water she'd put on the nightstand for him. They were next to his holster, gun and phone. "Sorry, but I don't have anything stronger."

With his hands a little unsteady, he opened the bottle and downed several of the pills. With even more unsteadiness, Jace stood while he tried to keep the sheet in place over his groin. When he wobbled, catching onto the headboard of the bed, Linnea hurried to him, propping the shotgun against the wall so she could slip her arm around him.

It was a bad time for her to notice how his bare skin felt. Warm and all man. *Naked.* Yes, a stupid time. Then again, she often had stupid thoughts when it came to Jace.

"Are you okay?" he asked.

That got her attention, and her gaze whipped up to his.

"You made a weird sound," Jace added.

Oh, that. Probably a sigh that went with the dopey thoughts of having him stripped bare and so close to her.

"Knee-jerk reaction," she said, trying to keep her voice level and light. "It's from all those years of making sure we didn't end up near a bed together."

The corner of his mouth lifted, and despite his pain-ravaged eyes, he still managed to look, well, incredibly hot. That was Jace. And she hadn't lied when she'd said they made an art form of avoiding each other.

His smile vanished. "Because of Gideon," he muttered.

Yes. It had been her brother's insistence that Jace keep his hands off her. In part because she was four years younger than the two of them. Also in part because Gideon didn't want his best friend *messing around* with his kid sister. Even though it had never made a lot of sense to Linnea, it clearly had gotten through to Jace, since he'd honored Gideon's demand.

Well, except for that one kiss.

It had happened a little over a decade ago, on her eighteenth birthday. A kiss that Jace had likely meant to be just a friendly peck when he'd found her in Gideon's barn while she was saddling one of the horses. But it had turned as scalding hot as he was. It had also ended when Jace had come to his senses and stepped back.

Way back.

And he'd never stepped toward her again.

Because that kiss, and the memory of it, always fuzzed her mind, Linnea pushed it aside and focused on the Texas-sized problems that were facing Jace and her.

"I need to keep watch," she reminded him. "Let me help you get into your boxers and jeans."

That, of course, meant seeing him in the buff again. When she'd taken off his clothes, she hadn't even thought about it. Linnea had been too scared that he might die. And he'd been unconscious. Well, he was alert now, and his gaze connected with hers as she brought over his clothes.

Once she had his feet and legs into his boxers and jeans, Linnea helped him up so she could shimmy the items up and in place. She zipped him and got more memories. Fantasies about unzipping him. She clamped her teeth over her bottom lip so that she didn't make that weird sound again.

Even though she didn't especially want him walking around, Linnea helped with his socks and boots when Jace reached for them.

"You can't wear the shirt," she said. "Well, not without me rebandaging you. I'd rather not do that, not until the wound's had some more time to close up."

He didn't argue with her about that. Jace was already back in cop mode, glancing around the room, and his attention soon landed on the keypad next to the front door.

"You have a security system," Jace said. "Will it alert a security company or the cops if it goes off?"

Good question. And it was one she'd already considered. "No. Basically, it's just a loud alarm meant to scare off any would-be burglars. Other than the guns and the ATV, there isn't much to steal around here, and the guns were in a hidden safe built into the floor."

Linnea made sure he was steady enough to stand alone, and picking up the shotgun, went back to the window. She turned and scanned the woods again. Nothing. But the wind had picked up, and it was tossing the branches around as the rain continued to batter the window. The whipping motion of the oaks and cedars would make it harder to see Gideon.

"I think the best plan is for me to take the ATV and go to Culver Crossing," she said. "But I can't do that until the lightning stops. Or until you can keep watch without keeling over."

When Jace didn't say anything, she turned to him and saw that he was giving her a seriously skeptical look. "You're a landscape designer," he pointed out. "You've got no training that can help if you were to meet Gideon along the way."

Linnea huffed. Not because she was dismissing what he'd said. It was true she had no firearms training, which was why she was holding a shotgun instead of the handgun she'd found in the floorboard lockbox. It would be easier to hit a target with a shotgun.

If she could hit it, that is.

She knew it wouldn't be easy to aim a gun at her brother and pull the trigger, but she couldn't just stand by and let Gideon kill Jace and her.

"Plus, if the road's out," Jace went on, "the ATV could get stuck."

"I'm strong," she pointed out. "All that dragging around plants, rocks and mulch have given me a few muscles. I managed to get you on the ATV."

Best not to point out, though, that it had been plenty hard, and there'd been moments where she hadn't been sure she could do it.

"If need be, I could run my way out of these woods. You can't run," Linnea added.

"No, but I can return fire if we get into trouble," Jace argued. "And I stand a better chance of hitting a target than you do."

It was a good argument. Well, it would have been if he hadn't had the gunshot wound. It wasn't on his shooting arm, thank goodness, but he was weak, and any movement could cause that wound to open up.

"You could bleed out before I get you out of these woods," Linnea reminded him. "Besides, I'm not sure you can shoot, much less shoot straight. You can't even stand up without help."

As if to prove her wrong, he picked up his gun from the nightstand and straightened his posture, pulling back his shoulders.

And what little color he had drained from his face.

Cursing him and their situation, she dragged a chair closer to the window and had him sit down.

"The main road isn't that far, only about a mile," she continued. Linnea tried to tamp down her argumentative tone. "I can get there on the ATV and call for help. Your deputies and the EMTs can figure out the best way to get you to a hospital."

That was the part of her plan that worked. What she

didn't feel comfortable about was leaving Jace alone while she got to the main road. Definitely not ideal, but they didn't have any other workable solutions.

Of course, this option wouldn't work until the lightning stopped. She could get through the wind and rain, but if she got struck by lightning or a tree falling from a strike, it could be fatal. First, to her, and then to Jace, since he'd be stuck here in the cabin.

He looked up at her, his color a little better now, and his eyes were hard and intense. "I can't let you take a risk like that. Gideon could ambush you."

"That's true," she admitted. "But the alternative is for us to wait here. Maybe for days until you're strong enough to ride out with me. That might not be wise since I suspect you need antibiotics for your wound before an infection starts brewing."

His jaw tightened, and even though he'd had plenty trouble standing, Jace got up. This time he didn't stagger, but she did notice the white-knuckle grip he had on his gun. "We'll see how I feel once the storm has passed."

In other words, he would insist on going with her. Linnea sighed. Obviously, Jace had a mile-wide stubborn streak and was planning on dismissing her *one workable option*.

"If you're hungry, there's some canned soup in the cabinet," she said, shifting the subject.

Jace didn't respond to that. However, he did step in front of her as if to shield her. And he lifted his gun.

"Get down," Jace ordered. "Someone's out there."

Chapter Three

Jace forced back the pain so he could focus. He'd seen some movement in the trees behind the cabin, and he figured it was too much to hope that it was a deer or some other animal. Yes, he'd shot Gideon, but that didn't mean his former friend hadn't made his way here to permanently silence Linnea and him.

"I don't see anything," Linnea said, her breath already too fast.

Obviously, she'd ignored his order for her to get down. An order that had been more cop training than the smart thing to do. If Gideon was truly out there, Jace might have to rely on Linnea's help. Again. She'd likely saved his life by bringing him to the cabin, and now he would need her for backup.

Blinking hard to clear his eyes, he tried to pick through the dense clutter of the trees and underbrush. Nothing. But he kept watching. Kept his gun ready, too.

And then he saw it.

Or, rather, saw *him*.

A man. He was wearing a dark green rain parka, and he was peering out from the trees, his attention aimed at the cabin. Jace's body jolted with the slam of adrenaline. He braced for the fight.

"That's not Gideon," Jace muttered, and he used his hip to nudge Linnea to the side so that she wasn't directly in front of the window.

"No. I think it's the man who came to see him," Linnea explained. "The one who showed up shortly after I confronted Gideon at his place."

Jace kept his gaze nailed to the guy. He wasn't moving, but with that bulky parka, it was impossible to tell if he was armed. "You don't know who he is?"

She shook her head, causing her sandy-brown ponytail to swish. "But like I said, he was arguing with Gideon."

So this could be one of Gideon's partners in crime. Jace figured there had to be at least one person who'd aided Linnea's brother with getting those crates of guns and cases of drugs from evidence storage. Or maybe Gideon's visitor had even been the one in charge of the plan that had netted Gideon a small fortune. It was possible this guy had been in on that fortune-making and had come here to help his partner cover up their crimes.

But Jace rethought that.

"You said you'd called Gideon's lieutenant at SAPD?" he asked Linnea.

She nodded and kept her attention on the man. "Lieutenant Bryce Cannon. But I know Cannon, and that's not him outside."

No, but it could be someone sent by Cannon. And that wouldn't be good, if the lieutenant was as dirty as Gideon. If so, then killing Linnea and him would go a long way to hiding their crimes.

"Crimes," Jace muttered under his breath. The throbbing pain in his shoulder and head cleared enough for

him to realize he should have already thought of something. "Toby."

Linnea gave him a confused glance. "Toby Conway?" she asked.

"Yeah," Jace verified.

Linnea knew him, of course. Most folks in and around Culver Crossing did because Toby had been in trouble with the law for pretty much all his life. In fact, Jace had arrested him for breaking and entering. For drug possession, too. But other than a short stint in jail for the B and E, Toby hadn't seen too much of the inside of a cage.

"Toby came to me," Jace continued. The man outside moved just a fraction, causing Jace to pause. But the guy didn't come an inch closer to the cabin. Nor did he aim a weapon in their direction. "Toby had a recording of Gideon offering him a piece of the action in the illegal gun racket. Gideon was sure Toby would be interested in something like that."

"But he wasn't?" Linnea asked.

"No. In fact, Toby was scared when he came to me. He'd let Gideon believe he would take part in the gun-running, but Toby had no intention of getting involved. Not in something that serious. That means Gideon could go after him to make sure he stays silent about the offer."

Linnea's quick breath let him know that she'd followed that through to a possible bad conclusion. Gideon could murder Toby. In fact, that could be happening right now while Linnea and he stood around, waiting for the guy in the parka to do something. They'd already wasted precious minutes that they might need to save Toby and anyone else in Gideon's or this man's paths.

"Keep back," Jace instructed, and he reached out to lift the window a fraction. Pain shot through him as fast and hard as a bullet, and he had no choice but to stagger back. "I want to call out to him," Jace managed to say.

Huffing, Linnea volleyed glances at him and the man, obviously trying to figure out if that was a stupid idea. Apparently, she decided to side with Jace because she shifted the shotgun enough so that she could unlock the window. The moment she lifted it, the alarm went off.

Linnea cursed, but her words were drowned out by the deafening sound. She had been right about the security system making a loud noise. It blared through the cabin, no doubt through the woods, too. It certainly got the man's attention, but he didn't run.

He came closer.

Linnea hurried to the security panel by the front door, turned off the system to silence it and ran back to the window. "Sorry, I forgot about the alarm."

Jace didn't mind. The alarm turned out to be just as effective as his shouting would have been.

"Gideon Martell?" the man yelled before Jace could say anything. "Are you in there? Is Linnea with you? I want to make sure she's all right."

It was hard to tell if their visitor was actually concerned about Linnea or if he was just trying to home in on a target.

"Get down," Jace told her. He'd needed her help to get the window open, but he wanted to handle the rest of this while she was out of target range.

Linnea gave Jace a quick glare, but she got down. Sort of. She crouched lower but stayed right by the window.

"I'm Jace Castillo, Sheriff of Culver Crossing," Jace yelled. "Who the hell are you, and what do you want?"

Because Jace kept his attention on the man, he saw the guy's posture relax a little. "ATF Special Agent Lionel Zimmerman. I'm going to reach under this rain gear and get my badge."

Again, Jace watched as Zimmerman brought out his badge and held it up. Of course, Jace couldn't get a good look at it from this distance, but it appeared to be a gold badge from the Bureau of Alcohol, Tobacco, Firearms and Explosives.

Appeared to be.

Jace wasn't just going to trust this guy based on what might or might not be real credentials.

"What do you want?" Jace repeated.

"I need to make sure Linnea Martell is all right," Zimmerman answered without hesitation. "Is she with you? Is Gideon here?"

Jace ignored the agent's questions and went with two of his own. "Why do you want to check on Linnea? How do you know her?"

Zimmerman wasn't so quick to answer this time. "I don't know her personally, but I know her brother." He paused. "Gideon's in a lot of trouble, and I'm worried he might have tried to hurt his sister."

Not yet, but Gideon had sure as hell tried to *hurt* Jace. "What kind of trouble is Gideon in?" Jace pressed, fishing for as much info as he could get from this guy.

Every little bit might help Jace figure out if Zimmerman was who he was claiming to be. Too bad they didn't have a working phone or internet so he could do a quick run on this guy.

Zimmerman muttered some profanity. "Why don't

I come in so we can talk? I'd rather not discuss this while standing out in the rain, and I really do need to make sure Linnea is all right. Tell me if Gideon and she are with you."

Jace debated what to say. One thing was for certain—Zimmerman wasn't getting inside until Jace was sure he was indeed a federal agent, one who wasn't swimming in the same dirty water as Gideon.

"Explain to me about Gideon's trouble," Jace repeated. "Then you convince me that you're here to help, not hurt."

Even with the distance between them, it wasn't hard to tell that Zimmerman wasn't pleased about that. "Gideon's been selling items confiscated during busts and arrests conducted by the San Antonio PD and the Texas Rangers. The Bureau has reason to believe that he's now on the run and will try to eliminate anyone who might have proof or knowledge of his wrongdoing."

That meshed with Jace's theory. "Does that mean Gideon's trying to eliminate you?" Jace fired back.

"Yes. And you." Zimmerman paused again. "We've had Gideon's place under camera surveillance. We saw the feed when you went to his place to confront him. We saw him run, and you went in pursuit."

Jace wanted to know if Zimmerman had also seen him get shot. Or if he'd seen Jace shoot Gideon. But Jace didn't want to give Zimmerman those sort of details.

"Since you knew I was in trouble, it would have been nice if you'd sent me some backup," Jace responded.

"We did. Obviously, it took a while to get out to Gideon's place, and I started a search of the area where I last saw the two of you. I've been looking for both of you." Zimmerman paused again. "I'm guessing Gideon's not with you. Where is he?"

That was the million-dollar question, and if Zimmerman was being straight with them, then it meant he hadn't found Gideon's body.

"Gideon's not here," Jace finally said. "I don't know where he is. And yeah, he tried to kill me."

"What about his sister?" Zimmerman quickly asked. "Did Gideon try to kill her, too?"

"Not yet. But I suspect that's because he hasn't gotten the chance. You're not going to have a chance to do that, either," Jace warned him.

Zimmerman nodded, and it looked as if he added a frustrated sigh. "After what you've been through, I don't expect you to just trust me, but you can't stay here. It's not safe, with Gideon at large. I've got a Jeep parked on one of the ranch trails. It's not too far from here, only about a half mile, and Linnea and you could come with me. I could get you both back to town where you'll be safe."

Jace didn't dispute their safety once they were back in Culver Crossing. He could assign deputies for Linnea's protection detail and get himself to a hospital so a doctor could check his injuries. But leaving with Zimmerman could be many steps past a stupid move.

"Tell him to go get his Jeep," Linnea whispered. "Tell him you're injured and that you need him to bring it closer. Then, once he's gone, we'll leave, too. I don't see that we have a choice about staying here."

Neither did Jace. If Zimmerman was dirty, he'd try to kill them—either here in the cabin or once he had them in his vehicle. Of course, telling the agent that he was wounded might spur Zimmerman to charge the cabin without any further conversation. If that happened, then Jace would have to kill him.

"Gideon shot me," Jace called out to Zimmerman. He was going to take Linnea's plan and tweak it a little. "Go back to your Jeep and drive until you have phone reception. Then call the EMTs. They'll figure out a way to get to me."

Zimmerman stayed quiet several long moments. "How bad are you hurt?"

"Bad enough that I can't go walking through the woods. Not bad enough that I can't shoot straight. Go ahead," Jace insisted. "Leave now and get me some medical help. Then we can look for Gideon."

More hesitation from Zimmerman. "But what if Gideon comes after you while I'm gone?"

"I can shoot straight," Jace repeated. *Probably.* "Hurry. The sooner I'm out of here, the sooner I can help you find Gideon and Linnea."

But Zimmerman didn't hurry. "Linnea's really not with you?"

"No," Jace lied. "But we need to find her. Go now."

Zimmerman nodded, and he finally got moving. Jace had no idea how long it would take the agent to get to his vehicle. Or even if Zimmerman was truly headed in that direction. If he wasn't, then Zimmerman could be planning on circling around so he could sneak up on them and try to get into the cabin.

"We have to leave right now?" Linnea asked, but it didn't sound nearly as much like a question as it did a huge concern.

Which it was.

"Yeah. Zimmerman might go for backup. The wrong kind of backup," Jace emphasized.

She made a sound of agreement, hurried away from the window and pulled a rain poncho from the closet. Linnea put on a dull green hooded windbreaker and then draped the poncho around Jace. Since both items were still wet, he figured she'd used them when she'd rescued him.

"It's the best I can do," she said. "You can't put your shirt back on. Even if we could get it on, we'd risk opening up your wound."

Jace had already figured that out, and while the poncho was plenty bulky, it was still a challenge to get it on. A painful one. Hell. His shoulder felt as if someone was stabbing him with a knife. His head wasn't faring much better, and he hoped the pain didn't interfere with what he had to do.

He had to get Linnea to safety.

"This way," she instructed after she picked up the shotgun.

She led him out the front door. Not fast. Both of them paused in the doorway to look around. Thankfully, there were fewer trees in front of the cabin, which meant fewer places for someone to hide, but it was still possible for a person—mainly Gideon—to be lying in wait.

When they didn't see anyone, Linnea and he went into the yard. There were downed limbs from the storm, and the ground was a muddy bog. Still, they slogged their way through to the shed. Linnea used a remote that she took from her pocket to open it, and Jace saw that she'd been right about the size. It was plenty big enough to hold her car, the ATV and other equipment.

"I'll have to drive," she insisted.

Jace didn't argue with her. Couldn't. Besides, he

wanted to keep his shooting hand free in case they ran into trouble.

The ATV had only one seat, which meant Linnea ended up in his lap. The pain was almost great enough for him not to notice the contact. Almost.

After she anchored the shotgun next to them, she started the engine and backed up. She didn't dawdle, but like him, let her gaze fire all around when she bolted away from the shed. That jostled Jace around and took care of the lust he was feeling for Linnea. The pain roared through him.

He blew out some sharp breaths, trying to steady himself, trying not to pass out. Losing consciousness sure as heck wouldn't do them any good.

The rain battered at them, but she maneuvered the ATV around the downed limbs and debris and kept on the road for about an eighth of a mile. Then Jace saw that the storm had indeed washed away enough of the dirt and gravel surface. There was now a huge ditch cutting through what had once been the road.

Slowing down, Linnea went around it, taking the ATV off the road and into an area thick with underbrush. Some of the bushes whipped at them as they passed, but she was finally able to cut around the ditch and get back on the road on the other side. It wasn't exactly smooth sailing after that, but she was able to pick up speed.

Even though his mobility was practically squat, Jace turned as much as possible so he could look behind them. No signs of Zimmerman or Gideon, and he prayed it would stay that way.

They hadn't gone far when Jace saw another spot where the road had washed out. Linnea went around it, and he tried to steel himself up for even more pain when the ATV bobbed over the uneven surface. Steeling didn't help much, but Linnea soon got them around it and headed toward the main road. Almost immediately, though, she had to stop again and climb off the ATV to move a tree branch that was blocking their path.

That was Jace's cue to take out his phone, and relief washed through him when he saw that he finally had cell service. It was only one bar, but while he kept watch, he pressed the number for the sheriff's office. More relief came when one of his deputies, Glenn Spence, answered on the first ring.

"Jace, where the hell are you?" Glenn asked just as Linnea got back on his lap. Jace positioned the phone so that she could hear the conversation.

"Long story." Jace was about to request that his deputy send out an ambulance and backup, but Glenn continued before he could say anything else.

"Jace you need to get back here right now." Glenn's words ran together. "All hell is breaking loose."

Chapter Four

Even though Jace hadn't put the call on speaker, Linnea was practically head to head with him, and she had no trouble hearing what his deputy had just told him.

All hell is breaking loose.

Since that pretty much described the last twenty-four hours of her life, Linnea wasn't sure she could handle another dose of trouble. Especially since her own woes weren't over.

Jace and she weren't anywhere near safe yet, not with her brother and heaven knew how many of his lawbreaking cronies ready to gun them down. Plus, they had to worry about the ATF agent, Zimmerman. If he'd found the location of the cabin, then he knew about this road, and that meant he would at least consider the possibility they could use it to try to get away from him. Zimmerman might be able to come up on them from behind.

Jace groaned, probably a reaction to his pain and the news he'd just heard from his deputy. News that was no doubt important, but Linnea had her own priorities, and right now getting out of the woods with Jace was at the top of her list. That was why she didn't stop driving.

"Jace is hurt and needs help," she blurted out before

Jace or Glenn could say anything else. She glanced around and tried to pinpoint their location. "We're on Smith Road, about two or three miles from the main highway. Get somebody out here ASAP. We're on an ATV and heading to the main road now."

She continued in that direction, trying to eat up some of the distance to get them out of the woods. She also kept watch, but sweet heaven, it was hard to see what she might need to see. Not only was the filmy curtain of rain stinging her eyes, but there were way too many thick trees, deep ditches and shrubs that tangled and blended with the landscape. A sniper would have his pick of places to hide and lie in wait.

"Boss?" she heard Glenn say. "You're really hurt?"

"I am," Jace confirmed. "I'll fill you in when I get to the office. What's going on there?"

"Hold a second and let me call dispatch so I can get you some help," Glenn insisted.

Linnea drove on. Because of all the debris and washed-away parts of the road, she was going practically at a snail's pace, which, of course, was making them an easy target.

"All right." Glenn's voice came back on several long moments later. "Crystal and some EMTs are headed your way. They'll turn on Smith Road and just keep going until they find you."

Crystal was Deputy Crystal Rankin, and Linnea would be thankful to have that kind of backup. Despite Jace's assurances that he could fire a gun even with his injuries, Linnea just wasn't buying it. Since her own aim was in question, as well, they needed all the help they could get.

"Tell me what's wrong there at the sheriff's office," Jace asked.

Glenn certainly didn't jump in with an explanation. Odd, considering how anxious he had been when he first answered Jace's call.

"Uh, is that Linnea with you?" Glenn asked.

Linnea was surprised the deputy had recognized her voice. She'd met Glenn, of course, but since he'd moved to Culver Crossing only a couple of years earlier, she didn't know him well and had only spoken to him a few times. So, why would Glenn have assumed she was the one with Jace?

Jace hesitated, too. Long enough for Glenn to continue.

"Was it Linnea who hurt you?" the deputy pressed, and every word of that question dripped with concern.

She hissed out a breath. Linnea hadn't understood the concern in Glenn's voice, but she sure as heck got it now.

"No," Jace snarled. "Why the hell would you ask that?"

Linnea wanted to know the same thing, and she figured whatever Glenn's answer was, it wouldn't be good.

"Because, well, because Toby Conway's body was found at his house," Glenn said. "He was murdered, boss. Not an easy death, either. A gut shot and two more shots to his kneecaps."

That felt like a punch to her own gut. Not because Linnea cared about or even liked Toby, but because she was very much afraid that Gideon had done this.

And that made her brother a killer.

She bit back a sob and tears. Neither would help now,

and she continued to maneuver the ATV, inching them closer and closer to the EMTs and backup.

"There's more," Glenn continued a moment later. "Right before he died, Toby scrawled out a message that we found next to his body. He said it was Linnea who shot him and left him to die."

Linnea automatically hit the brakes, and this time the gut punch was a lot worse. "What?" she managed to say into the phone.

"He claimed you killed him," Glenn spelled out.

Linnea tried to mentally latch on to that. Tried to make sense of it. She couldn't. But apparently Jace didn't have any trouble working through his thoughts, because he sounded like a cop when he snapped out the next question to Glenn.

"When did Toby die?" Jace demanded.

"The ME just got the body, so we don't have a time of death yet," Glenn answered without a moment's hesitation this time. "But it appears to have been late last night or very early this morning."

Either time meant she didn't have an alibi. Well, she did. She'd been taking Jace to the cabin and trying to keep him alive during that time frame, but Jace wouldn't be able to verify that since he'd been unconscious.

"I didn't kill Toby," Linnea insisted. "I didn't."

"We'll get it straightened out," Jace assured her. "My guess is Gideon killed Toby and tried to set up Linnea."

Since Glenn didn't question why Gideon would have done that, it meant the deputy at least knew about her brother being a fugitive. Of course, he did. Everyone would know that the ATF was on his trail. Maybe Glenn would then follow this through and at least consider that a dirty cop would continue being dirty and eliminate Toby, the man who'd ratted him out to Jace.

"We found a knife and an earring at the scene of Toby's murder," Glenn went on. "I sent them to the lab to be analyzed."

They wouldn't be hers. But Linnea immediately rethought that. Maybe they were. Maybe they'd been taken from her house. It wouldn't have been hard for Gideon to get in since he had a key and knew the code for her security system.

"I've never even been to Toby's," she muttered, but Linnea didn't add more. Jace was right that they could work out all of this later. It wasn't the time for her to try to prove her innocence while she still needed to get Jace to those EMTs.

"Toby said in the note he left that Linnea is the one who sold the weapons and drugs," Glenn explained. "That she used Gideon's ID and badge to get the stash from the SAPD storage."

That was so outrageous a claim that it dried up any hint of tears or sobs. Yes, Gideon had done this all right, and he was going to try to pin the blame on her. Fury raged through her, followed by the sickening dread that her brother was the monster she was beginning to fear he was.

"You'll have Toby's note analyzed, to make sure he actually wrote it?" she asked. When Glenn made a sound of agreement, Linnea added, "Even if it is his handwriting, that docsn't mean he wrote it voluntarily. He probably would have written any and everything if someone had a gun to his head."

Again, that got a sound of agreement from Glenn. Just in case Jace had any doubts whatsoever about her innocence, she glanced back at him to repeat that she hadn't done any of the things Toby had claimed in his note, when she saw him lift the edge of the poncho and look at his shoulder.

Blood.

The wound had obviously reopened, and blood was seeping out of the bandage and onto his forearm. Added to that, Jace was shivering now. That could be just because of the rain, but it was also possible he was going into shock. It was one of the things the medical book had said could happen.

"Tell the EMTs to hurry," Linnea ordered Glenn. "Jace is hurt bad." And she got the ATV moving as fast as she could. Every minute counted now.

"I will," Glenn assured them just as Jace ended the call.

With plenty of effort Jace put his phone in between his stomach and her back, probably to keep the rain off it, and then she felt him shifting his gun, which must've strained him even more.

"How far to the main road?" he asked, his breathing labored now.

"Not far," she lied.

At the pace they were going, it could be another twenty minutes or so before they got there, but hopefully that time would be shortened considerably since the EMTs were heading their way.

"Lean your head on my shoulder," she instructed. "You're not looking your best, Hotshot."

"Hotshot," he repeated in a mumble.

She kept her attention on the road, but Linnea thought maybe Jace attempted to chuckle. He remembered that was what she'd called him when she was a teenager. The nickname she'd given him because he'd been so darn good at pretty much everything. Working with the cutting horses, bull riding, football—you name it, Jace had excelled at it.

That included snagging her attention and never letting go.

Linnea suspected that part of Jace's drive to be the best stemmed from his miserable childhood. There'd been a whopping big scandal when his father's affair with a wealthy married woman had led to the woman's husband committing suicide. That, in turn, had caused Jace's parents to split, with neither one of them taking much interest in him after that. It was one of the reasons he'd spent so much time hanging out with Gideon.

"I'm not feeling like a hotshot right now," he added.

Linnea made a sound of agreement and thought Jace's voice seemed weaker. She reconsidered that, though, when she felt him move. With surprising speed, he shifted his position, bringing up his gun.

That gave her a jolt of adrenaline, but before she could even say anything, Jace hooked his uninjured arm around her waist.

"Get down," he snapped.

He didn't wait for her to do that, though. Jace pulled her off the seat and onto the muddy road. It was just in the nick of time. Because a bullet slammed into the front end of the ATV.

Linnea hadn't needed anything to get her heart pounding and her blood racing, but that did it. The fear quickly replaced her shock and confusion, and she knew exactly why Jace had done what he had.

They were under attack.

She hadn't even seen the gunman, but she could certainly hear him. A third shot ricocheted off the ATV, the sound of metal bouncing off metal and pinging through the woods.

Jace got them moving again, though she could hear his grunts and groans of pain. He rolled them right into a water-filled ditch that was about three feet deep. Not ideal, but it was a lot better than being on the ATV, where they could have been shot.

Of course, they could still be shot.

Hindsight sucked, because only minutes earlier, Linnea had been thinking how easy it would have been for a sniper to hide. And she'd been right. She hadn't even seen anyone. But Jace obviously had, and thankfully, he'd reacted in time to save them. Although the save had probably come with a Texas-sized price tag attached to it.

Jace's groans were louder now, and he arched against the pain, causing his phone to drop into the water before Linnea could latch onto it. However, she did manage to grab his gun.

Another shot came their way. It didn't hit the ATV this time but instead smacked into the ditch and sent mud and gravel flying right at them. She couldn't be sure, but she thought the gunman had shifted his position.

Moving closer to them.

Or rather moving in for the kill.

"Stay down," Jace warned her when she started to lever up.

Linnea hadn't even thought about staying down, not with a possible killer closing in on them. But she forced herself to stay put and listen. She didn't hear any footsteps. Only the rain and their heavy gusting breaths.

"Is it Gideon firing those shots?" she whispered.

"Don't know. I didn't get a good look at him."

So it could be a lackey. Or Zimmerman. Heck, it could be a hunter with poor eyesight who'd mistaken them for deer. But Linnea knew that was just wishful thinking on her part. After what had happened to Jace, it was obvious this was yet another attempt to do away with the lawman who'd tried to arrest her brother.

Since the shooter obviously knew their exact location, Linnea decided to try something. Probably something stupid. But maybe there was a vein of brotherly love left in Gideon.

"Gideon?" she called out, and she held her breath, waiting for him to respond. Praying that the sound of her voice would bring him back to his senses.

No answer. Well, not a verbal one anyway. But there was another blast of gunfire, and this one came even closer to Jace and her. So much for coming back to his senses. Instead, it seemed to serve as a reminder that he wanted them dead.

"Hand me my gun," Jace said, and despite the fact that he had no color left in his face, took it from her.

"I have a better chance of shooting him than you do," Linnea insisted.

But she might as well have been talking to the rain, because Jace climbed over her, putting himself in front of her like a shield. Later, she'd give him some grief over trying to protect her this way, but giving grief could get them both killed. Right now, she gave Jace the quiet he needed to focus.

And focusing was obviously what he was doing.

He didn't make a sound, but he lifted his head a fraction. Listening. Linnea tried to do that, as well, but she certainly didn't hear a gunman coming their way. However, Jace must have, because he levered himself up, and in the same motion, took aim at something.

And he fired.

The sound roared through her ears and head, and Linnea thought she might have cried out. Hard to tell, though, because the gun blast was the only thing she could hear. It echoed and expanded, filling her with throbbing pain.

Apparently, Jace didn't seem to have that problem. He shifted a couple of inches. Aimed. Fired again. And again.

Linnea tried to push aside the pain and figure out if he'd hit his intended target. She couldn't tell. But she did hear something else. Something she definitely wanted to hear.

A siren.

It was the wail of an approaching ambulance, and she thought maybe there was a cop's siren in the mix, as well. Relief surged, but Jace clearly wasn't on the same page with her. She heard him curse, and he practically climbed over her to get out of the ditch.

"The SOB's getting away," Jace spat out.

Linnea didn't want that. She wanted the snake caught. Even if the snake turned out to be her brother. But Jace certainly wasn't in any shape to go in pursuit.

That didn't stop him from trying, though.

Jace made it out of the ditch and even got a yard or so before she saw him drop down onto his knees. Mercy, he was going to kill himself by bleeding out if she didn't stop him.

She first tried to latch onto the side of the ditch so she could get out, but her hands just slid through the mud. Cursing, she grabbed some tree roots that were poking through the side of the ditch, and used them like a rope to start climbing.

Despite his injuries, Jace had made it look easy. It wasn't. Her boots bogged into the mud, and her hands were slick, so she lost her grip a couple of times. It seemed to take hours for her to finally make it to the top. She hit solid ground and started moving. Fast. The moment she reached Jace, she took hold of him and pulled him into her arms.

Linnea heard it then.

Over the wail of the sirens, the rain and Jace's ragged breath, she cursed the running footsteps of their attacker getting away.

Chapter Five

Pain. That was the one sensation that came through loud and clear for Jace. Unfortunately, his mind wasn't nearly so clear, and it took him a moment to push through the agony and realize that he wasn't back in the cabin. Or in the ditch with a gunman shooting at Linnea and him.

He was in the hospital.

Before he even opened his eyes, he could smell the antiseptic in the air and hear the pulsing beeps of a machine. A machine he realized was monitoring him.

"Hell," he grumbled.

He hadn't wanted to be brought to the hospital. He'd spelled that out to the EMTs when they'd arrived. They were to treat him so he could get back to work. Of course, everything was fuzzy after he'd given that order, and he was positive that he'd lost consciousness. Hard to argue with EMTs when you were out like a light.

Speaking of lights, the ones overhead caused him to wince in more pain. Jace gathered his breath, steeled himself and blinked until his eyes could adjust to the brightness. Even then, there was pain, but it was a drop in the bucket compared to his shoulder. Only then did he remember threatening the EMTs so they wouldn't give him any pain meds.

Obviously, that hadn't been a smart thing for him to do.

Wincing, he lifted his head and looked around, hoping he was safe here. Glenn would have seen to that, Jace assured himself. But his deputy wasn't around. No medical personnel, either. However, Linnea was in a chair, staring at him from over the rim of a to-go container of what smelled like the flowery tea that he knew she liked to drink. She was wearing green scrubs, and she set aside a newspaper that she'd had on her lap.

"What's a four-letter word for somebody who does something stupid?" Linnea asked, getting to her feet and putting her hand on his chest to stop him when he tried to get up.

He frowned. "I'm not up to helping with a crossword right now."

"The answer is *Jace. J-a-c-e*," she spelled out.

His frown deepened. Jace had figured she would dole out some TLC or at least ask how he was feeling, but Linnea definitely had no such ideas. She seemed riled.

"You tore open your gunshot wound when you jumped out of that ditch," she continued. "You left cover to charge at a guy who was shooting at you even though you were in no shape to shoot back."

Oh, that. He certainly hadn't forgotten about it, but what he'd done had been pure instinct and training.

"I'm a cop," Jace reminded her. "I didn't want the idiot getting away." He paused, muttered some choice curse words when he remembered how all of that had played out. "The shooter got away, didn't he? Was Crystal or one of my other deputies able to find him?"

"He got away," Linnea confirmed. "Because Crystal and the EMTs were more concerned about putting you in the ambulance and getting you here to the hospital so the doctors could save your life."

Linnea stared at him with slightly narrowed eyes. Then she sighed. Softened. There was no other word for her. The tightness in her face went slack, her mouth trembled and concern pushed aside the anger in her eyes.

Concern for him.

Yeah, Jace got that, too. He hadn't been close to dying, at least he didn't think he had been, but Linnea had saved him. Not just by taking him to the cabin but also putting him on that ATV and driving him out of those woods. If they'd stayed at the cabin, the gunman could have pinned them down and sent a hail of bullets through the flimsy wood walls.

Because Linnea had saved him and because he knew he'd scared her spitless when he jumped out of that ditch, he reached out, took her hand and gave it a gentle squeeze. Even that small movement hurt, and she noticed, too. She reached for the intercom button on his bed.

"Wait," Jace said. He wanted to talk to a nurse or doctor, but he needed to get some info from Linnea first. "Is this room secured? Are you safe?"

She nodded. "The hospital security guard is right outside your door."

That was a start, but the Culver Crossing Hospital wasn't large enough to have a full team of security guards. If the gunman who'd tried to kill them wanted to get into his room, all he'd have to do was create some kind of distraction to pull the security guard away from the door. Jace might not be able to protect

Linnea if that happened. Especially since his gun was nowhere in sight.

"I need to talk to Glenn," he said.

"Glenn just left about twenty minutes ago," Linnea informed him. "He's making arrangements to send over a reserve deputy who'll stay until you're discharged."

Which would happen soon. Jace would insist on that. "I need my gun. Where is it?"

The softness on her face wavered some, and while Linnea didn't exactly roll her eyes, she looked as if that was exactly what she wanted to do. "Glenn took it with him. You weren't allowed to be armed when you were unconscious. Hospital rules. It's a security risk."

"Well, I'm conscious now, and I want my gun back," he snarled. He reached for his phone, which was always in his pocket.

It wasn't there, of course, and he remembered that he'd dropped it in the bloody ditch. He also didn't have a pocket. Or jeans. Or boxers, for that matter. He was naked except for a green gown that he was certain would show his bare butt when he stood.

"Our clothes were wet," Linnea explained as if she knew exactly what he was thinking. "You had to be stripped down again, and your gunshot wound had to be cleaned and stitched."

Jace had some vague memories of all of that. More memories of pain, too. And of some kind of medication being put in his IV. An IV that was still in the back of his hand.

"Someone drugged me," he recalled.

"*Someone*—" she repeated, mocking his tone, "—aka Dr. Garcia—gave you meds so he could tend your wound without you passing out or yelling from the pain.

He then dosed you with plenty of antibiotics so you wouldn't get an infection."

"I wouldn't have yelled," Jace growled, and to prove it, he sat up. Oh, man. The pain was indeed bad, but he stayed upright on sheer willpower. "How long have I been here anyway?"

"A little while." She huffed and said, "About five hours," when he continued to stare at her.

"Five hours with a killer at large and our lives at risk." He definitely wouldn't be thanking Dr. Garcia for dosing him up. "I need to call Glenn and get an update on the investigation."

A murder investigation at that. Jace had only gotten the broad strokes when it came to Toby, but there should be plenty of details by now.

"Glenn will be back soon, and he'll fill you in," Linnea assured him. "And bring you your weapon." She gently took hold of his good shoulder and eased him back down. "But as for updates, I've already told you the gunman's still at large. Gideon, too," she added. "Of course, Gideon could have been the gunman."

That was true, and Jace would have given up his paycheck to have gotten a glimpse of the shooter's face. If it wasn't Gideon, then it was likely his partner in crime. Or maybe a hired hitman. But still, Jace wished he knew what he was up against. The more hired guns, the greater the threat.

"Glenn ran a background check on Zimmerman," she added. "He didn't find any obvious signs that he was dirty."

"I want Glenn to keep looking," Jace snarled.

"So do I, and he will." She paused. "I didn't kill Toby," Linnea stated while she continued to stare down at him. She seemed to be looking for any signs that he doubted her.

He didn't.

"I know," Jace assured her. "His death is on Gideon or whoever he's partnered with."

"Maybe another cop," she provided. "Or somebody else in law enforcement like Zimmerman."

Yeah, it was the *somebody else* that was eating away at him. Jace knew the threat Gideon could pose, but now he'd have to look at others he didn't know.

Jace kept the eye contact with her because this was something Linnea needed to hear. "When I was chasing Gideon, he never once tried to convince me that he was innocent. Just the opposite. He seemed fine with dirtying his badge and putting guns in the hands of criminals who could use them for heaven knows what. He wants us both dead. Best for us to get past that and focus on stopping him."

He hadn't exactly sugarcoated that last bit, the bit she truly needed to take to heart. Jace didn't pretty up the next part, either.

"If it comes to a showdown between Gideon and me," he added, "I'll have to kill him."

She nodded, swallowed hard. "I know. If it comes down to us or him, I expect you to kill him."

Her voice broke. The tears came. Tears that she cursed and tried to blink back and bat away by fanning her hand in front of her face. Jace couldn't fault her for those tears. He was torn up about this, too.

"I didn't see this in Gideon," Jace said. "Didn't know he was capable of doing something like this." There was an implied *Did you?* at the end of that.

Linnea shook her head. "When I found out, I didn't want it to be true."

Their gazes held, and she swiped away a tear that she hadn't managed to stave off, just as the door opened. Jace automatically braced himself for a fight, and he took hold of Linnea's arm, instinctively wanting to move her behind him. Of course, he couldn't manage that since he was in bed, but he soon realized that it wasn't necessary.

Dr. Ed Garcia came in.

He'd known the doctor most of his life—everyone in Culver Crossing did—and Dr. Garcia had stitched him up a couple of times before this. He trusted the doctor despite the dose of pain meds he'd administered.

Dr. Garcia gave Jace a long once-over, made a sound that could have meant anything, before he glanced at Linnea. "I need to examine Jace," he told her. "You can wait with Hal, the security guard, if you want."

"No, she can't," Jace insisted before she could say anything. "Linnea's in my protective custody."

The doctor lifted an eyebrow and motioned toward the huge bandage peeking out from the top of the gown. "Are you in any shape for protective custody work?" he asked, some dryness in his tone.

"I'll protect her," Jace said as a way of avoiding the question. He wasn't sure he wanted to know the answer to that, but Jace figured if it came down to another gunfight, he'd do what was necessary.

Even if it hurt like hell.

He had an easier time interpreting the next sound the doctor made. It was a definite *suit yourself*, with a layer of skepticism tossed in.

"FYI," the doctor continued as he lowered the front

of Jace's hospital gown and lifted the bandage to take a look at the wound. "Linnea did a decent job of fixing you up."

Jace knew that, and he gave Linnea a nod of thanks. He might not have died if she hadn't found him, but if Gideon or one of his cronies had gotten to him first, his chances of survival wouldn't have been good.

"You're lucky," Dr. Garcia went on. "The bullet cut through some muscle but not the bone. It's a clean through-and-through. Now that you're stitched up, I suspect you'll heal fast enough. At least you will if you take it easy for a couple of days and wear a sling so that your arm doesn't move around a lot."

That was mostly good news, especially the part about him healing fast. But the taking it easy wouldn't happen. Nor was it necessary. He'd been shot in his left shoulder, and he didn't need that part of his body to fire a shot to defend himself and Linnea.

"Your pain meds have worn off." The doctor pressed the bandage back in place. "I can have a nurse bring you another dose."

"No." And Jace couldn't say that fast enough. "I need a clear head, not one clouded by drugs."

"Your head won't be so clear if you're hurting," the doctor mumbled, adding another grunt that seemed to say, "Suit yourself."

Jace would indeed suit himself, and that started with him getting out of here. "I have to get back to work, so I need you to discharge me."

"The earliest I can release you is tomorrow." The doctor huffed when Jace opened his mouth to object to that. "You were shot and lost a lot of blood. Like I said, Linnea did a good job patching you up, but we have to take precautions. One day," he emphasized, his gaze drifting to Linnea. "And I'll arrange it so she can stay with you if she wants."

"It's what I want," Linnea rushed to say.

Jace seriously doubted that was because she had a yen to sleep in a chair by his hospital bed. Nope. Her wish to stay might not even be tied to her protective custody. Knowing Linnea, she probably wanted to be there to help him fight off Gideon if he showed up. That had Jace reconsidering if he should have her go with one of his deputies.

"If you're staying, I'm staying," Linnea insisted, staring at Jace.

So, either she'd developed ESP, or for a second time today, she'd rightly interpreted his thoughts.

"He's staying," the doctor insisted right along with her. "Make sure he doesn't overdo it."

"I will," she assured Dr. Garcia, though Jace knew there was no way she could back that up.

"I need to get out of here," Jace insisted, but the doctor didn't respond. Not verbally anyway. Dr. Garcia wrote something on a chart that he slipped into a slot on the door, and left.

Jace immediately shifted his attention to Linnea, and cursed. The profanity wasn't aimed at her, though, but rather the doctor, who'd clearly not listened to him.

Using his right hand, Jace threw back the cover, sat up and swung his legs to the side of the bed. Oh, yeah. The movement hurt, but it was something he was sure he could work through.

Well, he was almost sure.

"I need my gun, a phone and a laptop." He snapped out the words. "The sooner I get started on this investigation, the better. In fact, I need crime scene photos of Toby's murder. And if Glenn hasn't done it already, I want a crime scene team out to the area where Gideon and I traded bullets."

Staring at him, Linnea walked closer, and closer, until she was standing between his legs. It was a darn effective way of stopping him from getting off the bed, since he'd have a hard time moving her.

"Remember that time you kissed me?" she asked, mentally throwing him off balance.

Jace had expected a lecture as to why he couldn't get or do all those things he'd just grumbled about. Or an attempt to placate him by saying she'd see what she could do about the two easiest items on his list—a phone and a laptop. But nowhere in the possibilities of her responses had he considered that she'd bring up that kiss.

"I was eighteen," she continued when he gaped at her. "You took my hand, laced our fingers together and leaned in. Only lips to lips. That and our hands were the only physical contact, but you made it count." She smiled almost wistfully, as if savoring the memory.

Jace was savoring it, as well. A little too much. She'd tasted both hot and sweet. Oh, and forbidden. Definitely that.

He tried to shift the conversation and therefore the memory avalanche. "You're trying to distract me, to stop me from being so pissed off."

No wistful smile this time. It took on a sly edge. "Did it work?"

It had. And that wasn't a good thing. No way did he need to be thinking about that kiss or kissing her again.

But he was.

That made him feel both sick and brainless. Her life

was at risk, and he didn't need the distraction of this, well, heat between them. It had always been there, but it had kicked up several serious notches. Maybe because of the shared danger. Nearly dying together had a way of bulldozing through any barriers, including those that should have stayed in place.

Again, he went for a conversation shift and a complete realignment of his thoughts. "I need to get out of here," he repeated.

"You need to heal," she reminded him right back. "How are you going to protect me if you're too hurt to stop the bad guys?"

Well, at least she hadn't said, *How are you going to kiss me if you're too hurt?* That meant she had more common sense than he did right now. Still, Jace focused on the things he needed—and no, kissing Linnea wasn't anywhere on that list. He was about to ask for her help in getting a phone and a laptop, when there was a knock at the door.

Again, Jace moved, and this time he actually made it off the bed and to his feet. He wasn't a hundred percent, maybe not even fifty percent, but he didn't fall on his butt. Nor was there a threat. Because it was Glenn who poked his head in and smiled when he saw Jace standing.

"Didn't expect you to be out of bed," the deputy commented, stepping inside.

"He's not supposed to be." Linnea moved in again, taking hold of Jace's hips and pushing until he sat down.

Jace frowned and nudged her away so he could talk to Glenn. Or rather give Glenn some orders. "I want my gun, a phone and laptop."

"Sure, boss. Figured you would." Glenn set a backpack on the small table next to Jace's bed. "I added a change of clothes that I got from your locker. A charger cord, too, for the phone."

"Thanks," Jace mumbled, reaching for the backpack. Then, shifting and reaching again with his good arm. "I wish Dr. Garcia was as efficient as you are."

Glenn put his hands on his hips. "Guess that means he's not springing you loose, huh?"

"Not today." Jace didn't waste much time on the scowl he aimed at Glenn. Instead, he got busy taking out the items from the backpack. "But that doesn't mean I can't get some work done. I want any reports you have on Toby's murder."

The deputy nodded but suddenly looked very uneasy, and that discomfort was definitely aimed at Linnea.

"It's all right," Jace assured him. "Linnea didn't kill Toby, so it's okay if she hears what you have to say." Besides, Jace was holding to his rule about not letting Linnea out of his sight.

"Okay," Glenn said, gathering his breath. "Along with being shot three times, Toby was also stabbed in the chest, and the knife was left at the scene. The knife appears to have been taken from a knife block in Linnea's kitchen."

Linnea groaned. "I guess Gideon or whoever did this wanted to make sure the cops looked at me for this. But along with the note that Toby left, it's too obvious."

She seemed surprised and relieved that both Glenn and Jace nodded in agreement. Linnea studied their expressions and shook her head.

"So, why would Gideon have done that?" she asked. "First of all, my house is less than a block off Main Street, where he could have been spotted."

"Maybe Gideon had someone else break in," Jace suggested. "Or if he wasn't hurt that bad, he could have sneaked into the place last night. You don't have neighbors behind you, so he could have gone through your backyard."

"Yes," she muttered but then shook her head again. "Gideon's a cop, and he'd know the scene would look like an obvious plant. A blatant attempt to make me look guilty. Why wouldn't he throttle back on that?"

Jace had already turned this over in his mind when he first spoke to Glenn on the phone about it. "I figure Gideon knows we'll be looking at him no matter what so-called evidence is left or found at the scene. He's the one with a strong motive to kill Toby. Not you."

"Well, according to that so-called evidence, I stole the guns and drugs," she reminded him.

"And that's just dirt to muddy the waters," Jace answered. "There's absolutely no evidence that you used his badge to go into warehouses and steal confiscated items. No evidence that you'd know how to fence such things even if they came into your possession. Right, Glenn?"

"Right," the deputy verified. "I'm sorry, Linnea." He scrubbed his hand over his face. "I know it must hurt for you to hear all the things your brother's done."

"It does hurt," she said under her breath. "It hurts even more to know that he wants Jace and me dead. Gideon's basically thrown away the first three decades of his life as if they didn't matter." She paused again. "Why?"

"Money," Jace and Glenn answered together. "Lots of money," Jace emphasized.

And with that reminder, he thought it'd be easier for

Linnea to suss out her brother's motive. Gideon had always loved the finer things, but his family had been ranchers and hadn't always had a lot of ready cash to give him those things. Jace, and probably Linnea, as well, had overlooked Gideon's thirst for more, more, more, but that thirst had likely been the reason for what was going on now. Added to that, Gideon was cocky enough to believe that he'd never get caught.

Silence settled over the room for several long moments before Glenn cleared his throat, obviously pulling himself back from his thoughts about Gideon.

"I've set up a schedule so your door will be guarded by the reserve deputies," Glenn explained. "The Mercy Ridge Sheriff's office called and offered to help us with that if needed."

That was a surprise since the sheriff of the neighboring town of Mercy Ridge was Barrett Logan, and Jace and he weren't exactly pals. Of course, that non-pal status wasn't based on anything recent that had happened. Years ago, Jace's dad had had an affair with Barrett's mom. An affair that had ended disastrously and created a couple of decades of bad blood between the families. But obviously, Barrett didn't let bad blood get in the way of offering help to a fellow officer.

"I'll call Barrett and thank him," Jace said. Heck, he'd even take Barrett up on his offer if it meant keeping Linnea safe.

"Anything else you need me to do?" Glenn asked a moment later. "Anything else you need at all?" He extended that question to Linnea.

She shook her head. "A nurse gave me a toiletry kit and another pair of scrubs. That'll be enough for tonight. Maybe tomorrow, I can go to my house and get some things."

Jace didn't offer her any hope on that. "Even if the CSIs are done, it's not safe for you to go back there. Gideon could be watching the place."

Though that last part was a stretch. There was enough gossip in Culver Crossing for Gideon to have heard exactly where Jace and Linnea were. It would be gutsy to come after them at the hospital, but Gideon had already proven the gutsy side of himself by trying to gun down Jace.

"All right, then I'll head out," Glenn said as he tipped his head to the backpack he'd brought in. "All the reports on Toby are in your email, and I'll make sure you get any updates. Call me when you're sprung tomorrow to let me know where you'll be going."

Jace started to say that he'd be heading to his office. Which he would do. But it wasn't a place where Linnea could stay long-term, and that meant Jace had to give it some thought.

"I'll call you," Jace assured him.

Glenn turned, opened the door and practically ran into the wide-shouldered man who'd been about to knock. Jace instantly recognized him. Lieutenant Bryce Cannon, Gideon's boss at San Antonio PD.

"He said he's a cop," the security guard relayed. "And I had him show me his badge. I wouldn't have let him in without asking you first, though."

Jace slid his hand over his gun, which was still in the backpack. He didn't know Bryce that well, had only met him a time or two at cookouts and such at Gideon's. Jace had heard nothing about him to make him believe he was dirty. Still, best not to take chances, because Gideon had had help on the criminal path he'd taken, and he could have gotten that from his boss.

"Sorry to bother you," Bryce said, stepping inside the room.

Linnea knew Bryce, as well, and had probably socialized with him a lot more than Jace had. In fact, Jace had heard Gideon mention something about Bryce and Linnea dating. But that had been a while back. Years ago. So, obviously, things hadn't worked out between them.

She moved closer to Jace, putting her body right next to his. Glenn must have picked up on the suddenly tense vibe, because he stayed put.

"Did you find Gideon?" Jace asked the lieutenant.

"No. Not yet, but I've got plenty of men out looking for him."

Men who could be in league with Gideon. This was definitely not the time to trust anyone who'd worked with him.

"But that's not why I'm here," Bryce continued. His attention wasn't on Jace but on Linnea. "There's a problem, and I wanted to let you know what was heading your way."

Because the back of her hand was touching his, Jace felt her go stiff. "What problem?" she asked.

Bryce took a moment before he responded. "There's an ATF agent, Lionel Zimmerman."

"I met him," Linnea said when Bryce didn't add more. "Is he dead?"

Bryce blinked, clearly surprised by her question. "No. He's very much alive. Or at least he was a half hour ago when he called me. He wanted to give me a heads-up that he'd be coming to Culver Crossing this afternoon."

"Why?" she pressed.

"I'm sorry, Linnea." Bryce lowered his head, shook it. "But Zimmerman's coming here to arrest you."

Chapter Six

Linnea figured she should be shocked or furious with what Bryce had just told her, but she could thank the bone-weary fatigue from spent adrenaline for keeping her response low-key.

Unlike Jace.

He cursed, belting out some very bad words along with shooting eye daggers at Bryce. "Zimmerman can go to hell. He's not arresting Linnea." Jace growled out more profanity. "She didn't kill Toby. She was framed."

Bryce dragged in a weary-sounding breath. Weary because he might have thought of himself as just the messenger of this bad news. "Zimmerman wants to arrest Linnea for what he believes is her part in the transfer and sale of the guns and drugs that Gideon stole," he reminded Jace.

It wasn't the first time today that she'd been accused of that. It was in the "dying" note that Toby had left. A note that had yet to be verified as the real deal. Linnea suspected that Gideon had planted other "evidence" just in case the cops and feds needed more ammunition to look in her direction.

"I'm sorry," Bryce told her, and his tone practically

screamed of the old intimacy between them. And there had been some intimacy.

Sort of.

She'd dated Bryce for about a month, and before that, they'd hung out whenever they were at Gideon's at the same time. They'd never had sex, though. She just hadn't been that into him, but Bryce had apparently been into her.

When she ended things, he hadn't exactly turned stalker, but he'd called her multiple times to ask her to reconsider. Had sent her flowers. And had even talked Gideon into trying to sway her into giving him another chance.

It hadn't worked.

And when Bryce hadn't gotten her to cave, he'd turned petty by insulting her to mutual friends. He'd also given her the cold shoulder and even some nasty glances when they ended up at the same social functions. That was why things were awkward between them, and that *intimate* tone only made it more so.

Linnea hoped that Bryce wouldn't use this mess of a situation to try to rekindle things between them or to vent more of his venom about her. But she pushed that possibility aside. For now. She pushed everything aside except for this latest development.

"Zimmerman must think he has proof of my wrongdoing if he plans to arrest me," Linnea pointed out.

"He's not arresting you," Jace snapped.

"I agree," Bryce said, giving a nod to Linnea to let her know he was addressing her comment, "but that's Zimmerman's plan. He says he got eyewitness statements from an anonymous source that detail your involvement."

That didn't improve Jace's mood. "His anonymous

source is Gideon," he snarled. "Or maybe Zimmerman himself. Because any idiot who'd plan to arrest Linnea on evidence like that is suspect at best."

"I agree," Bryce repeated, and his quietly spoken agreement finally had Jace simmering down. "I'm not even sure Zimmerman managed to get a warrant for an arrest. I doubt he did. He's riled though because in his mind, you sneaked out of the cabin after he offered you help."

"Help I couldn't trust," Jace pointed out.

"I know," the lieutenant agreed. "But I suspect he plans to come here, throw his federal weight around and try to take Linnea into custody for questioning. I know you won't let that happen," he quickly added before Jace could object.

Maybe it was all that awkwardness playing into this, but Linnea didn't think Bryce was paying Jace a compliment. It seemed to be more of an…observation. One with undertones that she could spin back to their breakup. Crud. Did Bryce think Jace and she were together? If so, she didn't want any jealousy, even tiny bits of it, playing into this.

Bryce shifted his attention back to her. "You shouldn't be arrested," he stated. "Because Zimmerman might be as dirty as Gideon."

Since Jace and she had already come to that conclusion, that wasn't exactly a news flash, but she was hoping that Bryce had something to back up that accusation. Of course, she'd also considered that Bryce might be her brother's partner in crime. If that was true, then he was even more dangerous than Gideon. After all, there wasn't a statewide search going on for Bryce. He could use his badge to come and go as he pleased.

Including into Jace's hospital room.

Thank heaven Glenn had put Jace's gun in the backpack. But maybe it wouldn't be necessary for them to use it.

"Please tell me you have any shred of proof that Zimmerman and Gideon have teamed up," Jace said.

Bryce shook his head. "But I do have a lead." Again, he looked at Linnea. "Tammy Wheatly is missing, and I think she's on the run with Gideon."

"Tammy," she repeated on a groan, and she looked at Jace to fill him in.

"I know who she is," Jace said before she could explain. "She's Gideon's criminal informant turned girlfriend."

Linnea pulled back her shoulders. She'd known about the CI part but not the other. "Gideon and Tammy are involved?"

"Yeah," Jace answered as Bryce made a sound of agreement.

It was Bryce who continued. "Though *involved* maybe isn't the right word for it. I think it was just sex for Gideon." He stopped, his forehead bunching up. "It could be a whole lot more for Tammy. Gideon mentioned that she was getting clingy."

"Clingy?" Linnea repeated on a huff.

This was the first she was hearing about any of this, but it shouldn't have surprised her. Gideon didn't make a habit of discussing his sex partners with her. Especially a sex partner who shouldn't be one.

"Did either one of you tell Gideon that it wasn't a smart idea for a cop to sleep around with a CI?" Linnea threw out there. "I mean, the *C* in CI stands for *criminal*."

"I counseled him about it," Bryce answered. "He agreed to end things with her. That was two days ago."

That was the day before her brother had tried to kill Jace. So maybe there hadn't been time for a breakup. It was also possible that Gideon had never intended to end the relationship with Tammy.

She studied Bryce's expression. "You think Tammy helped him with his illegal guns and drug operation. You believe she could still be helping him."

"I do," Bryce said without hesitation. "Tammy's finished her parole for drug possession, but according to some of the other CIs, she's kept up with her old contacts. She'd be able to get the drugs to buyers. Maybe the guns, too. That's why I wanted to talk to her, but when I went to her place in San Antonio, her landlord and neighbors said they haven't seen her in days."

That didn't necessarily mean that Tammy was with Gideon, but it was possible. It was also possible that the woman was just off with friends. Still, it was suspicious.

"I'm getting a warrant to have some detectives go into Tammy's place," Bryce continued a moment later. "If she's really involved in this, she might not have left anything incriminating behind, but maybe we'll get lucky."

Linnea figured it would have to be some major luck if Tammy left anything that would lead them to Gideon's current location. Still, it was worth a try.

Bryce volleyed some glances at Jace and her, and Linnea thought that meant he had something else on his mind. And she was right.

"I've arranged for a safe house for Linnea," he finally said to Jace. "In fact, I think it would be a good idea to take her there now. That way, she can stay out of Zimmerman's way while I work on killing any warrant he might have managed to get. It's the smart thing to do, what with Gideon after her."

"Gideon's after Jace, too," Linnea quickly pointed out.

Bryce nodded. "But Jace is a cop and can take care of himself. I'm not so sure he can take care of you right now." He sighed when she just stared at him. "Linnea, this isn't a personal offer. It's something I feel I need to do. I owe you," he amended. "If I'd uncovered Gideon's dirty dealings sooner, he'd be behind bars, and you wouldn't be in danger."

"Maybe," she agreed in a mumble. She added some volume to her voice, though, when she continued. "But even with Gideon in jail, hurt or incapacitated, I'd still be in danger because none of us believes that my brother was acting alone. Whoever got to Toby could get to me."

"And that's my point," Bryce practically snapped. "You're a target here. You need to be in a safe house."

She glanced at Jace, who'd stayed quiet through all of this. A huge surprise, since he usually had an opinion on such things. But he hadn't needed to voice this particular opinion for her to know where he stood. Jace and she were of one mind when it came to this.

"Thank you, but no," she told Bryce. "I won't be going to a safe house." At least not one that he'd arranged for her.

Bryce's mouth didn't exactly drop open, but his expression showed his surprise. "I'm offering you a chance at safety. A chance to live."

"Yeah, I got that," Linnea told him, "but I'd rather take my chances here with Jace."

"Jace is hurt," Bryce snapped. "He can't protect you if someone comes barging in here."

Linnea shrugged and tried to look totally unbothered by the fact that what he'd said might be true. "Jace protected me just fine when we were in the woods and a sniper tried to take us out." She paused, met his gaze head-on. "I'm not going to a safe house with you," she repeated.

Bryce threw sharp glances at them again, but this time his eyes were slightly narrowed. "Okay. Fine." He opened his mouth, closed it and then shook his head. "The offer stands if you change your mind."

With that, Bryce turned and walked out. Or rather, he stormed out. He was obviously riled that she hadn't taken him up on his plan.

"I'll head back to the office and see if there are any updates," Glenn muttered, stepping out.

Linnea looked down at Jace and realized that he'd slid his hand over the gun in the backpack. "I take it that you didn't want me to go with Bryce?"

"No, I didn't," he said right off. "I don't trust him. Actually, there aren't many people I trust right now."

"I hear you," she muttered. "My list of people I trust is pretty short and has just one name on it. Yours. Maybe Glenn's, too, but for right now, it's just you."

"Put Glenn's on the list," he advised. "The rest of my deputies, too." Jace looked away, cursed. "Bryce was right about one thing, though. I might not be able to fight off someone who breaks in."

This wasn't a pity party. Jace wasn't the kind of guy who indulged in self-pity. And both of them knew there was truth to what he'd just said.

"You might not be able to save me," she admitted.

"Then again, maybe no one can. Or heck, maybe I can save myself and you."

Because she wanted to lighten the mood some, Linnea flexed her arms and motioned toward the slightly ripped muscles there. Slightly. He looked at her, but there was no lightening of his mood.

"Am I going to have to talk about that kiss in the barn again to distract you?" she teased.

His hand reached out, extremely fast for someone recovering from a gunshot wound. He took hold of her wrist, drew her down to him, and he very much distracted her by kissing her.

Linnea definitely hadn't seen that coming, and the feeling of his mouth on hers nearly knocked her off her feet. It robbed her of any common sense, too, because she forgot all about the danger. Forgot about her brother. Heck, she forgot how to breathe. But, man, oh man, she could taste and feel.

There it was. That trickle of heat, like warm honey making its way from her mouth to the rest of her. Making her tingle. Making her want things that she was certain Jace could give her. Linnea wasn't sure how Jace could manage such things with only some lip-to-lip contact. Then again, this was Jace. He had her number when it came to such things.

He didn't deepen this kiss. Didn't use his tongue or touch her except for the grip he had on her wrist. And that grip just melted away when he leaned back, and she stared into those stormy gray eyes.

Jace didn't say a word. He just stared at her, clearly waiting for her reaction. Of course, he could see her flushed face. Could hear her ragged breathing. Could almost certainly see the pulse throbbing in her throat, and he would know that the rest of her was doing some throbbing, too.

"Did that distract you?" he asked.

Except he didn't just ask, he drawled it. Hotshot was back. But the attitude didn't last long. It vanished as quickly as it'd come. Jace laid his head back on the bed and looked as if he wanted to curse as he had when Bryce had been there.

"A distraction isn't a good thing right now," he spelled out for her. "I need to be working on the investigation."

Linnea resisted saying something along the lines of *No, it wasn't a good thing, but the kiss was amazing.* It had been. Both amazing and incredibly hot. Instead, she reached into the backpack and took out the laptop. Best to put the kiss aside and forget that it had happened.

Or rather try to forget.

She was reasonably sure she'd remember it for the rest of her life. Ditto for the first one he'd given her. But what might be the hardest for her to forget was the future kisses that she very much wanted from him.

"Since typing might be hard on your arm," she said, "I can do whatever computer searches you need."

He stared at her for a moment. Maybe because he was having that whole forgetting problem, too, but Jace finally nodded.

"Send Glenn an email," he instructed. "His name and addy are in my contacts. Ask him to do a full background on Tammy. I want to know everything about her, and if SAPD hasn't put a BOLO on her, I want that done, too."

While Linnea was pulling up that info, she considered something. "If Tammy isn't with Gideon, she could be dead. Gideon might be tying up any loose ends." And a woman who was privy to his crimes would indeed qualify as a loose end.

Jace nodded so fast that it was obviously something he'd already considered. "It's possible, but if so, Gideon managed to cover some ground fast. Toby's here in Culver Crossing, and according to Bryce, Tammy's house is in San Antonio. Of course, Gideon or his partner could have had Tammy meet them somewhere."

True, and Tammy might not have realized her loose-end status until it'd been too late. Still, if what they feared hadn't happened, and they managed to find the woman, she could perhaps tell them the identity of Gideon's partner and Gideon's whereabouts. The DA might be willing to make her a deal in exchange for info that could bring down a dirty cop and a criminal operation.

Linnea fired off the email to Glenn and turned to Jace to get instructions on what she should do next, when there was a knock at the door. A moment later, the security guard peered in.

"Sheriff Castillo," the guard said. "You got a visitor, and he says it's real important."

"Who is it?" Jace asked, and he slid his hand over his gun again.

"It's me," their visitor said, and even though Linnea wasn't that familiar with his voice, she still recognized him.

Zimmerman.

The agent stepped around the guard and flashed his badge. His gaze zoomed right to Linnea.

"Miss Martell." Zimmerman whipped out her name. "You need to come with me now."

Chapter Seven

Even though Jace was nowhere near steady, he got out of the bed, standing in front of Linnea. He also drew his gun.

That didn't cool down the hot anger in Zimmerman's eyes.

"Do I need to give you a closer look at my badge?" Zimmerman snarled at Jace. "Do I need to remind you that I'm an ATF agent and that you ran out on me at the cabin when I was trying to help you?"

"ATF agents can be dirty, just like cops," Jace pointed out. "Linnea's brother almost certainly has a partner, and since I don't know you, it could be you."

That didn't help with the anger, either. Muscles tightened and flexed in Zimmerman's jaw. Jace figured the same thing was happening on his own face. He was sick and tired of dealing with badge slingers that he wasn't sure he could trust.

"I'm taking her into custody," Zimmerman insisted. "At best she's a material witness to her brother's crimes. At worst, she's working with him. I intend to find out which."

Linnea started to move out from behind Jace, probably because she wanted to look Zimmerman in the eye to return some verbal fire. Jace was all for verbal fire, but Zimmerman was armed, and if he pulled that standard-issue Glock, then Jace wanted himself between the agent and her. That was why Jace shifted—causing him enough pain to make him have to bite back a grimace—so that he was in front of her again.

"At best, you have a boatload of speculation about Linnea," Jace shot back at the agent. "At worst, your intentions, whether good or bad, could get her killed. The second she walks out of this hospital, someone could try to gun her down."

He heard Linnea's slight shiver of breath. She'd already no doubt considered this, but it was likely a kick to the teeth to hear it spelled out like that.

"Considering I'm not a patient in the hospital, I can protect her a lot better than you can," Zimmerman argued. He motioned for Linnea to step out. "You're coming with me."

"She's not." Jace didn't raise his voice, but the hard stare he gave Zimmerman let him know this was not up for negotiation.

Since Bryce had just left the hospital only minutes earlier, he probably hadn't had time to learn anything that would help put a stop to Zimmerman. But Jace wasn't going to wait for Bryce to lend a hand.

Zimmerman huffed. "She can help me find her brother. She can put an end to this just by cooperating with me."

"Clearly, I have a different opinion about that," Jace countered.

"I don't know where Gideon is," Linnea spoke up, and much to Jace's frustration, she stepped around him so they were side by side. "If I did, I would have already told Jace. I trust him," she added after pausing a heartbeat. "I don't trust you. No offense. But right now, your badge is a huge negative."

"You don't have a choice," Zimmerman insisted, and he took a step toward her. "I'm taking you into custody."

"Enough of this," Jace growled. "Show me your warrant, and then I can start the calls to get it blocked."

That stopped the agent in his tracks, and even though he wasn't quick to admit it, Zimmerman's narrowed eyes told Jace what he needed to know.

There was no warrant.

"Without a warrant, you have no grounds to take Linnea," Jace added, and he tried not to sound too smug about that.

Oh, that didn't please Zimmerman. "I'll have a warrant by morning."

"Then, you can come back, and I'll start those calls to block it," Jace said just as fast.

"And in the meantime, her brother is as free as a bird." Zimmerman flung an accusing finger at Linnea. "If she'd just cooperate, we could get him off the streets so he can't go after someone else. You of all people should know that, since Gideon's the one who shot you."

Jace shrugged. Regretted it. Oh, man. He really needed to do some fast healing. "I'm well aware of who shot me. Well aware, too, that you're on a fishing expedition to help bolster your investigation. Linnea isn't going on that expedition with you."

"Tomorrow she will," Zimmerman snapped.

"Then come back tomorrow when you have the warrant," Jace *invited*. In the meantime, he'd go ahead and start those calls to block Zimmerman in any way he could. If the calls failed, Jace would get her out of the agent's reach.

And yeah, that wasn't just bending the law. It was breaking it.

Still, having her stay with him was his best shot at keeping her alive.

"Uh, boss," someone said from the door. It was Deputy Crystal Rankin, and she was giving Zimmerman the hard eye. She also set a large leather bag on the floor and rested her hand on the butt of her service weapon. "Is there a problem?"

"No," Jace assured her, though his body language no doubt indicated otherwise. "Agent Zimmerman was just leaving."

Despite Jace's tone of "don't let the door hit you in the ass on the way out," Zimmerman didn't budge. He stood there, shifting his gaze from Linnea, to Jace, then to Crystal. He definitely noted the way Crystal had now gripped her gun, and he must have decided that this wasn't a fight he was going to win.

"You can't block this," Zimmerman said to Jace, and it sounded like a warning. "This investigation is under my jurisdiction now."

"Really. *Yours*?" Jace challenged. "What about San Antonio PD? Seems they'd want to go after one of their own."

Plus, there was the part about Toby being killed in Culver Crossing. Toby might have been a screw-up, but he definitely qualified as one of Jace's own.

"SAPD is running their own Internal Affairs investigation, but this is now a federal case. My case," Zimmerman said like he was speaking gospel. "You'll be getting official word on that very soon."

Zimmerman didn't seem to be bluffing about that, so Jace settled for saying, "All right. But without a warrant, you're leaving. If you refuse, my deputy and the security guard will escort you from the building."

As expected, the agent didn't like any of that. Also as expected, Zimmerman tried to intimidate him with a stare down. It didn't work. Jace kept up his own stare and motioned for Crystal and the guard to get Zimmerman out of there. Crystal reached for the agent's arm, but Zimmerman threw off her attempted grip with far more force than necessary.

"I'll be back," Zimmerman said. That was a warning, too. But he finally turned to leave.

Jace heard Linnea release the breath that she'd no doubt been holding too long, and they watched until Zimmerman was out of sight. Only then did Crystal shut the door. Only then did Jace get back in the bed. It was best not to risk a slam to his dignity by falling on his butt.

"You want me to have him followed, to make sure he leaves the hospital?" Crystal asked.

He considered it and shook his head. "He'll leave, and maybe now he knows he can't just walk in here."

Jace was also hoping that Linnea and he wouldn't be in this room much longer. He needed to get out so he could take her someplace where people he didn't trust couldn't get close to her.

Crystal nodded but cast an uneasy glance at the windows. Jace had done the same himself, a little while ago. The blinds were down, but it wouldn't take much for someone to figure out what room he was in and start blasting. That was yet another reason to take Linnea elsewhere.

But where?

That was the million-dollar question, and he didn't have an answer yet. That was something else he had to work out before morning, because one way or another, that was when Linnea and he would be leaving the hospital.

"I'll be standing guard outside your door for a while," Crystal explained. "Bennie will relieve me at midnight."

Bennie Waterman was another of his deputies, one with a ton of experience and a level head. Ditto for Crystal. Glenn had chosen well when he'd worked up the schedule for guard duty.

"No one gets in here without you asking me first," Jace emphasized.

Crystal gave another nod, and she made a sound to indicate that was understood. "The CSIs finished up at Toby's a little while ago," she said. "They found some blood on the knob of the back door. The lock had been compromised, so that's how we think the killer gained access to the house."

Jace had yet to see photos of the crime scene, but he suspected that because of the manner of death, there would be lots of blood in and around Toby's body. It was highly likely that some of that blood had gotten on the killer, and he or she had transferred some to that knob on the way out.

"The blood was on both the front and the back of the knob," Crystal added. "There was also blood inside the lock, maybe transferred there when the intruder picked it."

Well, that caused Jace to amend his theory and hinted at another possibility. One that could be a huge break in the investigation. The blood inside the lock could mean the person who'd entered had already been bleeding. If it wasn't Gideon's partner or hired gun who'd killed Toby, then Gideon himself could have done the deed.

"It could be the killer's blood," Linnea concluded after glancing at Crystal and him. "It could be Gideon's."

"Could be," Jace agreed, and he looked up at Crystal. "Light a fire under the lab to make sure it gets processed ASAP."

"I will. I brought my laptop with me so I could get some work done." The deputy picked up the leather bag that she'd set on the floor when she'd seen Zimmerman, and tipped her head to the windows. "Now that I'm relieving the security guard, I'll ask him to patrol the grounds. That might discourage someone from trying to get close."

It might, and Jace gave her the go-ahead nod, along with a thank-you as Crystal left the room.

"You shot Gideon," Linnea said once Crystal had shut the door. "But he'd know better than to leave a trace of himself on that doorknob or inside the lock. Or anywhere else in the house, for that matter." She stopped and some of the color drained from her face.

"What's wrong?" he immediately asked.

Linnea held up her left hand, and he saw the small bandage just below the base of her fingers. "Day before yesterday, I cut myself when I was opening a bag of mulch. The job was near Gideon's place, so I went there to get cleaned up. I wiped away some blood with some paper towels, cleaned up and threw the bloody towels in the trash."

"Gideon was there?" Jace wanted to know.

"Yes. He's the one who handed me the paper towel

roll so I could tear off some sheets." She looked a little ill when she sank onto the side of the bed next to him. "The cut wasn't bad, but there was blood." Linnea paused. "That happened the day before I found out what he'd been doing."

She didn't have to ask the question that was on her mind. Jace had followed this through to one possible conclusion.

A bad one.

That Gideon had used those paper towels to plant her blood on the doorknob and inside the lock. If so, it meant that after Jace had shot him, Gideon could have gone back to his house to get the bloody paper towels. Or maybe Gideon had had someone retrieve them to be used at Toby's. Either way, it could be Linnea's DNA that turned up when the lab ran the tests.

Hell.

"This could give Zimmerman ammunition to get that warrant for my arrest," Linnea muttered.

It could, but Jace could still argue that this was a setup, that Linnea had been with him in the cabin when Toby was murdered a good twenty miles away. That was why he needed to press the medical examiner to get a more exact time of death. It could be critical info in fighting Zimmerman.

And that led Jace to something they needed to consider.

"If things don't go our way with Zimmerman," he said, "you and I might have to take a trip."

She stayed quiet a moment. "We might have to go into hiding."

It twisted at him to consider this because the bottom line was that it would mean breaking the law. He believed in upholding the law, but it wouldn't be justice to hand Linnea over to a federal agent who could allow her to be murdered.

Jace held her gaze a moment longer, silently letting her know that yes, they'd go into hiding if Zimmerman gave them no other choice. Maybe, though, he could find another ATF agent, one he trusted. He didn't like the fact that Zimmerman had shown up at the cabin so soon after the shooting. And that Zimmerman was pushing so hard to try to take Linnea into custody. Maybe he was just doing his job, but Jace had to consider the agent might be trying to get Linnea into a position where he could silence her.

He took out his phone to get started on finding another ATF agent, but before he could make a call, it rang.

Apparently, Glenn had transferred Jace's contacts to this replacement phone, because the deputy's name popped up on the screen.

"Boss," Glenn said the moment Jace answered. "Gideon's been sighted."

Since the situation with Zimmerman was still in his head, it took a moment for that to sink in, and Jace put the call on speaker so that Linnea could hear. This was definitely something she'd want to know.

"Where?" Jace asked.

Oh, yes, she wanted to know. She not only moved closer, but Linnea also pulled in her breath.

"On a security camera outside a convenience store in Bulverde," Glenn explained.

That was about twenty miles away. Not far at all.

"You're sure it's Gideon?" Jace pressed.

"Positive. Gideon called the sheriff's office about

twenty minutes ago and said I should check the feed from that particular security camera. The store manager cooperated and sent it to me right away." Glenn paused. "Boss, it's something you're gonna want to see. I'm sending it to your laptop now."

Jace put his phone aside so he could take the laptop, and sure enough, the moment he checked his messages, he spotted the video file that Glenn had just emailed him. The deputy had apparently done the work of going through the feed so it started with a man moving into camera range. A man wearing a black San Antonio Spurs cap and dark sunglasses.

It was Gideon.

Linnea made a slight gasp, and judging from the muttered profanity that followed, it was a sound that she wished she'd managed to stifle. It had to be a shock to see the face of a brother who wanted her dead, but she had probably hoped she'd steeled herself up better by now. Jace was thinking there wasn't enough steeling in the world for her to see that face.

"He's alive," Linnea said under her breath.

Yeah, he was.

Jace froze the frame and zoomed in, checking Gideon for any signs of a gunshot wound. He certainly wasn't bloody or hunched in pain, but he was wearing a bulky windbreaker, outerwear that wasn't needed since they weren't in the middle of a storm. So Gideon might have used the windbreaker to cover up a bandage. Or it could be that Jace had been wrong, and he hadn't managed to shoot him after all.

He hit the play function again, and Jace watched as Gideon looked straight up at the camera. In the same motion, the man pulled a sheet of paper from inside the windbreaker.

"Something's written on it," Linnea quickly pointed out.

He'd noticed that, too, and was already zooming in. There were only five words, followed by ten numbers, but they were written so large that they took up almost the entire sheet of paper.

"Jace, we have to talk," Linnea read loud, and she repeated the numbers that Gideon had on the makeshift sign he was holding.

"A phone number," Jace mumbled.

"Yes, but it's not Gideon's number. Well, not his usual one. But he's probably using a burner cell so his location can't be tracked."

That was Jace's bet, too.

"Please tell me cops were sent to this location," Jace said to Glenn on the phone.

"They were. They're on the way now," Glenn assured him. "I'm guessing, though, that Gideon won't be there."

"No," Jace agreed, "but let me give him a call and see what he has to say. I'll record the conversation and send it to you to be analyzed."

He ended the call with Glenn, and once he had the recorder function on, Jace quickly pressed in the numbers that had been on the sign. Since it rang, it was indeed a phone number. A working one, because on the fourth ring, the call transferred to a message.

"Jace," the message said. Definitely Gideon's voice. "I've been set up. I had to say what I said to you in the woods. If I hadn't, we would have both been executed on the spot."

He glanced at Linnea to see how she was reacting, and she had the same skeptical look that Jace was certain was on his own face.

"In a day or two, I'll call you with a time and a place for a meeting," Gideon went on. "I have proof I'm innocent, and I'll give it to you then. In the meantime, protect my sister. Because, Jace, Linnea is the reason all of this is happening."

Chapter Eight

Linnea is the reason all of this is happening.

Though she'd tried to tell herself that her brother's message was an attempt to muddy the investigation, Linnea hadn't been able to push the possibility of it aside. It was one of the reasons that she hadn't gotten much sleep. That, and the fact that she had spent the night in a recliner right next to Jace.

He'd occupied plenty of her thoughts, too.

Those thoughts proved she was off-kilter. Way off. Even the threat of danger hanging over them hadn't stopped her from remembering that Jace and she would no doubt be sharing tight quarters for a while. Tight quarters that certainly wouldn't give her space to recover from the effect he was having on her.

Like now, for instance.

It was barely past six in the morning, a time that Jace had decided was when they needed to leave the hospital. He'd already spoken to the nurses about getting Dr. Garcia in to sign his release papers. He had also set up transportation with his deputies and asked them to secure her house—where they'd be going until he could come up with another solution.

The temporary solution caused her stomach to jitter

some. After all, someone had broken into her house and stolen the knife used in Toby's murder. Still, it made more sense to go there than to Jace's. His ranch was outside of town, and her place wasn't that far from the sheriff's office. The deputies would be able to get there in minutes if there was a problem.

Unfortunately, it might take a killer less than minutes to finish them off.

To ready himself for their departure, which Jace apparently thought would happen very soon, he'd already managed to remove his hospital gown and was attempting to dress himself in the clothes that Glenn had brought over the day before. That meant he was naked.

Well, mostly.

While sitting on the edge of his bed, he'd gotten on his boxers while she pretended she was blind, but he was struggling with the jeans. On a sigh, Linnea ditched the blindness pretense and went to him.

"You know," she muttered, "this is going to give me inappropriate thoughts about you."

She caught onto the waist of his jeans and pulled them up. And yep, there were indeed some inappropriate thoughts. Some touching, too. Linnea tried not to notice all the interesting parts of him. Of course, everything about Jace was interesting.

When she zipped him up, she lifted her head and collided with his gaze. He was watching her, and he appeared to be fighting a smile. Of all the reactions he could have had, that wasn't an especially bad one. It was better than pain. Or heat.

But it didn't last.

The heat came when his gaze dropped to her mouth. He didn't kiss her, but it made her wish he would. Instead, he did the responsible thing and looked away. He reached for a blue button-up shirt, but Linnea didn't even let him attempt that on his own. Not with that huge bandage on his shoulder. She got his good arm in the sleeve and got to work easing on the shirt on the other side.

"Linnea is the reason all of this is happening," she said, repeating what Gideon had told them in that recorded message.

Reminding Jace of that was a distraction ploy because she knew all the moving around had to be painful, but she also did want to open up another discussion about it. When she'd tried the night before, all she'd gotten from Jace was a growled, "Gideon is the reason all of this is happening."

Jace looked up at her, repeated his words from the night before. He added, "This isn't your fault."

Linnea wanted to believe that. She truly did, but it was yet something else to eat away at her.

"No one was holding a gun to Gideon's head when he ran from me," Jace went on. "No one went into those woods with us. If someone had been with him, I would have seen or heard something."

That was true. But there was something else she wanted him to consider.

"The person wouldn't have had to be there to threaten me," she suggested. "Playing devil's advocate here, but what if someone else threatened to kill me, and that's the reason Gideon stole those guns and drugs?"

There was no way Jace's look could have gotten any flatter or be filled with any more skepticism. However, he didn't call her an idiot for considering that. He just sighed.

"He's your brother, and he probably wants you to have doubts about his guilt," Jace explained. "That way, he can get close enough to finish us off."

But then he paused. Cursed. And he shook his head.

"Trust me," Jace said, looking her straight in the eyes, "if there's a chance Gideon has been set up or forced to do these crimes, I'll find out."

"I do trust you." Linnea didn't have a single doubt about that.

"But?" he challenged.

"No but." She finished getting his arm into the shirt and began to button it. "I just wish, well, I just wish," she settled for saying.

He nodded, stared at her for a moment, and then finally broke the eye contact so he could tip his head toward his boots.

"Help me with those," he said, "and maybe we can get out of here before Zimmerman or Bryce show up."

She certainly hadn't forgotten about those two. Zimmerman just might have that arrest warrant with him. As for Bryce, if he was truly a dirty cop, then he could make a return visit to try to figure out the best way to go after them.

While Linnea helped Jace put on his boots, she also glanced up at him. This time, though, it was to see if he was in as much pain as he had been the night before. Maybe. But if so, he was doing a better job of covering it up.

"What if Dr. Garcia won't discharge you?" she asked.

"I'm leaving whether he does or not." Jace took a shoulder holster from the backpack. He must have realized he wouldn't be able to get it on with his injury, so he put it away and instead slipped his gun into the back waist of his jeans.

Getting ready in case they were attacked.

It was only a couple of blocks from the hospital to her house, but it was also broad daylight. A sniper might try to pick them off. She got such a clear image of that happening that it was probably why she nearly jumped when there was a knock at the door.

"It's me," Glenn said from the other side. The deputy raised an eyebrow when he came in and spotted Jace already dressed. "You okay, boss?"

"Fine," Jace said and didn't even pause before he jumped right in. "Update me on the investigation."

Glenn nodded as if he'd expected to do just that. "The lab folks aren't real happy with us, but I got them to put our evidence at the top of the heap." He looked at Linnea. "It was your blood on the doorknob and in the lock at Toby's house."

She didn't come close to jumping this time, because it was exactly what she had expected him to say. Still, it stung—especially if Gideon had been the one to do this.

"I had a CSI go over to Gideon's and check to see if there were any signs of bloody paper towels in the trash," Glenn went on. "Nothing. But they are going to test the trash can. If there are any traces of your blood in it, then it'll back up your statement."

Linnea huffed. She apparently needed such things to prove her innocence. Of course, Jace didn't believe she was guilty, so he was on her side.

"I didn't send Zimmerman or anybody else a copy of the lab report," Glenn explained. "If it comes up, I'll just say we got so busy what with you out on medical that I forgot to copy them."

"Good," Jace mumbled, and he showed some signs of weariness when he scrubbed his hand over his face. "What about the feed from the security camera at the convenience store?" he asked. "Did the lab guys get to study that?"

"Only a quick glance, but I had a good look at it, and I enlarged a couple of the images and printed them out for you." Glenn pulled two photographs from an envelope he was carrying and handed them to Jace.

Linnea hurried to Jace's side to study them. The man was definitely her brother, but then she hadn't had any doubts about that. In one image he was reaching inside his windbreaker, and Linnea didn't think it was the overhead street light that made him look so pale. Plus, his face was sweaty. Not the kind of perspiration from a hot night, either. He looked hurt, and his forehead was bunched up as if wincing.

"I was pretty sure I'd shot him," Jace remarked. "Guess I was right."

Yes, and it made her wonder if Gideon had gotten medical care. There would have been alerts at the hospitals in case he showed up at one of them, but he probably had friends with enough training to help him out. After all, she'd been the one who'd tended Jace's injuries.

Jace moved on to the second picture, and in this one, Gideon had moved back the windbreaker even further to take out the sign. And she saw it. The blood on his shirt.

"He's hurt but mobile," Jace said, studying the picture. "Or faking an injury to make us believe he's not as much of a threat."

Linnea hadn't gone there yet, but she would have worked her way around to it. Everything Gideon did right now was suspect.

Glenn took out some other papers from the envelope and gave them to Jace. "That's for Linnea's order of protective custody. You said you wanted that on file in case Zimmerman came in and demanded that she go with him."

Linnea hadn't heard that particular request, but she had been aware that Jace and Glenn had emailed and texted many, many times since Jace's arrival at the hospital. Jace glanced over the papers, took the pen that Glenn offered him and signed it.

"That'll hold up against a warrant?" she asked.

Glenn shrugged. "It's something we can take to a judge to maybe stop you from being transferred to ATF custody."

She didn't like that *maybe*. And that brought her to another concern. "Zimmerman could just show up at my house."

"He could," Glenn quickly agreed, "but the idea is to stop him before he gets that far."

Linnea nearly asked what happened if they didn't stop him from getting that far, but she would just have to trust Jace and Glenn on this. And keep her own gun ready. If it hadn't been stolen or confiscated during the CSI search, she had a snub-nosed .38 in her closet. Ironically, it was one that Gideon had given to her years ago.

Jace handed the signed protection order and photos back to Glenn. "What about a time of death on Toby? Do you have one yet from the medical examiner?"

"Night before last, around midnight," Glenn readily answered. "When Linnea was with you."

Yes, she had been, but with Jace unconscious, he wouldn't have known that for certain.

"She was with me," Jace verified. "And what about Tammy? Anything new on her?"

Glenn's face brightened a little. "Yes. One of Tammy's neighbors said the lights were on in her apartment late last night, and he called SAPD because he knew they were looking for her. However, before the cops could show up, the neighbor said someone came out carrying a suitcase. He was pretty sure it was Tammy."

So the woman was alive. Too bad the cops hadn't gotten there a little sooner, and they could have taken her for questioning. Then again, if Bryce was dirty, he might have made sure Tammy never got the chance to be interrogated.

"Was anyone with Tammy?" Jace asked, and Linnea knew he meant Gideon.

"No, not that the neighbor saw, but he said it's possible someone was waiting for her in her car. It was dark, and she hadn't parked in her usual space in front of her door. She'd left her car at the edge of the parking lot where there isn't much light."

No way had Tammy done that by chance, so maybe she had been trying to conceal whoever had been in the vehicle. Though it was possible she was just trying to sneak in and out without anyone noticing. Plenty of people, including cops, could have seen her walking across a parking lot. After all, Bryce had said he intended to get a warrant to search Tammy's place.

Jace stayed quiet a moment, obviously giving that some thought. "It would have been stupid for Gideon to go there with her."

It would have been, but maybe Gideon had risked it if Tammy had needed to get something important from her apartment. Perhaps money or cash. Or weapons.

There was a quick knock at the door, and as he'd done before, Jace automatically stepped in front of her. Glenn pivoted, too, and took the stance of a lawman about to draw his gun. But it wasn't a threat. It was Dr. Garcia who came walking in.

The doctor took one look at Jace and frowned. Then he sighed as if in resignation. "Will it do any good whatsoever to tell you that you need another day of bed rest?" Dr. Garcia asked.

"None," Jace answered without hesitation. "I'm leaving." He shifted his attention to Glenn. "Is the cruiser ready to take Linnea and me?"

"It is," Glenn replied. "You want me to move it closer to the exit doors?"

"I do. Linnea and I will be out in just a few minutes."

That was no doubt Jace's way of telling the doctor that he wasn't going to wait around, and that was probably why Dr. Garcia sighed again.

"Okay." The doctor scribbled something on Jace's chart. "I'll phone in a script for some pain meds. Linnea, will you be able to check the wound and redress it the way you did before Jace got to the hospital?"

She nodded, though she wondered if she should say no and try to talk Jace into staying put a little longer. "Is it safe for Jace to leave?" she asked. "Will it cause some damage for him to move around?"

"Not necessarily damage, but it'll slow the healing process." The doctor scrawled something else on a notepad and handed it to her. "That's my cell number if you have any questions about the wound or the meds."

"I won't be taking the meds," Jace insisted.

The doctor looked resigned to that, too. "Then, at least take it easy and get plenty of rest."

Of course, everybody in the room, including the doctor, knew that wasn't going to happen. Once they got to her place, Jace would launch into what would turn out to be a long workday as he took up the investigation.

"I'll move the cruiser," Glenn said after the doctor walked out. "I'll text you when I'm ready."

Jace muttered a thank-you and began to gather up the things to put in the backpack. Here was something she could do to stop him from moving around too much, so she took the laptop from his and added it to the other items already in the bag. She'd barely gotten it zipped up when Jace's phone rang.

"That couldn't be Glenn already," she muttered. And it wasn't.

"It's me," the caller said the moment Jace answered.

Even though the phone wasn't on speaker, Linnea had no trouble hearing the voice.

Gideon.

Chapter Nine

A lot of emotions went through Jace when he heard his old friend's voice, but the trust he'd once gotten from their friendship wasn't one of them. Despite what Gideon had said about being set up, Jace had some serious doubts.

"Where are you?" Jace asked him, and he hit the record function on his phone so he could go over every bit of this conversation later.

Of course, Gideon didn't jump to answer that. He not only paused for several moments, but Jace also thought he heard another voice. One murmuring in the background. Of course, that could be part of the ruse. If a ruse was indeed what Gideon had in mind. Or maybe Tammy was with him, though Jace couldn't tell if it was a man's or woman's voice.

"I need to set up a meeting with you," Gideon continued long seconds later. "We have to talk."

"So you said last night when you called." Jace didn't bother to take the sarcasm out of his tone. "Do you really believe I'm going to meet you and give you the chance to try to kill me again?"

"Hey, I'm risking the same thing," Gideon fired back. "You could use this meeting to gun me down, too. I just need to give you some proof that I'm innocent, and it has to be done face-to-face."

Jace huffed, but before he answered Gideon, he shot a quick glance at Linnea. As he'd expected, she was hanging on every word. Like Jace, she was probably trying to analyze everything she was hearing. Thankfully, what she wasn't doing was making any attempt to try to talk to her brother. No way did Jace want to confirm to Gideon that Linnea was with him.

"You said Linnea is the reason all of this is happening," Jace reminded Gideon. "What the hell does it mean?"

He heard Gideon take a deep breath. "I think it goes back to Bryce. Things ended badly between them, and I think it caused something to snap."

Jace huffed and rolled his eyes. "Because Linnea wouldn't keep dating him?" And yep, he added even more sarcasm. "That's the reason a cop would commit a laundry list of crimes?"

Gideon gave a huff of his own. "Bryce had a thing for Linnea for years, and when she went out with him a couple of times, he thought it was going to be the start of something big. The start of their future together."

It sounded like a crock to Jace, but again he glanced at Linnea to see if she thought that theory was even in the realm of being possible. She shrugged. Definitely not a flag-waving declaration of Bryce's innocence.

Hell.

A lieutenant in SAPD could have definitely set up something like this. Could possibly be pulling the strings even now. But then Jace remembered the taunts Gideon had tossed out during their gunfight.

"To hell with Linnea. She's the one who ratted me

out," Jace repeated. "That's what you said. And more. You also said, as far as you were concerned, Linnea could die right along with me."

"I was wired," Gideon insisted, "and the person who set me up was giving me messages, telling me what to say."

Jace jumped right on that. "If you were getting messages, then you know if it's Bryce or not."

"No. He was disguising his voice. But I believe it was Bryce," Gideon quickly added. "That's why we have to meet, so I can give you what I have."

"And what is it exactly that you have?" Jace snapped.

"Statements from CIs—"

"You mean from Tammy?" Jace interrupted.

Gideon paused. Or maybe it was a hesitation as he tried to figure out the right way to spin this. "Yes, from her and others. I've got statements from three people who say I wasn't part of the illegal operation."

As Linnea had done earlier, Jace didn't bother to point out the criminal part of the CI's title. "You'd better have more than the hearsay of CIs."

"I do. I have the login sheet for one of the warehouses where I supposedly took some guns. I have an alibi for that time."

Jace groaned but also tried to listen to the background sounds. No more mutterings. No sounds of traffic or machinery, either. "Let me guess—Tammy is your alibi?"

"She is." There was some defiance in Gideon's voice now. "But I have a receipt for the dinner we had. I can give all of this to you when we meet."

There was no *when* to this. "Why meet with me?" Jace challenged. "If you're truly innocent as you say you are, send the evidence to San Antonio PD, and they can deal with it."

Gideon didn't pause this time. "Bryce has friends throughout the force. I don't know whom I can trust there."

Jace wanted to curse and tell Gideon exactly what he thought of this idiotic demand for a meeting. But more than that, he needed information from Gideon. For starters, his location. Then, his partner or partners in crime. He seriously doubted that Gideon was just going to volunteer that, so Jace intended to keep him talking.

"How'd Bryce set you up?" Jace asked.

This time, Gideon didn't hesitate. "By duplicating my badge and using a disguise to get into those warehouses to steal the guns and weapons."

"Convenient," Jace muttered. "I haven't been able to confirm who tried to set up your sister, but that's exactly what her accuser claimed she'd done."

"Not Linnea." Gideon's voice was barely audible this time, but it sounded as if there was some regret or maybe doubt in his voice. "She's in danger, Jace. She needs to be protected."

Linnea opened her mouth, but before she could say anything, Jace shook his head to silence her—even though he knew it had to be hard for her just to stand there and listen to this.

Jace's phone dinged with a text from Glenn, letting him know that he was ready with the cruiser, but Jace didn't want to have this conversation as Linnea and he walked through the hospital. He wanted to be on full alert because it was entirely possible that this call was meant to distract them to make it easier for Gideon or a hired gun to murder them. Jace sent a quick text to Glenn to let him know they'd be out soon.

"You can't trace this call," Gideon said. He'd apparently heard the clicks of the text. "I'm using a burner."

"So I figured." Jace decided to move this along because there was another possibility for things to go wrong here. Gideon could be using this as a stall tactic to keep Linnea and him in the hospital room so someone could shoot through the window.

Damned if they did, and damned if they didn't.

"Let's assume I might be interested in meeting with you," Jace continued. "When and where would this take place?"

"Today. This morning if possible. The sooner the better," Gideon added so fast that his words ran together.

"All right," Jace said. "Meet me in my office in one hour."

Gideon laughed, but there was definitely no humor in it. "I'm not going to make it easy for you to kill or arrest me. I don't trust you any more than you trust me."

Finally, he was certain Gideon had spoken the truth. "Yet you want to meet with me," Jace reminded him.

"I *have* to meet with you," Gideon emphasized. "I have to give you this evidence so you can start clearing my name. It's the only way for Linnea and me to be safe."

Jace scowled over "the only way." He could do things to minimize Linnea being attacked again, but first and foremost, those things involved keeping her away from Gideon and his hired guns.

"When and where do you want to meet?" Jace pressed when Gideon didn't say anything else.

"I'll call you back with an exact time and location."

Yeah, and Jace was betting that time and location would allow Gideon to set a trap. Or rather try to do that. So Jace turned the tables on him.

"Meet me in two hours at the place where I first kissed Linnea," Jace told Gideon.

As he'd expected, that got a reaction from Linnea. She pulled back her shoulders and stared at him as if he'd lost his mind. Gideon might have been doing the same thing, because he suddenly got very quiet.

"The barn at my family's ranch," Gideon finally muttered.

Bingo. Though Jace hadn't known that Gideon had been aware of that kiss or the location of it. Obviously, Linnea and he hadn't been as discreet about that as he'd thought.

"The place is empty," Jace reminded him. "There's no one around to get caught up in friendly fire if things go wrong."

That part was true. The ranch had literally been for sale for two years now, since Linnea's parents had been killed in an interstate collision while coming back from a vacation. Because both Linnea and Gideon already had their own places and hadn't wanted to live there, they'd put it up for sale.

"Swear to me that you won't just ambush me and gun me down," Gideon said.

Now it was Jace's turn to be surprised. "You'd take my word on that?" he asked.

"I would." Gideon sounded confident about that when Jace knew there was no way in hell he was. Obviously, Gideon was willing to say whatever it took to get a second chance at tying up loose ends.

Maybe.

And it was that *maybe* that was eating away at Jace.

"I won't ambush you or gun you down," Jace promised. "But if it's a trap, then all bets are off."

"Deal," Gideon assured him. "But two hours won't work for me. I'll call you back with a time." And with that, he ended the call.

Jace stood there a moment, staring at the phone and wondering what the hell kind of game his former friend was playing.

"Come on," he told Linnea. "Let's get out of here before our luck runs out with Zimmerman."

Nodding, Linnea scooped up the backpack before Jace could, and she was right on his heels when he headed out. Crystal was just outside the door, obviously waiting for them.

"Glenn filled me in," the deputy said. "We can go this way to get to the cruiser."

This way was down the hall past the patients' rooms, past a nurse station and then into a waiting area. One that Glenn had cleared, from the looks of it, since there was no one around.

Good.

With fewer people, there'd be fewer distractions. Still, Jace continued to fire glances all around them as they made their way to the exit through the ER.

Glenn had pulled the cruiser practically up the sliding glass doors, and had even opened the back door so Linnea and he could just slide in. Linnea got in first and moved across the seat to make room for him. It took Jace a little longer, and he felt every movement and tug of the stitches in his shoulder. Hell. He needed to get past this pain fast.

"I had a couple of the reserve deputies go through

Linnea's place," Glenn said when he drove away. "They're waiting there until you're tucked away inside and have the security system on."

That was the plan that Jace had gone over with Glenn the night before. Now Jace had to hope that it wasn't a stupid plan that would put Linnea and him in the sights of a killer.

"You believe Gideon?" Linnea asked him. It was a question that Jace had definitely expected. "You really think he has evidence to clear his name?"

"I think he has statements and such. I also think what he has isn't worth a thimble full of spit."

She made a sound of agreement and glanced away. But not before Jace saw something very dangerous in her eyes.

Hope.

Hope that her brother wasn't dirty, that this had indeed all been a setup. Jace didn't want her, or himself, thinking that way.

"Gideon wants to meet with me," Jace told Glenn, and he caught his deputy's surprised look as Glenn glanced in the rearview. "I told him I'd meet him at the barn on his parents' property."

"You won't go there," Glenn immediately said.

"I won't go there," Jace assured him. "Gideon probably won't, either. But he could have plans to have a sniper along the route." Jace stopped, rethought that. "Unless his game plan really is to try to convince me that he was set up. Either way, I won't be going to the barn."

"But what happens when Gideon calls back?" Linnea asked.

Jace still had plenty of things to work out about that,

but he knew the gist of what he had to do. "I'll try to arrange to meet at another location, one where I can control the timing and the security. He probably won't go for it, but that would be the way I stand a chance of taking him into custody."

Linnea stayed quiet a moment, but like Jace, she was watching their surroundings. Unlike the ER waiting area, there were plenty of people out and about on Main Street. And yeah, some of those people had noticed him in the cruiser and would no doubt guess they were either going to Linnea's house or his. He wasn't sure though that any of the locals would share that info with Zimmerman or Bryce. There was plenty of gossip in Culver Crossing, but there was just as much distrust of outsiders.

"I need to work out a safe way for Gideon to get me copies of what he considers evidence to clear his name," Jace went on when Glenn turned onto Bluebonnet Lane, the street where Linnea lived.

"Maybe I can help with that," she offered. "I could talk to him and arrange for a meeting place where he'll feel protected enough to show up. If I'm there, he'll know it's not an ambush because you wouldn't risk me being in the middle of possible gunfire."

He considered it, shook his head and then shrugged. Nodded. No way would Linnea be part of any meeting with Gideon, but maybe she could go at her brother from a different angle than Jace could. Through talk, not action. Blood ties could maybe work better than friendship, and she might be able to use those ties to get Gideon to show up so he could then spill whatever it was he claimed he had.

Glenn slowed when they approached Linnea's house.

It was a single-story limestone-and-white cottage with a much larger lot than what most other residents had this close to Main Street. The houses, including hers, were on several acres, which meant there was plenty of space between her neighbors and her. Plenty of land-scaping, too.

She'd obviously turned her yard into a showcase for customers.

There were pecan and oak trees mixed with mountain laurels. The right mix. Everything looked balanced, with the swirls of color in the flowers that dotted the yard and curved around the stone walkway toward the porch. Jace had no idea what the flowers actually were, but there were beds of red, purple and white.

"The place looks good," he said, staring past the landscape to see any potential problem areas. There was a cluster of crepe myrtles that could turn out to be a hiding place for a gunman, and Jace made a mental note to keep Linnea away from the windows on that side of the house.

"Thanks. I haven't had a chance to weed in a while." She was no doubt seeing the work that needed to be done. Probably seeing the security pitfalls, too, because she added, "I have blackout shades we can pull down on the windows."

They'd definitely use those, and if they were still there come nightfall—which was highly likely—they wouldn't be turning on lights and advertising exactly where they were in the house.

Glenn pulled into Linnea's driveway and parked next to a cruiser that was already there. Jace immediately spotted the two reserve deputies on the porch. Darnell Hough and Manuel Rodriguez. Both had once been full-time deputies in the department but had retired. He trusted them, but Jace would check the place for himself to make sure they hadn't missed anything.

"The CSIs didn't break the door when they went in," Glenn explained. "In fact, they found the front door unlocked and the security system turned off."

Linnea's mouth tightened. "Whoever broke in to get the knife and earring probably did that. I always lock up the place tight, and I don't have a spare key hidden for someone to find."

Jace didn't doubt that, but at least this meant they'd have no trouble getting into her house now. He suspected she'd left her keys and purse at the cabin when she'd been trying to get them out on the ATV.

"You'll need to change the codes for the security system once we're inside," Jace reminded her and he got an immediate nod.

"I can do that on the panel box by the door," she assured him.

With all of them still keeping watch, Linnea and Jace hurried to the porch, and Jace took a moment to thank the reserve deputies before Linnea and he went inside. First things first, he locked the door and had her engage the security. Then, he went through the place room by room.

It wasn't an overly large house, but it was a decent size. A combination eating, living and dining area with three bedrooms and two baths. He knew the layout because he'd been here a couple of times. Once to help her move in and again when Gideon had brought him over for dinner.

Obviously, the CSIs had rifled through the place, leaving some cabinet doors and drawers open. On a sigh, Linnea set down the backpack and went to close them. Along the way, she started lowering the shades.

Jace lowered some, as well, while he made his way through the house, checking the locks on the windows and doors. He didn't have any trouble finding Linnea's bedroom. Or seeing the unmade bed and the clothes tossed on the floor. Jeans, a tee along with a skimpy pink lace bra and panties.

He was frozen there, imagining what she'd look like wearing those when he heard her footsteps behind him. And her gasp. She hurried around him, practically knocking him down to scoop up the clothes and toss it all into a laundry basket that was on the floor of the adjoining bathroom.

"I take it the intruder didn't leave those things on the floor," Jace commented.

"No." And he could tell from the dread in her eyes that she didn't like that he'd seen them.

"The CSIs and deputies saw them, too," she grumbled. "Trust me, if I'd known my life was going to Hades in a handbasket, I wouldn't have left my dirty clothes lying around."

For some reason, that made him smile. Of course, his head was still swimming with images of Linnea wearing them, and not wearing anything, so he knew he wasn't thinking straight. If he had been, he wouldn't have asked the next question.

"You wear underwear like that all the time?" he blurted out.

Yeah, definitely a stupid question.

"All the time," Linnea verified, and she flashed him. A quick lift of her scrub top to reveal a swatch of pale blue lace. A bra that barely covered her nipples and left plenty of her breasts exposed. "And yes, the panties match."

She didn't flash those, and the disappointment of missing out on that must have shown in his eyes.

"Why did this have to happen now?" she asked on a huff.

"This?" Jace repeated, though he knew exactly what she meant. He just didn't want to be the one to say it, but when Linnea fanned her hand over first him and then herself, he added, "Oh, *that*."

"Yes, that," she verified with another huff. "We're in danger. My brother wants us dead. On top of that, you've been shot and are in no shape to do anything about *this* or *that*."

He smiled again, but it was tinged with a grimace this time. Because he now knew exactly how Linnea looked in that skimpy lacy underwear.

"You kissed me in the hospital," she reminded him. "Why didn't you do that sooner? And no, I don't mean the kiss in the barn. Why didn't you kiss me in those dozen years in between?"

"Gideon," he answered without hesitation. "He told me you were hands-off. He thought it'd mess with our friendship to have me hit on his kid sister."

She released a low, slow breath. One that made him notice the rise and fall of her breasts. "That's stupid."

He nodded. "Especially stupid because it turns out that criminal activity messed with our friendship a hell of a lot more than me hitting on you would have."

Linnea gave him a considering stare, her eyes examining him as if she was trying to decide what to do. Jace knew what he wanted to do. He had relived both of those other kisses and wanted the memories of a third one.

Hell, he wanted to have sex with her so that he'd have those memories, too.

Her gaze dropped, over and up, taking him in and still debating what to do. Jace fixed that by brushing his mouth over hers. Oh, and there it was. The heat. It rippled over his skin and made him forget all about danger, pain and gunshot wounds.

Which, of course, was bad.

Thankfully, he didn't have to muster up enough willpower to stop because his phone did that for him. When he saw Crystal's name on the screen, Jace answered it right away.

"Anything wrong?" Jace immediately asked her.

"No," the deputy assured him just as fast. "I'm back in the office, and I thought you'd want to know that Zimmerman didn't get his warrant. Not yet anyway."

Well, that was a plus for Linnea and him, but Jace figured the ATF agent would continue to push. If he wasn't out to kill Linnea, then Zimmerman was obviously obsessed with taking her into custody.

"There's something else," Crystal went on. "As I was leaving the hospital, one of the nurses told me that Lieutenant Cannon called to check on Linnea and you. They wouldn't give him any info even when he tossed his badge and rank around, so he said he'd be here later this morning, that it was important he talk to you."

"Apparently, I'm a popular guy," Jace muttered. "If he shows up at the office, just tell him I'm on medical leave."

He had no intentions of telling either Bryce or Zimmerman about Gideon's call. Not yet anyway. If they were dirty, they already knew about it. If they were trying to coerce Gideon, then it might spur them to murder him. That meant Jace had no reason to have a conversation with either man.

Jace finished his call with Crystal and turned back to Linnea. This time, he did some steeling up and forced himself not to think of hot underwear, kisses or sex. What they had to do was critical to stay alive, and it started with talking about Gideon.

"We need to work out what we're going to say to Gideon when he calls back," Jace explained, making sure he sounded as serious as this talk was. "We need to convince him to turn himself in. Now, how do we go about doing that?"

"I can tell him I love him." Linnea answered so fast that it was obvious she'd already given this some thought. "I can remind him that I could be killed if he doesn't try to put an end to the threat."

Jace considered that. Nodded. Gideon had loved his sister. Maybe he still did. And maybe they could use that. Of course, it was just as likely that Gideon would try to use Linnea's love for him to gain any ground he thought could be gained.

Jace's phone rang again, but this time he didn't recognize the number. He hit answer and hoped like the devil that it wasn't Zimmerman or Bryce. It wasn't. It was a woman.

"I'm Tammy Wheatly," the woman said. "Are you Sheriff Castillo, the one who's looking for me?"

"I am," Jace verified, and then he immediately asked. "Where are you?"

"I need to talk to Gideon right now," Tammy went on, obviously not answering his question.

Welcome to the club. "About what?" Jace pressed.

The woman let out a hoarse sob. "Tell Gideon that

it went wrong. Tell him that he has me, and that he's going to use me to get to Gideon."

"He?" Jace questioned.

"Just tell Gideon what I said," she insisted.

Jace was just as insistent. "Tell me who has you and where you are."

But he was talking to the air because Tammy had already ended the call.

Chapter Ten

With the laptop next to her, Linnea sat on her bed and listened to the water running in the tub in her bathroom. Jace was in there, taking a bath, something that he'd assured her he could do without her help.

But she wasn't so sure.

That was why she kept her ear turned in that direction while she went over the latest info that Glenn had sent to Jace and then Jace had shared with her. Not the actual official reports but rather a sanitized summary that wouldn't technically violate any procedures.

Scanning through the summary, Linnea could see that the deputy hadn't actually given them any new information, but Glenn had certainly been thorough in his follow-ups. He and the other deputies were still working on the traces for the phones that Tammy and Gideon had used, but they hadn't gotten anywhere on that. Nor had there been any sightings of either her brother or the CI. Since it was going on 3 p.m., it meant it was forty hours or so since anyone had laid eyes on Gideon.

In another part of the summary, Glenn had written that no evidence had been recovered from the woods where Jace and she were attacked by the sniper. No footprints, tire tracks or even any spent shell casings.

That was the bad news. However, there was good news, too, and it was in Glenn's next report. Not an official one that would go in the police files but more like a memo to his boss.

According to that memo, Zimmerman still hadn't gotten a warrant to take her into custody. Definitely good, and Linnea thought his chances of carrying through on that particular threat were growing slim. She sure hoped so anyway. There was enough to worry about without the threat of an arrest hanging over her.

She glanced at the bathroom door again when she heard some moving around. From the sound of it, Jace was getting out of the tub. So it'd been a short bath, less than ten minutes, but he had told her that he wasn't a bath sort of guy. He preferred showers, but because of his wound, he'd opted for the tub so his bandage wouldn't get wet.

Since Crystal had dropped by earlier with an overnight bag of clothes and essentials that she'd gotten from Jace's, he would have something clean to change into. If he could actually get into them, that is. Considering she'd had to help him get dressed at the hospital, Linnea waited for him to ask her to do the same now. But nothing. Until she heard a sound that had her getting to her feet.

A moan.

She knew a moan of pain when she heard one. She went straight to the door. It was slightly ajar, something that Jace had insisted on so he'd hear her if she called out to him. Linnea had wanted it open, as well, in case he slipped in the tub. Well, he hadn't slipped, and he'd even managed to get on his jeans, but he was wincing while trying to get on his shirt. At least he'd taken the two over-the-counter pain pills that she'd left out for him.

"What's a four-letter word for as stubborn as a mule? *J-a-c-e*," she spelled out while he scowled at her.

"I can put on my shirt," he insisted.

"Stubborn *J-a-c-e*," she repeated.

Linnea took the shirt from him and couldn't help glancing down at his bare chest. It probably violated personal rules to gawk at him like that, but it was hard to be this close to him and not notice that he was built. Of course, this wasn't the first time she'd been well aware of that.

He didn't balk when she helped him maneuver his arm into the sleeve, and she had to admit that he probably could have done it by himself. He was moving a lot better than he had just hours earlier, and the wincing had been just that one-time deal.

"I don't mind helping you," she pointed out.

When she looked up at him, he was staring at her. "You've undressed and dressed me more than—" He stopped, cursed, shook his head.

Linnea considered how to fill in the blanks on that, and she came up with one pretty fast. "A lover," she supplied. "Though I suspect your lovers only do the undressing part."

Jace didn't disagree with her about that. "Usually that's the way it works," he said. Definitely a drawl. A sexy-as-sin one that made the heat in her body go up some significant notches.

She saw that gleam in his eye spark into a fire, and while Linnea liked both the spark and the fire very much, she felt she had to remind him of something. So she ran her fingers over the edge of his bandage. Because she thought she'd hurt him, she nearly jerked back her hand when a muscle flickered in his jaw.

But it wasn't pain.

Nope.

She got confirmation of that when he leaned in and kissed her.

This was about as personally dangerous as things could get between them. They were alone, their bodies touching, and everything inside her was begging for more. More that she was certain Jace could give her if he hadn't had that gunshot wound. Still, she settled for this. This kiss. The feel of his mouth on hers. His taste when his tongue skimmed over hers. The man had certainly made an art form out of kissing.

She leaned in closer, careful not to touch his shoulder, but of course, that left room for a lot of other contact. Specifically, the front of his jeans against the front of hers. Each touch lit new fires and fanned the ones that he'd already started with his mouth.

Jace apparently had plans for a lot more fires today because he hooked his good arm around her waist, lowering his hand to her butt, and pulled her even closer. Oh, yes. This was an art form, too.

Her body molded to his, and she got a jolt of pleasure when she felt his erection. Of course, it was going to have to stay in his jeans, but she allowed herself the thrill of thinking how it would be with him. Amazing, she was sure. Heck, he could probably even manage amazing with a bum shoulder.

He pulled back from the kiss but kept the rest of the body contact, and he stared down at her. "You know this is a mistake," Jace said. "Because of the timing," he clarified. "But later, after the investigation is finished, it won't be a mistake. Understand?"

She did indeed, and Linnea nodded. But she couldn't help but think of the reality of that. Their lives had changed. Would never be the same. They'd be able to get past what happened, but there was no doubt a long, hard road ahead of them. Still, it was nice to know that Jace would be at the end of that road.

And they'd have sex.

Linnea had no doubts about that. It would happen. But apparently not now. Even if Jace had continued the kissing and touching, it would have had to stop because someone rang the doorbell.

Just like that, the heat vanished, and Jace scooped up his gun from the counter. "Stay here," he insisted, and he stormed out, looking very much like a gunslinger about to face a showdown.

Since it was a showdown he might not be physically up to, Linnea followed him. Not to the door, though. She stayed back in the hall and watched him go to the front window. He peered out the edge of the curtain. And cursed. A moment later, she realized the reason for his profanity.

Because it was Zimmerman.

"I know you're in there," Zimmerman called out. "We need to talk."

Jace didn't answer, but he kept his gun ready.

"I'm not here to arrest Linnea or take her into custody," Zimmerman went on after a loud huff. "I just need to show you something. It's about Gideon."

"You're not coming in," Jace told him, "and I'm not going out there. Whatever you have, you can leave at the sheriff's office, and I'll have one of the deputies bring it to me."

Jace moved away from the window, and Linnea suspected he'd done that so that Zimmerman wouldn't be able to pinpoint his location. Though it would be plenty stupid for the agent to start firing at them in broad daylight where any one of her neighbors would see and hear him.

"I want to talk to you about it," Zimmerman argued, "not to one of your deputies."

"That sounds like a personal problem to me. That's the only offer you'll get from me on this." Jace glanced over his shoulder at her. Seeing his narrowed eyes, Linnea stooped down where she wouldn't be an easy target.

"I can't believe you don't want to see what I have about Gideon," Zimmerman went on. "Unless you believe your old friend is innocent."

"It has nothing to do with my old friend, his innocence or guilt," Jace said, and then he moved again to the other side of the door. "You're a risk, Zimmerman, and I've had my fill of risks."

The agent made a sound of outrage. "I'm not dirty like Gideon."

"Then stop pressing to come inside a house where you're not welcome." Jace went to the kitchen window and looked out.

Linnea's stomach clenched because she realized this could all be a ploy by Zimmerman to distract them while someone tried to break in. If that happened, the security alarm would go off.

Unless Zimmerman had somehow managed to disarm it.

"I'll get my gun," she whispered to Jace, and she hurried back to her bedroom to take it from the closet.

By the time she made it back to the hall, Jace was in the far corner of the living room, glancing out the window at the side yard. He must not have seen any kind of threat because he merely shook his head.

"Zimmerman, how'd you get the copies of this so-called evidence?" Jace threw out there, still moving. This time to the other side of the house.

"I did my job with a thorough investigation," Zimmerman answered, and unlike Jace, he seemed to be staying put.

Jace huffed. "How'd you get it?" he repeated.

Linnea couldn't see Zimmerman's expression, but she doubted he was happy with Jace's refusal to let him in or his cop's tone.

"I heard buzz that Gideon was trying to get statements from CIs," Zimmerman finally snarled. "And from the security guards at the warehouses where the guns and drugs were taken."

Since that jibed with what Gideon had said, Linnea suspected there would have been a least some talk about it. You couldn't stir up that kind of hornet's nest without creating a buzz.

"I've got statements from CIs and the guards at the warehouse," Zimmerman went on. "But they sounded coached. Maybe intimidated. I think Gideon threatened them. Maybe somebody else did threats, too."

That got her complete attention, but Linnea figured Zimmerman was just going to try to tie her to this. To accuse her of cobbling together lies or half-truths to save her brother.

"If Linnea can't hear me, ask her if Gideon ever

said anything about his boss being dirty?" Zimmerman pressed.

"No, he didn't," Jace answered for her. "Do you think Lieutenant Cannon is in this with Gideon?"

Zimmerman definitely didn't jump on that particular train. "I don't know. But I don't think Gideon pulled this off alone. Personally, I think he'd turn to family for that kind of help."

And there it was. Zimmerman was back to accusing her of aiding and abetting her brother. Jace must have been as tired of it as she was, because his next huff was considerably louder.

"Leave now, Zimmerman," Jace demanded. "If you want me to see those statements you've got, then take them to the sheriff's office."

Jace moved across the living room to the window that would allow him to see the front yard and the street. Several moments later, she saw him release the breath he'd been holding.

"Zimmerman's going," he relayed to her. But he continued to stand there and watch even after Linnea heard the sound of a car engine and someone, Zimmerman probably, driving away.

"You didn't see anyone else, did you?" she asked.

Again, he shook his head but then stopped. "What the hell?" he mumbled, and Jace braced himself as if preparing for a fight.

Oh, mercy. That caused her heart to jump to her throat. "Did Zimmerman come back?"

"No, it's a woman."

"A woman?" she repeated, but before Linnea could press him for more, she heard someone call out.

"It's me, Tammy," a voice called out. "I got away from him, but I need help. He'll come for me again."

"She's coming on the porch," Jace said, and he hurried to another window to look out. "Her clothes are torn, and she looks like she has injuries. Call Glenn and ask him to get out here. I want an ambulance, too."

Jace tossed her his phone, and she scrolled through to find Glenn's number, all the while asking herself what the heck Tammy was doing here at her house.

"You have to let me in," Tammy insisted, banging on the door now. "I'm hurt, and he'll come after me."

"Who? Gideon?" Jace demanded. "Is he the one coming after you?"

"No, not Gideon. Not Gideon," the woman repeated through her sobs. "Lieutenant Bryce Cannon. He's not just part of this crime scheme. He's the leader of it."

Chapter Eleven

Lieutenant Bryce Cannon.

Jace definitely didn't like the way the man's name kept coming up in connection with Gideon's crimes. And since Gideon seemed to have a partner in those crimes, Jace figured it would have made things easier for him if his boss had been in on it.

"How bad do you think Tammy's hurt?" Linnea asked, and thankfully she hadn't gone to the window or door to see that for herself. She was still in the hall, and her knuckles had gone white because of the hard grip she had on her gun.

"Hard to tell. There are some bruises on her arms and face, and her dress is torn, but I don't see any blood."

However, what Jace did see were tears and plenty of them. The woman had dropped down onto the porch step and was crying with loud, hiccupping sobs. Her gaze fired all around the yard, the nervy gaze of some-one ready to jump out of their own skin.

Jace did feel for her and hated to see anyone hurt. Well, anyone hurt who didn't deserve it. And he wasn't sure yet if Tammy deserved it or if this was all just a scam. Just like he hadn't wanted Zimmerman to come in, though, Jace had no intention of letting her in Tammy, either. Crying was going to be her golden ticket to come inside and try to go after Linnea or him.

He continued to stand by the window, and Jace watched as the cruiser pulled into Linnea's driveway. It hadn't taken Glenn but just a few minutes, and Jace heard the howl of the ambulance sirens right behind him.

"Stay put," Jace warned Tammy when she got up to run. "My deputy will take you to the hospital where you'll be safe." Where she wouldn't be able to attack, either, but Jace didn't spell that out for her.

"He'll come after me," Tammy howled. "Lieutenant Cannon will kill me."

But she didn't run, not even when Glenn approached. However, Tammy did eye the badge with fear and wariness. Jace had no idea if the emotions were real or not. Since the woman had spent some time behind bars, it was possible that she'd learned how to put on a show, one to convince them that she was a woman in danger.

Jace disarmed the security system so he could crack open the door and speak to Glenn. "This is Tammy Wheatly, a possible material witness along with being Gideon's CI and lover. Yeah, you heard that right," Jace added when Glenn raised an eyebrow. "Ride with her to the hospital."

Which he would be able to do very soon because the ambulance pulled to a stop, and two EMTs rushed out.

"Stay with her at all times," Jace continued with his instructions to Glenn. "When Tammy's medically cleared, bring her back to the sheriff's office. I'll use the cruiser to get Linnea and me there, and we'll wait for you. I want to interview Tammy myself."

Glenn gave him another raised eyebrow. "You think that's safe to go into your office?"

"Not especially," Jace muttered.

But after having Zimmerman and Tammy show up, he figured everyone in Texas must know his location. Besides, he really did want to personally do Tammy's interrogation. He was getting bits and pieces from Gideon and Zimmerman, but it was possible that Tammy had the whole picture.

Jace went back in the house, engaged the security and watched as Glenn and the EMTs got Tammy moving. He also tucked his gun away so he could finishing buttoning his shirt. There was still pain every time he moved his left arm, but it was a lot better than it had been that morning. He credited the bath and ibuprofen for that. Linnea, too. Kissing her was darn effective in helping him forget the pain. Then again, kissing her made him forget a lot of things.

Like common sense.

Maybe it wasn't good common sense now to take her away from her house, but he had an uneasy feelings about staying here. If Tammy was some kind of decoy or distraction, Gideon, Bryce or whoever the heck was after them might be gearing up to shoot into the house. Jace was hoping they'd have second or third thoughts about trying something like that at a police station.

Jace looked back at Linnea, who was still in the hall. "Are you ready to go?"

"Yes." She glanced down at her gun. "Should I bring this with me?"

"Please tell me you have a license for that?" he muttered, but then he waved that off. It might be a good deterrent to a sniper if he saw that both Jace and Linnea were armed. "Bring it."

He had a lockbox in his desk, and he could secure it there. Best not to have any civilian weapons in easy reach since they'd be bringing in Tammy. She was officially a person of interest in this tangled mess. For now anyway. But that could change if Jace found a reason to arrest her.

Jace waited until the EMTs, Tammy and Glenn were in the ambulance before he disengaged the security system and got Linnea out to the cruiser as soon as they'd locked up the house. He said a lot of prayers in that short run they made to the vehicle, and the prayers must have worked, because no one fired shots at them.

"You'll question Bryce?" Linnea asked. She still had a tight grip on her gun, and she was keeping watch.

"I will." And that was another reason he wanted to be in his office. He didn't want Bryce inside Linnea's house any more than he wanted Zimmerman in there. But Jace had to talk to the lieutenant, and like with Tammy, he wanted that to be a formal interview.

Jace parked in front of the sheriff's office and glanced around to make sure there weren't any people lurking around whom he didn't know. Main Street looked as it always did this time of day. Traffic was practically nonexistent, and there was a handful of people going in and out of the shops and businesses. Jace certainly didn't get a bad feeling like the one he'd had at Linnea's.

He hurried Linnea inside and took her into his office so he could secure her weapon. "You might as well get comfortable," he told her. "It could be a while before Glenn gets back with Tammy, and I've got to call Bryce."

"I want to hear what he has to say," she insisted, and she sank down into the chair next to his desk.

Jace sat, too, and even though the jostling around was giving him some jabs of pain, he made sure he kept that pain off his face. He didn't want Linnea snarling out any more "four-letter word" jabs.

Putting his phone on speaker, he tried calling Bryce but then cursed when it went straight to voice mail. Jace left a message for the man to call him ASAP, and then he located the directory for San Antonio PD and got the contact info for Bryce's boss. Captain Katelyn O'Malley. Jace didn't get through right away to her, either. He had to work his way through her admin, but the captain finally came on the line.

"Sheriff Castillo," she greeted. "How can I help you?"

"I'm trying to get in touch with Lieutenant Cannon. It's important," Jace emphasized. "Any idea where he is?"

The captain didn't answer right away. "Important?" she questioned. "Is this about Detective Gideon Martell?"

"In a roundabout way."

And Jace, too, paused to figure out how much to tell her. He didn't know Captain O'Malley, but he had heard that she was a good cop. Still, she was a boss, like him, and he understood the need she might have to protect her people. Hopefully, she wouldn't protect someone who'd betrayed his badge.

"There's a CI, Tammy Wheatly, who just showed up in Culver Crossing, and she claims that Bryce is after her, that he took her captive. I don't have a lot of details," Jace quickly added, knowing that the captain would probably have questions, "but I need to speak to Bryce and get his side of this."

"Of course," she said.

Her voice was cop-flat. But Jace suspected there was a whole lot of emotion going on with those two little words. She definitely wouldn't like that she had another officer, especially one with rank, who could be tied to Gideon.

"According to the schedule, Lieutenant Cannon should be in his office," the captain explained after he heard the clicks of a computer keyboard. "I'll track him down and have him contact you after he speaks with me."

Bryce wouldn't care much for being called into the captain's office. Jace didn't like it much, either. He wanted to throw some questions at Bryce and gauge his reaction before the man had time to think about his answers. Still, Jace couldn't exclude the captain or blame her for wanting first crack at one of her men. But Jace doubted Bryce would make a confession just because his boss, or Jace, pushed him on Tammy's allegation.

No.

There was way too much at stake for that, but there was always the possibility that Bryce might let something slip during an interview that would blow this investigation wide open.

"Oh, and Sheriff Castillo?" Captain O'Malley continued a moment later. "If you'd copy me on the statement from this CI, I'd appreciate it."

Jace assured her that he'd do that and ended the call.

"Bryce won't go on the run like Gideon," Linnea

immediately said. "He'll just deny whatever it is that Tammy says he did to her."

He made a sound of agreement and scrubbed his hand over his face. "And there might not be a reason for Bryce to run. He could be innocent, and this could be an attempt for Gideon to get the light off himself by making a fellow cop look dirty."

Linnea nodded. "But it doesn't get the light off him," she muttered.

No, it didn't, and while Jace thought Linnea might be having doubts as to whether or not her brother was guilty, Jace was almost positive that Gideon had not only broken the law, he'd crushed it.

Cursing, Jace got to work. It wouldn't do him any good to sit and stew while he waited to hear from Bryce, so he got started on pulling up the reports that he hadn't had time to study yet. He especially wanted to take a long look at the ones that dealt with the search at Linnea's. However, before he had time to even get started on that, his phone rang.

"It's Glenn," he told Linnea, and he put the call on speaker.

"Thought you'd want to know that the doctor took Tammy in right away for an exam," Glenn said. "But the EMTs told me they don't think her injuries are serious. Just some scrapes and bruises."

"I noticed. Has she said anything?" Jace asked.

"Plenty. In fact, she started talking in the ambulance and didn't hush while we were getting her into ER. Boss, she insists she was held captive in the barn on Linnea's family ranch."

Jace groaned, shook his head. "That's where Gideon wanted us to meet," he reminded Glenn.

"Yep, I thought that was interesting, too. Another interesting thing she had to say was that she didn't actually see Cannon, but that the guy holding her said he worked for him. Oh, and get this. Her captor wore a ski mask the whole time he had her so she didn't actually see his face."

Jace didn't bother to groan this time. It was exactly what he'd expected the woman to say. Maybe it was the truth that her captor had indeed told her Bryce was responsible. However, it was just as possible that Tammy was making all of this up in an attempt to help Gideon.

"There's more," Glenn went on. "Tammy claims she found a nail on the barn floor and jabbed it into this guy's arm. She says that's how she got away from him. But get this—she insists she dropped the nail right outside the barn door and that it's got the guy's blood on it."

Jace jumped right on that. "We need to get somebody out there to find it."

"Already made the call," Glenn assured him. "One of the CSIs was finishing up at Toby's, and I asked her to make a quick run over there."

"Good." Well, it would be if the nail actually existed. It could be part of the hoax. Still, if there was such evidence, it might be exactly what they were looking for. Because a hired thug could maybe lead them to the person who'd orchestrated all of this.

"I'll call you if the CSI finds anything," Glenn continued. "And I'll bring Tammy to your office as soon as the doctor releases her."

Jace ended the call but immediately got an incoming. From Bryce this time.

"What the hell game are you playing, Sheriff?" Bryce demanded the moment he was on the line. Jace didn't have to guess that the man was thoroughly pissed off.

"No game," Jace assured him. "I need to talk to you about Tammy Wheatly. I have her in protective custody, and she's made some, well, disturbing allegations about you."

"Anything she has to say will be lies, and I get called into my captain's office for that?"

"If what Tammy tells us are lies, then you've got nothing to worry about. Your captain will get that. But you need to come to my office right away so I can get an official statement from you."

"Oh, you'll get a statement," Bryce snarled. "I'll bring a lawyer with me, and we'll be there in about two hours. And afterward, I want to interrogate Tammy."

Jace didn't have to think about that. "I can't let you do that." Because if Tammy wasn't lying, then Bryce's mere presence could intimidate her. "But I'm sending a copy of the report to your captain, and I can do the same for you. Of course, that deal is off if you're part of what's going on with Gideon."

"I'm not part of it." There was such anger, and yes, some bitterness that went into that denial.

Jace ended the call and made a mental note to make sure Tammy had no contact with Bryce. They'd have to be under the same roof, but Jace would need one of his deputies to stay in an interview room with Tammy while he was talking to Bryce.

"He'll hold a grudge," Linnea said. There was no anger, just a weary kind of resignation in her voice. "If he's had no part in this, he could try to get back at you."

Jace raised an eyebrow. "Has he done that sort of thing before?"

"He badmouthed me after I stopped seeing him," she readily supplied. "He told people that I led him on, that I was sleeping around while I was seeing him." Linnea stopped, took a breath. "It was petty and mean. It stopped when Gideon told him to knock it off, though. Bryce apologized, telling me that he was just hurt, but I got the feeling that he wouldn't mind seeing me taken down a couple of notches."

Well, hell. That wasn't good, especially since Jace knew for a fact that Linnea wasn't the sort to lead a man on or sleep around.

"If Bryce is involved with these crimes," Jace said, "this could be the motive for why you were set up for Toby's murder. This way, he can get back at you as well as tie up loose ends so he won't end up behind bars."

Her eyes widened, and she groaned softly. "I'd like to think he's not capable of murder, but I thought the same thing about Gideon just a couple of days ago."

Yeah, so had Jace, and that was why he now had a gunshot wound in his shoulder.

He gave Linnea's hand a gentle squeeze and wished it was more. But this wasn't the place for hugs and such, even if they were meant just to comfort.

His phone rang again, and he glanced at the screen. It was Glenn. Jace hoped something hadn't gone wrong at the hospital. "Is everything okay?" he asked his deputy.

"You could say that. The CSI, April Gendry, went straight over to the barn, and within minutes, she'd found a nail by the door, right where Tammy said it would be," Glenn said, his words rushed together in excitement.

Jace was sure he'd get excited, too, depending on the

next answer he got from Glenn. "Please tell me there's blood on it."

"Oh, there's blood all right," Glenn verified. "And here's some better news. April has bagged it and is taking it straight to the lab. Boss, we just might have some answers real soon."

Chapter Twelve

Finally. That was the one word that kept running through Linnea's head while she paced across Jace's office. Once they had the blood examined, Jace and she might finally have the evidence to link all these crimes and attacks.

Of course, that finally might lead them right back to Gideon, but at least then she'd know.

Jace clearly wanted to know, as well, because he'd been on the phone with his deputies and the lab since telling her about the bloody nail. From what she could garner from the conversations, it would be processed as soon as the CSI arrived. Since the lab was in San Antonio, that should be any minute now.

Also from what she'd overheard, Glenn had arranged for a CSI team to go to the barn to look for any other evidence. That would take a little longer, but the CSIs would be on scene before nightfall. Then, maybe they could find other things, other little pieces of the person who'd held Tammy there.

Well, if she had indeed been held.

The bloody nail seemed like proof that she was telling the truth, but Linnea had to consider that it might be part of a setup. The trouble with that was the woman wouldn't have been able to gouge Bryce without him knowing, and he likely would have said something about that when he'd spoken with Jace.

Unless…

A sickening thought slammed into her. Was it possible that the blood on the nail belonged to her? That it'd been taken from those paper towels in Gideon's trash. She considered that.

Dismissed it.

She had a solid alibi, since she'd been with Jace for forty hours or so. No way could anyone say she'd held Tammy captive in that barn. But Linnea hoped and prayed this wouldn't come back to her.

Since her nerves were starting to fire on all cylinders, Linnea forced herself to stop pacing and sat back down so she could continue reading the reports of Toby's murder. It was a lot of jargon, but she got through the first couple of pages. Then froze when she saw the attached photo.

Oh, mercy.

It was Toby, and all it took was one glimpse for her to get confirmation that the man had had a very hard death. So much blood, and his lifeless face still carried a mask of pain.

She looked up when she heard Jace sigh, and he obviously didn't have any trouble seeing what had captured her attention. He merely reached down and closed the file. Then he took her by the hand, urging her to her feet. He gave his office door a little kick to close it and pulled her into the crook of his good arm.

Linnea nearly told him this wasn't necessary, that was she fine. But she practically melted against him. "Take a minute," he said, his voice a soothing whisper. "And then we'll go back to your place. This time though, I'll try to figure out a way to keep the visitors at bay."

She lifted her head from the crook of his neck and looked up at him. "But what about Tammy? You want to interview her. And Bryce."

"Tammy had a panic attack, and the doctor gave her a sedative," Jace explained. "He's keeping her in the hospital overnight and said I wouldn't get much from her right now, that he wants me to wait until the morning to talk to her. We'll have the lab test back by then, so the timing could work better anyway."

"Okay," she said. That did make sense. "But what about Bryce?"

Jace suddenly didn't look so calm and comforting. "Bryce's lawyer called and said he can't get here until around seven o'clock. Maybe even later. I rescheduled the interview for tomorrow morning because I don't want us driving back to your place in the dark."

Neither did she. That would give a sniper an even better opportunity to have another go at them.

"Besides, the same applies," Jace went on. "We'll have the lab results, and if the blood doesn't belong to Bryce, then I'll have time to try to connect the person to him. Or to Zimmerman," he added.

She certainly hadn't forgotten about Zimmerman. "Did you see any signs of injury this morning when he was at my house?"

"No, but he could have changed his shirt, and he didn't actually see Tammy, remember? She waited until after he'd left before she came running out."

That was true, and they didn't know specifically when Tammy had "escaped." It could have coincided with Zimmerman leaving to come to her place. Which brought her to something else on her mind.

"How'd Tammy even know to go to my house?" Linnea asked, but the moment she said it, she knew what the obvious answer was. "Gideon."

Jace nodded. "He could have orchestrated her captivity and brought her to Culver Crossing."

She saw the disappointment of that possibility in his eyes. Still, the nail had to mean something. But what that something was, they wouldn't know until they had the results.

Jace brushed a kiss on her forehead, probably because she looked as if she could use a little more TLC. Since she could, she kissed him. Not on the forehead, either, but on the mouth.

And yes, she got that TLC all right.

Along with the inevitable heat that came with kissing Jace. A distracting heat that shouldn't be happening since they were in his office and one of his deputies could come walking in. Still, she took her time, letting her mouth sink into his. It was a good kind of sinking that left her feeling a whole lot better. Unfortunately, the whole lot better ended pretty fast because his phone rang again.

The heat vanished when he glanced at the Unknown Caller on the screen. Jace did more than ease back then. He stepped away from her, hit the record function and then answered it.

"Jace," Gideon said. "We need to meet. I've got a time and place—"

"Tell me about Tammy," Jace interrupted.

"Tammy?" he repeated, sounding genuinely surprised by the demand. "What do you mean?"

"I mean tell me about the person who kidnapped her and held her captive."

"What?" The time, Gideon seemed shocked, and Linnea wished she could see his face to know if that shock was anywhere near the real deal. "Where is she? Is she okay?"

Those were the right things that someone might ask if they hadn't had a part in this, but Jace clearly had his doubts. He was scowling and shaking his head.

"Tammy's hurt," Jace answered after a long pause. A pause because he was likely trying to figure how much or how little to tell her brother.

"Who did this?" Gideon snapped. "Where is she? I need to talk to her."

Jace homed in on the first question. "I figured you could tell me who kidnapped her."

"I can't. I swear, I can't," Gideon insisted, his voice thick with worry. Or make that fake worry. "Where is she? Is she okay? How bad is she hurt?"

The rapid-fire string of questions made Linnea wonder if Gideon had feelings for the woman. Maybe. They had been lovers after all, and Gideon might not have gotten involved with her solely for her ties to criminals he could use to fence guns and drugs. However, if Tammy had truly been taken captive, it didn't meant Gideon hadn't had a part in it. It was possible that for some reason he'd set up Tammy's kidnapping, which had somehow gone wrong.

Perhaps his partner in crime had turned on him.

"I don't know who did this," Gideon insisted. "But I'll find out."

Jace cursed when Gideon ended the call. "I wanted to keep him on the line longer," Jace grumbled. "Every second of our recorded conversations could end up giving us clues to find him."

"Yes," she agreed. "But he'll call back. He said he had a time and a place for that meeting he wants with you. A meeting that won't happen, right?"

Jace looked at her, their gazes connecting, and she saw something in his eyes that she didn't want to see. "What's a four-letter word for stupid?" she snapped but didn't wait for an answer. "It's *Jace* if you're thinking about trying to use yourself as bait. You're in no shape to go head-to-head with Gideon."

His eyes narrowed a little. "It wouldn't be bait. But if Gideon knows I'll be there, then he'll come. When that happens, I can arrest him and put him in a cage."

Good grief. He was thinking about putting himself in the crosshairs. "Anything Gideon sets up could be a trap. He's a cop, and he would have already thought of the angles. He could set the perfect trap and kill you. Not because killing you would stop him from being charged with a whole host of crimes but because he wants revenge for you trying to arrest him."

She let the silence linger between them to give Jace a moment for that to sink in. It didn't. So Linnea went with her ace in the hole.

"Gideon could use a meeting like that to double back and come after me," she said.

Jace opened his mouth, maybe to argue, but they both knew he couldn't. Linnea truly believed Gideon wanted Jace dead more than her. However, getting to her would in turn draw out Jace. Then Gideon, or whoever was behind this, could kill them both.

The sound of his phone ringing shot through the silence, and Linnea was glad she'd had the chance to lay out her case for refusing the meeting, since she figured that was her brother calling back. But it wasn't.

"Glenn," Jace told her, and he hit Answer and put it on speaker.

"We got a problem," the deputy said. "April Gendry, the CSI who has the bloody nail, just put out a call for help."

"Help?" Jace snapped.

"Yeah." Glenn muttered a profanity. "The dispatcher heard what she's pretty sure were gunshots while April was on the phone asking for backup."

Linnea pressed her hand to her mouth and forced herself to breathe. Oh, mercy. This couldn't be happening.

Jace did some cursing, too. "Where'd she call from?"

"Just outside of Mercy Ridge. April was probably driving toward the interstate."

That made sense, since the CSI would have had to go through the small neighboring town to get to San Antonio.

"Mercy Ridge cops are on the way to the scene," Glenn added a moment later. "But April's not responding. Boss, it doesn't look good."

DOESN'T LOOK GOOD was a massive understatement. Jace had confirmation of that within a few seconds after being on the phone with Sheriff Barrett Logan.

"The CSI is dead," Barrett said.

Jace wished that he hadn't put this particular call on speaker, because Barrett's words caused the color to drain from Linnea's face. She'd already looked shaky after Glenn's heads-up, but she seemed truly distressed now.

"Two gunshot wounds to the head," Barrett continued. "According to your deputy, she was couriering some evidence to the crime lab, but that's missing."

Of course, it was. Maybe it had been taken to cover up whoever had held Tammy captive. But it was just as possible that it had been stolen to make law enforcement believe that was what had happened. Either way, they didn't have the piece of evidence that could have given them some answers.

But they might have another chance at that.

"I'm stretched for manpower right now," Jace told Barrett, "but I'd like to send over one of my deputies to have a look at the scene. Any objections?"

"None. I suspect the ATF will want in on this, too."

They would indeed, and Jace figured Zimmerman was already on his way there. Well, he would be if he was actually investigating this series of crimes instead of just trying to cover up his involvement.

"Deputy Darnell Hough will be there as soon as I can contact him," Jace assured Barrett.

Jace ended the call to contact the reserve deputy. He then exchanged texts with the other reserve deputy, Manuel Rodriguez, and instructed him to go to Linnea's house to do a search to make sure no one had gotten in. Jace didn't want to be surprised by a killer when he took Linnea home.

And home was exactly where she was going.

Jace didn't think she'd have an actual meltdown, but she definitely wasn't steady. Unfortunately, that unsteadiness would probably get worse because Jace didn't have much time to try to give her any reassurance. He had to put some other things in motion fast.

While he kept an eye on Linnea, he called Glenn and instructed him to beef up security for Tammy. If April had been a target, then the CI could be, as well. That meant using the hospital security guard since Jace didn't want Glenn doing bodyguard duty without a backup.

"We can go soon," Jace told Linnea. "We need to wait for Manuel to give us an all clear on the house, and since he's just up the street at the diner, it shouldn't take him long. I also have another call to make, and I don't want to do it in the cruiser." Once he was in the vehicle, he wanted his focus solely on the drive and getting Linnea safely home.

Linnea nodded and sat up straighter in the chair. Probably because she was trying to convince him that she was okay. She failed big-time. She was nowhere near being okay.

He made that call to get an entire CSI team out to the barn at Linnea's family ranch. Jace insisted they get there fast and go over every inch of the place.

And do that while keeping watch for a sniper.

Because anyone who would kill April and steal evidence wouldn't hesitate to make sure nothing incriminating was recovered at the scene.

"I keep thinking I could have done something to stop this," Linnea muttered. She squeezed her eyes shut a moment, and he could see her fighting to keep it together.

Jace wouldn't tell her that he had been thinking the same thing. That he should have done something. He should have anticipated there'd be a problem and had one of his deputies go with April.

But why had there been a problem?

How had the killer known to go after her and get that evidence?

Both were good questions, and while Jace didn't have

answers, not yet anyway, he could maybe do something to help Linnea. Maybe it would help him, too.

"The person responsible for April's death is the person who killed her," Jace spelled out. "Not you and not me."

"But Gideon might be, and I maybe could have..." Linnea trailed off and shook her head.

With her gaze locked with his, she stood and went to him. She didn't hesitate. She stepped into the arm that he circled around her.

"After this is over," she said, "I don't want this to be over."

Jace had to smile because he knew exactly what she meant. "I don't want it to be over, either." He paused and because he wanted to try to get her to smile, too, he added. "What's a four-letter word for this not being over? *Date*," Jace supplied just in case her mind was heading in a different direction.

"A date?" she repeated.

"Dates," he amended. "I want more than one."

Now she did smile, and it was a darn good thing to see. "Who knows, once you're all healed, maybe it could be more than a date."

That was like an invitation to certain parts of his body. Because, yeah, he wanted more than dates. "I'm feeling all healed now," he said, and brushed his mouth over hers.

He kissed her frown. "You're not all healed," she insisted.

Jace might have kissed her again to prove her wrong. Or rather to try to prove her wrong. But his phone dinged with a text message.

"It's Manuel," he said. "Your house is clear. He'll wait on the front porch for us like he did this morning."

"Are you okay to drive?" Linnea asked.

"Sure." That was his automatic answer, and it was probably true. He could steer with his good arm, but that would mean he wouldn't be able to keep his hand on his weapon.

"You can drive," he amended. It was another bending of the rules, but Jace figured this was a better-safe-than-sorry kind of deal.

He took a moment to drop another kiss on Linnea's mouth, and then he shifted his brain from her to the trip to her place. Gathering their things, he got Linnea her gun, which she tucked into the backpack. Jace then made a quick stop to let the dispatcher know where he'd be, and he went to the door to look out. He didn't see anything out of the ordinary, so Linnea and he hurried to the cruiser. However, he just put the key in the ignition when his phone rang.

Glenn, again. And Jace braced himself for what would no doubt be more bad news.

"Someone set the barn on fire," Glenn immediately said.

Jace groaned. Yep, definitely bad news. "What happened? Is anyone hurt?"

"Don't know yet. One of the neighbors saw the smoke and called it in. The fire chief just let me know about it because he wasn't sure if you'd be in the office."

"I'm on my way to Linnea's," he said as Linnea started driving. Jace kept watch while he considered something. "The CSI team wouldn't have had time to get there, so they probably weren't caught up in this."

Of course, someone else could have been. Maybe someone else the killer had wanted to eliminate.

"Once I'm at Linnea's, I'll make some calls and see what I can find out. Is Tammy still secure?" Jace asked when Linnea turned onto Bluebonnet Lane.

"She is," Glenn confirmed. "She's out like a light, and the doc says she might be that way for a while."

Good, because it meant the woman wouldn't try to escape or cause trouble. But that thought had barely had time to form in his mind when Jace heard something.

A loud popping noise.

His head whipped up, and he looked for whatever had caused it. And he prayed that it was a car backfiring, even though there weren't any other vehicles around.

"Keep moving," Jace told Linnea when she slowed down so she could glance around.

Linnea pressed the accelerator, but she'd only gone a few more yards when he heard the noise again. Louder, this time. And he had no doubts as to what it was.

Because a bullet slammed into the window.

Right next to Linnea's head.

Jace saw the safety glass crack into a spider's web, but it held in place. The bullet didn't get through. But a second one tore into those cracks, weakening the glass even more.

Cursing, Jace pushed her down, leaning over her to try to protect her. She hit the brakes, causing his arm to slam into the steering wheel. Jace could have sworn he saw stars, and the pain ripped through him. Gulping in some hard breaths, he fought to clear his vision. Fought, too, to figure out where the hell the shooter was.

He got a much better idea of that with the third shot.

It, too, came from the driver's side of the vehicle, and

it blasted into the rearview mirror. Again, just inches from where Linnea and he were. But it was still a miss, and the shooter had almost certainly been aiming for the window again.

"Stay down," he told Linnea when she started to get up.

"You're hurting, and I can return fire." And she somehow managed to get her gun from the backpack that was on the seat between them.

Well, she sure as heck didn't sound as rattled as she had been in his office. That would come later, though. He was sure of it, but for now Linnea looked ready to help him fight their way out of there. But Jace wanted to minimize the fight. They were in a residential neighborhood with houses. There could be kids around. Hell, this was a prime situation for a bystander to get killed.

"Just stay down," Jace repeated, "but ease up on the brake. I'll handle the steering wheel, and we can get to your house."

Maybe.

But the next bullet ripped through the window, leaving a fist-sized hole and showering Linnea and him with safety glass.

Jace didn't bother cursing this time or playing into that whole hindsight thing. Determined to stop this SOB, he looked through the front windshield to the area where he was sure the shots were coming from. And he saw something.

Or rather *someone.*

A man wearing a ski mask.

He had on black pants and an unbuttoned, bulky gray shirt, and he was crouched down by the side of a house. The guy was already getting into position to fire again.

Since the windshield was bullet-resistant, it wouldn't do Jace any good to return fire through it, and Linnea was in his way for him to get a good shot through the damaged window. Still, it would have to do.

"Stop the cruiser," Jace snapped, and in the same breath, he lifted his gun. Took aim.

And fired.

Jace saw the man stagger back as if he'd been hit. That was when Jace got a glimpse of what the guy had on beneath that bulky shirt.

A Kevlar vest.

Hell.

The chest shot certainly hadn't killed him. The assailant managed to pull the trigger again, and he got off another bullet. It missed the cruiser, going heaven knew where. Hopefully, not into someone's house.

Jace adjusted again, bracing himself on Linnea's back and shoulder, and fired. It was another chest shot, but this time the guy finally fell.

"Stay in the cruiser," Jace told her, and he spotted someone that he wanted to see. Manuel was running toward them.

"Watch Linnea," Jace ordered the deputy.

"You're not going out there," Linnea insisted, and she tried to hold him back.

"I have to do this. He's not dead," he said, throwing open the door. "He probably just got the breath knocked out of him, and I need to get to him before he tries to fire again."

Jace didn't wait for her to argue with him. Bracing his shooting wrist as best he could, he ran across the street and into the yard. He took aim at the gunman as he approached him.

There was blood on the sleeve and shoulder of his shirt. Blood, too, on the right side of the ski mask. The man was writhing in pain, with his gun only a couple of inches from his body.

"I'm Sheriff Castillo," he snapped, as he kicked the gun away. He also did a quick check to make sure the guy had no other weapons.

None.

With his gun still on the man, Jace studied him. Well, what he could see of him. And he suddenly got a really bad feeling in the pit of his stomach. Already knowing what he would see, Jace reached down and yanked off the ski mask.

Oh, hell.

It was Gideon.

Chapter Thirteen

Linnea sat in the passenger's seat of the cruiser and watched as the EMTs loaded Gideon into the ambulance. Her stomach was churning, the muscles clenched so tight that she thought she might get sick. Every nerve in her body felt raw and exposed.

Her brother had just tried to kill her.

There was no doubt about that. She'd seen Jace unmask him. Had seen Gideon fire at the cruiser. Not just once but several times, and his aim hadn't been off. If the glass on the cruiser hadn't been bullet-resistant, Gideon would have no doubt managed to shoot her in the head before Jace pushed her down.

"We'll follow the ambulance to the hospital," Jace said.

Linnea looked over at him as he opened the driver's-side door and raked the safety glass off the seat. Bits of that glass were glistening in his black hair and on his clothes. It was probably the same for her, but Linnea didn't have the energy to do anything about it. Her nerves might have been right at the surface but so was the exhaustion that went all the way to the bone.

"I would ask you if you're okay," Jace said, starting the engine. "But I know you're not."

"Neither are you," she muttered, knowing it was the truth. She could see the weariness in his eyes that was almost certainly showing in hers.

He grunted, possibly agreeing with her, and that was when she saw something else. Jace was keeping watch as they drove to the hospital. Keeping watch in case Gideon had brought his partner or a hired gun with him.

Maybe it was the exhaustion clouding her mind, but having to take such precautions riled her to the core. It wasn't enough that Jace and she had been attacked, again, or that Jace had had to shoot her brother. The danger was still there. And would be until they got answers to put a stop to it.

She prayed her brother could and would give them those answers.

Jace pulled into the hospital parking lot and parked behind the ambulance. He winced when he got out, and Linnea made a mental note to have his wound checked. Heck, it was possible he'd popped a stitch or two. Also possible that he'd gotten new injuries from the flying glass and debris. She hadn't been hurt, but she hadn't had to bolt out of the cruiser to stop them from being killed.

The EMTs rushed Gideon out of the ambulance, and Linnea got a better glimpse of him. His eyes were closed, he wasn't moving, but he was breathing.

And bleeding.

There was blood seeping from an open cut on the side of his head. It looked as if he'd been grazed by a bullet. Or maybe more than grazed. It was possible he had a gunshot wound there.

"Kevlar," she muttered when she spotted the vest.

"Yeah." Jace nodded.

She hadn't seen the vest during the gunfight with Jace, but that explained how Gideon had taken shots to the chest and was still alive. And she knew that Gideon owned such a garment because she'd seen it at his house.

The EMTs wheeled Gideon inside, and Jace and she were right behind them. They followed them to an examination room where the nurse, Arlene Halverson, tried to stop them from entering.

"He's my prisoner," Jace stated. "And he'll be charged with Toby's murder and attempted murder of Linnea and me. He's dangerous."

Obviously Jace's warning got through to the woman because Arlene's eyes widened, and she gave a shaky nod. "We'll use the restraints to make sure he doesn't leave the bed."

Arlene proceeded to do that after the EMTs moved Gideon to an exam table. Jace didn't actually go into the room, but he didn't budge out of the doorway, either. That gave Linnea a chance to get a look at Jace's bandage, and he didn't even try to stop her when she undid the top buttons on his shirt.

No blood.

That was somewhat of a miracle, considering all the moving around Jace had done when he was fighting to save their lives.

"I'm not hurting that much," he assured her as he plucked a bit of glass from her hair and flung it into the trash can.

Linnea returned the favor and got several pieces from the collar of his shirt. "But you're hurting," she stated, knowing it was more than *that much*.

"Once Gideon tells us that name of the person he's working with, I'm sure I won't feel any pain at all," he muttered, his attention still on her brother. Jace paused, groaned. "I really didn't think he'd go after you that way. I knew he wanted me dead. But I thought…" He stopped again, and Linnea saw the hard emotions tightening his face.

"You did what you had to do," she assured him, just in case Jace was having any doubts about that.

That brought his gaze directly to hers, eye to eye. "Yeah," was all he said.

She would have tried again to give him whatever reassurance she could, but his phone rang, and she saw Glenn's name on the screen. Jace gave Gideon another glance, maybe to confirm that he was indeed restrained, and he tipped his head for her to follow him several feet away.

"Just heard Linnea and you were here at the hospital," Glenn said. "You really brought in Gideon? That's what one of the nurses told me."

News traveled fast. Not exactly a good thing in this case, and that was probably why Jace moved her behind him. Her brother might be out of commission for the moment, but his partner could come in with guns blazing since Gideon had failed to finish them off.

"Gideon's here in the ER," Jace explained. As he was talking, Dr. Garcia came into the examining room and went straight to Gideon. "He's hurt and doesn't appear to be conscious."

"So he hasn't told you anything," Glenn concluded.

"He tried to kill Linnea and me, so I guess that's the message he wanted to get across." Jace shifted his attention to the waiting area, glancing around. No doubt trying to assess if there was any kind of danger.

"Linnea and I might be here for a while," Jace continued a moment later. "I need you to call and make sure Manuel's secured the crime scene. The shooting happened on Bluebonnet Lane, just about a block up from her place. Also, check and make sure no one was injured. It's possible some of the rounds went into one of the houses."

"I'll get right on that. The security guard is on Tammy's door, so should I go to the scene now?" Glenn asked.

Jace gave that some thought, probably evaluating if that was his best use of resources. After all, Manuel was a reserve deputy, and he would need help.

"Yes," Jace finally answered. "Go and make sure everything is under control, but then come back in case I need to get Linnea out of here."

She definitely didn't like the sound of that because she didn't want to go anywhere with Jace. Or without getting answers from her brother.

"Okay, I'm heading out the side exit now," Glenn continued. "In the meantime, I can give you an update. I just got off the phone with the fire chief, and he said from his preliminary exam of the barn, the device that started the fire was on a timer. And there was a camera positioned on a tree limb and facing the barn."

"A camera," Jace and Linnea repeated in unison.

"Yes," Glenn affirmed. "It'll be taken to the lab so they can see if it has prints or if it can be traced to anyone. The chief said the camera didn't have any dust or debris on it so it probably hadn't been there long. I'm guessing Tammy's kidnapper put it there to keep tabs on her."

Since Tammy had escaped—well, unless she'd

faked the abduction—that made sense. But something else didn't.

"Tammy said she gouged her captor with the nail and then ran," Linnea said, thinking out loud. "So, why wouldn't he have taken the camera with him before he went in pursuit? Or he might have thought he could get her, bring her back and deal with the camera then."

Jace made a sound of agreement, but she could tell from his expression that there were things about Tammy's kidnapping that didn't make sense to him, either.

"Whoever was watching from that camera," Jace added a moment later, "would have seen April retrieve the bloody nail. That could have been how he knew to go after her."

Mercy. That was true. So did that mean Gideon had been the one to kill April? Or had his partner done that while Gideon went after Tammy? She wished that was something she could ask her brother now. Then again, Gideon probably wasn't just going to volunteer the truth if he had indeed committed murder.

"I'll call you if there are any problems at the scene of the shooting," Glenn said before he ended the call.

Jace put his phone away just as Dr. Garcia stepped outside the room and looked at Jace. "I'll need to shut the door while I examine Gideon. And yes, I understand he's dangerous." He tipped his head to Gideon. "I'll keep the restraints on him."

"Good. What can you tell me about his condition?" Jace asked.

"He's alive but unconscious. He's lost some blood from what appears to be an older injury, maybe a gunshot wound. It was treated but not well. It'll need to be cleaned and stitched. Also, judging from the bruises on his chest, he might have some cracked ribs."

"That's from the impact of the bullets on the Kevlar," Jace explained. "What about the head wound?"

"Looks like a bullet graze to me, but I'll know more once I've had a better look at him and run some tests."

"I want him restrained during the tests," Jace insisted.

The doctor nodded, gave a weary sigh. "If we have to move him around, I'll make sure he can't escape."

"Make sure he doesn't grab whatever he can reach and use it to assault or kill you," Jace countered. "Yes, he's that dangerous," he added when the doctor's eyes widened. "How long will he be unconscious?"

"Don't have the answer to that. Head injuries are tricky, and he could be out for a while."

Jace stared at Gideon. "Is it possible he's faking being unconscious?"

"It's possible but not likely in this case," the doctor answered without hesitation. "He had no reaction when I touched his bruises. Or his eyelashes. An awake patient usually has an involuntarily blink response when the eyelashes are touched," he explained.

"Usually?" Jace pressed.

"*Usually* is as good a guarantee as I can give you," the doctor said on a huff. "Now let me examine him, and I'll be able to give you more." He paused. "Well, I can do that if he's under arrest. I'm walking a fine line with privacy concerns—"

"He's under arrest," Jace confirmed. "I'll Mirandize him and interrogate him the second he's awake."

Jace might have tacked on more instructions, but the sound of the ER doors opening had him pivoting in that direction. He drew his gun, causing her heart to jump to her throat. And she soon saw why he'd done that.

Zimmerman came rushing in.

The agent cursed when he saw Jace's weapon aimed at him. "You can put that away, Sheriff. I've heard you have Gideon, and I'm here to take him into custody."

"Take a number," the doctor grumbled. "He's not going anywhere until I release him." Dr. Garcia went back in the examination room and shut the door.

"What's Gideon's condition?" Zimmerman snapped, turning his attention to Jace. "What has he said?"

"Unknown and nothing," Jace provided, and his tone wasn't especially helpful. "And FYI, he just tried to kill Linnea and me, so he's going to answer to that first before you take him anywhere."

That caused Zimmerman to puff up his chest. "The ATF has jurisdiction."

"For the drugs and illegal weapons," Jace readily admitted, sliding his gun into the back of his jeans. "But this was a personal attack on Linnea and me, and it happened right here in my jurisdiction."

Clearly, that didn't please Zimmerman. His eyes narrowed as he spoke. "Any related crimes will be dealt with by the ATF."

Jace leaned in, so close that he violated the agent's personal space. "Gideon just tried to shoot his sister in the head. He opened fire in a neighborhood where he could and maybe did cause injuries. He's going to answer for that."

The stare-down continued for several long moments before Zimmerman finally looked away.

"What are you doing here anyway?" Jace demanded. "How'd you get here so fast?"

Jace hadn't softened his tone one bit, and that seemed to put Zimmerman's hackles back up. "I was in the area. I heard about the dead CSI, and I was on my way to Linnea's to ask you about it."

"So you were close by when Gideon opened fire on us?" Jace pressed. Still no softening, and in fact, that sounded like an accusation.

Which it was.

Zimmerman was high on their list of suspects as Gideon's partner in crime.

"I was about a mile away," Zimmerman snarled. "And no, I didn't have anything to do with it." He appeared to be gearing up to spew out more of an argument about that, but the sound of running footsteps stopped him.

Both Jace and he turned in the direction of the footsteps just as Tammy barreled out of the hall. Her green hospital gown was fluttering around her. Ditto for her hair, and her feet were bare.

And the security guard was chasing after her.

"Gideon?" the woman called out. "Where are you?"

Tammy bolted toward them but came to a quick stop when she spotted Zimmerman. She actually dropped back a step, allowing the guard to take hold of her arm.

"Sorry, Sheriff," the guard said with his breath gusting. "She got away from me after she heard one of the nurses say that Gideon was in the ER."

Jace gave the guard a look that would have made many people shrivel up. Obviously, he was riled. Along with being curious, too. Linnea hadn't missed the way Tammy had reacted to Zimmerman, and obviously neither had Jace.

"You two know each other?" Jace asked, volleying glances at both Zimmerman and Tammy.

"She's Gideon's CI," Zimmerman quickly volunteered.

"Gideon said I shouldn't trust you," Tammy said just as quickly. "Gideon didn't trust you," she added.

Zimmerman huffed. "He said that because he knew I was going to arrest him for all the crimes he's committed."

Tammy stared at him, every part of her body in a defensive pose now, and she shook her head. "Are you the person who hired that thug to take me?" But she didn't wait for answer. "Did he?" She made her plea to Jace.

Jace only shrugged. "To be determined," he answered, causing the anger to flare in Zimmerman's eyes again.

Just then, she saw Bryce come through the ER doors. Great. With Gideon here, the people who wanted Jace and her dead could be only a few feet away from them.

"I heard Gideon was brought in," Bryce said without greeting. Or without an explanation as to why he was there.

Jace picked right up on that. "I rescheduled the interview with you," he snapped, but Jace was looking at Tammy.

Or, more specifically, at Tammy's reaction.

She'd taken a step back when she spotted Zimmerman, but with Bryce, she actually maneuvered herself behind the guard as if using him for a shield.

"Is this the man who held you captive?" Jace came out and asked Tammy.

The woman cowered behind the guard, peering out to study Bryce. She stared at him for several long moments before her bottom lip started to tremble. "I don't know. Maybe. The man said he was working for Lieutenant Cannon."

"That's a lie," Bryce snarled. He shifted his attention to Jace. "Obviously, the person who had her lied. Or else she made up the story to try to smear me and take the blame off Gideon."

Since that could be the truth, Jace acknowledged it with a nod. "That's why I need to interview both Tammy and you. So I can get to the bottom of what happened."

"I don't want to be here with him. Gideon?" she called out again. Her voice was a lot softer now, barely a whisper, and there was a plea in it.

"Gideon can't answer you," Jace told the woman. "And even if he could, you're not getting in there to see him. Same goes for you," he told Zimmerman and Bryce. "Don't bother to give me the spiel about you being his boss and therefore you have the right to question him," he went on when Bryce opened his mouth. "Right now, Gideon is my prisoner."

Tammy frantically shook her head. "I need to see Gideon. I need to make sure he's all right."

"He's alive," Jace said while motioning to the guard. "Take her back to her room, and this time, make sure she stays there."

The guard did drag Tammy away while she continued to call out for Gideon. Either the woman was in love with Gideon, or else she was putting on a good act.

Jace didn't say anything else until Tammy and the guard were out of earshot, and then he turned to Zimmerman and Bryce. She figured, from the way Jace paused, that he was trying to decide how much to tell them. Or maybe he was deciding the best way to get them out of there. He moved protectively in front of her again, and he had his right hand tucked behind him so that he'd be able to reach his gun fast.

"Tammy claims she managed to gouge her captor with a nail," Jace finally said. "Would either of you like to show me if you have any injuries on your arms?"

Both men were wearing long-sleeve shirts, and while Bryce had his sleeves rolled up to the elbow, it was still possible the fabric was hiding a wound. A wound that might prove he was dirty.

Linnea didn't have to guess what the men's reactions would be, and she was right. Bryce cursed, and huffing, Zimmerman dismissed Jace's words with the wave his hand.

"I have nothing to prove," Zimmerman insisted.

"Neither do I," Bryce chimed in.

"Well, actually you do." Jace directed his comment to Bryce. "Tammy made the accusation, so I figure you want to clear you name."

"How? By letting you do a body search on me? I don't think so," Bryce quickly added. "And if you try, my lawyer will fight you on this. I'm a cop, a ranked officer," he emphasized. "I won't be treated like this."

The man certainly hit all the notes of someone who'd been wrongfully accused, but Linnea wasn't sure if it was bluster to try to cover up the fact that he was as guilty as sin.

"I have nothing to prove," Zimmerman repeated when Jace shifted his attention back to the agent. "The burden of proof in on you about that, and since you no longer have possession of the so-called weapon that

Tammy used to attack her captor, then you're barking up a very wrong tree."

"Maybe." Jace paused again. "But I do have something else. Something else that was found at the barn where Tammy was held."

Linnea went still, but she tried to keep her face blank. Maybe Jace was fishing to see if one of them would mention the camera. Neither man bit, though. But both were glaring and obviously waiting.

"Blood," Jace said. "There were a few drops in the same area where the nail was found. The firemen spotted it and collected it before the fire could bring down the barn. This time, I have a team taking the blood to an undisclosed location."

She moved to Jace's side and saw him smile. It was sly and a little mean. The kind of smile that said, "You're toast."

"Soon," Jace added, his voice a warning, "I believe we'll know if one of you is as dirty as Gideon."

Chapter Fourteen

"You lied to them," Linnea said the moment Jace got her out of the hospital and into the cruiser that Glenn had just dropped off for them. "You lied when you told Zimmerman and Bryce that there were blood drops found at the barn."

Yeah, he had, and Jace would continue to lie if it exposed any dirty dealings.

Even after Zimmerman and Bryce had left, Jace hadn't wanted to fill in Linnea on his "plan" while they'd still been at the hospital. Way too many chances for someone to overhear, and he hadn't wanted the talk to get back to Gideon, Zimmerman, Bryce or even Tammy. However, he had wanted Tammy to hear about the blood at the barn, and that was why Jace had instructed the security guard to tell her.

If Tammy was in on her own kidnapping, she would know it was a lie. And if she'd truly been taken captive, then it might give her some comfort to believe the person responsible could be caught.

"If Zimmerman, Bryce and Tammy are Gideon's partners, then they might try to get someone to the barn," Jace explained to Linnea. "That's why I texted one of the reserve deputies and told him to put up another camera. If anyone goes to that barn, we'll know about it."

That would be the best-case scenario. Well, if Gideon didn't confess, that is. The worst-case scenario would be if this lie backfired and caused Gideon's partner to attack them again.

Yeah, definitely the worst case.

When his lungs began to ache, Jace forced himself to release the breath he'd been holding. He also eased up on the grip he had on the steering wheel of the cruiser. And even though this wasn't the same cruiser that Gideon had shot into, just glancing out the driver's window was a gut-punch reminder of how close Linnea had come to dying. He could still hear the sound of the gunshots. Still see the hole in the glass where the bullet had torn through.

And now they were back, literally at the scene of the crime.

Jace drove past the yard that was now marked off with yellow tape with the warning Do Not Cross. The CSIs were in the spot where Gideon had finally gone down, and they were probably checking for spent shell casings or any other evidence that could be used to build a case against Gideon.

Of course, the biggest piece of that evidence was that Jace and Linnea had actually witnessed Gideon shooting at them. Maybe soon, Gideon would be able to confess that. After he regained consciousness. Something that Jace had to believe would happen. Officially, though, Gideon was in a coma, and Dr. Garcia had no idea just how long that coma would last.

He drove past the CSIs, past Crystal and Manuel, who were still going door-to-door and talking with Linnea's neighbors. Judging from the cars he spotted in driveways, most of those neighbors were now home. They'd likely rushed in from work, or wherever they'd been, to check on their loved ones and property.

"I don't see any masked bogeymen," Linnea remarked.

She said it almost casually, as if this drive wasn't eating away at her. But he knew it had to be. It certainly was getting to him. Although there was some comfort in knowing that there were plenty of law enforcement people and eyewitnesses around. That would make it harder for a gunman to come after them again.

He hoped.

"I don't see Bryce or Zimmerman, either," she added, her gaze flickering to the rearview mirror.

No, neither did he. But it was possible they were around somewhere, since both men had left the hospital before Linnea and him.

"Zimmerman and Bryce pretty much hightailed it out of the hospital," Linnea continued as Jace pulled into her driveway. "But if one of them is Gideon's partner, they might try to find a way to get to him."

That was also part of the worst-case scenario. Linnea and he stood at least a chance of protecting themselves against an attack. An unconscious Gideon couldn't lift a finger to try to stop a killer. That was why Jace had Deputy Darnell Hough guarding Gideon's room. Jace had also given Darnell an order to call him the moment Gideon woke up.

"I'll keep a deputy inside his room," Jace assured her.

He was stretched for manpower, with the multiple investigations going on, but guarding Gideon wasn't an option. He could be the ultimate loose end for someone looking to silence him permanently.

There was also the problem with Tammy. Jace didn't like the woman being near Gideon, and she'd already proven that she could get away from the security guard. Hopefully, though, Tammy would only be staying overnight in the hospital, and then Jace could get her in for questioning. Depending on how she answered those questions, he'd either arrest her or offer her protection.

Since Crystal had already checked the house to make sure no one had broken in, Jace got Linnea inside, and they immediately locked up. According to the security system panel, all windows and doors were armed. That would give them a warning if there was indeed a break-in, but Jace was praying that whoever wanted them dead was done for at least the day. Linnea was clearly wiped out and needed some time to recover from the adrenaline crash.

He got another reminder of the attack when he saw a piece of glass in her hair. As they'd been doing to each other, he plucked this one out, dropping it on the foyer table. What he didn't do was move away from her. He was battling an adrenaline crash, too, along with nerves that had been scraped raw.

Hell.

He'd nearly lost her today.

Jace didn't speak that thought out loud to her. No need. And maybe she was thinking the same thing about him, because on a heavy sigh, she leaned in and laid her head gently on his uninjured shoulder.

"If someone didn't want us dead," she said, "I'd suggest we have a very strong drink. Maybe a couple of drinks." Linnea paused. "Maybe lots and lots of drinks," she amended.

He wasn't much of a drinker, but Jace agreed. A couple of shots of whiskey might help level him out some.

"Can't risk a buzz right now," she murmured.

Jace agreed with that, too. "You could maybe take a hot bath and then we can eat. I could make you a cup of that hot tea you like."

She looked up at him and frowned. "Tea?"

He shrugged. "It's about the best I can offer you right now. That and one shoulder."

Her mouth twitched a little as if she was about to smile. But the smile didn't come. Instead, with the fatigue of the day on her face, she pressed her hand to his cheek. "The one shoulder sounds good," she said. "What can I offer you?"

Jace didn't think she was talking about hot beverages, but it wasn't an offer of sex, either. More like some hand-holding. Maybe a gentle hug or two combined with a pep talk to try to convince them that they'd get through this. That soon, all would go back to normal.

Except Jace didn't think normal was going to cut it anymore for him.

No.

Going through all of this with Linnea had changed things for good. This wouldn't end with them going their separate ways. He'd kissed her, had her body pressed against his. Had wanted her more than his breath.

Still did.

It was the *want* that had him kissing her, but Linnea must not have seen it coming. She made a quick sound of surprise, a sound that he captured with his mouth as he sank into her. Tasting and upping that *want* to a need.

"You're in no shape for this," she muttered against his lips. But her voice wasn't a protest. More like a mix of silk and heat.

An invitation.

Or so he thought until she eased back a little and repeated, "You're in no shape for this."

He brushed the front of his jeans against hers to give that heat another bump. It worked. Jace saw the flush form on her cheeks. Heard the shivery breath she released. Her eyelids fluttered down for a moment.

"We could just talk sex," she suggested. "It'd be like phone sex."

Jace gave her a flat look. "And that would take care of this ache I have for you?"

"Probably not." She exhaled another of those breaths, along with a little moan, when he bumped her again. "But it would save your shoulder from hurting."

"My shoulder's fine," he assured her. At the moment, that wasn't a lie. He wasn't feeling any pain whatsoever.

To prove that to her, he kissed her again and started backing her into the living room. They might not be able to have sex the old-fashioned way in a bed, but there were plenty of other ways.

"This'll be better than lots and lots of drinks," he told her.

Since he still wasn't sure he'd convinced her of that, Jace just kept on kissing her. Just kept on moving her toward the sofa. As he lowered his mouth to rain kisses on her neck, he found a spot right below her ear that had her moaning again.

The right kind of moan, too.

Heat was right there, rippling off her skin, and the heat had gone hot by the time they reached the sofa. Jace first put his gun on the coffee table and then shifted so that he sat down first. He pulled her onto his lap. All in all, it was a darn good place for her to be. It didn't put any pressure on his shoulder, and it put them center to center.

Jace kept up the kisses but went lower this time. Down to the base of her throat. Then, lower. He kissed her breasts through her top, but soon that wasn't nearly enough. The top had to go, and with her help, he shucked it off her.

And stopped when he saw the bra.

Oh, man. He was toast. The bra molded against her breasts so that her nipples were peeking up over the tops of the black lace. Yeah, black lace. He hadn't realized he had a weakness for such things, but apparently he did. He didn't even wait to get a taste of that, and he took both that lace and her nipple into his mouth.

Not only did Linnea moan again, she also wiggled closer, pressing the center of her thighs right against his erection. The pleasure shot through him, and he knew this was going to have to move a little faster than he'd planned.

Linnea was on board with the faster because she reached between them and unzipped her jeans. Showing some incredible balance, she managed to lever herself up and shimmy out of her jeans, all without leaving the couch.

Her panties were black lace, too, and the sight of them caused Jace to groan. If he hadn't already been rock-hard, that would have done it.

"You can see right through that lace," he told her. "That's not a complaint."

She smiled, a siren's smile, took his hand and slid it

into her panties. Jace had planned on going there anyway, but that sped things up.

He touched her. Watched her. The way her mouth opened. The rise of her chest as her breathing quickened. The wet heat as he stroked her. It didn't take many of those strokes before he felt her muscles respond and contract, and he might have sent her flying right then if she hadn't caught onto his hand to stop him.

"No," she said. "I've fantasized about you for way too long for this to be solo. I want us together on his."

Fantasized, huh? Later, Jace would ask her about that, but for now he apparently had to free himself from his jeans. He didn't have time to figure out the logistics of that because Linnea got started on it. She shoved down his zipper, sliding both his jeans and boxers off his hips and freeing his erection.

She looked down, smiled.

"Oh, yes," she said, her voice low and silky. "You're living up to my fantasy."

Jace hoped like the devil that the living up continued, but he had to steel himself up when Linnea leaned to the side to shimmy out of her panties. He was dead sure the image of her doing that would stay with him for a long, long time. Along with giving him plenty of fantasies of his own.

"Condom," he managed to say just as Linnea was about to get back on his lap. "In my wallet, back pocket."

She went right after it, her hands and movements more than a little frantic now. There was some bumping involved, possibly bumps that involved pain, but Jace was past the point of no return. The moment Linnea retrieved the condom, he opened the packet and got it on. Good thing, too, because Linnea didn't wait even a second before she straddled him again.

And took him inside her.

"I've got this," she assured him.

She did. As if to make sure he didn't move around too much, Linnea anchored one hand on his good shoulder and used her other hand to grip the back of the sofa. And she moved.

Mercy, did she.

Linnea created a slow, deep rhythm. Then, not so slow. Then, fast. And faster. Until his pulse was thick and throbbing. Until there was so much need for her that Jace wasn't sure he'd ever get his fill of her.

Apparently, she had her own need for him because with that quickened pace, he felt her muscles squeeze against his erection. Her fingers dug into the sofa while her hips pumped as if to drain every drop of pleasure from this.

Which she did.

As the climax rippled through her, Jace savored the moment for just a heartbeat before he followed her.

Chapter Fifteen

Linnea was thankful for the slack, sated feeling that came with great sex. Thankful for the great sex, as well. Maybe there'd be plenty more of that in her future, but for now, she was just glad that her brain and nerves weren't on full throttle. She needed the lazy calm even if she knew it was only temporary.

Apparently, Jace was having his own "lazy calm" because he didn't seem in much of a hurry when they'd finally gotten up from the sofa. He'd made a quick stop in the hall bathroom and had come out with his clothes back in place. That had been Linnea's cue to get dressed, as well.

And Jace had watched her do that.

He was especially attentive when she slipped on the bra and panties.

Normally, she would have felt the need to cover all her body flaws, which were plentiful, but it was hard to think of flaws and such when there was a hot cowboy giving her an equally hot look.

She was so having him again—soon.

Judging from the smile he flashed her, he knew exactly what she was thinking and wanted to return the favor.

"Please don't say anything about this feeling weird," she told him. "I mean, because you've always thought of me as Gideon's kid sister."

His smile turned a little sly. "Linnea, I quit thinking of you as a kid more than a decade ago. And no, this doesn't feel weird." He paused, his forehead bunching up as if he was giving it some thought. "It feels—"

His phone rang.

Linnea groaned and wanted to insist that he finish what he'd been about to say. However, when he looked at the screen and muttered, "It's Glenn," she knew he had to take the call. He did and put it on speaker.

"Everything's okay," Glenn said right off, probably because he knew they'd be expecting the worst. "I did just have a run-in with Zimmerman, though. He came to Gideon's room and tried to barge his way in. He left when Crystal showed up to bring me some dinner. It's my guess he didn't want to take on two deputies."

Good. Linnea was glad Zimmerman hadn't gotten in with Gideon, because if the ATF agent was Gideon's partner, he could have tried to kill him. Zimmerman might have risked that with just Glenn, but Crystal was some extra insurance. Of course, that didn't mean Zimmerman wouldn't try again.

"Was Bryce with Zimmerman?" Jace asked.

"No. Haven't seen him. But I do have some news about Gideon. That's why I'm calling. The doc is in there with him now, but Gideon opened his eyes a couple of minutes ago."

Linnea hadn't expected that to hit her like a heavyweight's punch. She wanted her brother to regain consciousness. Wanted him to confess all. But she hadn't steeled herself up enough. Just like that, her "lazy calm" vanished, and she got a full reminder of the danger still facing them.

"Gideon didn't say anything," Glenn continued. "He just moaned and tried to lift his hands. He's still re-strained," he quickly added. "That's when I called for the nurse, and she had a doctor come in. They asked me to step out while they examined him."

"Stay right there," Jace instructed. "Do you know the nurse and doctor?"

"I do. It's Dr. Garcia and Ashley Dorman. After Zimmerman tried to get in here, I thought maybe he'd try to send in someone posing as medical staff."

"Zimmerman or Bryce. Or, hell, anybody working with Gideon." There was plenty of frustration now in Jace's voice, and his jaw had gone tight.

"Is Gideon still in the ER, or has he been moved to a room?" Jace asked.

"He's in room 119. It's not far from the nurses' station."

Probably because they'd want to keep an eye on him. But the fact that her brother wasn't in ICU probably meant his condition wasn't that bad.

"Linnea and I are coming back to the hospital," Jace said a moment later. "Tell Dr. Garcia that I'll need to speak to Gideon ASAP."

"Will do. Crystal's back at the office. You want me to have her follow you to the hospital?"

Jace opened his mouth, and Linnea was pretty sure he'd been about to say no. But when he looked at her, he must have changed his mind. "Yeah. I want to leave as soon as she gets here. I don't want to give Gideon any time to try to concoct a story to try to make us think he's not as dirty as I know he is."

"I'll call Crystal now," Glenn said. "Be careful, boss. I don't like that Zimmerman and Bryce are out there."

Neither did she, and she knew Jace felt the same way. But what Jace was lacking was any kind of proof that would get one or both men off the street and behind bars. Maybe Gideon could give them that proof.

Linnea hurried to the bathroom to freshen up, and when she came back into the living room, she saw Jace putting his gun in the waist of his jeans. It sickened her that they had to take such measures just to step out of the house. But being outside could be the opening a sniper needed to fire shots at them.

Jace went to the front window to keep watch, and because she knew it was what he'd want her to do, Linnea stayed back. It was ironic that just minutes earlier, she'd been so happy. So pleasured. Now Jace and she were facing reality again.

"I'll talk to Tammy, too, while we're there," he said, keeping his attention on the yard and driveway. "I can also find out from her doctor if her condition is really serious enough for her to stay overnight. If she's not in on this, I want her moved to a safe house."

There was something in his voice, something she couldn't quite put her finger on. "You're worried someone will try to kill Tammy."

"It could happen, but I'm more worried she'll try to kill somebody," Jace clarified. "She doesn't have access to a weapon, but since she got away from her security guard to run to the ER, she might be able to sneak something past him." He dragged in a long breath. "If she has to stay in the hospital, I'm calling the Texas Rangers to assist in guarding her."

That was a good idea, but it tightened her chest to

think that Tammy might be a killer. A killer in the very place that Jace and she were about to be. Still, they had to go. They had to talk to Gideon.

"Crystal's here," Jace said.

Jace and she went through the now familiar routine of disengaging and then rearming the security system locks before they hurried out to the cruiser. Crystal was indeed there, also in a cruiser, and she followed them out of Linnea's driveway.

The CSIs were still at work, processing the scene of the shooting, and some of her neighbors were milling around, no doubt trying to find any tidbit or gossip that would let them know what had gone on here today. If the whole story wasn't out yet, it soon would be. There'd likely even be talk about Jace and her spending "so much time" alone in her house.

As a rule, Linnea couldn't bother with that kind of speculation. However, she couldn't stop herself from speculating about Jace.

And no, this doesn't feel weird, he'd said. *It feels—* She thought maybe he'd been about to say something like "good." There was a chance, though, that it had felt wrong. Not at the time they'd been having sex, of course. He'd enjoyed that as much as she had. But he was a cop to the bone, and he was probably thinking how unsafe it was to be so distracted.

And it was.

But so were her feelings for him.

Yes, there were feelings. Deep ones. The attacks and the danger hadn't fueled those feelings, but it had made her see that life was too short, too littered with pitfalls not to go after what she wanted.

"I'm falling in love with you," she blurted out.

Linnea wasn't sure who was more surprised by her confession—Jace or her. The timing sucked, of course, and she'd just contributed to that whole distraction problem, but life was indeed short. If Jace and she didn't make it through this, then it was something she wanted him to know.

The muscles in his jaw stirred, and he gave her a long glance. "I'm a bad bet right now."

"I'm not exactly a good one," she pointed out. "It's just something I wanted you to know."

Obviously, that didn't please him, because his jaw muscles got even tighter. "We'll talk about this later," he said, pulling into the hospital parking lot.

Yes, they would, but Linnea had a horrible thought. One that clawed away in her belly. The thought that there might not be a later. But no way would she hit Jace with that gloom and doom right now. She simply nodded, tried to give him a reassuring look, and they got out of the cruiser as soon as he'd parked it.

As they'd done on their previous visits, Jace and she scanned the waiting room. No one was there today, and the reception desk had a sign that said Be Back Soon, Please Take a Seat.

They moved past the desk and went straight to the hall where there were about a dozen rooms. Jace spotted the security guard, Melvin Carter, in front of what was no doubt Tammy's room. Unlike some of the other hospital guards, Melvin wasn't past his prime. Jace figured the guy was only in his early forties and was in good shape.

"Make sure she stays put," Jace warned the guard.

Linnea and Jace didn't stop. They continued down the hall, which forked off into two smaller wings, each with only four rooms. They went to 119, where Glenn was standing.

"The doctor and nurse just left," Glenn explained. "Dr. Garcia wouldn't give me an update, though."

"I'll get it from him," Jace muttered, and walked into Gideon's room with Linnea right behind him.

Her brother's eyes were closed, but he looked better than he had when he'd been brought out of the ambulance. There was more color in his face, and his head wound didn't look as serious. There was a gash, but it'd been cleaned and stitched.

"I listened at the door," Glenn told them, "but I didn't hear Gideon say anything. The nurse mentioned that he was still unresponsive. Hope I didn't get you here for nothing."

Jace didn't comment on that. He went to Gideon's bed and stared down at him. "You said you saw him open his eyes?" he asked Glenn.

Glenn nodded, and both Linnea and the deputy also moved closer. She watched Gideon's eyelids, looking for any sign of movement.

And she saw it.

Just a flicker, maybe an involuntary one, but Linnea leaned down and got right in his face. "You tried to kill me," she bit out, feeling the anger snap through her like a bullwhip. "Open your damn eyes and tell me why you did that."

Linnea didn't expect for that to work, and that was why she was shocked when it did.

Gideon opened his eyes slowly. Cautiously. And she saw all those shades of blue. Shades that she knew very well because they were practically a genetic copy of her own. Ditto for his hair color, but hers had caught a lot more sun and had streaks that his didn't.

Her brother's gaze landed on her and then immediately shifted to Jace and Glenn. His attention settled on Jace as Glenn stepped out, no doubt to continue guarding the room.

"I need protection," Gideon croaked. His voice was hoarse, and she didn't think he was faking that. "I need a deal."

"You're not getting a deal," Jace informed him, and there was plenty of anger in his tone and expression. "But you are going to tell me who helped you steal and sell guns and drugs."

"I can't." Gideon swallowed hard, cleared his throat and repeated it. "If I tell you, I'm a dead man."

"Why? Who?" Jace demanded.

"I'll be a dead man," Gideon repeated.

Jace glared at him. "If I take my deputy off guard duty, anyone could come in here. Anyone," he emphasized, and it sounded exactly like the threat that it was.

Her brother's eyes widened, and while he might have been shocked that Jace would threaten to do something like that, Gideon seemed to at least consider the possibility.

"I want the name of your partner," Jace insisted. "I want you to tell me about any and every goon who's had a hand in getting your sister nearly killed."

Gideon stayed quiet, but there was plenty going on in his head. Linnea could practically see the fears and thoughts flying around in there.

"I need protection," Gideon insisted. "If you want me to testify, you have to keep me alive."

Jace hesitated, but Linnea figured he would agree

to some kind of protection, something he was already providing anyway. But Jace didn't get a chance to voice an agreement because the door opened.

"Boss, we got a problem," Glenn said. And Linnea's heart went to her knees when she saw that he'd already drawn his gun. "A nurse just told me that two armed men came in through the ER. They're headed this way."

JACE FELT THE punch of sickening dread. Hell. He'd brought Linnea here, hoping to get answers, but now he might have put her in another deadly situation.

"Stay back," he told Linnea, and hurried to the doorway, where both Glenn and he scanned the hall.

Nothing.

Not yet anyway. But Jace couldn't see the entire hall. If the gunmen were truly coming from the ER to get to Gideon's room, they'd have to go right past the security guard.

"Call for backup," Jace instructed Glenn. "I want every available deputy up here now, but tell them to approach with caution."

Now probably wouldn't be soon enough, though. The gunmen would have factored that in, that the sheriff's office was just up the street and that Jace would call in backup. That was probably why the thugs intended this strike to be fast, and anyone who got in their way would likely be killed.

"They're coming for me," Gideon snapped. "Get me out of these restraints so I can defend myself."

Jace couldn't do that for the simple reason this could be a ruse to rescue Gideon rather than kill him. If Gideon got free, he might try again to kill Linnea and him.

"This is Sheriff Castillo," Jace called out, ignoring Gideon. "Stay in your rooms and get down. Melvin," he added to the security guard, "you've got armed men coming your way. Get in the room with Tammy and block the door."

Jace had figured his warning would garner some attention. And it did. There were some gasps and screams. The sounds of people scrambling to get out of the path of whatever was coming their way. Maybe the patients, visitors and medical staff would all stay down. But he'd no sooner had that thought when he heard something else. Not a blast.

But it was gunfire.

Jace was certain of it. It was the swishing sound that came when a bullet was fired through a silencer.

Glenn cursed, obviously knowing exactly what that sound was. Maybe the one that followed, too, because Jace was pretty sure the hard thud was because someone had dropped to the floor.

Someone who'd been shot.

His guess was that it was Melvin. If the guard hadn't managed to get in Tammy's room fast enough, he would have made an easy target. And a necessary one in the eyes of the attackers. No way would they want to leave an armed security guard who could return fire.

There were more screams, and Jace knew some of them were coming from Tammy. "No! No! No!" the woman shouted.

Jace didn't know if the woman was reacting to the guard being shot or if the armed men were now going after her. He couldn't just stand there and let Tammy be killed, but he also couldn't leave Linnea, since the gunmen were almost certainly headed straight for Gideon's room. He had a couple of seconds at most to figure out what to do, and whatever he came up with could have deadly consequences for any one of them.

"Stay here with Gideon," Jace told Glenn. "I'm getting Linnea away from here, and then I'll be back."

Jace didn't give the three of them a chance to tell him what they thought about that plan, but Linnea clearly didn't like it because she started shaking her head. Gideon just kept shouting for Jace to get him out of the restraints.

"Move fast and follow me," Jace said.

He gave Linnea one last glance, hoping to reassure her that he'd do his best to get her out of this. He peeked into the hall, and while he still couldn't see the armed men, he could hear what was no doubt their footsteps. They were indeed heading this way.

The moment Jace had Linnea in the hall, he maneuvered her in front of him. Not easily. He had to keep his shooting hand free, which meant he had to take hold of her with his left hand. The pain shot through his shoulder, watering his eyes and nearly knocking the breath out of him. But that didn't stop him. He kept her moving.

They raced past the nurse station. No one was around, but there was a closed door directly behind the desk. Maybe that was where everyone had taken cover. He considered trying to get Linnea in there, too, but that would mean pounding on the door since it was almost certainly locked. That would take time and would alert the gunmen to where they were.

Jace ruled out sending Linnea to the emergency exit. It would get her out of the hospital, but it was possible there were other thugs waiting in the parking lot. Since she wasn't armed, she'd make an easy target.

"Go in there," Jace insisted.

It was just three doors down from Gideon's, and the room was empty. He practically shoved her inside and turned to run back to Glenn and Gideon.

But it was too late.

The gunmen rounded the corner of the hall. They were dressed all in black and had on ski masks and Kevlar vests. They immediately took aim at him. And fired. The bullet tore a chunk out of the door frame as Jace hurried inside.

A thousand thoughts went through his head. None good. The shooters had obviously seen him and would be coming this way. Well, they wouldn't if they stopped first at Gideon's room. If that happened, they'd try to take out Glenn before they did whatever else they'd come to do.

Backup had to be on the way by now. His deputies wouldn't just come barging in without assessing the situation. An assessment that was necessary, but it would eat up precious seconds. Those were seconds that Linnea and he didn't have.

"Get in the bathroom," Jace whispered to Linnea. That way, there'd be another door and wall between the shooter and her.

But Linnea didn't head there.

Instead, she scurried across the room and latched onto a metal IV pole that she probably intended to use as a weapon. Jace wanted to believe that it wouldn't be necessary, but the bottom line here was a really bad one. If the gunmen got past him, they'd kill Linnea. He doubted the IV pole would do much to stop them, but it was better than nothing.

He cursed himself for getting her into this. Cursed Gideon for starting this whole chain of danger. Later, if there was a later, he could tell Linnea how sorry he was that this was happening. For now, though, he focused all his energy on saving her.

He tipped his head to her, motioning for her to get behind him. Thankfully, she did do that, but he didn't know whether she'd stay put or not.

I'm falling in love with you.

Her words came back to him now, and they were a chilling reminder that she might do anything to try to save him. Anything that would include sacrificing herself. No way would Jace let her do that.

The footsteps in the hall slowed, and Jace risked sneaking a look outside again to pinpoint the gunmen's location. His heart skipped a couple of beats when he saw them outside Gideon's door. The door was still closed, but it wouldn't stay that way for long. Jace knew he had to do something now.

He adjusted his position. Took aim. And he got lucky. Because the men's attention were on Gideon's door and not him. Jace took full advantage of that.

"Drop your weapons," Jace called out, and the moment one of them whirled in his direction, Jace fired. Because of the Kevlar vests, he didn't go for the chest. Jace aimed at the guy's head.

And he didn't miss.

His shot was dead-on. Literally. The gunman dropped like a stone, but before Jace could do the same to his partner, the second gunman got off a shot. It came so close to him that Jace could have sworn he felt the heat from the bullet.

The gunshot slammed into the wall, and the trigger-man didn't stop there. He kept firing. Kept coming right at them. He was pinning them down with the gunfire, and Jace knew once he reached the room, he'd be aiming those bullets right at Linnea and him.

Jace steeled himself up for the attack. He gripped his gun. Waiting. Praying.

Behind him, he heard Linnea's breath. It was gusting, and he knew every muscle in her body was tight and primed for a fight for their lives. Any second now, the gunman would come into view, and he'd fire at him, just as Jace had shot the would-be killer. Both of them might end up dying, but at least Linnea would be okay. He hoped so anyway.

Jace heard some moving around, but the footsteps no longer seemed to be coming toward them. That didn't loosen the knot in his stomach because it likely meant the guy was doubling back to go after Glenn and Gideon.

Then again, this could be the gunman's way of trying to lure Jace out.

It wasn't easy, but Jace stayed put. Listening for the sound of Gideon's door being opened. He heard something, but it sure as heck wasn't a door.

It was a scream.

"Let me go," a woman shouted.

Jace didn't think it was Tammy's voice, and a moment later he got confirmation he was right.

"Someone help me," she begged, and he was pretty sure it was Ashley Dorman, one of the nurses.

Moving to the other side of the door frame so he

wouldn't be an easy target, Jace peered out and saw the woman. It was Ashley all right, and the armed thug was behind her. He had Ashley in a choke hold, and his gun was pressed to her temple.

The nurse was a good twelve inches shorter than her captor, which meant there was room for a head shot to take the guy out. But for Jace to get that shot, he'd have to come out from cover. That might have to happen if things went downhill fast—and the conditions for that happening were prime.

"Sheriff, it appears you've got a decision to make," the gunman snapped. He sounded tough enough, but there were nerves in his voice. "Come out and bring Linnea with you or this lady dies."

Jace squeezed his eyes shut a moment and cursed. He'd seen the look of terror on Ashley's face, and even though he hadn't seen the gunman's face, Jace had no doubts that he'd shoot and kill the nurse. Of course, he'd do the same to Linnea and him if he got the chance.

"If you shoot her," Jace said, "you'll lose your shield. Then, I'll kill you just like I did your partner."

Jace was doing more than merely trying to reason with the thug. He was also alerting Glenn to what was going on. The gunman and Ashley were only a few inches from Gideon's door, and if Glenn came out now, he might be able to knock out the guy from behind. It wasn't without risks, but doing nothing was a bigger risk right now, and if they could take him alive, he might bargain to tell them who was behind this.

The guy bobbled a little, shifting his weight from one foot to the other. He was also firing glances all around. Apparently, he didn't have a plan for getting out of this situation without his dead comrade, and if he panicked, he could end up taking out others in an attempt to escape.

Jace looked out again and saw Gideon's door opening. Just a fraction. Glenn was no doubt trying to figure out the best way to take the guy down. Jace could help with that by keeping up a distraction.

"I'll take the nurse's place," Jace told the man. "Her for me."

"It's gotta be both Linnea and you," he fired back.

Jace jumped right on that. "Who gave you that order?"

"Like I'd tell you that," the gunman snarled.

"Well, you should tell me. You're the one taking all the risks here. Not your boss. You're the one who could be killed."

The gunman paused several moments, and he was no doubt thinking that if he talked, he'd soon be dead. But Jace was hoping that talking was exactly what this guy wanted to do if he had the right incentive.

Jace gave this another push. "Maybe we can arrange a deal," he offered. "Your testimony in exchange for a shorter sentence. Maybe even witness protection."

The man's next round of silence was actually a good thing. Maybe, just maybe, he could get through to them, and no one else would die today.

That thought had no sooner crossed his mind when Jace heard more footsteps. Someone was hurrying toward the junction of the hall. Since it could be his deputies, Jace was about to shout out for them to stay back.

But it was too late for that.

Jace saw Zimmerman rounding the corner, fast, and the ATF agent's eyes landed right on the hostage situation. Zimmerman already had his gun drawn. A gun he aimed at the thug.

And before Jace could do anything to stop it, Zimmerman pulled the trigger.

Chapter Sixteen

Linnea had no trouble hearing the gunshot, and it caused her to break into a cold sweat. For one horrifying moment, she thought Jace had been shot. For one horrifying moment her world had stopped.

Still gripping the IV pole, she moved out from behind Jace so she could see if there was any blood on him. It was hard to force herself to focus, to fight through the panic that was clawing through her. But there was no blood. Not on Jace anyway.

She couldn't say the same for the gunman in the hall.

He was in a crumpled heap on the floor, and there was plenty of blood already pooling around him.

Frozen in place, Ashley started screaming, and Linnea couldn't fault her for it. She hadn't actually seen what had gone on, but she'd figured it out from Jace's and the gunman's brief conversation. The gunman had taken Ashley hostage to try to bargain an exchange.

Ashley for Jace and her.

But it obviously hadn't worked, and the gunman had been shot. Not by Jace, though. Linnea was certain of that. She shifted her gaze to the other end of the hall and spotted Zimmerman. His attention was fixed on the dead guy, a guy he'd obviously just shot, and the ATF agent slowly lowered his gun to his side.

Ashley finally managed to get herself moving, and with her breath wheezing out in panic and fear, she ran to the nurse's station door and started pounding on it with her fist.

And then the chaos started.

Glenn bolted from Gideon's room and took aim at Zimmerman. So did the deputies, three of them, who came barreling around the corner. Their guns were ready, too, and with all the firearms aimed at him, Zimmerman stopped.

"Call off your men," Zimmerman warned Jace.

"I'll call them off when and if I'm sure you're not a threat," Jace shot back.

"I'm not a threat." Zimmerman's voice was as hard and cold as his eyes. "I just stopped one. I heard there were gunmen in the hospital. I saw one, one with a hostage, and I took care of it."

Jace was just as quick to respond. "Maybe you took care of silencing a hired gun who could have ID'd you as his boss."

Zimmerman cursed, and with his glare on Jace, he lifted his hands and walked toward them. "I saved a woman's life."

"If you'd waited just a few more seconds, I could have talked him into giving himself up."

The agent made a sound as if he wasn't buying that. But Linnea did. Jace had indeed been making progress with the gunman, and she believed he could have defused the situation and arrested the man. Maybe Zimmerman had wanted to make sure that didn't happen. Of

course, it could be that he'd unknowingly done someone else a favor by offing the guy.

Jace didn't say anything else until he was eye to eye
and practically toe to toe with Zimmerman. "I need you
to go to the sheriff's office and give a statement about
the shooting." Jace tipped his head to Darnell. "Take
the agent's weapon into custody. You'll get it back,"
he quickly added to Zimmerman, "once everything is
cleared up and the paperwork is done."

Linnea figured it was standard procedure to confis-
cate a weapon used in deadly force. That meant Jace
would have to do a statement, as well, since she was
pretty sure Jace had killed the guy sprawled outside
Gideon's room.

Zimmerman tossed another scowl at Jace, but he
didn't resist when Darnell took his gun and motioned
for him to follow. Linnea probably would have breathed
a little easier at having one less threat right there, but
her lungs were so tight that breathing any kind of easy
wasn't possible.

Oh, mercy.

This had been a bloodbath, and there was no doubt
that Jace and she had been the targets. Maybe Gideon,
too.

The moment Zimmerman was out of earshot, Glenn
finished up with a phone call and then stepped toward
Jace and her. "Crime scene unit is on the way. I told
them to expect to be here for a while."

Oh, yes. Two dead bodies. Or maybe more. Linnea
remembered the other shot she'd heard.

"What about the security guard outside Tammy's
room?" Linnea asked, and she could tell from the way
Crystal shook her head that it wasn't good news.

"He's alive, but it looks like he's lost a lot of blood," the deputy explained.

Yes, definitely not good, but at least he was alive.

"Manuel's on Tammy's door," Crystal went on, talking to Jace now. "Not sure we can spare him there for long, though. We'll need to take a lot of statements."

Jace nodded and blew out his breath as if to clear his head. "I need you to guard Gideon." He shifted his attention to Glenn. "Go ahead and coordinate what else has to be done. Statements and the medical examiner. I also need a sweep of the building to make sure no one else was hurt by any stray shots."

"I'll get right on that," Glenn assured him, and he moved away to talk to the other deputies. Crystal stepped over the dead guy to go into Gideon's room.

Jace turned, looked at Linnea, his gaze combing over her. He was making sure she wasn't injured. The same thing she was doing to him. They'd come out of this without a scratch. Well, none that showed, anyway. Linnea was certain she had enough to fuel nightmares for the rest of her life.

He surprised her by brushing a kiss on her cheek. "I have to talk to Gideon and Tammy," he said. "The chief of staff, too. I'll have to get patients moved from this part of the hall."

Because this was now a crime scene. She understood that. Understood also that this was just the start of a long ordeal. It would have been easier to swallow if they'd learned the name of the person who'd hired the gunmen, but Zimmerman had made sure that hadn't happened.

"Did you send Zimmerman to the sheriff's office to get him out of here?" she asked.

"In part," Jace admitted. "I wanted him away from you and off the street. He'll be at the office for at least a couple of hours. That'll buy me some time to finish up here and get you back to your house."

Where they wouldn't necessarily be safe. But Linnea didn't say that out loud. No need. But along with the adrenaline and the fear came the anger, too. So strong that it felt as if it might punch right out of her. Their lives had been torn to shreds, and she still didn't know why or who was responsible. But her brother did. In fact, Gideon could have been the one who'd hired these men.

"They didn't go into Gideon's room," she pointed out to Jace.

"No, they didn't." He agreed so fast that he must have already been giving that some thought. "But maybe Gideon told them to make it look as if that's where they were heading."

That was the possibility she'd reached, as well. And it was just as likely that her brother had hired more than these two.

Jace went to the dead man Zimmerman had killed, and he leaned down to lift the ski mask. The blood had spread now, and the sight of it turned her stomach as she got a better look at him. His head was seriously damaged with the gunshot wound, but Linnea could see his features well enough. A wide, cleanly shaved face and a large nose that had probably been broken at least a time or two.

"I don't recognize him," she said, swallowing hard and praying that her stomach settled soon. "Do you?"

Jace shook his head and patted down the man's pockets. "No wallet."

Which meant he had no ID on him. That probably meant they'd have to wait for him to be fingerprinted before they knew who he was. Well, they would unless Gideon could tell them.

Jace used his phone to snap a picture of the dead man, and he moved onto the second one. He also had been killed with a head shot, and this time Linnea had to just stop breathing and choke everything back down so she could force herself to get a glimpse of his face. Again, she didn't recognize him, but he had a teardrop tattoo just below his eye.

"A prison tat?" she asked.

"Probably." As Jace had done with the first man, he went through this one's pockets and came up empty again. He took another picture before he stood.

"I want to talk to Gideon," Linnea insisted, and she headed toward his room.

Jace didn't stop her. In fact, he was right behind her as they threaded their way through cops and the medical staff who'd come out of hiding to try to assist. Crystal reached for her gun when they stepped in, a reminder that everyone was still on edge. That included Gideon.

Gideon wasn't still struggling with the restraints, but his wrists were red. There was also sweat on his forehead. "Who's dead?" he immediately asked, directing his gaze and therefore his question at Jace. "Your deputy won't tell me."

"The gunmen didn't tell me their names before they tried to kill us," Jace said.

His voice sounded calm enough, but it was a dangerous kind of calm. Linnea could practically feel the anger coming off him in hot waves.

Jace went closer to Gideon's bed and used his phone

to show him the two pictures he'd just taken. Under normal circumstances, her brother probably had a better than average poker face—he'd been a cop after all—but she saw the recognition in his eyes.

"Who are they?" Jace demanded.

Gideon looked away, and for a moment Linnea thought he might stall. But he didn't. "Silas Beck and Teddy Monroe. They belong to a militia group that bought some of the weapons taken from the storage warehouse."

Linnea mentally replayed each word. Gideon hadn't exactly confessed to stealing those weapons, but at least now they had someone to question. Of course, members of a militia weren't likely to spill all to the cops, but maybe Gideon would do that now.

"Who's your partner?" Linnea demanded. "Who hired these thugs to come after us?"

This time, her brother did hesitate. A long time. "I want a lawyer, and I also want to speak to the Culver Crossing district attorney."

"You want a deal," she grumbled, and she didn't tone down the sarcasm.

Gideon looked her straight in the eyes. "I'm sorry for what happened. I'm sorry," he repeated when she huffed. "If I could go back and…" He stopped, shook his head and shifted his attention back to Jace. "Without a deal, I won't stay alive for long."

Jace glared at him. "And I'm supposed to be concerned about that?"

"You should be, what with that shiny, untarnished badge of yours." There was sarcasm in Gideon's voice, too, and a bitterness that sounded bone-deep. "You'll want to get to the truth, and the only way you'll get that is with the DA figuring out how to keep me safe. Then and only then will you get everything you need to tie all of this up in a neat little bow."

Muscles flickered in Jace's jaw. "You're not just going to walk on this. Even if you didn't actually murder anyone, there's conspiracy-to-murder charges—"

"I know what I'm facing," Gideon snapped. He volleyed glances at both of them. "I want to stay alive to make sure the right people go down with me."

Linnea stared at him, trying to figure out exactly who the right people were. Maybe it was a veiled threat against Jace and her. Or maybe he meant his partner and any other thugs they might have hired as hitmen. She just didn't know, and when Gideon turned his head away, she figured he wasn't going to clarify it.

She was right.

"I'm not saying anything else without a lawyer and the DA," Gideon insisted. "And you won't press because now that I've played the lawyer card, anything else you try to wheedle out of me could possibly be tainted and you might not be able to use against me in a trial."

Judging from the profanity that Jace muttered, that was true. "He stays in those restraints," Jace told Crystal. "When he tells you the name of the lawyer, make the call for him and hold the phone to his ear."

The deputy nodded and took out her phone. Jace didn't wait around. He put his hand on the small of Linnea's back to get her moving out the door. They stepped around the dead body and headed up the hall, away from the other deputies and the chatter.

"I'm sorry," Jace said as they walked.

While Gideon's apology had riled her, Jace's confused her. "For what?" But she didn't wait for him to answer. "For my brother being a selfish SOB who'd rather save his own skin than give you info that could get us out of harm's way along with putting his partner behind bars?"

There was no humor in his smile. A smile that faded as quickly as it'd come. "For that and for putting you through this."

"Oh, we're doing the hindsight thing now." She managed to sound a lot more flippant than she felt. But there was one thing she knew for certain. "This wasn't your fault. It's the selfish SOB's fault along with anyone else who had a part in this."

Jace gave her no indication that he believed that. However, he did give her hand a gentle squeeze as they approached yet more blood on the floor. This one was outside Tammy's room and had almost certainly come from the security guard who'd been shot.

Manuel was right by the door when they stepped in, and like Crystal, he also went for his gun. But he visibly relaxed when he saw Jace. Nothing, however, was relaxed about Tammy. She was huddled in the corner of the room and was sobbing, her face buried in her hands.

"She's been like that ever since I came in here," Manuel explained.

Tammy looked up, her gaze zooming straight to Jace, and she practically leaped off the floor. "Is Gideon okay? Is he hurt?" The words rushed out.

"He wasn't hurt," Jace assured her.

Her face was red, ravaged by the crying jag, and she shook her head. "I want to see for myself. I have to talk to him."

Jace didn't waste any time responding. "Not going

to happen. Gideon's in custody, where he'll stay until he's able to be transported to the jail."

That brought on more tears. "Just tell Gideon I need to see him. He'll figure out a way for that to happen."

Jace's sigh was pure frustration. "He'll be transported to jail," Jace repeated. "Once you've been interviewed and I'm convinced you had no part in the crimes or attacks, then you can make a formal request to see him."

Tammy seemed to skim over the first part of that. The part where she would have to get Jace to believe she was innocent. "Let's do the interview now," she insisted. "Then I can make the request."

"I don't have time for an interview now," Jace informed her, but then he stopped, stared at her. "Unless you can tell me the name of Gideon's partner."

Tammy did more headshaking. More crying. "I don't know. That's the truth," she insisted.

Maybe it was, and maybe these attacks had just left Linnea cynical, but she figured Tammy could easily know more than she was saying. If Gideon had asked the woman to stay quiet about naming his partner, Tammy would.

Jace turned to Manuel. "I need you to go to the ER doors and make sure no one else comes in the hospital. If a patient with an actual emergency tries to get in, call me first to clear it before you let them inside. I'm going to call Sheriff Logan in Mercy Ridge and ask if he can send over some deputies to secure the other entrances and exits."

Manuel nodded, then glanced at Tammy. "What about her?"

Jace didn't respond to Manuel but instead stared at

Tammy. "I don't have the manpower right now to make sure you do as you've been told and stay put. But you will stay put, understand? My advice is for you to get back in bed or wait in the bathroom until someone on the medical staff comes in and moves you to another room."

"But what if someone tries to come in and kill me?" she blurted out.

"I'm going to do my best to make sure that doesn't happen. That's the best assurance I can give you right now," he added when she opened her mouth, no doubt to protest that. "The bed or the bathroom," Jace reminded the woman.

Jace took out his phone as they left a still crying Tammy, and he scrolled through his contacts until he got to Sheriff Logan. He was about to press Call when the sound pierced through the hospital. A pulsing blare of noise.

"It's the fire alarm," Jace said right before Linnea caught a whiff of something.

Smoke.

Chapter Seventeen

Jace's hand froze on his phone. His head whipped up and he caught the scent of smoke. Along with the alarm, that confirmed they had a huge problem. Because no way would he believe this wasn't connected to the attacks that'd just happened.

He allowed himself a split second to curse the fact that he hadn't already gotten Linnea out of there. His chat with Gideon and Tammy could turn out to be a fatal mistake. Later, he'd deal with that and what Linnea would perhaps call hindsight. But he should have realized that Gideon's partner wasn't finished. And wouldn't be finished until all the loose ends were tied off.

Gideon was that loose end.

Jace considered having Linnea wait with Manuel and Tammy, but he didn't want her out of his sight. Besides, Tammy could be a loose end, too, and if he left her there, she could soon have to face another hired killer, one that'd have an easier time going after her without Jace around.

"Come with me," Jace told her, and he hoped like the devil that he didn't regret this.

With Linnea in tow, he started toward Gideon's room.

Unlike the gunfire, the alarms brought patients opening the doors to their rooms to see what was going on. Jace did some checking, as well, and while he did see some thin, ghostlike wisps of smoke floating in the hall, he didn't see any flames. That was good, but there were no guarantees it would stay that way.

It was possible Gideon's partner or another hired thug had actually set a fire, but it was just as likely this was a smoke bomb of some sort. After all, a killer wouldn't want to battle a blaze to get to a target. Just in case he was wrong about that, though, Jace went ahead and put in a 911 call to alert the fire department.

While he tried to keep watch all around them, Linnea went back to the fork of the hall. Just then they heard something else. Not gunfire, thank God. But someone yelling.

"Help me," a man said.

Jace saw the man come staggering through the smoke. And he recognized him. It was Eddie Coltrane, an orderly who worked at the hospital. He was wearing his green scrubs and had his hand clutched to his chest.

A chest now soaked with blood.

"Somebody shot me," Eddie told them, and he tumbled forward, collapsing on the floor.

"I need a doctor or a nurse," Jace called out. "I've got an injured man here."

He didn't race toward Eddie, though that was what his instincts were screaming for him to do. Instead, Jace took Linnea by the arm and put her back in the doorway of Tammy's room.

"Don't let anyone get to her," Jace ordered Manuel. He added a stern look to Linnea to make sure she knew he wanted her to stay put. Jace waited for her to nod, and then he hurried to Eddie.

Cautiously hurried.

Because, after all, this could be a trap. But no one jumped out at him. No one came up the hall with guns blazing.

Jace knelt beside the orderly, took one look at his chest and realized this wasn't a hoax. Eddie truly did have what appeared to be a gunshot wound to the chest.

"Who did this?" Jace asked him.

Eddie groaned in pain and continued to clutch his hands over his injury. "Don't know. Didn't see him. I was in the ER, about to head back here to help, and he shot me from behind."

Hell. The guy could be anywhere by now. Maybe coming this way.

But that didn't make sense.

Well, it didn't unless the attacker thought Eddie had seen something. Something that could point the finger at him. It was just as possible, though, that this shooting was some kind of ploy.

"We're evacuating," someone else called out. "We need to move everyone out of the hospital."

It was Dr. Garcia. The doctor was heading their way, and he sped up when he spotted Eddie. He crouched down next to the man, did a quick assessment and yanked out his phone.

"I need a gurney, stat," the doctor told the person he'd called. "I'm outside Room 106. Stat," he repeated.

Jace glanced around, trying to figure out what the hell to do. He couldn't just leave the doc and a bleeding patient here on the floor. If a gunman did come through, he'd finish them off. But he also needed to get to Gideon's room. Because Jace's gut was telling him that Gideon was right now the primary target.

"We're going to have to move Eddie," Jace insisted, and he ignored the doctor's protests while he motioned for Manuel to help him.

Together, Manuel and Jace lifted the man, and Jace got a jolting reminder of his own injury. He must have grunted in pain because Linnea rushed out to help, and together they got Eddie into Tammy's room.

They put him back on the floor, and Dr. Garcia rushed in to continue trying to help him.

"Change of plans," Jace told Manuel. "Stay with Dr. Garcia, Tammy and Eddie. Keep watch because someone armed could try to get up this hall. And alert the fire department that there's another shooter somewhere in the area."

Manuel's nod was a little shaky, but Jace believed the deputy would hold up if there was another attack.

Jace then turned to Linnea. "You can stay here, too—"

"I'm going with you," she insisted, and she took hold of his arm to get him moving.

That meant going back in the hall, and Jace was glad that the smoke was already dissipating. Hopefully, that meant there wasn't actually a fire. But even if there was, the fire department would be there soon, and with Manuel's warning about a possible shooter, maybe they would take precautions. Jace didn't want anyone else shot or dying today.

Especially not Linnea.

He had plenty of doubts about taking her with him, but the doubts would have been even bigger if he'd had to leave her behind. He trusted Manuel and the doctor, but they'd have to evacuate soon, and Jace didn't want Linnea outside unless he was there to help protect her.

Both of them checked over their shoulders as they hurried to the hall junction, and when they turned toward Gideon's room, Jace didn't see the mayhem he'd expected. He'd been gone only about fifteen minutes, but the medical staff had done a good job of clearing out people. Probably evacuating them since he could hear a lot of footsteps heading toward the emergency exit.

The bodies were still there. Not much could be done about them now. Probably on Glenn's orders, the dead guys hadn't even been covered up. That way, the bodies would have less of a chance of picking up stray trace and fibers—something the ME and crime scene folks would appreciate—but it made this trek to Gideon's room even harder. Linnea had seen enough blood and gore, and now she was having to deal with it yet again.

"Maybe they evacuated Gideon, too," Linnea muttered as they approached his room.

She was right, and that caused Jace to curse. Hell, he hoped that hadn't happened, but if it had, Crystal or Glenn would have likely called him. Still, it gave him a bad feeling. A feeling that caused him to position Linnea behind him when he used his forearm to ease open the door.

Jace drew his gun.

However, he'd no sooner done that when the door slammed right into him. Right into his shoulder. The pain knifed through him and nearly brought him to his knees. Worse, it cost him precious seconds. Because whoever had slammed the door into him, threw it open, latched onto Linnea.

And put a gun to her head.

LINNEA HADN'T SEEN it coming. She'd been focused on Jace, on reaching for him to make sure he was okay.

He wasn't.

Neither was she.

She felt the cold hard steel of a gun barrel against her temple and the choke hold of the arm around her throat. Someone had her. Someone who'd already hurt Jace, because she could see that his gunshot wound was bleeding.

Linnea rammed her elbow against the man who was holding her. And it was a man. The muscles in his chest were pressing against her back. He grunted in pain, but his grip only tightened, making it hard for her to breathe.

Jace made a quick move as if he might lunge for her, but her captor only dug the gun in harder. That stopped Jace, and he fired glances around as if looking for help.

But help wasn't there right now.

Crystal was on the floor, and her head was bleeding. Maybe she'd been shot, but Linnea prayed she'd just been knocked unconscious. Probably by the same man who had her now. Either way, the deputy likely wasn't going to just get up and help them.

"Don't kill her," Gideon spat out.

She glanced at her brother, who was still in bed. Still restrained. And he was staring at the man who had her.

"Don't kill her?" her captor repeated. "That's funny coming from you, considering you tried to shoot her."

Oh, mercy. Everything inside Linnea went still. Because she recognized the voice.

Bryce.

Of course, she hadn't forgotten that he was a top

suspect, but she hadn't expected for things to come down like this.

"I tried to shoot her because you said if I didn't, you'd do it yourself," Gideon insisted. "And that it wouldn't be *pretty*." Her brother spat out the last word like venom.

"It wouldn't have been. But you failed, Gideon. Your kid sister not only figured out your dirty deeds, she teamed up with the sheriff here to try to stop both of us." *Sheriff* had some venom in it, too. "If I'd left this to you, we'd both either be dead or behind bars—which for cops is the same thing."

It sickened her to think that this had all been because of greedy cops who'd broken the law. And one of those cops was her own brother. Yes, Gideon seemed to be in a bad place right now with his partner, but his own actions had brought him to this.

"Bryce," Jace said. "Let Linnea go. You can't keep killing people to cover up your crimes." Obviously, he was trying to bargain with the man.

"I'm not going to kill you. Not unless I have to," Bryce quickly amended. "But Linnea and you are going to help Gideon and me get out of this mess. We have to go somewhere and lie low for a while. I'm thinking to a country without extradition to the US."

"Help you how?" Jace insisted. He still had a grip on his gun, but he couldn't shoot because she was blocking his line of fire.

"The four of us are leaving," Bryce explained. "We're going to walk out of here, and I'll make sure none of your deputies or Zimmerman gets the chance to shoot me. That's because you'll tell anyone who asks that you and I are transporting Gideon to your office for questioning."

Jace shifted his position and nearly managed to stave off a grimace of pain. Nearly. "No one would believe I'd do that. Gideon is a patient here."

"Then, you'll have to convince them otherwise." Bryce's voice was as calm as a lake. Too calm. And it made Linnea wonder just how many times he'd done something dirty like this. "Remember, all the time you're doing that convincing, I'll have a gun on Linnea."

Bryce lowered his gun to the base of her spine.

"Do anything stupid," Bryce went on, "and I end her with a shot before I turn the gun on Gideon and you."

"And then you'll be arrested," Gideon quickly pointed out.

Bryce made a "yeah, right" sound. "But I won't be dead like you'll be."

"You will," Jace argued. "Because if you fire a shot, then I've got no reason whatsoever to hold back. And I *will* kill you."

Linnea tried to tamp down her pounding heart so she could think. So many things could go wrong in the next couple of minutes, but she had no idea if it was best to try to make a stand here or do that outside. Jace certainly didn't look as if he was in any shape to fight off Bryce, but it might be better than going into the parking lot where plenty of people could be killed if there was a gunfight.

"Jace, take off Gideon's restraints," Bryce ordered. "And remember that part about not doing anything stupid."

Still glaring at Bryce, Jace went to Gideon's bed. Since he could only use his right hand, he had to remove the restraints while also holding on to his gun.

Linnea watched as Jace took off Gideon's left restraint, and then he moved to the side of the bed to take off the other one. The moment he'd finished, Jace adjusted his gun so that it was aimed at Bryce again.

"You're going to want to be careful about where you aim that weapon, sheriff," Bryce warned him. "But I'll let you keep it for now. It wouldn't look right if somebody saw you, and you weren't armed."

No, it wouldn't. But if Glenn or maybe one of the other deputies spotted them, they'd still know something was wrong.

She hoped.

"Now, let's move," Bryce ordered. "We'll leave out the side emergency door and go to the cruiser you've got parked by the ER. Another smoke bomb is set to go off right about now. That'll cut down on visibility, so who knows, we might be able just to walk out of here without anyone noticing us."

She couldn't see Bryce's face, but Linnea could see her brother's, and Gideon was scared. She doubted that fear was all for her. No. Gideon probably believed Bryce would murder him as soon as they were out of there.

And she was betting that was exactly what Bryce planned to do.

Along with killing Jace and her. Because Bryce might not have to worry about fleeing or extradition if they were all out of the way.

Her brother got up from his bed. Not easily. Like Jace, he was clearly in pain, and Bryce was well aware of that. Still, she doubted that would stop Jace from trying to fight back if he got the chance.

"Sheriff, open the door," Bryce instructed. "I'll just

keep this gun on Linnea's back so you'll make sure to do as you're told."

She saw the debate Jace was having with himself. Their eyes met, and so many things passed between them. Things she wished they'd said. Time that she wished they'd had. But this wasn't over, and Linnea tried to let Jace see that on her face. It wasn't over. She wasn't going to lose him now that they'd finally gotten together.

"There's blood in the hall," she mouthed. "Don't slip on it."

Of course, she meant that for Jace. A way of letting him know that she intended to "slip" once they were out of the room. Bryce might still get the chance to shoot her, but maybe he wouldn't have time to turn the gun on Jace.

Before Jace could even reach for the door, it flew open. He dodged it this time and stepped back before it could smack into him. However, it did hit Linnea, and she staggered back. She felt the gun.

And figured she was a dead woman.

"Gideon!" someone shouted.

Tammy.

She came rushing into the room.

Linnea used the distraction to try to get away from Bryce, but he used his body to knock her to the side so that she landed, hard, on the metal bed rail. The pain shot through, but she tried to jump right back up so she could fight him off.

Fighting him off wasn't necessary, though.

Bryce latched onto Tammy's hair, yanking her back

against his chest. Putting the gun to Tammy's head, Bryce muscled Tammy out of the room.

And with Tammy in tow, Bryce started running.

Chapter Eighteen

Jace hurried to the door, ready to go after Bryce, to stop the man from getting away. But if he did that, it would mean leaving Linnea with Gideon. And that was too big a risk to take. He pivoted back.

And his heart dropped.

Gideon had a gun, and he was taking aim at Linnea.

Jace didn't think. He dived at her, catching onto her and dragging her to the floor. Barely in time. The shot that Gideon fired tore into the wall just above their heads.

Gideon walked to the end of his bed. Not easily. He was clearly in pain, gasping and holding his ribs with his left hand. He was trembling, too, but that didn't stop him from pointing the gun at them again.

Jace was dealing with his own pain, and it was crashing into him and robbing him of his breath, but it didn't stop him from aiming, either. He fired, and the shot didn't go into the wall.

It slammed into Gideon's shoulder.

Gideon seemed to freeze, and he looked down at the blood that was spreading across his chest. Directly above the bandage over the other gunshot wound he'd gotten from Jace.

"There was never any evidence to prove I'm innocent. Couldn't be. Because I'm not innocent," Gideon said. His voice was as shaky as the rest of him. "I'm supposed to kill you both, That's why Bryce tucked the gun under my pillow before you came in. I was supposed to kill you both and then escape."

So this had all been a ruse. One meant to eliminate Linnea and him while Bryce and Gideon got away. With no live witnesses, Bryce might not ever get what he had coming to him. And what he had coming to him was justice in the form of the death penalty or life in prison.

"You didn't have to go along with Bryce's plan," Jace pointed out.

"I know." Gideon groaned, repeated it. "But I also knew if I let you live, that you wouldn't stop looking for me. Neither of you would have. You would have just kept hunting until you found me."

Linnea stayed put on the floor behind him, but Jace couldn't risk looking back at her to see how she was handling all of this. But it had to be eating away at her.

Beside them, Crystal started to stir. Jace hoped the deputy was okay, but again, he couldn't check on her right now.

"You're not killing us," Jace warned Gideon. "And you're not escaping. Drop the gun, or I'll put another bullet in you. I'd rather not kill you in front of your sister, but I will if it comes down to us or you."

Gideon's laugh was nearly silent and had no humor in it. "It has come down to me and the two of you." He stopped, groaned and lowered his weapon to his side. "Things got out of hand. I never expected it to go this far."

Jace kept his gun aimed at Gideon, but what he

wanted to do was beat him senseless. And go after Bryce and do the same to him. Jace tried not to think of the lieutenant getting away. He'd deal with him later, but for now he had to focus on Gideon. He was no longer pointing a gun at Linnea and him, but Gideon still had hold of it and could decide to use it.

Or rather try to use it.

"You never expected there'd be consequences for murder?" Jace asked, and yeah, there were layers of his own bitterness over what Gideon had done.

"No one was supposed to die. When Bryce first came to me with the plan, it was all about the money. Money we thought we deserved after risking our lives for people who couldn't care less if we died."

So that was the motive, but now it was drenched in bitterness. Stealing goods and cashing them in came with a huge price tag.

"And Zimmerman?" Jace asked. "Was he in on this, too?"

"No. He's clean, but he was sniffing too close to us, so Bryce wanted to set up Linnea to try to get Zimmerman off our trail. I agreed because she knew what I'd done. She knew I was dirty. If I was going to ever have a chance at getting away, then I needed to make sure no one believed her."

That caused the anger to return with a vengeance. "Setting up Linnea for murder," Jace reminded him.

"I didn't kill anyone," Gideon quickly snapped back. "Bryce used his militia contacts to murder Toby and the CSI who was taking in that nail."

And Bryce had done that because he'd thought they were a threat, that they could point the finger at him.

"You tried to murder Jace and me," Linnea reminded

him. "You came close to succeeding. I hope it was worth it. I hope all of this was worth it." Her tone was many steps past just being bitter, and Jace couldn't blame her. This was her big brother, someone she'd once loved.

"No. It wasn't worth it," Gideon said.

He let go of the gun, and it clattered to the floor. Still holding his side, Gideon collapsed on the bed. He was bleeding but was still conscious.

Jace and Linnea practically sprang up. But Linnea didn't go to her brother. She helped Crystal up, supporting the deputy's weight and helping her to a chair. Jace hurried to the bed, and even though he doubted Gideon could muster up the strength for a fight, he scooped up his gun, tucking it in the back waistband of his jeans, and he clamped one of the restraints on Gideon's right wrist.

Jace heard the sound of running footsteps, and he cursed when he thought there might be another attack. But it wasn't a gunman who came to the door. It was Glenn. The deputy stepped in and cursed.

"I was coming to tell you that the fire was a false alarm," Glenn said, his gaze firing all around the room. "What the hell happened here?"

"Long story," Jace settled for saying. "Lieutenant Bryce Cannon is behind the attacks, and he just fled the scene, taking Tammy as hostage."

"Tammy," Glenn repeated like profanity. "Zimmerman's here. I just saw him by the back exit. You want me to alert him?"

Jace considered it but then shook his head. The seconds were ticking away much too fast. "Call for a doctor for Gideon and Crystal and stay with them. I'm going after Bryce."

"You're hurt and bleeding," Linnea quickly pointed out. She took Gideon's gun. "I'm going with you."

Jace didn't want to take the time to argue with her. They'd already lost precious seconds, but he didn't stop her from following him when they raced out the door. Jace didn't go toward the back emergency exit but instead went in the direction of the ER.

Linnea and he didn't pass anyone along the way, but Jace could hear the sirens of the fire truck. If the firefighters weren't already in the building, they soon would be.

The moment Jace got to the ER doors, he spotted the cruiser.

And Bryce.

Bryce's back was to them, and he appeared to be trying to pick the lock. Tammy was struggling, obviously trying to get away, but Bryce still had her in a choke hold.

"Drop your gun," Jace ordered, stepping outside.

Bryce went stiff, and Jace could see that the man wasn't going to do that. He pivoted, a movement that caused Tammy to scream even louder.

"I told you he was the one who had me kidnapped," Tammy insisted. "And now he's gonna try to kill me."

Not if Jace had any say in this.

"It's over," Jace told Bryce. "You're a killer, and you'll pay for what you've done."

"It's not over," Bryce snapped. But he was sweating, and his gaze swept all around, obviously looking for an out.

"It is." Jace glanced around, too. He didn't want anyone walking up on this to give Bryce another hostage. "We've pieced it together. You were head of the crime ring that stole those drugs and guns. When things started to go to hell, you did clean up. That included having Tammy kidnapped so you could keep Gideon in line."

That last part had been a theory, but Bryce didn't dispute it. "Gideon's weak. He should have killed you," he repeated.

"But he didn't." Jace went with another theory. "You killed the CSI and stole that nail because the blood on it would have been linked back to you. Not your blood," he clarified. "You wouldn't have done the dirty work of kidnapping Tammy yourself. I suspect that person was either a member of the militia like the hired thugs or maybe one of your CIs."

Bingo. It was the last one, and the anger over his crimes being revealed raged through Bryce's eyes. Yeah, it would have looked plenty suspicious for the lieutenant's CI to be connected to a kidnapping.

The fury continued to build in Bryce, and it came to a head when Bryce yelled, hurling Tammy toward Jace. The woman rammed into his shoulder, causing pain to knife through him. It took Jace precious moments just to get back his breath, and Bryce took full advantage of that.

The dirty cop turned to latch onto Linnea.

But Linnea stopped Bryce in his tracks by bringing up her gun and taking aim at him. "Move and you die," Linnea warned him.

Bryce's breath was gusting, and it seemed as if his every muscle had gone rock-hard. Primed for a fight. But he still had enough restraint left to take a long look at Linnea, no doubt trying to figure out if she would indeed pull the trigger.

She would.

Jace could see that on her face. And Bryce could see it, too.

"Put down your gun," Jace told him.

The moments crawled by, and Jace steeled himself to do what he had to do. Even though she would do it, he didn't want Linnea to take the kill shot. Didn't want her to have to live with that for the rest of her life. She already had enough baggage.

"Gideon should have killed you," Bryce finally said, and tossing his gun aside, he turned toward Jace.

Bryce moved fast. So did his hand as he drew his backup gun from a slide holster in the back of his jeans. Before Jace could fire, the shot blasted through the air. It hadn't come from his gun or the one Linnea had. But from the side.

And it was deadly.

A shot to the head that immediately killed Bryce.

"I heard what the lieutenant said," Zimmerman called out. He came from around the side of the hospital, his gun still aimed at Bryce. "I could see that he was going for his backup."

Jace nodded his thanks, and the agent moved in to help a sobbing Tammy get to her feet. That freed up Linnea to step back, but she didn't waste a second hooking her arm around Jace's waist.

"You're bleeding," she reminded him. "You need to see the doctor right now."

He looked at her to make sure she wasn't in shock. She wasn't. "You're thinking pretty straight, considering you just saw a man gunned down."

"I'll think less straight later when that hits me. For now, I'm getting you back in the hospital."

Jace didn't put up a fight about that. He was indeed bleeding and in pain. But he was feeling other things, too, things that were a lot stronger than the pain. And one of those things was the overwhelming relief that Linnea was all right. Despite all the attacks and the gunfire, she hadn't been hurt.

She led him to an exam room, had him sit on the table and reached into his pocket for his phone. No doubt to call for help. However, before she could do that, Glenn came to the doorway.

"You okay?" he asked Jace right off.

"Yeah." It wasn't a lie. He was a lot better than he had been forty-eight hours ago, when this whole ordeal had started. "Where're Crystal and Gideon?"

"A couple of nurses and Dr. Garcia are with them. Crystal's a little woozy but okay, so I came to check on you. What happened?"

Linnea made that call and requested that a doctor come right away. Jace knew he didn't need immediate attention, but he wouldn't turn it down. Once she'd put down his phone, she started unbuttoning his shirt to get a look at his wound.

"Bryce is dead," Jace explained to Glenn. "He was Gideon's partner."

Glenn nodded as if processing that. "You killed him?"

"No. Zimmerman did. He has Tammy now. How's Gideon?"

"Alive, and Dr. Garcia thinks he'll stay that way. He's got a lot of injuries, but none of them appear to be life-threatening." Glenn paused. "He asked me to tell you that he was sorry."

Linnea's hands froze on his shirt, and she looked up

at the deputy. "Sorry," she repeated, but it wasn't with bitterness or sarcasm.

However, there was sadness, and Jace thought that would be with her for a long time. Gideon might be alive, but he would no longer be a regular part of her life. Well, unless she visited him in jail. If she wanted to do that, Jace would support her. Heck, he'd go with her. Anything to ease what Gideon had put her through.

Glenn nodded again and then blew out a long breath. He tipped his head to Jace's bloody shirt. "How bad are you hurt?"

"Not bad." That was the truth, too.

Glenn studied him a moment as if trying to determine if that was true, and then his attention drifted to Linnea. There was something in Glenn's change of expression that had Jace following his gaze.

And that was when Jace saw that there were tears in her eyes.

He sighed, pulled her into his uninjured arm, and glanced at Glenn. "Could you give us a minute? And if the doctor comes, tell him we need a little time to steady ourselves."

"Sure," Glenn said, already closing the door behind him.

Now wasn't the time for a long heart-to-heart talk, something he very much wanted to have with Linnea, but he could try to reassure her that life would get better. He considered how to convince her of that and settled for kissing her.

Linnea responded. First with a soft sound of surprise. Then she sank into the kiss, giving him back everything and more than he was giving her. He'd kissed other women over the years, but nothing was better than being like this with Linnea.

When they were both a little breathless, Jace eased back and checked. No more tears, and some of the sadness was gone, too.

"Mission accomplished," he said. He pushed her hair from her face and left his fingers on her cheek.

"Well, it was accomplished if you meant to make my legs even wobblier and cause my heart to pound really fast."

She took his hand, pressed it to her chest. Yep, her heart was beating hard enough for him to feel it, and he was pleased some of that reaction was because of him instead of the nightmare she'd just been through.

Linnea glanced down at his shoulder. "We really should get the doctor in here to check that."

"I will, but first I need to tell you something." He'd hoped that the words would flow after that opening. They didn't. He mentally hemmed and hawed before he finally said. "You remember when you told me how you felt about me?"

She made a show as if she had to think about that, and even though she'd done that to lighten things up, it sent a pang of fear through him.

"I want you to keep on falling in love with me," he said.

Her eyebrow rose, and despite everything that'd just happened, a smile flirted with her mouth. "I think I can manage that." With that half smile, she kissed him.

And Jace could have sworn his legs got a whole lot wobbly, too.

"I think I can manage even more," she added with her lips still against his.

"Oh yeah? Like what?" He nudged her even closer to him.

"Like…what's a four-letter word for how I feel about you?" she asked.

"Love," he quickly supplied.

She nodded. "Already in love with you."

That unclenched his heart and made him feel a whole lot better. In fact, it was obviously a cure for his pain.

"That's more than four letters," he pointed out. "But it works for me, too. I'm already in love with you, Linnea."

"Good." Her smile was a lot brighter this time, and it made Jace feel as if everything was truly all right. "Prove it," she challenged.

Jace took her up on that challenge, and he made the next kiss slow, long and deep.

* * * * *

DISAPPEARANCE AT DAKOTA RIDGE

CINDI MYERS

For Jim and Loretta.

Chapter One

Courtney would like it here, Lauren Baker thought as she drove through the town of Eagle Mountain, Colorado. A lover of beautiful old things, Courtney Baker would have felt at home among the gingerbread-trimmed Victorian buildings and carefully tended flower gardens. She would have marveled at the snowcapped mountains that soared above the town and would have been eager to explore the shops and cafés along the town's main street.

Lauren drove slowly, scanning the clusters of people on the sidewalks for the flash of Courtney's bright blond hair. But of course she didn't see anyone who looked like her sister-in-law. She had known before coming here that finding Courtney wouldn't be that easy.

The crisp female voice from her phone directed her to turn left ahead, and a few minutes later she pulled her Prius to the curb in front of the Rayford County sheriff's office. Stomach churning with nerves, she checked her appearance in the car's rearview mirror and smoothed a hand over her streaked brown hair, then slid out of the car and headed up the walk to the entrance to the sheriff's department.

A bell chimed as she entered the small lobby. "Hello," woman said. "Can I help you?"

Lauren lowered her sunglasses and blinked at the white-haired woman behind the desk near the back of the lobby.

The woman peered at Lauren from behind purple-framed eyeglasses and reached one pink-painted nail up to fondle a dangling earring shaped like a leaping dolphin. "Did you need something?" the woman prompted.

Lauren approached the desk. "I'd like to talk to someone about a missing person," she said.

The woman's eyebrows—carefully plucked and painted on—rose above the rim of her glasses. She picked up the phone at her right elbow. "Deputy Ellis," she said. "I'm sending a woman back to talk to you." She replaced the receiver and pointed toward a hallway to their left. "Go down that hall and take the first right. Deputy Ellis is the good-looking blond in the uniform."

Deputy Ellis—who was indeed good-looking, in a way that made Lauren catch her breath in spite of her distress—was waiting at the door of an office a little way down the hallway. "I'm Shane Ellis," he said, offering a firm, warm handshake and a steady gaze from tawny eyes. He was a big man—easily six foot four, with muscular legs and arms, thick blond hair swept over one brow and sculpted features. "Let's sit down and you can tell me how I can help you," he said, and ushered her into the office.

He indicated she should sit in one of the chairs in front of the battered desk, then instead of sitting behind the desk, he took the chair next to her. "What's your name?" he asked.

"Lauren Baker," she said.

"What brings you to Eagle Mountain? I don't think you're from around here. I have a good memory for faces and I haven't seen yours before." In other circumstances Lauren might have suspected this was a pickup line, but there was nothing flirtatious in his manner. Maybe he was trying to set her at ease.

"I'm from Denver," she said. "I came here to look for my sister-in-law, Courtney Baker. She's missing."

Deputy Ellis's brow furrowed. "Why don't you tell me your story," he said. "Start at the beginning." He leaned over to pluck a small recorder from the desk. "I'm going to record this, if you don't mind. It will help me keep things straight."

"Of course." She wanted him to remember everything she had to say. "Courtney is my brother's widow," she said. "They were married only two years before he was killed, in Afghanistan."

"I'm very sorry for your loss," the deputy said.

She nodded. "Courtney was devastated. We all were, but she was so young—only twenty-one at the time, and she was pregnant with Ashlyn. Courtney didn't have any family living near us, so I tried to help her. She and I became close." She focused on her knotted hands in her lap, trying to breathe past the pain of loss that had a habit of sneaking up on her at the most inconvenient times. Loss of her brother, and loss of a woman she had come to think of as her sister.

"When did Courtney go missing?" Ellis asked.

"First, I need to tell you that about three months ago a man named Trey Allerton came to see her. He said he had served with my brother, Mike, that they were best friends. He had some photographs of Courtney he said Mike had carried with him, pictures Trey said he felt duty bound to return to her. He said Mike had talked about her a lot and he had asked Trey to look after her if anything happened to him."

"You didn't like him much," Ellis said.

She jerked her head up and found his gold-brown eyes fixed on her. Sharp eyes, but not without compassion. "No, I didn't like him," she said. "I didn't believe his story about being Mike's best friend. I still have every letter and email and text Mike sent and he never mentioned Trey Allerton. And I didn't understand why Trey would have pictures of

Courtney. The army had returned all of Mike's other personal belongings."

"What did Allerton want?" Ellis asked.

"He said he wanted to look after Courtney. If it had
been me, I would have told him to get lost, but Courtney
isn't like that. She—" How could she describe Courtney?
Needy wasn't the right word, though it was partly true.
Weak wasn't right, either. She had worked hard to pull her
life together and to take care of her daughter after Mike
died, showing a strength Lauren admired. "Courtney is
very trusting. She always believes the best in everyone.
She grew up in a small town, the only child of parents
who protected her from everything. And then she met my
brother and he protected her. Trey Allerton promised to
protect her and I think that appealed to her."

"Protect her from what?"

"I don't know. Life, I guess." She sighed. "Anyway, he
started hanging around, and within a week he was talking
about his plan to buy a place in the mountains and build
a ranch that could be a retreat center for disadvantaged
kids. He painted a glowing picture—he even said he and
Mike had planned to run the place together. Again—my
brother never said anything about this to me or to anyone
else that I could find. But Allerton made Courtney believe
everything he said was true. The next think I knew, he
had talked her into moving to Eagle Mountain with him
to start this ranch."

Ellis jutted his chin, considering. He had an energy, a
charisma that seemed out of place in a cop. But what did
she know? She didn't have a lot of experience with law
enforcement. "Did Allerton ask your sister-in-law to fi-
nance this supposed youth ranch?" he asked.

She felt a surge of elation. She had told him very little, but already Deputy Ellis had grasped the situation.
"Oh, yes."

"How much money? Did he name a figure?"

"I don't know. But he must have known Courtney has money. A lot of it. My parents died right after Courtney and Mike married and before he left for Afghanistan, and Mike arranged for a trust that will provide his widow and his daughter a very good income for the rest of their lives. It's not the sort of thing Mike would have ever talked about, but somehow Allerton found out about it."

"All right. So your sister-in-law and Trey Allerton moved to Eagle Mountain? When was this?"

"Two weeks ago," she said. "I had a couple of texts from Courtney, saying they had arrived in town and how much she loved it, and that they were going to talk to some people about buying land for the ranch. The last time I talked to her, shortly after they arrived here, she sounded off. She said she was fine and that I shouldn't worry, but the words didn't ring true—as if she was saying what Trey told her to say. Since then—nothing." She held up her hands. "She doesn't return my texts or phone calls, and there's nothing on her social media pages since then, either."

"And that's unusual?"

"Yes. Courtney posted multiple times a day to Facebook and Instagram, and she and I texted all the time." She leaned toward him, her gaze steady, trying to impress upon him the seriousness of the situation. "Something is wrong. I know it. I finally decided to come here to try to find out what's going on, but I need your help."

"Has anyone else heard from Courtney in the past week—other relatives or friends?"

"As far as I know, she wasn't close to any relatives. Her parents died shortly before she met Mike, and her grandparents have been gone for a while. She never mentioned any aunts and uncles or cousins she was in touch with."

"What about friends? Neighbors?"

Lauren shook her head. "No one has heard from her."

He studied her a long moment. She felt the intensity of his gaze, and forced herself to meet it with a level look of her own. "If you spoke to your sister-in-law and she said she was all right, that doesn't give us cause to go looking for her," he said finally.

"I know Courtney. I know she isn't all right." She leaned toward him. "Isn't there something called a welfare check? Can't you do that? Especially since there's a child involved?"

"Maybe." He leaned past her to slide a legal pad across the desk. "Let me get some details. Full name, description, things like that."

Lauren opened her purse and took out a five-by-seven studio portrait of Courtney, with two-year-old Ashlyn on her lap. "This was taken in May," she said.

Deputy Ellis studied the image of the young woman and the toddler, both with white-blond curls and large blue eyes. Ashlyn was laughing at something the photographer was doing, mouth open, eyes crinkled, hands in the act of clapping. Courtney's closed mouth curved slightly into a smile, but her eyes held the sadness that never really left her. For one so young, she had lost so much. Lauren was determined Trey Allerton didn't take even more. Lauren passed over an index card on which she'd written everything she knew about Courtney—approximate height and weight, cell phone number and social media handles. Lauren's contact information was underneath this. Ellis studied the list, then met her gaze again, his own questioning. "You know her Social Security number?"

"I helped her do her taxes last year and I still had a copy on my computer. I told you, we're close."

He nodded and placed the photograph and index card on the desk. "Do you have a photo of Trey Allerton?" he asked.

"Of course. I should have thought of that." She took out her phone and scrolled through her saved pictures, until she came to one of Courtney with Trey. She turned the phone toward Deputy Ellis. "I took this last month." There was nothing sinister about the image of Courtney with the handsome, smiling man, but looking at it now made Lauren uneasy. How could she convey to the deputy just how much she distrusted Trey?

"Do you know where Courtney and Allerton were staying in Eagle Mountain?" he asked.

"She said they were at the Ranch Inn."

"Are you staying there now?"

"No. I'm in a vacation rental. I took a leave of absence from my job, and I intend to stay as long as it takes to find Courtney."

"What's your job?"

"I'm a nurse practitioner."

He stood, and she rose also. "What do you think has happened to your sister-in-law?" he asked.

She fought back the jumble of horrifying images that had crowded her sleepless nights and tried to maintain an appearance of calm. She wanted this man to take her seriously, not to think she'd been overdosing on crime dramas and imagining the worst. "I think Allerton may have persuaded her to cut contact with me, in an effort to swindle her out of her money. He's already taken advantage of her trust and innocence."

"I'll try to help," Ellis said. "But if your sister-in-law left of her own free will, there's not a lot we can do. There's no law against not talking to your relatives."

"No, but I can't abandon her. I need to make sure she's okay." She met his gaze again with a fierce look of her own. "Whatever Trey Allerton says, I'm the person Mike asked to look after Courtney and Ashlyn, and that's a promise I have to keep."

He nodded. "I'll be in touch."

She left the office feeling empty and restless. She had

told Deputy Ellis everything she knew, but now she had to wait and trust that he was good enough at his job to find Courtney. He had struck her as sharp and competent.

She paused before getting into her car and looked up at the mountains that towered over the town. Courtney would love Eagle Mountain, but would Eagle Mountain love her?

"WHAT DID YOU say to her? She looked pretty upset when she left."

The door had scarcely closed behind Lauren Baker when Adelaide Kinkaid, office manager and Eagle Mountain's number one busybody, was at Shane's side, fixing him with a critical eye that always made him feel about ten years old. "Her sister-in-law has stopped talking to her," he said. "That's why she's upset. Not because of anything I said."

Adelaide pressed her bright pink lips together. Though she had to be pushing seventy, she dressed like someone fifty years younger, in bold colors and often downright garish accessories. But the look worked for her. "Did she know who you are? Is she a fan?"

"I'm a cop, Addie. That's all she cared about."

"Plenty of people still remember you," Adelaide said. "You can use that to your advantage."

Shane didn't see any advantage to being a *former* Major League pitcher, especially when it came to enforcing the law. When he did meet fans, they wanted to relive big games or, worse, talk about the injury that had sidelined him for good. They talked like his best years were over and he'd never do anything good again.

"Ms. Baker was worried about her sister-in-law," he said. "That's all that matters."

"She was very attractive," Adelaide said. "About your age."

Shane scowled. "I don't need you to find women for me,

Addie," he said. He'd dated models and actresses when he was a pro ballplayer. Since coming back home to Eagle Mountain to settle down, he'd enjoyed working his way through the slate of eligible single women. If anything, they were even more fun than the models and actresses. He liked women in general, and he was in no hurry to settle down.

Adelaide made a huffing noise. "I would never try to saddle some poor woman with the likes of you."

Sure she wouldn't. They both turned at the sound of footsteps down the hall, to see Sheriff Travis Walker coming from the employee entrance. Almost as tall as Shane, Travis had a rangier build, and a famously reserved demeanor. Locals joked that when the sheriff gave a speech, the whole thing fit on a single note card. He stopped in front of Shane and Adelaide. "Something up?"

"A young woman came in to report a missing person," Adelaide said, before Shane could answer.

Travis looked at Shane, waiting.

Shane retrieved the photo from his desk and handed it to the sheriff. "Her name is Courtney Baker. She supposedly came to Eagle Mountain with a man named Trey Allerton, then dropped off the map. She stopped posting to social media and doesn't return phone calls or texts. Her sister-in-law, Lauren Baker, says that is really unlike Courtney and she's worried something has happened to her."

Travis studied the photograph. "Who's the kid?"

"Ashlyn Baker—Courtney's daughter. She's two, and is supposed to be with her mother."

"Where's the baby's father?" Adelaide leaned in to look at the picture.

"He died in Afghanistan over two years ago," Shane said. "Lauren Baker is his sister."

Travis returned the photograph to Shane. "How does Ms. Baker know they were in Eagle Mountain?" he asked.

"Her last communication with Courtney was about two weeks ago, phone call saying they were here and staying at the Ranch Inn," Shane said. "She also said she was fine and not to worry, but Ms. Baker insists something about the conversation wasn't right. She asked us to do a welfare check, though to do that, I need to find Courtney. I thought I'd start by asking at the motel."

Travis nodded.

"Have you heard of Trey Allerton?" Shane asked. He glanced from Travis to Adelaide, including them both in the question.

"No, but I'll ask around," Adelaide said. "There are a few women in this town who make a point of noticing every new young man who comes to town—and some not-so-young ones."

"Shane has got this," Travis said. He left them and went into his office.

"I guess if anyone at the motel saw these people, they'll tell you," Adelaide said. "You have a way of getting people to talk." The phone started ringing, and she left to answer it.

Shane stood outside his office, Courtney Baker's picture in hand. Unlike her happy baby, Courtney looked sad, and a little lost. Could a washed-up baseball player turned sheriff's deputy really help someone like her? After all, sometimes people took a deliberate wrong turn in life and all you could do was step back and wait for the crash.

Unless you were the Lauren Bakers of the world. People like Lauren didn't wait for a crash. They rushed to set up roadblocks, threw tacks on the road to puncture tires and, if all else failed, enlisted the nearest cop to issue a speeding ticket.

That was Shane, duly enlisted. He returned to his desk, tucked the photo and the file card into an envelope, and put on the wide-brimmed Stetson that completed his uniform. Time to get to work and see if he still had what it took to bring in a win.

Chapter Two

Lauren had chosen her vacation rental based on its central location in town and its reasonable price. She had reserved the apartment for a week and hoped her search wouldn't take longer. But she had a month's leave from her job and was willing to devote all of it, or more, to finding Courtney and making sure she was okay. Lauren owed that to Mike.

"You should have everything you need, but let me know if you run out of anything." Brenda Prentice, an attractive blonde, led Lauren up the outside stairs to the garage apartment next to her stylish home not far from the sheriff's department. "The cleaners come on Wednesdays. They'll take the trash out for pickup Thursday morning." She unlocked the door, then handed Lauren the key. "There's a map of the town and some brochures about local attractions if you're interested." She indicated a notebook on the table by the door.

"I'm sure I'll be very comfortable here." Lauren set down her bag and surveyed the clean, well-decorated apartment. It was a nice step up from a motel room, but she wasn't picky.

"What brings you to town?" Brenda asked.

Lauren's first instinct was to make a benign comment about taking a break or getting away, but if she was going to find Courtney, she needed to talk to as many people as possible. In a town as small as Eagle Mountain, anyone might have seen Courtney or know something about her. "I came here to look for my sister-in-law," she said. "We've lost touch, and the last I heard, she was here in Eagle Mountain."

Brenda had an expressive face, and her look of concern now seemed genuine. "Who is your sister-in-law?"

"Her name is Courtney Baker. She's traveling with her little girl, Ashlyn. Ashlyn is two." Lauren pulled up Courtney and Ashlyn's photo on her phone—the same one she had given Deputy Ellis. "This is them," she said. "It was taken just a couple of months ago."

Brenda studied the picture. "I'm sorry, I don't recognize her."

Lauren pushed aside her disappointment. She had known that finding Courtney might not be easy. "She may be traveling with a man named Trey Allerton." She showed Brenda Trey's photo. "Is he familiar?"

Brenda shook her head. "But I can ask my husband. He's a sheriff's deputy."

The words jolted her. But she reminded herself that Eagle Mountain was a small town. "I stopped by the sheriff's department on my way into town and spoke to a Deputy Ellis," she said.

Brenda smiled. "Oh, Shane." The words carried a lilt of amusement and maybe admiration.

"What do you mean, 'Oh, Shane'?" Lauren asked.

Brenda shook her head. "Nothing. He's a good deputy. He's also the local heartthrob." She grinned. "He caused quite a stir among the local women when he joined the force six months ago."

"He promised to try to find out more about Courtney and Trey Allerton," Lauren said. "But I got the impression that unless I could prove a crime had been committed, the bulk of the search was going to be up to me."

"Do you think a crime has been committed?" Brenda asked. "Did Allerton bring your sister-in-law here against her will?"

"I don't know." Lauren suppressed a sigh. "I just know that I haven't heard from Courtney at all in a week, and that's really not like her. And I don't trust Trey Allerton. I'm determined to stay in Eagle Mountain until I find them, or find out where they've gone."

"I have you down for a week here," Brenda said.

"Yes. I may need to stay longer."

Brenda shook her head. "I wish I could accommodate you, but this place is booked the rest of the summer. I can give you the name of a local real estate agent who might be able to help you with another rental. And I'll ask around and see if anyone I know has anything available."

"Thank you. Maybe I'll get lucky and I won't need it."

"I'll ask about your sister-in-law and Allerton, too," Brenda said. "It's hard for new people to come to a town this small without someone noticing them."

"I guess that's a good thing," Lauren said. "I didn't realize before coming here that Eagle Mountain was quite so small."

"You sound as if something about that worries you," Brenda said.

The woman was definitely observant. "No offense to Deputy Ellis or your husband," Lauren said. "But does the sheriff's department in a town as small as Eagle Mountain have the resources to deal with this if it turns out to be a crime like kidnapping?"

"I think they probably are better equipped to handle a case like this than many larger departments," Brenda said. "Since we don't have much serious crime around here, the officers will have more time to devote to the search for your sister-in-law. Also, the officers tend to know everyone in the county. Someone new or anyone who is acting oddly will stand out. And the small-town stereotype of everyone knowing what everyone else is doing can be an advantage in any kind of investigation."

"I guess you have a point," Lauren said, though her doubts lingered.

"I'll leave you now, but my number is in that notebook." Brenda indicated the notebook on the table again. "Call me if you need anything at all or have any questions. And I'll let you know if I hear anything about your sister-in-law."

"Thanks."

When she was alone again, Lauren carried her bag into the bedroom, intending to unpack. But instead of opening the bag, she sat on the end of the bed and pulled out her phone. She pulled up Courtney's cell phone number and tried for the hundredth time to call. A mechanical voice informed her that the party she had called was unavailable and her voice mailbox was full.

She scrolled to her last texts from Courtney. Dinner with Trey tonight. He says he has big news about the ranch. I'll fill you in later.

Then, two days later, after numerous unanswered texts and calls from Lauren, she received a new message. Sorry. Super busy. We're going to see property for the ranch.

Allerton had painted a glowing picture of the ranch he and Mike had dreamed of opening—a place in the Colorado mountains where disadvantaged and troubled youth could come for fresh air, exercise, attention from caring adults and lessons in life skills. Courtney, who loved children and had a soft spot for anyone in need, had latched on to his appeal that this would be a way of securing her husband's legacy, and using his family money to do real good in the world.

Except that Mike had never once mentioned the idea of this ranch, to Courtney or to his sister. When Lauren had pointed this out, along with the fact that Allerton had no credentials that qualified him to run this kind of program, Courtney had dismissed her concerns. Mike probably hadn't wanted to tell her until he and Trey had worked out all the details, she had argued. And they could always hire professional counselors and therapists to work with the kids. The important thing was to find a place to build the facility and make the dream a reality.

Right. And all that took was money. Lots of it. Which Allerton didn't appear to have, but Courtney, thanks to Mike's generous trust, did.

Everything about Trey Allerton rubbed Lauren the wrong way. His smile was too broad, his words too glib, his charm too overdone. But Courtney saw none of that. He got to her by talking about Mike, sharing stories of their time in Afghanistan that Courtney was hungry to hear.

Courtney believed every word the man said, but Lauren wasn't that trusting. Maybe it came of her medical training and knowing how often people lied about the simplest things, from their weight to how many drinks they had a week, to the severity of their symptoms. Little of what Allerton said rang true to her. He obviously had known Mike. He knew plenty of personal details that convinced Courtney, but Lauren couldn't picture her brother being friends with someone like Allerton. Mike had disdained pretense and posturing. Growing up with wealth had given him a good eye for someone who was interested only in his money, something he and Lauren shared.

But Courtney trusted everyone. The only daughter of a minister who had spent most of her life in a small town in the Midwest, Courtney saw the good in everyone. She'd never encountered real evil, so she never looked for it in others. Mike loved that about her, but he also recognized she was vulnerable. "Look out for Courtney while I'm deployed," he had told Lauren. "Don't let anyone take advantage of her."

Lauren had solemnly promised to do so. But she had failed to keep her promise when it came to Trey Allerton.

She scrolled through the texts from that last week, cryptic messages with Courtney pleading she was busy and couldn't talk. Don't worry. I'm fine. We're in a beautiful place called Eagle Mountain. And get this—the motel we're staying at is the Ranch Inn. I think that's a good sign, don't you?

What are you doing there? Lauren had replied.

Trey says I shouldn't talk about it yet. Don't worry. Everything will be fine.

Those last words sent a chill through Lauren. Everything was not fine, and the very fact that Courtney kept insisting it was made Lauren believe her sister-in-law knew she was in trouble, even if she wasn't ready to admit it.

"TAYLOR, YOU ARE just the person I needed to speak to." Shane leaned over the front desk of the Ranch Inn motel and grinned at the young woman behind it.

Taylor Redmond flushed pink. "Why would you want to talk to me, Shane?" she asked. "Do you think I'm guilty of something?"

"We're all guilty of something," he said.

She giggled. "I'm always glad to see you, Shane. What can I do for you?"

"I'm looking for a woman who stayed here recently. Name of Courtney Baker. She would have had a two-year-old girl with her, her daughter. And she might have been traveling with a man named Trey Allerton."

Twin lines formed between Taylor's eyebrows as she thought. "Those names don't sound familiar, but let me check our records." She moved to the computer terminal at the end of the counter and began typing. A few seconds later, she shook her head. "I'm not showing anyone registered under either of those names. Are you sure she was staying here?"

"This is her picture." He handed over the photo Lauren had given him. "Does she look familiar?"

Taylor's face brightened. "Oh, I remember her. Her little girl was so sweet. But she said her name was Allen. I never heard her first name. Just Mr. and Mrs. Allen. She and her husband and daughter stayed here earlier in the month." She turned to the computer once more and began typing. "They checked out eight days ago."

"What's his first name?"

"Troy. Troy Allen. Mister and missus. No first name for her. But I heard her call the little girl Ashley, I think."

"Ashlyn?"

"Maybe. Something like that. Why? Have they done something wrong?"

"Not that I know of." He slid the photograph back into its envelope. "Did everything seem okay with them? I mean, did the two of them get along and seem comfortable with each other?"

Taylor frowned again. "I guess so. I mean, they seemed normal to me, but I only saw them for a few minutes. What's going on? You can tell me."

"I'm just trying to get in touch with them. Did they say where they were headed next when they checked out?"

"I never talked to them. They just left the key in the room on their last day. The bill was already paid, but a lot of people do that."

"Thanks, Taylor. You've been a big help."

She leaned across the counter toward him. "Before you go, I was wondering if you're planning on going to the Fireman's Ball July Fourth weekend."

"They're still doing that?" Shane had memories—some

of them rather hazy—of attending the annual ball in the years before he was recruited to the majors.

"Oh, for sure." Taylor's eyes sparkled. "You know Eagle Mountain goes all out for the holiday. The town is packed with tourists. The ball kicks off everything."

"I wouldn't miss it," he said.

"Then maybe I'll see you there." She fluttered her eyelashes.

He took a step back. "Maybe you will," he said, and hastily retreated. Not that he didn't like Taylor, but she couldn't have been more than nineteen. Ten years younger than him, which wasn't so young, but a man in his position in a town this size had to be careful. So far, he'd stuck to women close to his age and older, never letting things get too serious. He wasn't ready to settle down yet, but he didn't want to get a reputation as a player who used women. He tried to remain friends with every woman he had ever dated and so far had succeeded.

Back in his cruiser, he made note of the information Taylor had given him about Courtney Baker and Trey Allerton. Apparently, Courtney hadn't behaved like a woman who was traveling with a man against her will. Lauren Baker might not approve of the man her brother's widow was associating with, but so far, Shane hadn't found evidence of a crime.

Except—why would a man who had nothing to hide check into a motel with an assumed name? Instead of focusing on Courtney Baker, maybe Shane should dig deeper into Trey Allerton's background.

Chapter Three

"This is a picture of my sister-in-law, Courtney, and her daughter, Ashlyn. They were in Eagle Mountain a couple of weeks ago. I was wondering if you remember seeing them in your store?" After visiting six stores along the town's main street Tuesday morning, Lauren had her spiel down pat. She passed the copy of Courtney and Ashlyn's photograph to the woman behind the counter of the toy store. The window display of a doll's tea party was the kind of thing that would have caught Courtney and Ashlyn's attention and might have enticed them in to browse, or even make a purchase.

The woman, a trim sixtysomething with fashionably cut short white hair, adjusted her silver-framed glasses and studied the photograph before handing it back to Courtney. "I'm sorry. I don't remember anyone like that. Such a cute little girl. And the woman is very pretty, too. I think I would have remembered if I had waited on them."

"Thank you for taking the time to look." Lauren tucked the photo back into her purse. She had received similar answers from the other five shops on this side of the street.

"Is something wrong?" the woman asked. "Why are you looking for them?"

"I believe they're missing," Lauren said. "I'm doing everything I can to try to find them."

"Have you contacted the sheriff's office?" the woman asked. "Maybe they can help you."

"The sheriff's department is looking, too," Lauren said.

"I hope you find them," the woman said, then turned away as a customer approached the counter.

Lauren left the store and studied the next one: a shop specializing in cigars and imported tobacco. Not the sort of thing to attract Courtney's attention, and as far as she knew, Allerton didn't smoke. Next in line was a café, the Cake Walk. A steady stream of people filed in, as it was almost lunchtime. Would one of them remember seeing Courtney and Ashlyn? And how upset would the owners of the café be with Lauren if she interrupted customers' meals to ask?

"I've never eaten anything here that wasn't good." A familiar voice sounded just behind her. She looked over her shoulder and saw Deputy Shane Ellis. He touched the brim of his Stetson in a gesture that was a little old-fashioned and completely charming. "I was just heading in for lunch," he said. "Would you join me?"

Her first instinct was to say no. She wasn't interested in socializing with this man, or with anyone, really. But lunch would give her a chance to find out what he had done so far to locate Courtney, and maybe to impress upon him that her sister-in-law wasn't behaving normally. Lauren believed Courtney really was in trouble, and she needed Deputy Ellis to believe it, too. "Thank you," she said, and forced a smile. "I'd love to."

He held the door open and touched her back lightly to usher her inside. Again, the gesture was mannerly, not intrusive. It made her feel cared for, a little vulnerable and a lot uncomfortable. She sat at an empty table and pulled up her chair before he could help her. He took the seat across from her, amusement in his eyes. "You can relax," he said. "I don't bite."

She wanted to deny that she was tense, but that was clearly a lie. "I'm not used to being in a situation like this," she said.

"Having lunch with a man?" He quirked one eyebrow. "Or with a cop?"

"I'm not used to being in an unfamiliar place, looking for a missing loved one," she said.

"Well hey, Shane!" The waitress, young and blonde, her hair in a ponytail, smiled at Ellis, ignoring Lauren entirely. "It's always good to see your handsome face in here."

"Hello, Dee," he said. "How's life treating you?"

"Well enough, though it could be better. What can I get for you?"

Shane looked at Lauren. "Do you need more time?" he asked.

Lauren turned to study the chalkboard that listed the day's special. "I'll have the soup and a house salad," she said.

"The green-chili burger for me," he said.

"Gotcha."

Dee moved away, and Shane turned to Lauren once more. "I heard you've been asking questions around town."

Had he been following her? Or had someone called the sheriff's office to report her? "I didn't come here to sit in my rental and wait for other people to do all the work," she said. "I thought if I could locate someone who had seen Courtney and Ashlyn, it would help me put together a time line of their movements."

"You're free to talk to anyone you want," he said. "Have you found anyone who remembers seeing your sister-in-law or her little girl?"

"No one remembers seeing them, and that in itself strikes me as wrong. Courtney loved to shop. And she especially loved cute little stores like the ones here in Eagle

Mountain. She couldn't pass one by without stopping. Yet no one remembers her coming in to any of them."

"She and Allerton checked out of the Ranch Motel eight days ago," he said. "I don't think it's that unusual that people don't remember a customer they may have seen only a few minutes more than a week ago."

"Someone would have remembered Courtney," Lauren said. "You saw her picture. She's gorgeous. Striking. And Ashlyn is adorable. Someone would have remembered if they had been in one of those stores." The server returned with their drink orders.

"Thanks, Dee," Shane said, and was rewarded with a dazzling smile. Maybe he didn't see the disappointment in the server's eyes when he turned back to Lauren, but Lauren did. Brenda Prentice hadn't been kidding when she said Shane was the local heartthrob.

"How do you know they checked out of the motel eight days ago?" she asked.

"I had the desk clerk check the registration records at the motel."

"I asked, and no one had heard of Courtney or Allerton," Lauren said.

"They weren't registered under their real names." He studied her over the rim of his glass, not saying more.

"How were they registered?" she prodded, annoyed that he was making her ask.

"You're not going to like the answer," he said.

"I don't like any of this, but I still want to know the truth."

"They were registered as Mr. and Mrs. Troy Allen."

She sucked in her breath. "This is worse than I thought, if he talked her into marrying him," she said.

"Do you think she would do that?" he asked.

"No!" She wanted to protest that Courtney was still too much in love with Mike to marry someone else, but her brother had been dead more than two years. Courtney had every right to fall in love and marry again. Just because the idea hurt to think of didn't mean it couldn't happen. "I don't think she was in love with Trey," she said. "She never talked about marrying him, but maybe that was because she knew I disapproved. And she may have thought he offered her and Ashlyn the kind of security and companionship she hadn't had since Mike died." She shook her head. "But I still can't believe it."

"Maybe they weren't married," he said. "People lie about that kind of thing because they think it looks more respectable. Or because they don't want to attract attention or for a host of other reasons." He took a long sip of tea, then set down his glass. "For what it's worth, I didn't find any record of their marriage with the state of Colorado, though it sometimes takes a few weeks for the state to get the information from various counties. And if they were married in New Mexico or Nebraska, or another state, it wouldn't show up in a search of state records."

So he had been busy. "I'm impressed with what you've learned so far, Deputy Ellis," she said.

"Please, call me Shane," he said. "And is it okay if I call you Lauren?"

"Of course."

Dee returned and slid a steaming plate in front of him. "One green-chili burger for the hottest man in town," she said. She delivered Lauren's salad and soup without comment.

"Thanks." Shane picked up the burger. Dee lingered a moment, but when he said nothing else, she moved on.

He took a bite of burger and Lauren tried the soup. After a moment, Shane said, "I looked for a criminal record for Allerton, under both Allerton and Allen. I didn't find anything, but I've got some more feelers out."

"I had a friend check his military records," Lauren said.

"He did serve in the same unit as Mike, and he was honorably discharged."

"You've saved me a step, then."

Loud laughter from across the room made them both look over. A young woman with bright auburn curls, wearing an orange sundress with a print of blue-and-green parrots, swept into the café, trailed by two similarly striking women, all laden with shopping bags. They laughed loudly, catching the attention of everyone in the room. "Dee, show us your best table!" the redhead called, then joined the others in a new fit of giggles.

Dee scowled at them. "We only have one table, Talia," she said. "Take it or leave it."

"Well." Talia tilted her head, considering. "I suppose if we take it, that will automatically make it the best table."

More laughter as the trio followed a still-scowling Dee to the corner table. Lauren met Shane's gaze. "Who is that?" she asked.

"Talia Larrivee." He picked up his burger again. "I guess you could say she's the closest thing we have around here to a socialite."

More laughter erupted from the table as Dee arrived to take the women's order. "What makes her a socialite?" Lauren asked.

"She's Evan Larrivee's daughter."

"Evan Larrivee of Larrivee Software?"

"The same. He has a second home—or maybe a third or fourth home—just outside of town. I haven't been out there, but I hear it's quite the place."

"I'm sure you could charm her into showing you around the place if you really wanted to see it," Lauren said. "You seem to have most of the women in this town eating out of your hand."

"Not Ms. Larrivee." He popped a French fry into his

mouth, looking thoughtful. "I'm not rough around the edges enough for her. A little too much of a straight arrow."

"You seem to know a lot about her." Lauren tried to look unconcerned. Why should it matter to her what kind of relationship Shane had with the lovely Talia Larrivee?

"We've had a few encounters." He met her eyes. "Official ones."

"As in—she committed a crime?"

"Nothing major. And her father can afford the best lawyers to get his little girl out of trouble. But it's another reason she doesn't much care for me."

"How disappointing for you. She's very pretty. And rich."

"But not my type." His eyes met hers again, whiskey brown and mesmerizing.

Her heart beat a little faster and she found herself uttering the first thought that came to mind. "What is your type?"

"I like someone who's loyal. Someone who's competent and cool under pressure. Someone smart."

"I notice you don't mention beauty."

He shrugged. "Most women have something attractive about them. But yeah, I'm shallow enough to admit looks matter."

"Good luck finding this paragon," she said.

"Oh, I don't know. You seem to have a lot of those qualities." He pushed back his chair and stood. "I'll pay at the register," he said. "And I'll let you know if anything develops in the search for your sister-in-law." He touched the brim of his hat again, then turned and sauntered away.

Lauren's weren't the only pair of female eyes on the deputy, but she was pretty sure she was the only one whose mouth was hanging open in shock.

Dee stopped by the table. "Can I get you anything else?" she asked. "More iced tea?"

Lauren pulled her gaze away from Shane's retreating back. "No, thank you."

"So, how do you know Shane?" she asked. "Is he an old friend?"

"No. My sister-in-law is missing and he's looking for her."

"Oh!" Dee's expression brightened. "So this was just a business lunch."

"Yes."

"Still, if you have to do business, why not with a guy like Shane?" Dee's attitude was friendly and confiding now. "He puts most other guys in this town to shame, but he's not full of himself, like you might expect." She began gathering up the empty plates and cutlery. "I couldn't believe my ears when I heard he was coming back to town. He could have gone anywhere—why here? And to be a deputy, of all things." She shook her head.

"Why are you surprised he's a deputy?" Lauren leaned back to allow Dee to retrieve her empty glass.

"I would have expected him to get work as a broadcaster, or maybe a coach." Dee added the glass to the bus tub and balanced the tub on one cocked hip. "I mean, isn't that what ballplayers do when they retire?"

"Wait a minute, he was a ballplayer? Basketball?"

"You didn't know? He was a pitcher. For the Colorado Rockies. A good one, too, until he tore up his arm." She shook her head. "Such a shame. You think he looks good in that deputy's uniform—you should have seen him in pinstripes. You sure you don't need anything else?"

"No, thank you." Lauren stood.

She made her way across the crowded café, aware of a few eyes watching her, though most were focused on Talia and her two friends as Talia loudly regaled them with a story about a drunken attempt at skinny-dipping in a nearby swimming hole. "The water was ice-cold!" she shrieked.

Lauren told herself she should show Courtney and Ashlyn's photo to the rest of the stores on Main, but she had lost the heart for it. Instead, she made her way back to the rental and booted up her laptop.

A search on the name Shane Ellis filled her screen with articles about the Colorado Rockies' ace pitcher, including dozens of pictures—mostly of Shane in uniform, but a few of him at parties or charity events, often with an attractive woman on his arm. The man she was familiar with looked a little older, a little less…*glamorous*, the best word she could think of. She had met Shane the small-town deputy. These pictures were of Shane the celebrity. The star athlete.

She opened the top article in the search and read about his retirement from professional baseball. It included an overview of his career: top pick while he was still in college, meteoric rise through the minor leagues, nomination for a Cy Young Award as a rookie pitcher, helped lead his team to the playoffs his second year, culminating with a career-ending injury. Surgery. A comeback attempt. Then the announcement that he was leaving baseball.

She sat back, trying to digest everything she had just read. She had to agree with Dee—it seemed odd that Shane had decided to become a small-town law enforcement officer. He had known fame and wealth, he was good-looking and charming, and he probably could have done anything he wanted with his life. Instead he had retreated to this out-of-the-way place. Why? How did prowess as a pitcher translate to crime solving?

Chapter Four

After lunch, Shane slipped through the back door of the sheriff's office and headed for his desk, hoping to catch up on some paperwork before Adelaide realized he was there. The office manager had a habit of sending members of the public to him first. "You're so good with people," she said when he had protested.

But Adelaide had ears like a cat's and he had scarcely sat down before she hurried to his side. "There's going to be a sheriff's department versus fire department baseball game on the Fourth to raise money to spruce up the Little League fields," she said.

Inwardly, he cringed, though he kept his expression neutral. "I hadn't heard," he said.

He pretended to read through the report on his screen, though the words were a blur.

"Better get your pitching arm warmed up," Adelaide said.

"Doesn't the department have a regular team? Maybe they won't want me."

Adelaide's laughter was more of a hoot. "Of course they'll want you. And they'll need you to win. The fire department has some real sluggers on their team."

Tension settled between his shoulders. "I'm not a Major League pitcher anymore," he reminded her.

"You're miles better than anyone else around here."

"Better at what?" Sergeant Gage Walker strolled into the space devoted to the deputies' desks, which was generally known as the bullpen. The irony of going from one bullpen to another wasn't lost on Shane. Gage's brother, Sheriff Travis Walker, followed him into the room. Taller, blonder and definitely more outgoing than his brother, Gage had a sharp sense of humor and a quick mind.

"I was just telling Shane about the annual sheriff's department versus fire department ball game for the Fourth of July," Adelaide said.

"Those smoke eaters won't know what to do when they see the heat you bring," Gage said.

"It's been a while since I've pitched," Shane said.

Gage clapped a hand on his shoulder. "Then you'd better start practicing."

The front door buzzer sounded. "I'd better go see who that is," Adelaide said.

"I'll go with you," Gage said and followed her out of the room.

"Are you okay with pitching in the game?" Travis asked. "Does the arm still bother you?"

"Not really." Most of the time his arm felt fine. "But I don't have the speed and power I used to."

"This isn't the majors," Travis said. "The fire department has a few pretty good hitters, but anything you throw is going to get past them."

The sheriff's interest in the game surprised Shane. Travis was always so focused on his work first and his family second. He rarely engaged in debates about sports, though Shane had heard he'd been a pretty good athlete in high school. "What's at stake here?" Shane asked.

"Bragging rights, mostly. But the fire department has beat us the past four years running. It would be nice to take the title back."

"I'll do what I can," Shane said.

"You're liable to draw a crowd when word gets out you'll be on the mound," Travis said. "Does that bother you?"

Some. Only because people would expect to see the ace he'd been, not the above-average amateur he was now.

"Nah, it's okay," he lied.

"Anything new on the missing woman?" The sheriff was all business again.

Shane filled him in on the information he'd gleaned from computer searches and the motel, and what he'd learned from Lauren at lunch. "The sister-in-law thinks Trey Allerton was after Courtney Baker's money. She's positive something shady is going on."

"See if you can find out what that is," Travis said. "But don't neglect more pressing business. This may be a case of a woman who wanted to get away from her late husband's family and start over. It happens."

"I'll keep that in mind."

Alone once more, Shane tried to focus on the motor vehicle accident report he needed to complete, but his mind kept going back to the grief in Lauren's eyes when she spoke of her dead brother and his missing wife. Lauren didn't come across to him as a controlling relative. She was reserved and serious, but loyal and caring, too. She probably thought he was out of line, telling her she was the type of woman who interested him, but he'd hoped the confession—all truth—would shake her enough to get her to loosen up and trust him more. They were on the same side, both wanting to find her sister-in-law and niece safe and happy, but he could tell Lauren didn't believe he'd do a good job.

Others probably shared her doubts. He wasn't blind to the fact that everyone still saw him as a ballplayer first and a law enforcement officer second. He'd been a good player, gifted even—you had to be to make it to the majors.

Did he have the talent it took to be a good officer? Could he find Courtney Baker? He wouldn't mind seeing Lauren look at him the way female fans had sometimes regarded him when he wore a baseball uniform.

"WEEK-TO-WEEK RENTALS can be hard to come by in the summer. That's our busy season. But I might have a couple of places that would suit you," Mallory Workman said when Lauren stopped by Workman Realty on Wednesday. Mallory had the weathered skin of someone who spent a lot of time outdoors. She wore a pearl-button Western shirt, pressed slim jeans and pink cowboy boots, and a gold rodeo buckle Lauren suspected was the real deal. "I was state barrel racing champion in ninety-six," she said when she noticed Lauren taking in the buckle. "It's been a while, but I still ride, and I help train girls who are just starting out."

"I appreciate your help finding a place for me to stay after my week at Brenda Prentice's place runs out," Lauren said.

"Brenda is a real sweetheart," Mallory said. She sat at her desk and pulled up a form on her computer. "Let me get a little information from you and we'll go from there. I know you said week to week, but about how long do you think you'll need the place?"

"I wish I knew," Lauren said. "It really depends on whether or not I can make contact with my sister-in-law."

"You got a picture?" Mallory asked. "I know pretty much everyone in town, and between my job and the rodeo I meet a lot of people who come through here."

Lauren handed over the photograph of Courtney and Ashlyn. Mallory studied it a long moment. "She's got the kind of looks that would make most people do a double take," she said after a moment. "And that little girl is a real doll."

"Here's a photo of the man they're supposed to be with," Lauren said, showing Trey's picture. "He's about six feet tall, and he can be very charming."

"And I'm guessing not a nice guy, from your tone of voice," Mallory said.

"I don't know him well," she admitted. "But it worries me that Courtney came here with him, and then cut off all communication. I haven't heard from her, and neither has anyone else who knows her."

"I haven't seen either of them around," Mallory said. "But I'll keep my ears open and let you know if I hear anything. What were they doing in Eagle Mountain?"

"Trey Allerton, the man Courtney is allegedly with, said he was looking for land in the mountains to open a ranch for disadvantaged youth. Kind of a summer camp setup, I guess."

"I haven't had anyone contact me about anything like that, but I'll ask around. All the agents here in town are friendly, and even though we're competitors, we share information and help each other out."

"Thanks. I'd really appreciate it."

"Now, let's get your information."

They had almost finished completing the form when the door to the office opened and Shane Ellis strolled in. "Hello, ladies," he said, touching the brim of his hat. His gaze fixed on Lauren. "We seem to keep running into each other."

"Lauren was just telling me about her missing sister-in-law," Mallory said. "I'm going to talk to some other agents in town and see if any of them got a call from this Trey Allerton."

"You're one step ahead of me," Shane said. "I was stop-

ping by to ask if you'd met Allerton on his quest for his
kids' ranch."

"You know where else you might check?" Mallory said.
"You should look up recent sales at the courthouse. Maybe
he already bought something."

"Would there have been time for that?" Lauren asked.

"You'd be surprised how quickly deals can close sometimes, especially if the buyer has cash."

"I don't think Allerton had that kind of money," Lauren said.

"What about Courtney?" Shane asked.

Lauren sucked in her lower lip, thinking. "I don't think
so. The terms of her trust limit what she can withdraw cash
for, but maybe I can do some checking."

"You do that, and I'll check at the courthouse," Shane
said. "Mallory, you'll let us know if you hear anything
from your competition?"

"Of course." Mallory's smile warmed. "And if I do you
this favor, you'll owe me one."

He sat up straighter. "What's that?"

"One dance at the Fireman's Ball," Mallory said. "You
are going, aren't you?"

"Wouldn't miss it."

Mallory turned to Lauren. "If you're here for the Fourth
of July, you should plan to go to the dance. And there's
a parade, and fireworks. Oh, and a baseball game." She
grinned at Shane. "The annual rivalry between the sheriff's department and the fire department. That should be
very interesting this year. I assume you're pitching for the
sheriff's team?"

Shane shifted from foot to foot. "I guess so."

"I went to a Rockies game when Shane was pitching
once," Mallory told Lauren. "It was thrilling. The team
won, too. Made me feel proud to see a hometown boy
doing so well."

"Yeah, well, I'd better get over to the courthouse before they close for lunch," Shane said.

Lauren stood. "I'll go with you."

Neither of them said anything until they were on the sidewalk. "You don't like talking about your baseball career, do you?" she said.

He shrugged. "I'm not one to live in the past."

The Rayford County Courthouse was an elegant structure made of large blocks of red native stone, three stories tall with a gray slate roof and galleries of long windows. Inside, their steps echoed on scarred hardwood floors. They passed through a metal detector and a guard inspected Lauren's purse, then Shane led her down a long hall to a door marked County Clerk.

"Hello, Frieda," Shane greeted the plump woman behind the counter, her blond hair in braids that reached almost to her waist, her lips slicked with bright pink gloss.

"Well, Shane Ellis, you handsome thing." Her voice was a honeyed Southern drawl. "What can I do for you?"

"This is Lauren Baker," Shane introduced her. "Lauren, Frieda Patterson, our county clerk. Frieda knows everyone and everything in the county."

"Everyone ends up in this office at one time or another," Frieda said. "If they buy property or get tags for their car or get a new RV, they've got to see me, so yes, I know everyone." She narrowed her eyes. "So who are you looking for?"

"A man named Trey Allerton," Shane said. "He came to town about three weeks ago to look for property to start a youth ranch. Do you remember any transactions like that?"

Frieda shaped her bright lips into a pout. "I haven't recorded any sales of big property or ranch land in the past month," she said. "What did this guy look like?"

Shane looked to Lauren. "Trey is about six feet, slim, with sandy hair and brown eyes," she said. "He can be

very charming. He might have had this woman with him."
She showed the photo of Courtney and Trey on her phone.

Frieda considered the photograph and shook her head.
"I haven't seen them," she said, and returned the phone
to Lauren. "But the man sounds familiar. But it wasn't a
sale—it was a lease."

"Tell us about that," Shane said.

Frieda shook her head. "Not without permission from
the landlord."

"Could you ask the landlord for permission to share that
information with local law enforcement? Or give me their
name and I'll contact them myself."

"I don't know how that would go over," she said. "Let
me call them and see. I'll get back to you."

"Could you do it now?" He gave her his most charming smile.

"All right." She returned the smile. "Give me a minute."

She retreated to a back room and returned a few moments later. "Mr. Russell is always happy to cooperate
with the sheriff's office," she said.

She moved to a computer terminal and began typing.
"The man you're looking for wasn't using the name Aller-
ton," she said after a moment. "He called himself Allen
Troy Allen."

"That's the name he used when he registered at the
motel," Shane said.

"You should have said," Frieda chided. "I'd have remembered him sooner." She typed some more, and a
printer behind her whirred. She collected the printout and
laid it on the counter.

Lauren and Shane leaned over to read it. "This description of metes and bounds doesn't mean much to me," Shane
said. "Can you translate it into plain English?"

"It's a section of the Russell Ranch," Frieda said. "Samuel Russell agreed to lease sixty acres to Allen Entertain-

ment, Inc., for five years. They came in together to do the deal and Sam didn't look upset about it or anything."

"Thanks, Frieda."

"Anytime, darling." She slid the paper toward him. "I'm looking forward to seeing you pitch on the Fourth," she said. "I never got to see one of your games in person, but I watched you on TV."

"This won't be that exciting," he said.

"It will be for us," she said. "You're the closest thing we have to a celebrity."

He managed a pained smile, then he and Lauren left the courthouse. "I'll check out this property and let you know what I find," he said when they were outside again.

"I have a better idea," she said. "Take me with you."

"I can't take a civilian on sheriff's business."

"Civilians do ride-alongs with law enforcement officers all the time," she said. "Besides, so far we're following each other around town, covering the same ground. Wouldn't it be easier if we worked together?"

"When you say it like that, it makes perfect sense."

"I'm a very sensible person."

"Yeah. I like that about you." His eyes met hers and she felt a tug inside, like a guitar string snapping. Something letting go that she didn't understand—but didn't exactly want to run away from.

Chapter Five

The Russell Ranch sprawled across six hundred acres of sagebrush and pinion foothills and grassy valleys shadowed by towering mountain peaks. Shane eased the sheriff's department SUV down the rutted gravel road that led to the main entrance to the ranch. Lauren, beside him in the passenger seat, looked up at the massive iron gate with the Double R brand at its center. "Who owns the ranch?" she asked. "And why would they lease part of it to Trey Allerton?"

"Samuel Russell owns the place," Shane said. "He's third or fourth generation to ranch here. He had a son, Brock, but he was killed in an accident right after I graduated high school. He has a daughter, Willow, who was a few years behind me in school."

"Is there a Mrs. Russell?" Lauren asked.

"She died when the kids were pretty little. Sam never remarried, that I've heard, anyway. As for why he would lease the land, I intend to ask him."

He lowered the driver's window and pressed the call button on the intercom by the driveway.

"Hello?" a man's gruff voice demanded.

"Mr. Russell? This is Deputy Ellis. We spoke on the phone earlier."

"Gate's open. Come on up." As he spoke, the gate

swung to the side. Shane raised the window and drove through. He drove another quarter mile before the ranch house came into view—red brick with green gables and shutters and a sharply pitched slate roof. He parked the SUV in the drive and a man walked out to meet them.

Samuel Russell had thick white hair, a deep tan, the bowed gait of a man who had spent a life on horseback and the deeply wrinkled face of someone who lived outdoors in all seasons. He shook hands with Shane and nodded to Lauren. "You said on the phone you wanted to talk to me about Trey Allerton, but there's not a whole lot I can tell you," he said.

"Anything you have to say might help us," Shane said. He squinted into the bright sun. "Is there someplace inside we can talk?" he asked.

"Sure."

Russell led the way up the steps and into a large entry tiled with red-brown Saltillo tile. He walked down a short, carpeted hallway and opened the door to an office, with a desk, computer and printer, and a pair of worn upholstered armchairs. Russell sank into one of the chairs. "This is where I met Allen when he came to talk to me about leasing that section of land. That's how he introduced himself—Troy Allen, though the name on all the paperwork was Trey Allerton."

"That didn't strike you as odd?" Shane asked.

"Sure. But people do a lot of odd things. My brother's name is Robert, but no one ever calls him that. Even his checks say Shorty Russell on them. This Allerton fellow's business was Allen Entertainment. My lawyer looked everything over and says the agreement is all aboveboard, so I don't guess I care what a man chooses to call himself."

Lauren sat in the chair across from him and Shane leaned against the desk. "How did he find out about the land?" Shane asked. "How did he know it was available?"

"I'd told a few people I'd be open to the right offer," Russell said. "Nothing formal, but word gets passed around. He probably heard about it from one of the real estate agents in town. They're always on the lookout for another deal. But he could have just as easily heard it down at the local bar, somebody running their mouth."

"But he contacted you, you didn't contact him, is that right?" Shane asked.

"That's right. He called me up and said he was looking for a place to start a ranch to host disadvantaged kids. A summer camp, or something. I told him the land wasn't much good for actual ranching, but it would probably be fine for that. So we arranged for him and his business partner to come see it."

"His business partner?" Lauren leaned toward him. "Who was that?"

"He never addressed him by name in my hearing," Russell said. "He was a little older than Allen, short and stocky, with dark hair. Rough looking."

"How do you mean?" Shane asked.

"He wore a long-sleeved shirt, but the cuff slipped up and I could make out tattoos down to his wrist. I'm no expert, but they looked homemade to me, like the kind men give each other in prison." He met Shane's gaze. "I've hired a few ex-cons to work for me before. I believe in giving a man a second chance. Sometimes it works out, sometimes it doesn't."

"Did Allen have a woman with him?" Lauren asked. "A young blonde woman, and a little girl?"

She offered the photo of Courtney and Ashlyn, and Russell nodded. "The woman was with him. Hard to miss her. No little girl, though. But there was another woman, about her age, but taller, with long red hair and a kind of restless manner. She was hanging on the tattooed guy pretty good and was acting—I don't know—off. Like maybe she was on something."

"You think she was on drugs?" Shane asked.

"I don't know. She was just—fidgety, and kind of spacey."

"Do you know the women's names?" Shane asked.

"Sorry, I don't."

"What happened when the four of them came to see you?" Shane asked.

"I drove them out to look at the place. Mr. Allerton did all the talking. He said he liked the place and offered me cash—ten thousand down and another ten thousand in two weeks."

"Why not the whole twenty thousand up front?" Shane asked.

"He said he was waiting on a check for some work he'd done."

"And you agreed?" Lauren said.

"I didn't see any reason not to," Russell said. "The land is still mine, and if he violated the terms of the lease, I could kick him out."

"Did he pay you everything he owed?" Shane asked.

"He paid the first ten thousand," Russell said. "The rest isn't due for another week." He narrowed his eyes. "Are you trying to tell me I shouldn't hold my breath for that money?"

"Did Allerton tell you what his plans were for the property?" Shane asked. "Did he intend to live there?"

"He said he might move an RV onto the place to live in, and he wanted to build some cabins for the kids and other workers to stay in. I reminded him any buildings stayed with the property, and he agreed to that—didn't even blink. Which I thought didn't make him the shrewdest businessman in the world, but what did I care about that? I figured, in the end, I could wind up with a nice bunch of cabins on the land. Maybe I could turn it into a guest ranch or something."

"You didn't think Allerton's youth ranch was going to pan out?" Shane asked.

"Maybe it would, maybe it wouldn't. He was a good talker, but I thought he might be full of hot air. But like I said, I didn't see that I had a lot to lose."

"Did either of the women say anything?" Lauren asked.

Russell shook his head. "Not a peep. And nothing from the other man, either. Allen talked enough for all three of them."

"How many times did you meet with him?" Shane asked.

"Twice—that first time he came to see the place, and again when we closed the deal. He came alone that time, with a cashier's check for the first payment. He didn't run his mouth as much that time, just did the paperwork, handed over the check and thanked me. A couple of other times after that I saw vehicles—a truck and a blue sedan—headed back toward the property he leased."

"When was the last time you saw them?" Shane asked.

Russell rubbed his chin. "I guess it's been a week or so, maybe a little less." He shrugged. "He and his friends didn't make any trouble, so I didn't have any reason to keep track."

"I'd like to see the property he leased," Shane said. "Then I may have more questions for you."

Russell stood. "You're welcome to drive back there. Just continue on this road past my gate, up a hill and around a big curve. You'll cross a cattle guard and that's the western boundary. There's an old trailer house back there, but it's not really fit to live in. I told Allen if he wanted to get rid of it, he'd have to pay to have it hauled away. He didn't have a problem with that."

"Thank you, Mr. Russell." Shane handed the rancher one of his business cards. "Let me know if you hear from Mr. Allen, or if you think of anything else."

"What's he done, that you're so interested in him?" Russell asked.

"The woman he's with is my sister-in-law," Lauren said. "She's my brother's widow, and I haven't heard anything from her for over a week. I want to make sure she's all right."

"She looked fine when I saw her," Russell said. "If that's any comfort to you."

Shane put a hand to Lauren's back and urged her toward the door. "Do the other people Russell described—the man and the woman who were with Trey—sound like anyone you know?" Shane asked when they were in the cruiser again.

"No," she said. "Mike never brought any other friends over when he and Courtney visited my place, and I never saw anyone else when I was with them at Courtney's house. I don't remember her mentioning anyone else, either."

She sat back, arms folded over her chest. "I can't believe Russell would lease his property to someone he hardly knew."

"He thought it was a way to get money from a section of the property he's not utilizing right now," Shane said. "And maybe Allerton impressed him with his plans to use the place to help kids."

"I don't believe Allerton has any intention of helping children," Lauren said. "I think he just said that to get to Courtney. Everything about the man struck me as phony, but she refused to see it." She crossed her arms over her chest and stared straight ahead.

"What did she say when you told her your opinion of Allerton?" Shane asked.

"She said I was upset because Trey survived and Mike didn't, and that I didn't want her to be with any man but Mike."

He winced. "Any chance she was on to something?"

She sat up straighter, and he could almost feel the chill from the cold look she sent him. "This didn't have anything to do with Mike. I'm a good judge of character, and I recognize a snake when I see one."

"So if Courtney had decided to leave with a different man—someone you like—you wouldn't be here now looking for her," he said.

"If she ran off with this man and then stopped all communication with me and with all of her other friends, yes, of course I'd be concerned and I'd be searching for her. The fact that I don't like Allerton makes me even more afraid for her."

"Just making sure," he said. "I believe you, but I need to be able to justify devoting my time to driving out here with you. We haven't established a crime has been committed."

"Maybe we'll get some answers at the ranch," she said.

They both fell silent, gravel popping beneath the tires the only sound. This part of the ranch looked more used up than the other land, thick stands of silvery sagebrush and clumps of prickly pear cactus choking out the grass, signs of overgrazing. Shane rolled down the driver's window a few inches, bringing in the smell of sage and the raucous fussing of a flock of pinion jays.

Lauren pulled out her phone. "No service," she said.

"Maybe that's why you haven't heard from Courtney," he said.

"Surely she has to leave the ranch sometime," Lauren said. "Staying out here with just Ashlyn and Allerton for company would drive her crazy. Courtney isn't really a country girl. She likes her fancy coffee and professional manicures and getting her hair done once a month."

She made a good case for something to be wrong, but was that merely because she couldn't accept that her brother's widow had moved on? If they found Courtney and Ashlyn happily ensconced in a cozy cabin, getting the property ready to welcome a bunch of disadvantaged children, would Lauren be able to accept that, and move on herself?

The SUV rumbled across a cattle guard, and the silvery branches of a dead pinion marked the turn onto the twin ruts of a drive that twisted through a stand of sagebrush, then ended abruptly at a leaning trailer house. The trailer's siding, faded turquoise streaked with rust, bore several large dents, as if a truck or other vehicle had collided with it. The screen door—minus all but a remnant of screen—stood open, and the windows, dirty and uncurtained, looked onto a rocky clearing.

"Stay here while I check this out," Shane said.

But as soon as he was away from the SUV, Lauren came after him. "Courtney doesn't know you," she said. "She might not answer the door."

He had a feeling no one was going to answer the door here. The trailer didn't look as if anyone had lived in it for the last decade. He climbed the three wooden steps to the door, his boots making a hollow echo with each footfall. He knocked firmly, then waited. Lauren stood on the step just below him, her shoulder brushing his arm. "I don't hear anything," she whispered.

He knocked again, and when no answer came, he tried the doorknob. It turned easily in his hand and swung open with a creak worthy of a nightmare.

The carpet in the living room had once been avocado green, the color discernable now only in bright patches where furniture had once stood. The only items in the room now were a broken plastic patio chair and an overturned cardboard box that had once held paper towels. "Hello!" Shane called. "Anybody home?"

Absolute silence met his inquiry. He moved forward, one hand hovering near his gun, constantly scanning the empty room for any sign of movement. They checked the kitchen, to the left of the living room, a rust-streaked sink and yellow laminate countertops identifying its function. Beyond that was a bedroom, with no bed, only a stack of newspapers. The top one was dated five years previous. "I don't think anyone has been here in a long time," he said, dropping the paper onto the pile once more.

Lauren moved past him, into the bathroom, with its plastic tub and shower combo and toilet. "Nothing but dirt in here," he said.

"Wait a minute." She bent and retrieved something from the tub.

Shane stared at a doll, about six inches high with long purple hair. The doll wore a pink dress with a yellow daisy embroidered in one corner. Lauren's hand holding the toy trembled, and when he met her gaze, he was shocked to see her eyes filled with tears. "Ashlyn was here," she said. "This is hers. Why would she have left it behind?"

Shane acted on instinct, not as a cop, but as a man who hated to see another person in distress. He put an arm around her shoulder. "It's good to know she was here," he said. "It means we're on the right track. And children forget things. They get distracted. Finding it here doesn't mean anything bad happened."

She nodded, her eyes still fixed on the doll. "You're right." She took a deep breath. "They were here. So where did they go?" She looked into his eyes, tears gone, the determination he had admired so much returned. "And how are we going to find them?"

Chapter Six

Lauren stared at the little doll, a clear picture in her mind of Ashlyn playing with it. She had fallen in love with the purple-haired toy and carried it everywhere. "Ashlyn isn't careless," she said. "She wouldn't just leave her doll behind."

"Maybe something else distracted her and she laid the doll down, thinking she'd come back to her," Shane said.

"So why didn't she come back?" Her imagination could think of a dozen different reasons Ashlyn and Courtney would have failed to retrieve the doll, none of them good.

"I don't know," he said.

She smoothed the doll's hair, then offered it to him. "I guess you'll want this," she said.

He didn't take the doll. "You should keep it."

"But don't you want to log it in as evidence?"

He frowned. "Evidence of what?"

"It proves Ashlyn was here," she said. "And if she was here, Courtney must have been here."

"Yes, it could be proof that they were here," he said. "But Mr. Russell already told us Allerton came here. He had a legitimate lease, so him being here isn't a crime." He looked around the empty trailer. "There's no sign of a struggle, or of anything illegal here. I don't have any reason to treat this as a crime scene."

She wanted to argue with him, to protest the facts that Ashlyn and Courtney weren't here now and that Ashlyn had left behind her beloved doll were proof that something was wrong. But that was only her instinct. She had no real evidence that this was so. "What are you going to do?" she asked.

"I'm going to try to learn more about the man and the woman who were with Allerton and Courtney when they visited Mr. Russell."

Relief surged through her. "Then you're not going to give up."

"I'm not going to give up," he said. "But this can't be my only focus."

"I understand." She didn't want to. The fate of her sister-in-law and her niece felt so important to her. But she had a job that placed many demands on her, too. It would have been irresponsible for her to devote all her energy to one patient when so many other people needed care. It was the same with law enforcement. "I'm grateful for anything you can do," she said.

"Are you ready to go?" he asked.

She nodded.

They left the trailer and made the drive back to town in silence. Lauren stared out the window of the SUV, taking in the beautiful but wild scenery—vast stretches of wooded mountainsides or open valleys carpeted with wildflowers, with no houses or other people in sight. What if Courtney and Ashlyn were lost somewhere out in that wilderness? Or what if they were trapped with Allerton and the mysterious couple Mr. Russell had mentioned, desperate to get away but unable to do so?

"I'm sorry I can't do more to help." Shane interrupted her thoughts as they neared the sheriff's department. "Television and movies make it seem like a department can throw everything they've got at a single case, especially a missing person. But we can't really do that in real life." He spoke gently, as if he didn't want to upset her any more than she already was.

She turned toward him and managed a faint smile. "I know," she said. "I don't like it much, but I understand. I'm going to keep doing everything I can on my part to find them, too."

He parked in front of the sheriff's department and shut off the engine, but when she started to open the door, he put a hand on her arm. "Don't do anything reckless," he said. "If you find out something you think is important, tell me about it. Don't go rushing into a situation that might be trouble."

"I won't, but—"

"No buts," he said. "I know I said I couldn't make this a priority, but I don't want you thinking you should act on your own because you don't want to bother me or because you think I won't pay attention. I will pay attention. To you."

His hand on her arm was warm and firm, almost a caress. She heard the care in his voice and saw it in his eyes, and her heart fluttered, unsettling her. "Thank you," she said, and opened the door.

He took his hand away. "I'll touch base with you soon," he said.

She nodded. "Thanks." She'd look forward to talking to him again. And not just because of the case. There was something special about this man who was so considerate of her feelings, and so earnest in his desire to help. He didn't fit her image of a famous athlete or a small-town cop.

She returned to the rental apartment, intending to start calling the list of potential rentals Mallory Workman had emailed to her. Instead, she found herself replaying their conversation with Samuel Russell. He'd said that Troy

Allen / Trey Allerton had paid him the first lease payment and promised another $10,000 in two weeks. Nothing about Allerton had indicated to her that he had much money. He drove an older-model pickup truck that was well cared for but not expensive. He dressed well but not extravagantly. And he never talked about having money. That didn't mean he didn't have substantial savings or an inheritance, but he had always stressed the need for Courtney to "invest" in the ranch with him, telling her this was what Mike would have wanted.

She took out her phone and punched in a number. "Addison, Simmons and Clark," a woman's crisp voice answered.

"Mindy? It's Lauren Baker."

"Lauren! It's always nice to hear from you. How have you been?" Mindy Archeleta, office manager for the law firm that administered the Baker family trusts, responded with genuine warmth. In the years since Lauren and Mike's parents had died, the two women had become friends, occasionally meeting for coffee or lunch, and always taking time away from whatever business Lauren had with the firm to catch up personally.

"I'm fine," Lauren said. "How are you?"

"Crazy busy as always," Mindy said. "But in a good way. Jax is playing Little League this year, can you believe it? It's just T-ball, but he's so stinking cute in his uniform, swinging at the ball. Darrell is helping coach the team, and seeing my two guys together out there on the ball field makes me all gooey inside."

"Send pictures," Lauren said. "I bet little Jax is adorable."

"Darrell looks pretty good in his uniform, too," Mindy said. "Though I'll keep those photos to myself."

Lauren laughed.

"What can I do for you this afternoon?" Mindy asked.

"I wanted to refresh my memory on the terms of the

trust," Lauren said. "I'm allowed to draw out money to buy a home, right?"

"You are. Are you thinking of buying a new place?"

Lauren crossed her fingers. Here was where things got a little tricky. "I've been playing around with the idea," she said. "I've seen the place Courtney is interested in and the area is so great. And I'd love to stay close to her and Ashlyn."

"Somewhere in the mountains, right?" Mindy said. "In the southwestern part of the state?"

Adrenaline jolted Lauren, but she managed to keep her voice even. "That's right. Eagle Mountain. I'm here right now. The place is gorgeous."

"Then I guess that request was legit after all," Mindy said.

"What do you mean?" Lauren asked.

"Oh, some man called here last week and asked about getting money from Courtney's trust to buy a ranch out that way. He said he was Courtney's representative. I told him I needed authorization directly from Courtney herself and that we couldn't authorize withdrawals over the phone anyway. Which goes for you, too. You have to come into the office and sign a bunch of papers, and I have to notarize them and everything."

"That's good to know," Lauren said. "Who was the guy? Did he say?"

"He wouldn't give me his name, which is one reason I thought the whole thing was bogus. I mean, you wouldn't believe the scams some people try to pull."

"It was probably her real estate agent, getting ahead of himself," Lauren said.

"Probably. When you talk to Courtney again, tell her we're happy to help her out, but she has to come into the office."

"I will. And thanks for the information, Mindy."

"Anytime. When you get back in town, call me and we'll have lunch. I'll bore you with too many details about Jax's ball games and my own struggles with this new spin class I'm trying. It's supposed to give me a killer bod but so far it just makes me feel inadequate."

"We'll get together soon," Lauren said, and ended the call.

She stood up and began to pace, too agitated to sit still. She'd been right in thinking that Allerton needed Courtney's money to pay for his ranch. He must have been the mysterious "representative" who had called Mindy to ask about withdrawing money from the trust.

She wanted to do a little more digging before she spoke to Shane about this. She needed to make a strong case in order to keep him investigating. She could do a lot on her own, but she really needed—and wanted—his help.

SHANE REPORTED FOR work Thursday morning feeling less than alert. He'd spent a restless night worrying about Lauren. So far, he hadn't seen any evidence that her sister-in-law had done anything other than take up with a perhaps unsuitable man of her own free will. She'd cut contact with everyone for her own reasons, and while that could be a sign of an abusive situation, it also could indicate that she was trying to make a clean break with her old life as Mike Baker's widow and start over again in a new place, with a new man.

But Lauren believed firmly that something was wrong, and Shane wanted to help her. Partly as a way to prove himself as a law enforcement officer, and partly because he was starting to care about this tough but vulnerable woman who was so loyal to her family and so determined to do right by them. And, he had to admit, continuing to investigate this case was a ready-made way to stay close to Lauren, something he very much wanted to do.

He walked into morning roll call to find most of his fellow officers already in place. "Way to go, Ace!" Gage said, and several others applauded.

Shane ignored them and took his seat. "Something tells me our star player hasn't seen the posters for the Fourth of July matchup," Dwight Prentice said. He swiveled his chair and pointed to the bulletin board at the back of the room.

Shane stared at the poster, which featured a shot of him from his playing days, in uniform and grinning at the camera. He leaned closer and suppressed a groan. The photo was the one from his official baseball card the last year he played, taken a few months before he injured his arm. He wore the cocky grin of a man who had the world by the tail and didn't plan on letting go anytime soon.

"Addie says tickets are selling as fast as they can print them," Gage said. "The boys down at the fire station are already whining about how it's not fair for us to bring in a professional."

"I'm not a professional anymore," Shane said. "I'm just a cop."

This brought hoots of laughter from some in the room. Travis, who had been leaning back in his chair observing the banter, cleared his throat and stood, and everyone settled in their seats, facing forward again.

"We've got a few new things to look into this morning," the sheriff said, consulting a clipboard in front of him. "Mountain Aire Boutique filed a shoplifting complaint against Talia Larrivee. The shop's owner, Marsha Raymond, called this morning and said either Talia or one of her friends is robbing her blind and we need to do something to stop it."

"Did she catch them in the act?" Dwight asked.

"No. But she says every time they come into the store, something turns up missing," Travis said.

"Does she have a security camera?" Gage asked. "Maybe she could catch the thefts on film."

"She says she can't put a camera in the changing rooms—her customers would object."

"So no proof, just what she thinks is going on," Gage said. "What did you tell her?"

"I told her we couldn't act on suspicion alone," Travis said. "I told her she had the right to bar Talia and her friends from her shop, but she said she couldn't do that because they spent too much money there."

No one asked why a woman who had the money to afford anything in that shop would steal. For most shoplifters, it was more about getting away with something than getting an item for free. For some people, it was a compulsion; for others, a cheap thrill.

"This isn't the first time someone has complained about Talia being light-fingered," Dwight said. "But no one has been able to catch her in the act."

"Someone caught her one time," Gage said. "Over at the hardware store. Fred Wilkins was red-hot about it, too, but Talia's daddy showed up to pay for the items she stole and smooth Fred's feathers."

"More like grease Fred's palm," Dwight said.

"In any case, if you see Talia shopping in town, it wouldn't hurt to keep an eye on her and her friends," Travis said. "But be subtle. We don't want any complaints of harassment." He consulted the clipboard again. "Shane, where are you on that welfare check on Courtney Baker?"

Shane sat up straighter. "I tracked Courtney Baker and her companion's movements. They were registered at the Ranch Motel as Mr. and Mrs. Troy Allen. Trey Allerton and another man, whose name I don't have—Allerton introduced him as his business partner—struck a deal with Samuel Russell to lease a section of Russell's ranch for five years. Russell said Courtney visited the ranch with Russell, his business partner, and another woman I haven't been able to identify. I visited the property with Lauren Baker, Courtney's sister-in-law, and in an abandoned mobile home on the property, we found a doll Lauren said belonged to her niece, Ashlyn. I haven't learned anything more."

"Have you found any indication of foul play or anything illegal?" Travis asked.

"No, sir. Registering at the motel under a false name is suspicious, but it's not against the law."

"We'll keep our ears open, but I don't hear anything in what you've told us that sounds like a crime."

"No, sir. Lauren thinks her sister-in-law is acting out of character, but Mr. Russell said she didn't seem distressed when he saw her, and the clerk at the motel says the same."

"Brenda rented her old apartment to Lauren," Dwight said. "She thinks her concern for her sister-in-law and niece is legitimate, for what it's worth."

"Concern isn't enough for us to launch a full investigation," Travis said.

"I'd like to continue to follow up on this in my spare time," Shane said. "I'd like to find out more about the other couple who were with Allerton and Mrs. Baker at the Russell Ranch."

"That's fine," Travis said. "But don't make it a priority." He consulted the clipboard again. "Item number three…"

Shane forced himself to pay attention to the details of ongoing cases, a couple of BOLOs that had come in overnight and some housekeeping issues they needed to address. By the time the meeting ended, he had largely put Courtney Baker out of his mind.

But when he returned to his desk, he was startled—and pleased—to find Lauren Baker waiting for him. She stood as he approached. "Adelaide told me I could wait here for you."

"I see you're on a first-name basis with our office manager," Shane said.

"She insisted," Lauren said.

He settled behind the desk. "It's always good to see you."

She sat also, but her hands remained restless, clutching at the purse in her lap, or reaching up to smooth her hair. "Is something wrong?" he asked.

"I've found something," she said. "Maybe something important. Trey Allerton tried to get money from Courtney's trust."

He pulled out a notebook so he could make notes. "How did you find this out?" he asked.

She told him about calling the law firm that managed the trust and chatting up her friend, the office manager. "I checked Courtney's bank, too. Her checking account has been emptied, but that happened three weeks ago. Her savings account still has a little in it, but that money hasn't been touched."

"That information has to be confidential," he said. "How did you find it out?"

She flushed. "I told you I did Courtney's taxes last year, right? She gave me her online passwords so I could download all the transactions into my online accounting software. I told her she should change the passwords after I was done, but she never did."

"So she took money out of her checking account," he said. "How much money?"

"Less than a thousand dollars."

"How much is in savings?"

"About five thousand. There are some other accounts—a college fund for Ashlyn, a medical savings account and a retirement account. They're with a different bank and I wasn't able to check them."

"You didn't have the passwords?"

"They require a new password every three months."

He suppressed a grin. Clearly, Lauren had tried to hack into those accounts and been thwarted. He admired her determination, if not the not-exactly-legal approach to gathering information.

"This is all very interesting," he said. "But it doesn't prove that anything is wrong."

She scooted to the edge of her chair and leaned toward him. "Why did Allerton—or whoever the man was—call the trust fund to inquire about withdrawing money, and not Courtney herself?" she asked. "And why didn't Courtney follow up on the request for the money? Was it because she had refused to do so? Or because she couldn't?"

Chapter Seven

Shane had no answer for Lauren's question as to why Courtney had never followed up on the request to withdraw money from her trust fund. He had asked her to share anything else she learned, and promised to keep searching for more information about Courtney and Ashlyn and Trey Allerton. But she heard the reluctance behind the promise. He didn't really believe Courtney was in trouble.

Lauren wasn't going to give up, though. Thursday afternoon, she walked to the Eagle Mountain Medical Clinic. A dark-haired woman at the front counter greeted her. "Hello. Do you have an appointment?"

"I'm Lauren Baker, from Denver," she said. "I'm a nurse practitioner, and I wondered if I could speak to the clinic director for a moment." She handed over one of her business cards.

The woman—her name tag identified her as Rebecca—stood. "I'll see if Ms. Cox is free."

Lauren took a seat in the waiting room. Across from her, an elderly couple flipped through magazines. Next to them, a woman cradled a fussy toddler. The room was simply furnished, the chairs and tables slightly worn, but the magazines were of recent issue and everything was clean. It looked like a typical busy clinic, one that devoted funding to patient services rather than decorating, probably because there wasn't excess funding to go around.

"Ms. Baker?" A middle-aged woman with short dark hair streaked with silver, dressed in a navy pantsuit, approached.

Lauren stood. "I'm Lauren Baker."

"Linda Cox." She offered her hand. "Let's go into my office."

Ms. Cox led the way to a small office crowded with a desk, one visitor's chair and a row of filing cabinets. "What can I do for you, Ms. Baker?" she asked.

"I'm looking for this woman and her little girl." She passed over the photograph of Courtney and Ashlyn. "That's my late brother's widow, Courtney Baker, and her daughter, Ashlyn. They've been missing for several weeks now. The last anyone heard from them, they were in Eagle Mountain. I wondered if either of them had been seen in your clinic."

Ms. Cox studied the picture for a moment, then laid it on the desk between them. "As a nurse practitioner, you're aware that patient information is confidential."

Lauren tightened her hands on the arms of the chair. "I'm not asking you to divulge particulars, or anything about a medical condition," she said. "I'm only asking if they were seen at this clinic. I'm trying to track their whereabouts."

"Have you consulted the sheriff's department about this?" Ms. Cox asked.

"I have. But they tell me they can't devote much time to the search if there's no evidence of a crime having been committed. But I know Courtney. She wouldn't have cut off communication with me and with everyone else she knows if something wasn't wrong."

Ms. Cox stood and picked up the photograph. "Give me a moment."

Lauren clenched her hands in her lap and tried to focus on taking deep, slow breaths. She reminded herself that if Ashlyn and Courtney hadn't been seen at the clinic, it meant they were well, which was a good thing. But if they had been seen, it would be one more clue to what they had been doing here—and with whom.

Ms. Cox returned to the office, along with a young African American woman. "This is Tina, Dr. Folsom's nurse. She helped care for your niece when she was here two weeks ago," Ms. Cox said. "She can't give you any medical information, but there may be other questions she can answer."

Lauren stood, heart beating fast. "Ashlyn was here? Was her mother, Courtney, with her?"

Tina nodded. "Her mother was with her, and a man. I wasn't sure what his relation to them was, and he didn't say."

"What did the man look like?" Lauren asked.

Tina frowned. "He was white, with brown hair. Kind of tall." She shrugged. "It's been a while, and my focus was on the patient."

Lauren longed to ask what was wrong with Ashlyn. Why had she been seen? But confidentiality rules prevented the clinic from providing any of those details. "How did they seem?" she asked. "I mean, were they relaxed or nervous? Did they seem afraid of the man or comfortable with him?"

"The woman was concerned about her daughter, but not unduly so. And she didn't seem afraid, no." She glanced at Ms. Cox. "Was this some kind of abusive situation and I missed it?"

"Was it?" Ms. Cox asked.

"No," Lauren said. At least, Trey had never shown any sign of violence toward Courtney or Ashlyn, but that might have changed. "But it didn't strike you that she was trying to get away from him or anything?"

Tina shook her head. "She and I were alone in the exam room with the little girl before the doctor came in. The man stayed in the waiting room. If she had wanted to say anything to me, or to Dr. Folsom, she could have."

"Did she mention where they were going after they left the clinic?" Lauren asked.

"Not that I remember."

"Was Ashlyn going to be okay?"

Tina looked to Ms. Cox again. The director nodded. "She was going to be fine," Tina said. "It wasn't anything serious."

"Thank you," Lauren said.

"You can go back to work now, Tina," Ms. Cox said.

When they were alone again, Ms. Cox said, "Was that helpful?"

"It verifies they were still in town then," Lauren said. "And that they were okay." That was all good, but it didn't tell her why Courtney didn't answer calls or texts or post to social media.

Ms. Cox closed the door leading to the hallway. "Now I have a question for you," she said.

"All right," Lauren said.

"Would you be interested in moving to Eagle Mountain, to work for us?"

Lauren blinked, taken aback. "Nothing like that ever crossed my mind."

"Think about it," Ms. Cox said. "When you walked in and gave your card to Rebecca, I thought you had heard through the grapevine that we were looking to add a nurse practitioner. I hoped you had come to apply for the job."

"I'm very flattered," Lauren said. "But I'm happy where I am."

"If that changes, give me a call." Ms. Cox handed over

her own card. "We have a good practice here, lots of variety and a good team. And Eagle Mountain is a wonderful place to live. I'm happy to provide more details anytime."

"Thank you." Lauren stood. "And thank you for telling me about Courtney."

"I hope you find your friend and your niece," she said. "If I hear anything else about them, I'll let you know."

"Thank you."

Lauren left the clinic and was walking back toward her rental when a familiar voice hailed her. Shane pulled his sheriff's department SUV to the curb beside her. "You look like you just lost your best friend," he said.

"I dropped by the medical clinic," she said. "Ashlyn was seen there two weeks ago."

His look of genuine concern touched her. "What happened?"

"Confidentiality laws prevented them from telling me any details, but they assured me she's going to be okay. She was seen for something minor."

"Then why do you look so down?"

She hugged her arms across her stomach. "The nurse who took care of Ashlyn said Trey was with them. He stayed in the waiting room while Courtney and Ashlyn went back. It was the perfect opportunity for Courtney to ask for help if she needed it but the nurse said she seemed fine."

"That's good," he said. "Isn't it?"

"It is—but if everything was going so well, why did she stop returning calls and texts from everyone she knew back in Denver? And why did she stop posting on all her social media?"

"I don't know," he said. "You want to get coffee somewhere? I'd like to keep talking, but I'm holding up traffic."

She realized two other vehicles were patiently idling behind his SUV. "Sure," she said, and climbed in.

"Did you learn anything else at the clinic?" he asked as he pulled in to the flow of traffic once more.

"Not really. But they offered me a job. Apparently, they want to add a nurse practitioner."

"Are you going to take the offer?"

"No. I'm happy where I am." She'd been at the clinic in Denver for five years. Like any job, it had its drawbacks, but overall it was a very good position. She had no reason to want to change.

"You mind if I ask a nosy question?"

"Isn't that what cops do?"

He chuckled. "We do. You don't have to answer if you don't want to, but if you have this big trust fund from your family, what are you doing working as a nurse?"

"A nurse practitioner. I enjoy my work. I'd never be comfortably living off my parents' money. And what about you?"

"What about me?" he asked.

"I looked you up online. You made a lot of money when you played professional ball."

"And paid a lot of taxes and blew a lot on expensive vacations and gifts for family and friends."

"So you blew it all?"

"Not all of it. I had smart people who talked me into investing some. And I have a house."

"A house in Eagle Mountain?"

"Yeah. Would you like to see it?"

"Yes," she said, surprising herself with the answer. "Yes, I would."

SHANE HAD PURCHASED his house while he was still pitching, thinking he would use it as a retreat during the off-season, or a place to stay when he came home to visit family. He had retreated here, all right—to recover after his surgery, and again when he had been released from his contract and officially retired from the only job he had ever really wanted to do.

He pulled in to the driveway and cut the engine and waited for Lauren to say something. The log cabin, with its twin dormers and broad front porch, sat in the shade of tall spruce trees. It was large, but it wasn't elaborate or modern, or even very new. "It's not what I expected," she said.

"You thought I'd have some modern mansion, or a swinging bachelor pad." He'd heard similar comments before.

She flushed. "I guess so."

"Come on. I'll show you around."

He led the way along a flagstone path, up the steps and across the porch. She stopped to stroke the arm of a wooden rocker. "This is beautiful."

"I got it from a local guy who makes handmade furniture."

The front door led directly into a great room, which took up most of the downstairs. Light poured from large windows on all sides, onto wood plank flooring. He'd furnished the room with comfortable leather furniture, a large entertainment center and a wall of bookcases. A dining table and chairs from the craftsman who had made the rocking chair filled one side of the space, in front of the island that separated the kitchen area. "There's a master suite through there," he said, pointing to a hallway off the living area. "And three more bedrooms and two baths upstairs."

Her gaze fixed on him, a softness in her expression that made him feel shaky inside. "What?" he asked.

"You didn't buy a house," she said. "You bought a family home."

He shrugged. "I'd like to have a family—one day."

He led the way back over toward the seating area. "Did I hear right that you're from Eagle Mountain?" she asked

"That's right," he said. "I went to high school here. My mom and dad live across town."

"Do you have any brothers or sisters?" she asked.

He settled onto the sofa, and she perched on the adjacent love seat. "I have a sister. She's in Minneapolis."

"Why did you decide to come back here instead of staying in Denver?" she asked. "I assume that's where you lived when you played."

"I had an apartment there, but I guess I'm not much of a city guy. I like the mountains and the woods. And I hated Denver traffic."

"I guess no one likes the traffic," she said.

"What about you?" he asked. "Are you from Denver originally?"

She shook her head. "Lincoln, Nebraska. But I've lived in Denver for almost five years."

"Do you like it?"

"I do. Not the traffic, but I have a nice apartment close to work, and I really enjoy my job."

"It's good to have work you enjoy."

"Do you enjoy your work? Being a sheriff's deputy is very different from playing professional baseball."

He leaned his head back against the sofa and looked up at the ceiling. "When the club decided not to renew my contract, my whole world changed." He hadn't talked much about that time, but he found himself wanting to tell her. "I'd never thought about being anything but a ballplayer. Shortsighted of me, I guess, but when you're on top, you think you'll never fall."

"That must have been hard."

He shrugged. "I was upset, but I was only twenty-eight. I had to figure out something to do with the rest of my life. I saw that the sheriff's department here was hiring, so I did a ride-along."

"What drew you to that choice?" she asked.

He'd heard variations of that question before, usually phrased along the lines of "Why would you want to be a cop?" said with a tinge of horror. "It's nothing like what you see on TV, all excitement and danger and everything," he said. "I mean, you train for that stuff, but most of the time it's interacting with people, keeping an eye out for trouble and helping people out. I liked that. I wanted to be a part of the community again, to do something that really made people's lives better. I know some law enforcement get a bad rap and there have been problems other places, but this is a good group of officers here. It seems like a good fit, though I guess I'm still finding my footing."

"People like you," she said. "And people in town are proud of you. Everyone I've talked to has good things to say about you."

A familiar regret pulled at him. "They're proud of what I was."

"I don't know about that." She tilted her head, letting her gaze sweep over him. "All the women in town think you're pretty hot stuff."

He let out a hoot of laughter. "You're one to talk. I've already had three men ask about you."

"You're kidding!"

"I'm not. You have to remember that men still outnumber women in a lot of small towns out here. Someone new always sparks interest. Dating in a small town is risky because you can run through all the potential partners pretty quickly."

She looked amused. "And have you run through all the potential partners?"

"I'll never tell." He stood. "I need to change out of this uniform, then how about I fix us something to eat? I skipped lunch and I'm starved."

"All right."

"Feel free to look around more if you want."

Shedding the utility belt, weapon and ballistics vest lightened him by ten pounds and was always a relief. He thought about taking a quick shower, but settled for sponging off and changing into jeans and a T-shirt. When he returned to the great room, Lauren was standing in front of the bookcase. "You like detective novels," she said by way of greeting.

"Real-life crimes are seldom as easy to solve, but I've always liked figuring out puzzles." He moved to the kitchen. "Grilled chicken okay?" he asked.

"Sounds good." She moved to the other side of the island and watched as he unwrapped chicken thighs and mixed up a quick marinade. When he took out salad greens, she said, "You still eat like an athlete."

"I still have to stay in shape," he said.

"Have you ever had to chase down a criminal?"

"I chased a shoplifter down Main just a couple of weeks ago. A teenager. I think he was surprised an old guy like me caught him."

She laughed. "I saw a poster for a baseball game on the Fourth of July," she said. "Sheriff's department versus fire department. There was a picture of you in your Rockies uniform."

"I've been drafted to pitch for our side." He tore lettuce and added it to a bowl. "Apparently, the sheriff's team has lost to the fire department for the past four years and I'm supposed to stop the slide."

"No pressure."

He sent her a grateful look. "Everyone still thinks I'm the pro ace, but if I was, I'd still be on the mound, not sitting in a cruiser."

Her gaze shifted to his arm, and the scar that wrapped around his elbow, white against his tan. "Does it hurt to pitch?"

"It hurt to throw the ball as hard and fast, and for as

long, as I needed to do in the majors." He began slicing a bell pepper. "But I can pitch to a bunch of amateurs. It just won't be the spectacle people seem to expect."

"I wouldn't know the difference, and I'll bet a lot of other people are the same." She slid onto a bar stool. "I'd offer to help you with dinner, but you look like you've got everything under control."

"I do." He pulled out a tomato and began cutting it into chunks, and decided it was past time to shift the conversation away from himself. "Besides visiting the clinic, what else did you do today?"

"I followed up on some rental referrals and found a place that agreed to rent to me week to week for as long as I want. I'll move in tomorrow," she said. "I don't have to be out of the Prentices' place until Monday morning, but this way Brenda can rent her apartment out for the weekend. Apparently, there's a big demand."

"How did you luck into your new place on such short notice?"

"It's not a regular rental," she said. "It's a detached cottage where the owner's mother lived until she had to go into an assisted living facility last month. She wants to fix it up and rent it out but hadn't gotten around to it yet. But Mallory talked her into letting me have it, as long as I'm not picky, which I'm not."

"Then it sounds like a win for everyone." He picked up the bowl of chicken. "Come on outside."

While the chicken grilled, she helped him set the table on the patio. They ate grilled chicken and salad and drank iced tea. When they had finished, she walked to the deck railing and looked out at his view of a wooded valley.

"It is beautiful here," she said.

"I like it." He joined her at the railing, close, but not quite touching. He caught the scent of her perfume, something floral with a hint of citrus. Feminine and stirring.

"I don't just mean your house, I mean the whole area."

"Thousands of tourists can't be wrong."

She turned toward him. "But is beautiful scenery enough? It's great for a vacation, but to live your whole life?"

"I guess that depends on what you value, what fulfills you. That isn't the same for every person. And the answer isn't the same throughout a person's life. But for me, right now, it's enough."

"You don't think you're missing out on some things?"

Should he be glib or honest? He chose honesty. "Someone to share it with, maybe. If I had that, I think this would be just about perfect."

"I think that could make almost anything perfect," she said. "If you found the right person."

Their eyes met, and he felt a pull somewhere around his heart. There was something about this woman that caught and held him, not like a trap, but more like a warm embrace. Did she feel it, too? He moved closer and put his hand on her shoulder. She continued to look steadily into his eyes, almost daring him to move in nearer still.

So he did. She tilted her head up in invitation, and his lips met hers in a slow, sweet kiss that sent heat spreading through him.

Her fingers gripped his shoulder, a gentle, insistent pressure, and he wrapped his arms around her, their bodies pressed together, soft to hard, curve to plain.

Then she was moving away again, easing out of his arms, her face flushed, her breathing a little shallow. "That was nice," he said.

"Yes." She looked around, everywhere but at him. "But I think I'd better go now."

His first impulse was to tell her she didn't have to go, but he thought better of it. "I'll get my keys."

They were silent on the drive back to her rental. He

parked out front and unfastened his seat belt. "You don't have to get out," she said.

"I'll walk you to your door," he said, not leaving room for argument.

At the door, he waited while she dug out her key. "Thank you for dinner," she said.

"Thank you," he said. "You're good company."

"So are you."

"About that kiss," he began.

"You don't have to apologize."

"I wasn't going to apologize. I enjoyed it. A lot. And I wouldn't mind repeating it sometime. But I didn't want it hanging between us, if it made you feel awkward or pressured or…whatever."

At last, she looked at him again. "It was a good kiss," she said. "I'm just not interested in starting something when I'm not going to stick around. I'm here to find Courtney and Ashlyn, and then I'm going back to Denver."

"Denver isn't so far away," he said.

"I know." She bit her lower lip. "I have a bad habit."

He waited, but when she didn't say more, he prompted. "What is it? Do you bite your nails? Are you a closet smoker?"

A smile flirted with the corners of her mouth. "I have a bad habit of falling for men. Falling too hard, too soon. It's…awkward when things don't work out."

Was she saying she was falling for him? The idea made him a little light-headed. He brushed his hand down her arm. "It was a nice kiss," he said. "I'm not expecting more. You don't have to, either."

She nodded. "But I think we should stick to looking for Courtney."

"All right." That was a reason for him to see her again.

As for the rest—he might not have expectations, but he could hope. It was a subtle difference, but one he could build on. And if they fell, maybe they could do it together.

Chapter Eight

The next day Lauren moved to her new rental. She did laundry and paid a few bills, filling her time with these mundane tasks to avoid thinking too much about Shane and the kiss they had shared.

It had been a good kiss. The kind she'd like to repeat. The time she had spent at his house, having dinner and getting to know each other, had been some of the best hours she'd had since Mike died. She really liked Shane, but that worried her. She'd fallen too hard and fast for men before, and the breakups had really hurt. She didn't want to go through that pain again.

She was still pondering all this when her phone rang in late afternoon. She didn't recognize the number. "Hello?" she answered, prepared to hang up on a telemarketer.

"Lauren? It's Mindy, from Addison, Simmons and Clark."

"Mindy!" Lauren relaxed. "What can I do for you?"

"I'm not at work and I'm calling from my personal phone, so this isn't an official call," Mindy said. "I probably shouldn't even be talking to you about this, but I'm worried."

Lauren perched on the arm of the floral sofa in the rental. "What's wrong?" she asked. "What are you worried about?"

"Courtney called the office this morning."

Lauren stood again, too agitated to sit. "Is she all right? Did she say where she was calling from?"

"Don't you know where she is?" Mindy asked.

Lauren remembered that she hadn't told Mindy that Courtney was missing. "I haven't seen her in several weeks," she said. "She left town and hasn't been answering my calls or texts. I've been worried sick about her."

"Now I'm even more concerned," Mindy said.

"Why did she call you?" Lauren asked.

"She wanted money from her trust. But not for a house purchase. She said she needed it for medical bills for Ashlyn. And then she started crying."

Lauren's stomach clenched. "What did she say was wrong with Ashlyn?"

"She didn't say. At least not to me. I was hoping you'd know."

"This is the first I've heard about Ashlyn being ill. She was fine when I saw her last." She took a deep breath, trying to rein in her emotions and think logically. "How much money did she ask for?"

"She said she needed ten thousand dollars right away. Mr. Simmons talked to her and said he'd arrange for the funds to be made available. You really don't know anything about this?"

"No." The clinic here in Eagle Mountain had said Ashlyn's visit to them wasn't for anything serious. Had it turned out to be serious after all? "Can you find out where she wanted the money sent?"

"That's supposed to be confidential information," Mindy said. "You know that."

"This could be really important," Lauren said. "I don't trust the man she was hanging out with before she left Denver. I need to find her and make sure she's all right."

"I'm not supposed to snoop, but I'll admit I did," Mindy

said. "I was that concerned about her. You won't tell anyone where you got this information, will you?"

"Not a soul," Lauren promised.

"All right, then. I looked on the computer and she requested the money be wired to a bank in Telluride."

Telluride was only about an hour from Eagle Mountain. So Courtney was still in the area. "Did she leave an address for where she's staying, or information on how to get in touch with her?"

"If she did, it's not in her computer file. And I can't snoop around on Mr. Simmons's desk. I don't want to lose my job."

"Thanks for letting me know all this," Lauren said. "I really appreciate it."

"Let me know what you find out," Mindy said. "I hope Ashlyn is okay."

"I hope so, too." They said goodbye and Lauren sank onto the sofa, feeling hollowed out. Mindy had said Courtney was crying. Her sister-in-law wasn't one to fake something like that. She wasn't manipulative or in the habit of lying to get her way.

She took out her phone and studied it a minute. She had thought it would be a good idea to stay away from Shane for a few days, to give them both time to cool off a little. But she needed his help now. She dialed his cell phone and listened to it ring. After five buzzing rings, a mechanical voice transferred her to Shane's mailbox. "Courtney contacted the trust fund administrator and asked for ten thousand dollars to be wired to a bank in Telluride," Lauren said. "She told them she needed the money for Ashlyn's medical bills. How can we find out where they are, and if Ashlyn is okay?"

She hung up, fighting down panic. Fear gripped her—fear for her niece, and for Courtney. She had promised

Mike she would look out for his widow and his little girl, but right now she was failing miserably.

"COME ON, SHANE, you're gonna show those smoke breathers what real heat feels like!"

"Whoo, Shane! Smoke 'em!"

Shane gave a half-hearted grin and walked toward the mound on the high school baseball field at this first official practice Friday evening, which a number of people had gathered to watch. Baseball wasn't a first-tier sport in a mountain town, where even June games could be snowed out and spring training often had to be moved indoors because of cold weather, and the field showed it. A family of ground squirrels had colonized left field, and the chalk lines for the bases ran over clumps of weeds.

Then again, the players weren't professional level, either, ranging in age from nineteen to fifty, the latter being a reserve deputy who had bragged that he had been a pretty good player back in college. A few decades and many cheeseburgers ago, Shane thought.

Dwight was catching, and fired the ball to Shane on the mound. Shane rubbed it up, the familiar feel of leather comforting. He wound up and hurled a strike over the plate. The crowd applauded and whistled. They were easily impressed, since Shane hadn't even put much energy behind that first warm-up toss. He tossed a few more, gaining confidence. Dwight pantomimed a stinging hand and gave Shane a thumbs-up. "I'm ready," Shane said. "Let's get this show on the road."

The sheriff strode to the batting box and assumed his stance. "Whatever you do, don't hit him!" someone on the sidelines called, and everyone around him laughed.

Shane pitched a strike and Travis didn't move. "Strike one!" the umpire—Bud O'Brien, owner of the local garage—called.

Travis fouled off the next pitch, then Shane threw a ball. He ended up striking out the sheriff, and the next two batters. As he walked off the mound, the spectators cheered. "You looked great out there," Gage said, and slapped him on the back.

"How's your arm?" Dwight asked.

"It's fine," Shane said. "It feels good." It had felt exhilarating out on that dirt mound, too, looking down on the batter's box, cleats digging in as he executed his windup. But it felt a little like cheating, too. Pitching to most of these guys was like pitching to Little Leaguers. He didn't have to bring his best stuff to beat them.

Which was just as well, his ego reminded him. Because his best stuff was long gone.

Gage took over pitching for the next group of batters. He didn't have Shane's speed, but he was pretty accurate, and though fireman Al Tomlinson hit a high fly, Deputy Jamie Douglas caught the ball and fired it back to first.

Shane turned his attention from the game to the crowd filling the rickety bleachers. "Hey, Shane!" Taylor Redmond called and waved to him.

He nodded and looked past her to another group of women. Talia Larrivee and her posse. With a thick-set man with a moustache whom Shane didn't recognize.

Adelaide sidled over to him and followed his gaze to the bleachers. "Who are you looking for?" she asked.

"Nobody," he lied. He had hoped Lauren might show up to watch the practice, but why should she? It sounded as if she didn't follow baseball, and he wasn't sure how she felt about him since that kiss. She had liked the kiss, and she had wanted it at the time, but afterward, she'd been upset. Whether because she had decided she didn't like him that much, or she liked him too much, he wasn't sure.

"Who's that with Talia Larrivee?" he asked.

Adelaide squinted. "I don't know, but I can find out."

"Adelaide, no!"

But she ignored him and made a beeline for the bleachers. A moment later, she stood in front of the couple. The man looked from Adelaide to Shane. He was too far away to clearly make out his expression, but Shane was pretty sure the man wasn't too happy to know a deputy had been asking about him.

Adelaide made her way back to Shane. "He told me his name was none of my business, but right before I got to them, I heard Talia address him as Tom."

"Next time you should be more subtle," Shane said.

"Why? Sometimes the direct approach gets the best results."

"Shane! You're up!"

He headed for the mound, pushing aside thoughts of the mysterious Tom, or Lauren or anyone else.

Two hours later, practice ended and he headed for his house to shower and eat whatever he could find in the refrigerator. He'd turned down an offer to go out with a couple of his teammates, not eager to deal with the crowd of locals who had gathered around to congratulate him. They all wanted to talk about his days as a player, and that wasn't history he cared to relive.

He started to undress, and when he pulled out his phone, he saw that he had missed a call from Lauren. Surprised, and pleased, he punched the code for his voice mail.

"Courtney contacted the trust fund administrator." Tension stretched Lauren's voice and his chest tightened as the message continued. "How can we find out where she is and if Ashlyn is all right?"

He punched in Lauren's number. "I got your message," he said when she answered. "I'll be over in a few minutes and we'll talk about this."

Chapter Nine

Twenty minutes later, Shane was at the door of Lauren's rental. His hair was damp, curling at his temples, and he smelled of soap. "Did I pull you out of the shower?" she asked.

"I had just finished ball practice."

"How did it go?"

He took her hand and squeezed it, his touch gentle and reassuring. "It went fine, but you didn't call me to talk about baseball. What's going on with Courtney?"

"My friend at the lawyer's office called to tell me Courtney got in touch with them. But please don't tell anyone that's how I heard about this. My friend could get into real trouble for breaking a client's confidentiality. She could lose her job."

"I don't see any need to bring her into this," he said. "At least, not now." He led her over to the sofa, the floral upholstery something his grandmother might have owned. "Let's sit down and you can tell me everything. Something about the call concerned your friend enough that she got in touch with you."

Lauren nodded and sat, her hands fisted in her lap. "Courtney said she needed ten thousand dollars right away to pay medical bills for Ashlyn. But the nurse at the clinic here in town said they saw Ashlyn for something minor.

And she's always been a healthy child. But what if she's been in an accident, or she has cancer or something?" She swallowed tears. Now that Shane was here, she was on the verge of giving in to the wild fears that ricocheted through her.

"Isn't Ashlyn covered by medical insurance?" he asked.

The question was like a stiff breeze clearing away fog. "Yes," she said. "She and Courtney are both covered by the military's health insurance—Courtney until she remarries, and Ashlyn until she's twenty-one." She shook her head. "I don't know why I didn't think of it before."

"I can't think of any situation where a medical facility would demand ten thousand dollars before they would treat Ashlyn," he said. "So Courtney wasn't telling the truth about why she needed the money."

Lauren sagged with relief. "So Ashlyn probably isn't sick."

"I don't think so," he said. "I think Courtney made up that story—or maybe Allerton or someone else made it up and convinced her to call and ask for the money, after their first attempt to get cash from her trust failed."

"I don't know how much the man who called before asked for from the trust," she said. "But he said it was to buy a house, and that would cost hundreds of thousands. Why ask for only ten thousand this time?"

"That's the amount of the payment Trey Allerton owes Sam Russell for the lease," Shane said. "Did your friend indicate whether or not the lawyer agreed to send the money?"

"I'm not sure she knows," Lauren said. "I was so upset I forgot to ask. But the information about a bank in Telluride, where Courtney wanted the money sent, was in the file, so that may mean they were going to send it. And I'll bet the lawyer got her contact information, too—a telephone number where he could reach her, and maybe an address, too."

"It would be helpful if your friend could pass that information to us."

Lauren shook her head. "She says it's not in the file, and she's too afraid of losing her job if she's caught snooping in the senior partner's office. But you could find out."

He frowned. "How am I supposed to do that?"

"If you call and say you're searching for Courtney, that she's a missing person, don't they have to give you whatever information they have?" But the look on his face—somewhere between pity and frustration—told her she was wrong.

He raked one hand through his hair. "Look. No attorney is going to reveal information about a client without a warrant requiring him to do so. And no judge is going to authorize a warrant without probable cause that a crime has been committed."

"What kind of proof?"

"A threat. A cry for help. Some evidence that Courtney is in real danger."

"Everything about this situation is wrong," she said. "Courtney and I are friends. We're like sisters. She's closer to me than she is to any of her blood relatives. She wouldn't disappear like this unless she was in big trouble."

"I believe you," he said. "But it's not enough for a judge."

"Courtney wouldn't lie," she said. "She's the daughter of a preacher, and she's the most honest person I know." Her stomach hurt. "So someone either forced her to say those things to the lawyer, or Ashlyn really is ill."

"I don't think Ashlyn is ill," he said. "Do you think Allerton could persuade her to lie for him?"

"I don't know. I don't want to believe it, but if he threatened her or Ashlyn…" She shook her head, not wanting to finish the thought.

"Sometimes people will do uncharacteristic things for people they think they're in love with," he said.

"Courtney isn't in love with Trey Allerton."

"She might believe she is." The gentleness in his voice and his eyes didn't soften the blow of his words. "She's a young woman. She's probably lonely. You've said Allerton came across as charming. He's good-looking. He paid her a lot of attention. She wouldn't be the first person to be taken in under those circumstances."

"I don't believe it. Courtney can be very naive and trusting, but she's not stupid." But was she refusing to believe Courtney had real feelings for Allerton because that was true—or because admitting the possibility felt like a betrayal of her brother? "If you can't get a warrant to get Courtney's contact information from her lawyer, what can you do?" she asked.

He was silent for a long moment, then he said, "I'd like to talk to Samuel Russell again. If he's received the ten thousand dollars Allerton owes, it isn't proof the money came from Courtney, but it is suspicious. And I should speak to any neighbors in the area. Maybe one of them saw or heard something that will give us a clue about the nature of Courtney's relationship with Allerton. I'd also like to find out more about the other couple Sam Russell saw with Courtney and Allerton."

Her spirits lifted a little. "Those are all good ideas," she said. "What can I do to help?"

"Check in with other family and friends and see if Courtney has contacted any of them in the last week or so. I'll let you know what I find out, but don't expect to hear anything right away. I have to do my investigating when I'm off-duty. This isn't an official case."

"Because we don't know if a crime has really been

committed," she said. "I get it." She buried her face in her hands, overwhelmed. "I feel so helpless. And I'm worried if we take too long to find them, Courtney or Ashlyn could end up hurt."

"Do you think Allerton is violent?" he asked.

"I think he could be. I just don't know." To her horror, she started to cry. She jumped up, trying to choke back the tears, but Shane stood also and pulled her into his arms.

"It's okay," he said. "We're going to find them."

She gave in to the sobs, great waves of them. She hadn't wept like this since the weeks right after Mike died. Amid the storm of emotion, she was aware of Shane's strong arms encircling her, of his strong shoulders supporting her. She smelled the clean cotton of the shirt she was soaking with her tears, and felt the soft brush of his lips against her hair. She wanted to cling to him, reveling in the comfort and security of his touch, letting his strength make her stronger. How long had it been since she had felt so cared for?

But was it real affection driving those feelings, or only her need? Doubt was like a burr under her clothes, a distraction she didn't welcome. She pulled away and wiped at her eyes with her fingers. "I'll be okay," she said. "You should go. You must be tired after working all day, then playing baseball."

"It was just a practice," he said. "I'm fine. I can stay awhile longer."

She sniffed and forced a smile. "Really, I'm okay."

He looked as if he wanted to argue but apparently decided against it. "Call me if you need anything. Anytime. I mean it, understand?"

She nodded, and the smile was genuine this time. "Thanks for coming over. Talking to you—and knowing you're going to help—means a lot." She leaned in and kissed him—on the cheek, the rasp of beard stubble against her lips sending a jolt of heat through her.

His eyes met hers, and for the briefest moment she glimpsed how much he wanted her, and she caught her breath. Then he turned away. "We'll talk tomorrow," he said, and left. But she remained frozen in place for a long time, stunned by the strength of his feelings for her—and by her own desire for him.

SAMUEL RUSSELL WELCOMED Shane into his kitchen the next morning. The rancher didn't remark on the early hour— just after eight, but the older man had probably been up hours. In Shane's experience, farmers and ranchers rose at first light or before, in order to do all the work living on the land required. "How about some coffee?" Russell asked as he led the way into a kitchen that looked untouched since the 1970s.

"That would be great." Shane wore jeans and a Rayford County Sheriff's Department T-shirt. He didn't go on duty until three and hoped to learn as much as he could from Russell and his neighbors before then.

Russell brought two mugs of coffee to the square wooden table and sat, and motioned for Shane to do the same. "What can I do for you?" he asked.

Shane cautiously sipped the coffee. It was hot and strong and exactly what he needed. "Have you heard from Trey Allerton or his partner?" he asked.

"Yep." Russell blew on his coffee, then sipped. "Yesterday I got a check for ten thousand dollars." He set down the mug. "To tell you the truth, it surprised me. I haven't seen them around in a few days, so I figured the whole lot might have skipped town."

"Have you seen them since you received the payment?" Shane asked.

Russell shook his head. "Not a whisker."

"Is there anyone else living around here, maybe a neighbor who might have seen or talked to them?"

"You might talk to Robby and Becca Olsen," Russell said. "They have the property on the other side of the piece I leased to Allen and his bunch. They moved out here about a year ago from some city up north and said they were going to live off the land. I thought they'd last maybe a couple of months, but they're still sticking with it. I'll say one thing for them—they aren't afraid of hard work. They built a yurt, of all things, and put up a big greenhouse, got chickens and goats and pigs and who knows what else. I still think it's crazy, but they're nice enough, for all their odd ideas."

Shane finished his coffee, then went in search of the Olsens. He found them setting fence posts around a trio of beehives a few hundred yards from a forest green canvas yurt surrounded by a wood deck. Robby Olsen hailed Shane when he got out of his pickup. "Come on back!" he shouted, then went back to pounding in steel posts.

Shane walked past a chicken house and chicken yard, a pigpen where two very large spotted hogs grunted at him, and a plastic-covered greenhouse three times the size of the yurt. The purple-and-yellow beehives stood out amid the sunburnt grass where they had been situated, and as Shane neared, he heard a low hum from the hives and saw bees filling the air around them.

A young man in cargo shorts and no shirt stepped forward and offered his hand. "I'm Robby Olsen," he said. "Mr. Russell called and said you were coming to see us."

"I'm Becca." The woman, tall and thin, brown skinned with two long braids of black hair, smiled. She wore shorts and a tank top, her nose dusted with freckles.

"I'm Deputy Shane Ellis," he said. "I'm looking for the couple who are leasing a section of the Russell Ranch. I'm wondering if you'd seen them."

Robby removed his leather work gloves and slapped them against his hip, knocking loose a small cloud of dust. "There were two couples over there. They stopped by one day."

"When was this?" Shane asked.

Robby glanced at his wife. "It was this past Tuesday," she said. "I remember because that's my day to deliver eggs and vegetables in town."

"What can you tell me about them?" Shane asked.

"The two men did all the talking," Becca said. "The two women and the little girl didn't have much to say. I asked one of the women if she wanted some chard or onions, and she just shook her head and said, 'No, thank you.' I tried to draw her out a little, asking about where she was from and all, but she wouldn't hardly talk. The other woman, the redhead, just kept her eyes on the older dark-haired man the whole time and ignored me."

Shane took out his notebook and his phone with the photo of Courtney and Ashlyn. "Was this one of the women, and the little girl?" he asked.

The couple put their heads together to view the phone, then both nodded. "That was them," Becca said. "Cute little girl, but she was real shy. Her mother carried her the whole time. I offered to take her to see the chickens, but Mom said no."

"Did they give you their names?" Shane asked.

"The taller, younger man said his name was Troy," Robby said. "The older man was Tom. They didn't introduce the women."

"I thought maybe they were some kind of religious cult or something," Becca said. "But they were dressed normal. The redheaded woman wore a tank top and short shorts, and the other woman and the girl had on pretty sundresses with spaghetti straps. The men had on jeans and polo shirts."

"What did they want?" Shane asked.

"They said they were setting up a ranch on that piece of property next to us and wanted to introduce themselves," Robby said. "But when I tried to find out more, asked where they were from, what they planned to raise on the ranch, and things like that, they changed the subject."

"The way they were looking around, we thought maybe they were checking us out to see what they could steal," Becca said. She hugged her arms over her chest. "I got a bad vibe from the whole bunch. I didn't sleep well for a few nights after their visit, worried they would make trouble."

"What made you think that?" Shane asked.

"They weren't real friendly," Robby said. "And you just get a bad feeling about some people, you know?"

"What did they look like?" Shane asked.

"Troy was fairly tall, with sandy hair," Robby said. "I don't know about his eyes because he kept his sunglasses on the whole time. He was probably in his early thirties, maybe a little younger. The other guy was about forty, a good five inches shorter, and stockier, with dark brown or black hair and an olive complexion. The other woman had long red hair and high cheekbones and long legs."

"She looked like a model," Becca said. "And like she had money. Her clothes were simple, but they looked expensive, and she had gold and diamond jewelry—several rings and earrings and a couple of necklaces."

"Did they say anything about their plans?" Shane asked. "Any details about the ranch or whether or not they planned to live there?"

Robby shook his head. "Troy said he liked our yurt, that it looked more comfortable than the trailer that was on the place they were leasing from Mr. Russell."

"I drive by the entrance to that place a couple of times a week when I go into Eagle Mountain," Becca said. "I haven't seen any sign of anyone over there. I've been meaning to take Mr. Russell some vegetables and eggs and ask him about them, but we've been so busy I haven't had the chance."

"We're putting up an electric fence to keep the bears out of the beehives," Robby said. "We had a big sow snooping around here last week. She got a good jolt from the fence around the pigs and ran out of here."

"I hope that scared her off for good," Becca said. "But we know there are others out there."

Shane looked around, at the greenhouse and livestock, and the yurt, with its deck dotted with pots of flowers and brightly painted chairs. Behind the yurt he glimpsed a solar array. "You have a nice place here," he said. "Are you off-grid?"

"We are," Robby said. "We have a generator for backup, but mostly we run off solar. And we'd like to put in a wind turbine one day."

Shane took out a card and passed it over. "Let me know if Troy or Tom or the women stop by again."

"Are they wanted for some crime?" Becca asked. "Should we be worried?"

"The blonde woman's family is worried about her," Shane said. "I agreed to contact her if I could, and make sure she was all right."

"She looked okay when we saw her," Becca said. "I mean, she was clean and well-fed and didn't look upset about anything. She was just very quiet." She shrugged. "But some people are quiet. No law against that."

They said goodbye and went back to setting metal posts. Shane walked back to his truck. Was he wasting time, trying to track down Allerton and Courtney? Maybe some people would see it that way, but it would be worth all the hours and effort if he was able to give Lauren some peace of mind. Even hard truth would be better than not knowing.

Chapter Ten

Shane's text to Lauren on Sunday afternoon was cryptic: Meet me my place 6:30 to catch up.

Not exactly an invitation for a romantic rendezvous. She ought to be relieved that he was respecting her request to put some distance between them. Instead, she felt vaguely annoyed. How attracted to her was he if it was so easy for him to switch back to behaving as if their only connection was the case?

As soon as she responded that she'd be there, he replied: I'll get dinner.

Okay. Should she bring wine? Or dessert? Or was that too casual? Too intimate?

She ended up stopping at a bakery and picking up half a dozen cookies. She might have done the same for a meeting at the clinic. She was really overthinking this.

Shane was waiting for her when she arrived, fresh from the shower in jeans and a T-shirt, smelling of soap and aftershave, a combination that made her hyperaware of how masculine and sexy he was. Her gaze fixed on the hint of collarbone visible at the neckline of his shirt, the skin smooth over the bone and looking soft as velvet...

"Lauren? Are you okay?"

She blinked and met his puzzled gaze. "I'm fine." She took a step back and fixed her gaze on the kitchen table, where a bag from a local sandwich shop sat. "What did you get for dinner?"

"Sub sandwiches and chips." He followed her to the table. "There's water or beer, whichever you want."

"Water is fine." She pulled out a chair and sat. She was doing it again—getting obsessed with a man she had just met. Sure, he might profess to be just as interested in her, but those kinds of feelings never lasted. Real relationships took time to nurture and develop, and she didn't have that kind of time to spend in Eagle Mountain. She was here to find Courtney, and she needed to focus on that mission, not Shane.

"What have you found out about Courtney?" she asked when he returned to the table with two glasses of water.

"I stopped by the Russell Ranch before work yesterday." He settled into the chair across from her. "Mr. Russell hadn't seen her, or Trey. But he did receive a check for ten thousand dollars two days ago—the deadline for making the next lease payment. So I think we know how the money Courtney asked for was used."

A weight settled in Lauren's stomach. "I'm relieved Ashlyn isn't really sick, though I guess I already knew that. But it hurts to know Courtney lied. That isn't like her at all."

"Maybe you have an idealized version of your sister-in-law," he said. "It's not wrong to want to think the best of people, and she probably only showed you her best side. But that doesn't mean this other side of her hasn't been there all along."

"Maybe." Lauren popped a potato chip into her mouth and crunched it. Shane was a cop, and his job probably forced him to be cynical about people's intentions. But she knew Courtney wasn't dishonest. "I think Trey Allerton forced her to tell those lies," she said. "He either played on her sympathy and made her believe he was desperate and had to have her help, or worse, he bullied her or threatened her to make her do what he wanted." She met Shane's gaze, wanting him to see how concerned she was. "We won't know until we find her, and if he's threatening her, we really need to find her soon."

He nodded and picked up his sandwich. "I visited the neighbors who live on the other side of the property Allerton leased from Samuel Russell," he said. "A young couple who are homesteading the property, Becca and Robby Olsen. They live in a yurt, and they said Allerton, Courtney, Ashlyn and another couple stopped by there last Tuesday."

Lauren choked on the bite of sandwich she was chewing. As she coughed, Shane hurried around to pound her back. She took a swig of water and waited for the spasm to calm, then said, "Are they living at the ranch? Did you check there?"

"I stopped by there on the way out, but there's still no sign of them in that old trailer, or anywhere else that I could see." He returned to his chair. "The other couple with Allerton and Courtney sound like the ones Mr. Russell described—a dark-haired, stocky man and a tall redhead. They identified Courtney and Ashlyn from your photo. Becca said the redheaded woman with them had expensive clothing and jewelry and looked like a model."

"That sounds like Talia Larrivee," Lauren said. "That's how I would describe her."

Shane froze in the act of raising his sandwich to his lips. "I hadn't thought of that," he said. "And the man— forties, stocky, with dark hair and olive skin—that sounds like the man Talia was with at ball practice the other day. And she called him Tom. That's the name Allerton's partner was using. I feel like an idiot for not making the connection before."

"You've seen this man?" Lauren leaned toward him.

"Do you think Trey was with him then? Was he with another man?"

"He was with Talia," Shane said. "I didn't see him talking to or interacting with anyone else."

"But you were focused on playing baseball," she said. "Maybe Trey, and Courtney, too, were there and you didn't notice." She stood. "We need to talk to other people who were at that practice. Maybe someone noticed them. They can at least tell us if Courtney and Ashlyn are okay."

"They weren't there," Shane said. "And as of last Tuesday, at least, Courtney and Ashlyn were fine. Becca Olsen described them as clean, well-fed and quiet."

"I imagine prisoners get described that way sometimes." She sat back down. She hated this frustration, of knowing something was wrong but being unable to persuade anyone else of her suspicions. "How did Trey and Courtney end up with Talia and this Tom fellow?" she asked.

"I'm pretty sure Talia's father has a house in Denver. Maybe Courtney and Talia met there. They're close to the same age."

"And have nothing in common," Lauren said. "Courtney is a mom and a homebody. And she doesn't care about fancy clothes or jewelry."

"Opposites attract in friendship as well as romance," he said. "Or maybe Allerton and Tom know each other and Allerton brought him in because he needed a partner for his youth ranch."

"He told Courtney he and Mike planned to partner to build the ranch," Lauren said. "He wanted her to be part of the project in Mike's place. I really think that's the only reason she agreed to the plan—because she thought it was what Mike wanted."

He was giving her that look again—part sympathy and part skepticism. "I know you think I'm only seeing what I want to see," she said. "But Courtney is not in love with

Trey. Maybe she's physically attracted to him, and I get that she might enjoy having him pay attention to her. But I saw the way she looked at my brother, before and after they were married, and she never looked at Allerton that way. Not even close."

"Even if she isn't in love with him, she may have agreed to partner with him in the ranch because she wanted to help young people," Shane said. "Or she thought it would give her purpose in life, or allow her to make a fresh start or any of a dozen other legitimate reasons."

"But we'll need to talk to her to find that out," Lauren said. She crunched another chip. "So what do we do next?"

"I need to see what else I can find out about Tom," he said. "I'll stop by Russell Ranch and see if I can talk to Mr. Russell again."

"What can I do?" she asked.

"Get in touch with some of Courtney's other friends. Ask if they ever heard her mention Talia or Tom. And talk to your friend at the law office. Tell her to call you if Courtney requests more money from her trust."

"Should I tell her we suspect Courtney is lying about what the money is being used for?"

"I'll leave that up to you."

It felt like a betrayal, to accuse Courtney of lying that way. What she had done might even be illegal. "I don't think I'll say any more than I have to right now," she said. One day—she hoped soon—Courtney would want to come home and settle into her old life again. Lauren wanted to make that transition as smooth as possible.

"There's nothing else we can do tonight," he said. "Let's just enjoy our meal and talk about something else."

"All right. Tell me about this Independence Day celebration. I've seen posters around town. Besides the baseball game between the sheriff's department and the fire department, what else happens? Fireworks?"

He nodded and finished chewing. "There's a big fireworks show after dark, against the backdrop of Dakota Ridge. A parade in the morning."

"A parade? Like, with floats and marching bands?"

"One band, from the high school, and the floats are mostly just pickup trucks towing flatbed trailers with people on the back throwing out candy. But there are people on horseback and kids on bikes and people waving flags. It's one of those small-town things."

"It sounds charming," she said. "I'll be sure not to miss it."

"The history museum hands out lemonade and dresses in old-timey outfits in front of the museum," he said. "And the Elks sell barbecue in the park. The 4-H kids set up a carnival with face painting and little games and a dunking booth."

"When is the baseball game?" she asked. "And where is it?"

"The only field in town is at the high school," he said. "The game is at three o'clock on Sunday. They used to play in old-timey gray flannel uniforms and flat caps, but the uniforms wore out after a few years, and they were so hot and uncomfortable that guys refused to play if they couldn't wear jeans and T-shirts, so the committee gave in."

"Do a lot of people attend?" she asked.

"Seems like," he said. "Adelaide tells me they're selling tickets as fast as they can print them. She's looking for volunteers to sell concessions at the game. Sign up and you'll get in free."

"Maybe I'll do that." It would probably be better than watching by herself in the stands.

His phone rang, dancing across the tabletop as it vibrated. He picked it up and frowned at the screen. "It's the sheriff," he said.

She went to refill their water glasses while he answered the call. When she returned, he was holding the phone, looking disturbed. "What did the sheriff want?" she asked.

"He's asking everyone to report for duty," he said. "Evan Larrivee called and said Talia called him and said she was scared and in trouble. Now he doesn't know where she is."

Chapter Eleven

Sheriff Travis Walker assembled his force in the conference room at headquarters Sunday evening, his usual solemn expression betraying nothing. "Evan Larrivee called my personal number a little after six this evening to report that he had a very concerning phone call from his daughter, Talia. She told him she was afraid and begged him to come get her, but before she could say where she was, the connection broke off. He hasn't been able to reach her since."

"He called your personal number?" Gage asked. "Not Dispatch?"

"He didn't want to raise an alarm," Travis said. "But after talking to him, I think there might be reason for concern."

Several of the deputies exchanged looks. "What's happened?" Jamie Douglas, the force's only female deputy, asked.

"The last time Evan saw Talia was two days ago," Travis said. "She said she was going on a trip into the mountains with friends, but when Evan asked her who these friends were, her answer was 'You wouldn't know them.' He didn't hear anything from her until her frantic phone call this evening. He said she sounded really scared, but before he could find out more, the call ended. He couldn't say whether the call dropped, or someone took the phone from her."

"Where were Talia and these friends headed?" Dwight asked.

"She wouldn't say," Travis said. "Evan says that's unusual. He says Talia is always trying to shock him with stories about her wild adventures and rarely withholds information, though she's been known to embellish. He got the sense she was hiding something, and that worried him."

"She was at ball practice Friday evening," Gage said. "With a man I'd never seen before."

"Adelaide said she overheard Talia call the guy Tom," Shane said. "And I'm pretty sure the two of them were up at Robby and Becca Olsen's place, out by Samuel Russell's ranch, last Wednesday, with Courtney Baker and Trey Allerton."

Every eye in the room focused on him. "Courtney Baker is Lauren Baker's sister-in-law," Travis said. "Lauren came to Eagle Mountain from Denver to look for her and asked for our help, but we couldn't find any evidence of foul play, or that Courtney left with Allerton of anything but her own accord."

"In my spare time, I've been helping Lauren trace Courtney's footsteps," Shane explained. "Yesterday morning, I talked to the Olsens, and they told me about seeing Allerton and Courtney on Tuesday with a man called Tom and a red-haired woman in expensive clothes who looked like a model."

"That sounds like Talia," Gage said.

"I thought so, too," Shane said. Especially after Lauren had pointed it out to him.

"Talia has had a lot of different male friends," Dwight said. "Is there any reason to be particularly concerned about this one?"

"Evan said when he asked her why she wouldn't tell

him the names of the people she was with, she said, 'My new boyfriend wouldn't like it.' After he received that last call from her, he drove around town and found her car in the high school lot, and someone told him it's been there since Friday afternoon."

"Could this be Talia playing a trick on her dad?" Jamie asked. "Trying to get attention?"

"He says no, that he's convinced she was truly terrified when she contacted him," Travis said. "I want everyone to keep an eye out for her. Talk to people who might have seen her and follow up on any leads. If she's just rebelling against her father's authority with friends he wouldn't approve of, we'll find that out soon enough. But if she's in real trouble, we want to be in the best position to help her." He turned to Shane. "What were Courtney and her friends doing up by the Olsens?"

"Trey Allerton leased a section of the Russell Ranch that borders the Olsens' property," Shane said. "He says he wants to turn it into a retreat for troubled youth. He talked Courtney Baker into contributing money to the project, and he's introduced this Tom guy as his business partner."

"Any reason to suspect the retreat is a cover for something else?" Gage asked.

Shane shook his head. "There's no sign of any work being done on the property they leased, but maybe they're waiting for more funding or plans or something. The only thing suspicious is that Courtney Baker lied to get the money for the second lease payment. She told the lawyers who manage her trust fund that she needed ten thousand dollars to pay her daughter's medical bills. That's the exact amount of the payment Allerton made to Russell the day after Courtney withdrew the money."

"Did you talk to Sam Russell about all of this?" Travis asked.

"I did. He said Tom didn't say much—Allerton did all

the talking. But he said Tom had prison tattoos. He recognized them because he's had ex-cons work for him on the ranch."

"That surprises me a little," Gage said. "Not that Tom has prison ink, but that Russell hires ex-cons."

"He said he believes in giving people a second chance."

"Let's see if we can get a last name for Tom and find out if he has a criminal record," Travis said. "Shane, you come with me to talk to Larrivee. Let's see what he knows about Tom, and Talia's other new friends."

EVAN LARRIVEE HAD a shaved head, a neatly trimmed goatee showing the first signs of gray and the sagging features of a man who has not slept well. "I know Talia can be very high-spirited," he said when Travis and Shane stopped by his home to interview him. "She's done things before that worried me, but this feels different."

"You said before that your daughter is twenty-two," Travis said. "Has she gone off like this before?"

"I know what you're thinking," Larrivee said. "She's an adult. She doesn't have to report to me. But as long as she lives under my roof and I support her, she does." He visibly reined in his emotions. "That may sound antagonistic, and I don't mean it to. Talia and I have a good relationship. When she called me to ask for help, it's because she knew I would drop everything to get to her. If only I knew where she was." His voice broke and he looked away.

"What friends does she go off with?" Travis asked.

Larrivee pulled himself together. "Girlfriends, mostly," he said. "She has two or three she pals around with. But I already talked to them and they haven't heard from her, either."

"We'll need their names so we can talk to them," Travis said.

"Fine, but they don't know anything. You need to find the people she's with."

"Who is that?" Shane asked.

"If I knew that, I wouldn't have bothered you people," Larrivee said.

"But you believe Talia isn't alone?" Travis asked. "That she is with other people? What can you tell us about them?"

Larrivee shook his head. "I never met them. She mentioned a new boyfriend but wouldn't tell me his name. I finally got one of her friends to admit that there was a man, and she thinks his name is Tom, but she swore that's all she knew."

Travis pulled out his phone. "What's the friend's name?" he asked.

"Anne-Marie Winstead Jones," Larrivee said. "She said she saw Talia with the man once and he looked kind of rough."

"Rough how?" Shane asked.

Larrivee shrugged. "Just...rough. And older. Late thirties or early forties, she said." He pressed his lips together in a thin line.

"Has your daughter dated older men before?" Shane asked.

"No. And from what Anne-Marie told me, this guy was no looker. Talia can have her pick of men, but she's young. She likes to have fun. Which is another reason I don't understand her association with this guy. He's not her usual type."

"What is her type?" Travis asked.

"You know—young, like her. With enough money to show her a good time. And good-looking. She dates athletes—rock climbers, skiers, that kind of thing. She likes dare-devils and risk takers, but this guy sounded different."

"Is it possible this Tom targeted your daughter?" Shane

asked. "Maybe he charmed her because he's interested in her money."

"My daughter is used to dealing with fortune hunters," Larrivee said. "I taught her about them from the time she was a young teen. She's dated a lot of men, but if they show a hint of being interested in her money, she drops them like that." He snapped his fingers.

"You mentioned you believed your daughter left with more than one person," Travis said. "Who are the other people involved?"

"I don't know. Before she left, she said she was going off for a few days with friends. When I asked her who these friends were, she said she couldn't tell me, that her new boyfriend wouldn't like it. That set off all kinds of alarm bells, I tell you. But when I tried to question her further, she told me she'd call me later, and she hung up. Since then, all my calls go straight to voice mail and she doesn't respond to my texts, either." Some of the authority went out of his voice. "I'm really worried."

Travis made a few notes on his phone, then tucked it away. "We'd like to see your daughter's room," he said.

"This way." Larrivee led the way up a curving flight of stairs. "I already searched it. I didn't find anything but a little pot and some cigarettes. I don't approve of either and Talia knows it, which was probably why they were hidden, but they're not illegal here, so there's not too much I can do about them except order her not to use them in my presence."

Talia Larrivee's room—or rather, a suite of rooms—occupied a large portion of the second floor, with a bedroom, large sitting room, smaller dressing room and wardrobe, and an expansive bathroom. "Does she keep a datebook or diary?" Travis asked.

Larrivee snorted. "That's all on her phone, and she

has that with her. Though the tracking software has been turned off."

At Shane's startled look, Larrivee laughed. "I designed that software, Deputy. Of course I had it on my daughter's phone. But someone switched it off or removed it outright."

"Would Talia know how to do that?" Travis asked.

"She would," he said. "She might come across as an airhead, but my daughter is very smart."

"We'd like to have a look around, if you don't mind," Travis said.

"Don't you need a warrant for that?" Larrivee asked.

"I can get one, if that would make you feel better," Travis said, his expression deadpan, as usual.

"Nothing is going to make me feel better except finding my little girl," Larrivee said. He stepped back. "Go ahead. I've already seen everything in here, anyway." He moved to the door. "I'll be downstairs if you need me."

When he was gone, Travis pulled on a pair of gloves and moved to the desk. "What do you think?" he asked Shane.

Shane, who was slipping on his own gloves, said, "A twenty-two-year-old whose father still lays down the law and controls the purse strings, and who doesn't think twice about going through her personal belongings—I think most people would rebel against that at some point."

"So she could just be asserting her independence by going away for a few days with a man she knows Daddy won't approve of." Travis began thumbing through the books on the bedside table. "That doesn't explain the frantic phone call. And she seems to have crossed paths with another woman who left suddenly with a man her relatives—or one relative, at least—didn't like, who is also refusing to return calls." He shook his head. "I don't like coincidences like that."

"We don't know that any of them are breaking any laws," Shane said. He swept his hand under the edge of a bookshelf, searching for anything that might be taped under there.

"No, but they might be on the edge of illegal," Travis said. "I'd like to know for sure."

"The lease of the land from Russell is legitimate," Shane said. "Though there's no sign of any work being done on the place. Could the youth ranch idea be a cover for something else?"

"You say Courtney Baker has money?"

"Several million, according to Lauren," Shane said. "But most of it is tied up in a trust."

"Maybe Allerton thinks he can get control of the trust." Travis opened the top drawer of the dresser.

"Where does Tom come in?" Shane asked. "According to Russell, he didn't have much to say, but Allerton introduced him as his partner."

"Don't know," Travis said. He pulled out the drawer and lifted it up to peer under it. "There's something here."

Shane joined him, and Travis handed him the drawer, then took out his phone and photographed the bottom of it. He pocketed the phone once more and retrieved his pocketknife, which he used to pry off a small brown envelope that was taped to the underside of the dresser drawer. He laid it on the top of the dresser and, with gloved fingers, teased open the flap.

The picture inside was a woman, naked except for a lacy pink bra, her hands tied in front of her with rope, and more rope wound around and around her, a black cloth gag in her mouth. She lay on a bed, dark hair in a tangle on the pillow around her, her skin very white against dark sheets. She stared at the camera, eyes wide with terror.

"That isn't Courtney Baker or Talia Larrivee," Shane said.

"No." Travis slid the photo back into the envelope. "But

we need to find out who this is. Larrivee may be right—his daughter may be involved in something dangerous."

MONDAY MORNING, LAUREN inched her car along the rough gravel road that wound up the mountain, past the Russell Ranch. Had she missed the turnoff to the little trailer she and Shane had visited? It had seemed so easy to get to when she was with him, but today everything looked different.

She hadn't told Shane she planned to drive out here. If Courtney and Trey were leasing this place, then she had a right to visit, didn't she? Maybe she'd get lucky and Courtney would be here. Lauren would try to persuade her to come back to town with her. Maybe she would invite Courtney and Ashlyn to have lunch, and once she had them alone, she'd persuade her sister-in-law to return to Denver with her. At the very least, she could hear from Courtney herself what was really going on.

If Courtney and Trey weren't at the trailer or nearby, Lauren would do a more thorough search and hope to find evidence of where they might be. If she found anything, she'd share the information with Shane, but if she didn't, there was no need for him to know she had even been here.

The Prius rattled across the cattle guard, and she spotted the driveway to the right and turned in. Up a small rise and the trailer rose into view, ugly and abandoned. No vehicle waited in the driveway, and the windows stared vacantly at the barren yard. Lauren parked her car in the shade of a leaning juniper and got out, the echo of the car door slamming making her flinch. If Courtney and Allerton were anywhere within hearing distance, they would know someone had stopped by. She hoped they would come to find out who.

Every nerve taut, she crossed to the steps and mounted them. The door swung open easily, and she stepped inside.

At first glance, it seemed nothing had changed since she had been here with Shane. Trash still littered the mud-colored carpet, and the broken chair still leaned to one side in the corner. Lauren wrinkled her nose in disgust. If Courtney really was planning to live here with Trey and Ashlyn, she would have started cleaning right away. She would have thrown out every stick of furniture in the place and filled the rooms with simple, but tasteful, items she chose. The new furnishings wouldn't necessarily be expensive, but they would be comfortable, sturdy and pleasing to the eye. Courtney wasn't flashy or extravagant, but she had a knack for making a place into a home. Mike had always said that if he decided on a career in the military, Courtney would be able to make anywhere he was stationed warm and comfortable.

Lauren moved toward the bedroom and bathroom where she had found Ashlyn's doll when she had been here before. The first time she had met Courtney, she had been impressed by the young woman's combination of striking beauty and humble sweetness. And by how utterly besotted Mike was with his new girlfriend. Mike was handsome and outgoing and had dated many women, most of them very nice. But Lauren knew something was different between him and Courtney from that very first meeting. Mike couldn't take his eyes off Courtney, and when he spoke about her, his voice took on a tone of mingled pride and reverence.

"I think she's the woman I want to spend the rest of my life with," he had confided to Lauren a few weeks later. "I've never met anyone like her, and I think she feels the same about me."

Indeed, Courtney had been every bit as devoted to Mike. Had that devotion, even after Mike's death, colored her judgment? "Did Mike ever mention anything to you about Trey Allerton and this youth ranch?" Lauren had asked the last time the two women had spoken, after Courtney had announced that she had decided to be a part of Allerton's plans.

"No," Courtney admitted.

"Don't you think if this project was as dear to his heart as Allerton is trying to get you to believe, Mike would have said something to you?" Lauren asked. "He didn't hide things from you, did he?"

"Not that I know of, but maybe he was saving this to tell me when he came home. You know how generous Mike was, and how much he loved children. This is exactly the kind of project he'd be excited about."

Courtney was right. Mike would have loved the idea of a ranch in the mountains where kids could come to relax and get away from their problems, and maybe learn new coping skills or discover new strengths. But Lauren couldn't believe her brother had trusted someone like Trey Allerton. "I'm worried about you trusting too much in Trey," she told Courtney. "I think he's only interested in your money."

"The money isn't even mine," Courtney said. "It was Mike's money, and I want to do something with it to make him proud. I know you think I'm naive about people because I choose to believe the best in them, but I'm not stupid."

Lauren heard the hurt behind the words. "I know you're not stupid," she said, her voice gentle.

Courtney smiled and squeezed Lauren's hand. "Thank you for that. But sometimes your feelings show so clearly in your eyes. I'm going to be all right, you'll see. I don't even care if this wasn't Mike's dream. I know it's something he would approve of, so I'm going to do my best to make it happen."

"But how are you making it happen?" Lauren asked out loud. She looked around the deserted bedroom. "By lying to get money? By refusing to return calls and texts from the people who love you?"

A sound behind her made her turn around. A wiry man in dirty jeans and a faded plaid shirt stood in the doorway to the bedroom. "Who are you?" he demanded. Then he reached behind him and drew a pistol from a holster at his back and aimed the gun at her. "Around here, we shoot trespassers."

Chapter Twelve

Lauren froze, heart hammering, gaze locked on the gun. "What are you doing?" she asked, angry at the tremor in her voice but unable to control it.

"I asked you first. What are you doing here?" The rangy man jabbed the gun in her direction.

She flinched. "I'm looking for my sister-in-law, Courtney."

"What makes you think she's here? Nobody's here. You're trespassing on private property."

Lauren kept her gaze on the gun and stood up straighter, mustering her courage. "You're the one who's trespassing. My sister and her...her business partner leased this property from Mr. Russell."

"So you know about that, do you?"

"Who are you, and what are you doing here?"

"My name's King—Von King. Mr. Allen hired me to do some work on the place and to keep an eye on it while he's away."

Mr. Allen. He must mean Trey Allerton. "Where is he?" she asked. "I need to talk to him." She had nothing to say to Allerton, but she desperately wanted to speak to Courtney.

King shoved the pistol back in its holster. "It's above my pay grade to keep track of his comings and goings. And if you're such good friends with him, why don't you know?"

"I never said I was friends with him. But I'm good friends with Courtney."

"Who's Courtney?"

"She's the woman who's traveling with Allerton. Short, blonde, with blue eyes. She has a little girl."

The wicked glint in King's eyes made her shrink back. "So that's her name," he said.

"You've seen her?"

He leered. "A man's not likely to forget a woman who looks like that."

"I need to speak with her. Tell me Allerton's number and I'll call him."

"You keep calling him Allerton, but he told me his name is Allen."

She said nothing, merely glared at him.

King grinned, revealing gaps where half a dozen teeth were missing. "That's okay," he said. "My real name isn't King, either."

He turned away, his laughter trailing him all the way to his truck. He slammed the door, the engine roared to life and he raced away, kicking up a rooster tail of dust. Lauren leaned against the bedroom wall and stared out the window after him. Inside, she was shaking, with anger and with fear.

SHANE COULDN'T ERASE the image of that terrified bound woman from his memory, even long after he had left the sheriff's department and headed out to question Robby and Becca Olsen again. The image itself was disturbing enough, but why had Talia had it at all? And why had she concealed it under that dresser drawer? When they had shown the photo to Evan Larrivee, he had recoiled, visibly shaken. "I've never seen that before," he said. "It's not of anyone we know, I'm sure. Why would Talia have that?"

By the time Travis and Shane had left the Larrivee

home Sunday evening, Evan was already rationalizing the discovery of the picture. "It could have been taped under that drawer for years," he said. "I'm sure it has nothing to do with Talia."

Shane was sure the picture had not been there long. The tape holding it looked fresh, and the image itself wasn't yellowed or faded with age.

He passed the entrance to the Russell Ranch. He needed to talk to Russell again, but he wanted to interview the Olsens again first. They had seen Tom and company most recently. He tried to focus on the interview ahead. He needed the Olsens to go over every detail of their visit with Tom, Courtney, Trey and a woman he believed was Talia. He had a good photo of Talia to show them, and he hoped they would remember something one of the four had said to indicate where they might be staying.

He rounded a curve and braked hard as a car raced toward him, the driver straddling the center of the narrow gravel road, driving much too fast. He bumped the siren so that it let out a single whoop as a warning, and the car skidded to the side and came to a stop on the shoulder. He pulled alongside it and was startled to see Lauren, fumbling with her seat belt.

By the time he unfastened his own seat belt and opened the car door, she was standing alongside him. "Thank God I ran into you," she said. The words came out in a rush and she was breathless.

He slid out of the vehicle and took her by the shoulders. "What's wrong?" he asked. "What's happened?"

She glanced over her shoulder, then relaxed a little, as if she'd been worried someone was following her. "Did another car pass you, headed out?" she asked. "Or maybe a truck? Yes, I'm sure it was a truck."

"Yours is the first vehicle I've met," he said. "Come

on." He led her around to the passenger side of the cruiser. "Get in and tell me what this is about."

She slid into the seat, and he retrieved a bottle of water from a cooler in the rear of the cruiser, then returned to the driver's seat and handed it to her. She didn't open it but held it in both hands and turned toward him. "I drove out to the place Trey is leasing from Samuel Russell," she said. "I wanted to look at the trailer again and see if I could find any indication that Courtney had been there recently. Really, I was hoping she and Trey would be there and I could talk to them."

"Lauren—" he began, but she cut him off.

"If you're going to tell me I shouldn't have gone out there alone, don't waste your breath. I couldn't sit in that rental one more minute without doing something and I'm fine."

She hadn't been fine when she first flagged him down, but he decided he'd be better off keeping quiet and letting her talk. He merely nodded to indicate she should keep going.

"The trailer was open, so I went inside. Honestly, the place is a pit. I can't see Courtney in it—she's always kept such a nice house, and she'd be miserable so far from town, with no close neighbors."

"We don't know that they planned to live there," he said.

"You're right." She sighed. "And I didn't see any sign that anyone had been there since you and I checked it out on Wednesday. I was ready to leave when the man came in behind me and threatened me with a gun."

Anger and shock climbed up Shane's spine. "Are you okay? Who was this guy?"

"I'm fine." She knotted her hands together. "He scared me, but after I talked to him a bit, he put the gun away. He said his name was Von King, and that Trey Allerton—only he called him Troy Allen—had hired him to look after the place he was leasing from Russell. And then, before he left, he said his name wasn't really Von King."

"What did he look like?" Shane took out his phone and began making notes.

"He was medium height, thin and wiry, with thinning dirty-blond hair."

"How old?" Shane asked.

"I'm not sure. Forties? Maybe older, maybe younger. He needed a shave and his beard had some gray in it, but he looked like a man who spent a lot of time out of doors and had lived a hard life—leathery skin with a lot of wrinkles."

"What did he say to you?"

"He knew Courtney." She frowned. "He made some comment about how pretty she was. I tried to get him to tell me how to get in touch with her or with Trey, but he wouldn't answer. He just put the gun away and left. I did, too. I was worried he might follow me, but I don't know where he went." She opened the bottle of water and took a long drink, then settled back in the seat. "What are you doing out here?"

"I was on my way to speak to the Olsens," he said.

"Let me go with you," she said. "I want to know if they remember anything else about Courtney and Ashlyn."

He wanted to tell her to go back to her rental and wait for him, but her description of her encounter with Von King disturbed him, and he didn't think it would be a bad idea to keep her close for a little while longer. "All right," he said. "Do you want to follow me in your car, or ride in the cruiser?"

"My car should be all right parked here, shouldn't it?" She smiled. "I'll feel better riding with you."

The thought cheered him, though she was probably only saying that because he was a cop. They passed no other vehicles on the drive to the Olsens' and pulled up to the yurt a few moments later. "Hello!" Shane called as he climbed out of the cruiser.

"I don't see anyone around," Lauren said. Somewhere to their left, a chicken squawked, but otherwise, all was silent.

"Maybe they're in the house," Shane said. He strode to the front door and knocked.

No one answered. "What now?" Lauren asked when he returned to the cruiser.

"Let's see if we can find another neighbor," he said. "Maybe Allerton and company visited them, too."

He turned left out of the Olsens' driveway and continued on the same road, which became much rougher after they passed the fence marking the end of the Olsens' property. The grade grew steeper, climbing into the mountains near the tree line. They passed the weathered wooden frame and rusting cable of an old mine tram, and a pile of rubble that might have once been a cabin. "I can't imagine living in such rugged country," Lauren said. "It's beautiful this time of year, but I'm imagining how it must look in winter."

"There's a lot of snow at this elevation," he said. "And I'm pretty sure the county doesn't plow past Russell's driveway."

"How do people get around?"

"Snowmobile, or they plow for themselves. It takes an independent personality to live up here year round. But then, that's the type who end up here. They're willing to trade the inconveniences for cheaper land and few regulations."

He slowed as he neared a hand-painted sign at the end of a faint track leading across rocky ground. Full Moon Mine. No Trespassing. Owner Is Armed.

"Not exactly welcoming," Lauren said.

"No, but someone with an attitude like that is likely to remember anyone who stopped by." Shane swung the cruiser into the drive. He drove slowly for half a mile over increasingly rough ground, passing two more No Trespassing signs, one of which featured a drawing of a skull.

At the top of the hill, Shane stopped the cruiser in front of a shack made of split logs set on end, a rusting metal roof sloping steeply over a door made from a larger slab of wood. Shane maneuvered the cruiser so that it faced back the way they had come, and he left the engine running. "Stay here until I've checked this out," he said.

"You're making me nervous," she said, aware of the tension radiating from him.

"I'm just being cautious." As he exited the cruiser, the door of the shack swung open and a man dressed in canvas pants and a dirty gray shirt stepped out, a long gun cradled in his arms.

"You're trespassing," he said in a loud, clear voice. "You've got thirty seconds to get back in that vehicle and leave."

"Are you Martin Kramer?" Shane asked. He sounded relaxed, but his spine had stiffened, and one hand hovered over the pistol at his side.

"Who wants to know?"

"Deputy Sheriff Shane Ellis. I need you to put the gun down, sir."

"What are you going to do if I don't? Shoot me?"

"Please, put the gun away, sir," Shane said. "I'm looking for some people who may have stopped by here."

The wrinkles running across Kramer's face like gullies deepened, but he set the gun aside, leaning it against the wall of the shack. "I get all kinds of people come through here," he said. "You ought to do your job and arrest them for trespassing."

"Are you Martin Kramer?" Shane asked again. "I like to know who I'm talking to."

"I'm him," Kramer said. "What has this bunch you're looking for done?"

"I just need to talk to them," Shane said. "Have you had any visitors in the last couple of weeks? Two men, maybe with two women. They may also have had a little girl."

"Who's that in the car with you?" Kramer jerked his head toward Lauren. "Tell her to come out where I can see her."

"Come on out, Lauren," Shane said, his gaze still fixed on Kramer.

Lauren got out of the cruiser. "Hello," she said, walking around to stand near Shane. "I'm Lauren. One of the women we're looking for is my brother's widow. The little girl is my niece. I've been really worried about them."

"Is she the blonde or the redhead?" Kramer asked.

Lauren's heart lurched. "You've seen them? They were here?"

Kramer looked skyward. "What is it with you people who can't answer a direct question?"

"Courtney is blonde," Lauren said. She glanced at Shane. He hadn't moved, gaze still locked on Kramer, right hand near the pistol. This is what it's like being a deputy, she thought. Always alert for trouble.

"When were they here?" Shane asked.

"Three or four days ago. Two men—a big young guy who did all the talking, a shorter, darker man and two good-looking women and a little girl. I told them to clear on out, but the big one was like you—he didn't listen. He asked a lot of nosy questions about my operation—stuff that was none of his business. I had to fire a warning shot to get him to shut up and leave."

"Your operation?" Shane asked.

"My gold mine. I'm not some crazy hermit who thought it would be fun to live in a shack on a mountain. I work for a living. But it's not enough that I have to break my back in the mine—I've got to contend with trespassers and thieves?"

"Who's been stealing from you and what have they stolen?" Shane asked.

"That big guy with all his questions about the mine was a claim jumper or my name is Shirley Temple," Kramer said. "People think that kind of thing died out with the Old West, but greed never goes extinct."

"How would they steal your claim?" Lauren asked. "Did they threaten you?"

"They knew better than that," he said. "I had a gun and they didn't, or at least they didn't have one out where I could see it. But nowadays thieves don't need weapons to take what isn't theirs. They find out all about you and the claim, then they go on the computer and file papers and such, and the next thing you know, they've robbed you blind. I've known it to happen to other folks, but by gum, I won't let them do it to me."

"Did the man tell you his name?" Shane asked.

"He did not. He just launched right in with a spiel about how they were looking to buy land in the area and did I know of any for sale, and did I think any of these old mining claims around here were worth investing in and was I having much success on my own claim? The more he talked, the madder I got. And while he was going on and on, the other fellow was looking around at everything like he was taking inventory. A bunch of thieves for sure, ready to rob me blind."

Lauren couldn't see anything on the property worth taking, but that was beside the point. "What did the two women do?" she asked.

"The redhead hovered near the dark-haired guy, looking nervous. The blonde was fussing with the little girl, who was whining about wanting to go home. That little girl had more sense than the rest of them."

"This was on Thursday or Friday?" Shane asked.

"About that. I didn't mark it on the calendar."

"Did the man say where they had come from, or where they were headed next?" Shane asked.

"I didn't care enough to pay attention if they did," Kramer said. "I wanted them gone. The big guy didn't shut up until I fired my shotgun in the air."

"What happened then?" Lauren asked, trying to imagine the scene.

"The redhead screamed and latched on to the dark-haired man. The little girl started crying and the blonde picked her up, and the big guy swore at me. But he turned around and headed back to his car and the others followed him."

"What was he driving?" Shane asked.

"A black SUV. One of the big ones. New looking, with Colorado plates. I didn't get the number."

"Have you seen or heard from them since?" Shane asked.

"No. And I've been watching for them to come back. If they go near the mine, they'll be sorry."

"What do you mean by that?" Shane asked.

Kramer's scowl deepened. "Never you mind. If you find that bunch, I want to charge them with trespassing."

"They could charge you with threatening them with a weapon," Shane said.

"A man's got a right to protect his property. Now I've said all I've got to say." He folded his arms. "You can leave now."

"All right." Shane slipped a card from his shirt pocket. "If you see these people again, give me a call." He extended the card to Kramer.

"Don't have a telephone," Kramer said. "No service up here."

"I'll leave this, anyway." Shane laid the card atop a

nearby boulder. He waited for Lauren to get into the cruiser before he eased into the driver's seat, waiting until the last minute to turn his back on Kramer.

Lauren looked over her shoulder as they started back down the rough road. Kramer was cradling the shotgun again. She couldn't see his face, but she imagined him scowling.

Shane let out a long breath. "That could have gone badly," he said.

"The gun frightened me," she said.

"He meant it to. But I think Trey and the rest of them frightened him."

The observation surprised her. "Why do you say that?"

"He's one older man, up here all alone," Shane said. "There was fear behind his bluster, I'm sure of it."

"Do you think Trey was interested in stealing the mine?"

"You know him better than I do," Shane said. "What do you think?"

She pondered the question for the next few minutes, as Shane navigated the last half mile of the rough track. "I think he needs money," she said. "I still believe that's why he focused on Courtney. Maybe he saw another opportunity with the gold mine, though that doesn't really sound like a good source for quick cash."

"I'm trying to figure out Tom's role in all of this," Shane said. He shifted into a lower gear as they started down a steep slope.

"Trey introduced him to Mr. Russell as his partner," she said. "So maybe he supplied some of the money Trey needs."

"Why does Allerton need money?"

"For the youth ranch?" Though she hadn't believed he was serious about that project—it was just a way to play on Courtney's sympathies. "Do you think he might be involved in some kind of criminal activity?" she asked.

"I don't know," he said. "But I can't say he's acting like someone with nothing to hide."

"Courtney wouldn't have anything to do with him if she believed he was breaking the law," she said. "Not voluntarily." That was what worried her most—her sister-in-law and niece held hostage somehow by a man Lauren had never trusted.

They fell silent as they headed back down the mountain. As they passed the Olsens' yurt, the door opened and Becca Olsen ran toward them, waving her arms and shouting for them to stop.

Shane braked sharply and skidded to a stop. He and Lauren hurried out. "What's wrong?" Shane asked.

Becca's face was pale, her eyes red rimmed, as if she had been crying. "We were just going to call you," she said. "The most awful thing has happened."

Robby joined them and put an arm around his wife's shoulders. He was pale, too, his expression grim. "Becca and I were hiking in the wilderness area at the end of this road," he said, pointing back the way Shane and Lauren has just traveled. "The Sanford Mine trail. We were exploring some of the old mine ruins." He swallowed, Adam's apple convulsing. "We found a body. A woman. And I don't think she'd been dead long."

Chapter Thirteen

Shane called in for backup, then left Lauren with Becca while he and Robby drove to the end of the road. They parked at the trailhead for the Sanford Mine trail, then hiked another two miles to the mining ruins.

"The body is in there," Robby said, indicating a mostly intact cabin. Though the windows and door were missing, the rest of the structure looked sound. "In the back corner. We thought it was a pile of old clothes at first." He put a hand to his mouth.

Shane patted his shoulder. "You stay out here while I have a look." He approached the cabin, forcing aside emotion, focusing on the job. Nothing about the place looked disturbed. Nothing marred the slab of rock that served as a doorstep. Fallen leaves and the remains of a pack rat nest made of dried grasses and twigs littered the eight-by-eight room. He unclipped a flashlight from his belt and directed the beam into the corner.

The woman lay curled on her side, red hair obscuring her face, one arm stretched out in front of her. When he moved closer, he could see the red-black blood staining the back of her head. Carefully, he bent and lifted the hair away from her cheek.

Talia Larrivee stared up at him, her once lovely features rigid with shock.

Shane left the cabin and found Robby standing in the shade of a clump of aspens. Some of the color had returned to his face. "Did you find her?" he asked.

Shane nodded. "Did you recognize her?"

Robby pressed his lips together. "Maybe," he said after a minute. "But I only looked at her a minute. It was such a shock."

"I'm not asking for a definite identification," Shane said. "But did you think you had seen her before?"

He nodded. "I think she was one of the women I told you about," he said. "With Troy Allen. Not the blonde you showed me the picture of, but the other one."

Shane had suspected as much, but Robby added confirmation. "We'll need to get statements from you and your wife," he said. "And I'll need you to stay here with me until other officers arrive. Then I'll have someone take you back to your home."

"Yes, sir. Can I ask—how did she die? I mean, what was she doing up here—all alone?"

"I don't think she was alone when she died," Shane said.

"Do you mean someone killed her?" Robby's eyes widened.

"I can't say officially," Shane said. He probably shouldn't have said anything at all, but it was too late now.

"I saw the blood," Robby said. "I thought she might have fallen and hit her head."

"I don't think so." Not that he'd seen many gunshot wounds, but he was pretty sure that was what had killed Talia Larrivee. "We'll let the crime scene experts make that determination. I'm going to ask you not to talk about this with anyone except your wife. The same goes for her."

"We won't say anything," Robby said. "But do you think we need to be worried?" He wiped his mouth. "We've always felt so safe up here. Something like this—it's really shaken us up."

"I don't think you have anything to worry about," Shane said. "But it's always a good idea to be cautious. And if you see anyone suspicious, give us a call."

"We will." He stared toward the road, away from the cabin. "Someone should tell Mr. Kramer."

"You know him?" Shane asked.

"Well, not really know him." He grimaced. "He's not very friendly. But he's our neighbor and we get along okay." He laughed, though it came out more like a cough. "Becca brings him baked goods and stuff from our greenhouse and he likes that. I think we've convinced him that we're not after his gold."

"I'll stop by and have a word with him," Shane said. Until they ruled him out, Kramer would be on the list of suspects in Talia's murder. He'd admitted to arguing with the group Talia was a part of, and to firing a weapon on them. What if his bullet had struck her, and he'd tried to hide the crime by bringing her body here? He shook his head. He was getting ahead of himself, forgetting his training. First, collect the evidence. Study your findings, then start to develop a theory. Approaching the case any other way was asking for trouble.

LAUREN RAN TO meet the sheriff's department cruiser when it turned into Becca's driveway but drew up short when she realized Shane wasn't behind the wheel. Robby Olsen emerged from the passenger side of the vehicle, and the older man who was driving leaned over and addressed Lauren. "Are you Ms. Baker?" he asked. "Deputy Ellis asked me to give you a ride to your car. He's going to be tied up at the crime scene for a while."

"What's happened?" she asked, looking from Robby, who stood with his arm around Becca, to the older officer. "Who was the woman they found?"

"I don't know, ma'am," the officer said. "I'm a reserve deputy, called in to help shuttle people around and such."

Lauren had been on the edge of panic since Robby had made his startling announcement about finding a woman's body. She didn't think she could bear another minute of suspense. She turned to Robby. "Please, tell me," she said. "Did the woman have blond hair?"

Robby glanced at the officer, then shook his head. "She wasn't a blonde," he said. "Definitely not. But I promised Shane I wouldn't say anything else."

Relief almost buckled Lauren's knees. She swayed a little, then steadied herself. The dead woman wasn't Courtney. She'd confirm that with Shane later, but it was enough for now.

"We should get going," the officer said.

Lauren nodded. "Will you two be all right?" she asked Becca and Robby.

"We'll be fine." Becca forced a smile. "I'm better now that Robby is here. And we have plenty of work to keep us occupied."

"Thank you for waiting with me." She climbed into the cruiser, and the reserve officer executed a Y-turn and sped out of the drive, kicking up a cloud of dust and gravel. "This is the first really big crime we've had since I was hired," the officer said as he turned onto the road. "Most of the time they have me stopping speeders out on the highway or doing traffic control for funerals and things like that. Before Deputy Ellis asked me to transport Mr. Olsen and you, I got to help set up the crime scene barriers and watch the forensics team work."

"What do they think happened to the woman?" Lauren asked.

The officer pursed his lips. "I don't think I'm supposed to say."

"I'll ask Shane later, then," she said. "I'm sure he'll tell me."

"Well, I guess it would be all right to tell you, since you're his friend and all." He glanced at her, eyes alight with excitement. "I overheard a couple of the deputies saying she was shot in the head."

Lauren shuddered. "Do they have any idea who shot her?"

"Not that I heard, but we'll find out, I'm sure. I mean, if she's local, someone will know her, and they'll know who her friends and family are, and probably who her enemies are." He glanced at her again. "Strangers sometimes kill people, but most of the time it's someone the victim knew." He cleared his throat. "At least, that's what they taught us in the academy."

The dead woman isn't Courtney, she reminded herself. *Trey or Tom didn't kill her.*

But suddenly, it felt more urgent than ever to find her. She couldn't explain why she was so afraid Trey would harm Courtney, but it was a fear she couldn't shake.

The officer dropped her off at her car and headed back toward the crime scene. She drove to her rental, went inside and sank down on the sofa, suddenly too weary to stand. The events of the day, from being held at gunpoint by Von King to Martin Kramer threatening them with a shotgun, to learning that a woman had been murdered in the area where Courtney and Ashlyn had last been seen had drained her emotionally and physically.

Still, she jumped as if hit with an electric shock when her phone buzzed with notification of a text message. She hastily pulled it from her pocket, expecting to see a message from Shane. Instead, she received an even bigger shock when she saw the text was from Courtney.

Stop following me and go back to Denver. I'm fine, and I'm doing what Michael would have wanted. Ash sends her love. Court

She read the message through three times and began to tremble. She hit the button to dial the number and waited with the phone pressed tight to her ear as it rang once, twice…five times. Then silence. Not even a message that the voice mailbox was full. She texted: Courtney, call me, please.

But no answer came.

She paced the living room, clutching the phone and willing it to ring again. Finally, unable to bear this alone any longer, she sent a text to Shane. I heard from Courtney. I'm very worried. She says she's okay, but everything about the text was ALL WRONG.

SHANE STOOD WITH Travis as two attendants carried Talia's draped body past them to the waiting ambulance. "I'll need to notify Evan Larrivee before word gets out," Travis said.

"Do you want me to come with you?" Shane asked. Notifying a parent their child had been murdered had to be a law enforcement officer's worst duty.

"No, I want you to interview Martin Kramer again. Find out more about his encounter with Talia and the others. Then get back to the station and find out everything you can about him. And start the search for the people Talia was last seen with—Tom, Trey Allerton and Courtney Baker. Get their pictures and descriptions to the media and other agencies, and re-interview anyone they spoke to in the last week. Put out a description of any vehicles they may have been driving, too."

"You think one of them killed her?" Shane asked.

"I'm not making any assumptions at this point, but if they weren't responsible, I want to know why she wasn't with them when she died. They may know something that will lead us to her killer."

Shane looked around the mine ruins. "Why leave her here?" he asked. "It's out of the way but it's near a popular hiking trail, and these old ruins get plenty of visitors in the summer and fall."

"Maybe because her killer wanted her found, but not right away," Travis said. "Or because she was killed nearby and the killer was in a hurry to get rid of the body and leave."

"You don't think she was killed here?"

Travis met his gaze. "Do you?"

Shane shook his head. "No. There isn't enough blood, and the body didn't look like someone who had been shot and collapsed. It was more...arranged."

Travis nodded. "I think so, too. If we can find where she was killed, that might help us find the murderer."

"I'm still thinking about that photograph we found in her bedroom," Shane said. "It was hidden very carefully. Talia wanted to keep it, but she didn't want someone coming across it accidentally. Why?"

"Maybe she knew the woman in the photograph," Travis said.

"Or maybe she knew the person who tied up the woman and took the photograph," Shane said. "Maybe she came across the photo and kept it."

Travis nodded. "Go on. Why did she keep it?"

"Blackmail?" Shane guessed. "Or to use if that person tried to harm her?"

The sheriff frowned. "Maybe."

"Maybe her father knows something he isn't saying," Shane said. "Has Talia been in trouble before? Not here, but in other places they lived? Maybe as a minor, or something Larrivee managed to have suppressed?"

"Something that would have put her in contact with the

kind of people who would take a picture like that one?"
Travis nodded. "The kind of people who might kill her if
she threatened to tell what she knew." He pulled his keys
from his pocket. "I'll see what I can learn from Larrivee.
In the meantime, talk to Kramer and get started on that
search."

Martin Kramer didn't come out to greet Shane when
the sheriff's department cruiser stopped in front of his
shack. Shane waited in the car a moment before getting
out, but all around him was still and silent. He emerged
cautiously, aware that if Kramer had killed Talia, he might
not hesitate to shoot a law enforcement officer who came
looking for him.

"Mr. Kramer!" he called. "I need to talk to you again!"

No answer. Shane approached the shack at an angle, one
hand on his weapon. He pounded on the door and called
for Kramer again. No answer. Shane tried the knob, but it
wouldn't budge. Then he noticed the padlock on the outside
of the door, slipped through a hasp and fastened. Locked
from the outside, so Kramer probably wasn't inside.

He looked around the area, searching the ground for
any evidence of blood, or signs of a struggle. He spent
some time extending the search far beyond the house but
saw nothing out of order, not a broken branch or rock that
looked out of place, and nothing that looked like blood. He
started to return to the car, then noticed a well-worn path
leading away from the house. He followed the path and
after several hundred feet saw the black opening of a mine
tunnel. As he neared the tunnel, Kramer emerged, a five-
gallon bucket of rock in each hand. The old man glowered
at Shane. "What are you doing back here?"

"I had some more questions about the four people you
shot at a few days ago," Shane said.

Kramer set down the buckets and dusted off his hands.

"I didn't shoot at them," he said. "I fired over their heads. I wanted to scare them into leaving me alone."

"Are you sure you didn't hit one of them?" Shane asked. "Maybe the bullet ricocheted off a rock."

"If I had wanted to hit one of them, I would have. But I didn't."

"We found the body of one of the women at the mine ruins off the Sanford Mine trail," Shane said. "She'd been shot in the head."

Kramer recoiled, as if slapped. "Well, I sure as hell didn't shoot her. Which woman? How do you know it was one of the ones I talked to?"

"You said one of the women you saw was a tall redhead?"

"Yeah. So what?"

"This was a tall redhead."

"Well, she was alive and well last time I saw her." He picked up his buckets and pushed past Shane. Shane followed him toward the shack.

"What exactly happened after you fired the shotgun?" he asked.

"The big guy who'd been doing all the talking swore at me and got in the car and the others piled in after him. He peeled out of here, kicking up gravel. I never saw or heard from them again."

"You said if they came back, they'd be sorry. What did you mean by that?"

Kramer set down the buckets again and faced Shane. "Let's just say if they tried to go in the mine, they might end up with a half a ton of rock on top of them."

"You set up a booby trap," Shane said.

"Nobody could prove it wasn't an accident."

"What did you do before you came here to mine, Mr. Kramer?" Shane asked.

"None of your business."

"I can probably find out, so why not tell me?"

"I was a mining engineer. Doesn't matter who for."

"And you just decided to strike out on your own?"

"Some of us don't like working for other people." He picked up the buckets again. "I'm busy here and I'm tired of talking."

Shane let him go. Looking around the place, he had seen no signs of violence, and Kramer's shock at the news that Talia's body had been found seemed genuine—though maybe the man was a good actor. But Shane could find no reason to charge the old man with any crime. Better to collect more evidence and see where it led.

He was halfway to town when his phone sounded a text alert. He'd been out of signal range at the crime scene, and sometimes it took a while for messages to register once he was in range again. He hit the button to have the text read to him.

A mechanical voice indicated the message was from Lauren. "I heard from Courtney. She says she's okay, but everything about the message is all wrong."

He frowned and thought about pulling over to call and ask what was going on, but decided to wait until he was at the sheriff's department. He'd have a better phone signal and he could make a record of the conversation, as yet more evidence in what was turning out to be a serious case.

LAUREN DIDN'T WAIT for Shane to return her call. She drove to the sheriff's department and was waiting for Shane when he walked through the front door. She rose from the visitor's chair as Adelaide said, "Ms. Baker would like to speak with you, if you're available."

"I got your message." Shane touched Lauren's shoulder. "Come on back. I'll find somewhere we can talk."

They ended up in a small gray room she imagined was usually used to interrogate suspects, but right now privacy was more important than decor. She settled into one of the two chairs at the small square table and tried to ignore the camera and microphone hanging overhead.

"I'll be right back," Shane said. He left and reappeared less than a minute later with two bottles of water and set one in front of her. Then he sank into the adjacent chair. "How are you doing?" he asked.

I'm a mess was too frank a confession for her to make, and admitting as much might be all it took to lead to a meltdown. "I'm upset," she said. "But I need to stay strong, for Courtney and Ashlyn."

"The body we found wasn't Courtney's," he said. "I'm sorry—I should have told you that sooner."

She nodded. "Robby Olsen told me the woman didn't have blond hair. He wouldn't say anything else, but he told me that much. But I've been wondering—was it Talia Larrivee?"

The sudden rigid set of his jaw gave her her answer. "You don't have to tell me, if you can't," she said. "But I'm guessing it was. And the officer who drove me to my car said it was a murder scene. That means Tom or Trey may have killed her. We know she was seen with them."

"We don't know much at this point," he said. "We can't jump to conclusions."

He couldn't. But she could. But she hadn't come here to talk about that. She took out her phone, pulled up the message from Courtney and passed it to him. "That's the text I received from Courtney's number a little while ago," she said.

Shane read it, then laid the phone on the table between them. "She says she's okay. Don't you believe her?"

"Someone wants me to think she's okay," Lauren said. "But Courtney didn't write that message. Or if she did, someone made her get in touch to tell me to back off and she was letting me know the only way she could that she wasn't being sincere."

He frowned. "What makes you say that?"

She turned the phone so that she could read the message. "No one ever called Mike 'Michael.' Not even Courtney. Because his given name isn't Michael. It's Machiel—it's Dutch and it was my mother's father's name." She stabbed a finger at the phone. "She also never referred to Ashlyn as Ash. She hated that. She'd get really upset if anyone called Ashlyn by that nickname. She also hated when anyone called her Court. She would never sign her name that way—unless she was signaling me."

"You think she deliberately used the wrong names in order to let you know something was wrong?"

"Yes." She sat back, relieved that he understood. "I'm really worried. She's not telling me to leave her alone— she's letting me know she needs help."

"Did you try texting her back or calling her?"

"Of course I did. And she didn't answer. She may have been afraid to, with Trey watching her. Or he might have taken the phone away after she sent this message." She leaned toward him again. "Don't you see—this proves what I've been saying all along. Courtney and Ashlyn are in real trouble."

"We'll keep that in mind," he said.

That was it? She'd been expecting more of an answer. "What are you going to do?" she asked.

"We'll continue to search for Courtney and Allerton and Tom," he said.

He hadn't mentioned Talia—further confirmation that hers was the body the Olsens had found. "Can't you trace this text?" she asked. "Use technology to locate Courtney's phone and, we hope, Courtney?"

He pushed the phone toward her. "It's remotely possible that with a lot of time, effort and expense we might be able to determine an approximate location of a tower that transmitted the phone signal. But like everything else, it gets more complicated in the mountains, where towers are far apart and there are big dead spaces. And I'm pretty sure the technicians that do that kind of tracing have to send a message to her phone to do that. If she has it turned off or is in a dead area, they won't get the information they need."

"So what are you going to do?" she asked.

"We'll keep looking. We're going to distribute Allerton's and Tom's and Courtney's descriptions and photographs to other law enforcement agencies and to the media. We're trying to learn Tom's identity and background. We're asking anyone who has information about them to contact us. We're going to re-interview everyone who had contact with them and we're going to put every resource we can into finding them."

"Because you think one of them murdered Talia."

"One of them may know something that will help us find her killer."

She gripped his arm, and his eyes met hers. "If Trey or Tom killed Talia, then Courtney is in danger," she said. "And don't bother saying Courtney might have been involved in murder, because she wouldn't have been."

"She may be in danger," he said. "But we're going to do everything we can to find her."

"What can I do?" she asked.

"Let us know if you hear from Courtney again. Get in touch with her friends and other family and let them know to contact us if they hear from her." His eyes met hers. "I know it can be difficult to keep from thinking up the very worst-case scenario in situations like this, but don't tie yourself in knots that way. We have every reason to believe that Courtney and Ashlyn are still alive and well. Try to focus on that. And know that I will do everything in my power to find them."

She released her grip on him and sat back, drained. "I'll try." She knew he meant everything he said, yet it wasn't enough. But it was the best she could hope for.

Chapter Fourteen

Travis convened everyone involved with investigating Talia Larrivee's murder—most of the small department—at 8:00 the next morning. "I'll start with the medical examiner's report," he said when everyone was assembled around the long conference table. "Talia Larrivee died from a single gunshot wound to the head. The bullet was still lodged in her skull." He held up a clear evidence pouch showing the smashed lump of metal. "Two-twenty-five caliber."

"So not a pistol shot?" Gage asked.

"And not at close range." Travis set the evidence envelope aside. "Dr. Collins estimates she'd been dead approximately ten to fourteen hours when she was found, but she had probably only been in that abandoned cabin four to six hours. Lividity had set in by the time the body was moved. Before that, she lay on her back."

"So she was killed and either left lying where she fell or moved somewhere right away, and then to the mine ruins later," Shane said.

Travis nodded and consulted his tablet once more. "In addition to the gunshot wound, the report notes several recent minor injuries, including bruising on the side of the face, and cuts and scrapes on her palms and knees."

"Could those have happened when she was shot?"

Wes Landry, a recent addition to the department, asked. "Maybe she was running away and fell?"

"Maybe," Travis said. "Butch Collins was able to collect some fine gravel from the palms. It looks pretty typical for this area, but I'm going to send it off for analysis." He held up a second evidence pouch.

"It sounds like she was trying to flee her killer and was shot," Dwight said.

"That's consistent with the evidence," Travis said.

"Any luck identifying the man she's been seen with around town?" Gage asked. "Tom?"

"Not yet," Travis said. "Adelaide has a video appointment with a police artist this afternoon to try to come up with a likeness, since she spoke to him at ball practice on Friday. But it would help if we had a photograph."

"Tammy Patterson was at practice," Jamie said. "She had her camera with her and I think she took some photos for the paper. Maybe one of them shows Tom."

"Shane, go talk to her when we're done here," Travis said.

"Yes, sir."

"Here's something else that may or may not help us." Travis tapped his tablet screen. "We have a probable ID for the photograph of the bound woman found in Talia's bedroom. Samantha Morrison, twenty-two, disappeared two years ago from Colorado Springs. Her body was found in the mountains northwest of the city eight months later. El Paso County Sheriff's Department and the Colorado Bureau of Investigation have no leads in the case. They're going to dig a little deeper and get back to me, but nothing in their files shows a link to Trey Allerton, Courtney Baker or anyone named Tom. The only similarity is that her remains were found near the ruins of an old mine."

"It could be the same killer," Gage said.

"Or it could be a coincidence," Travis said. "Colorado

is full of old mines, and they make convenient disposal places for a lot of things. But we'll continue to look for other links. And so will other people. Evan Larrivee is offering a one-hundred-thousand-dollar reward for information leading to the apprehension and conviction of his daughter's killer."

Someone let out a low whistle. "That will bring a lot of loonies out of the woodwork," Dwight said.

"But it might bring real evidence, too," Travis said. "Adelaide is setting up a schedule for some of our civilian volunteers to handle phone calls on a hotline number Larrivee has established. We'll have to sift through it all, but maybe something useful will pop up."

The rest of the meeting consisted of presenting the evidence found at the mine site—almost nothing—and updates on an outstanding burglary, a fraud investigation and plans for the upcoming Fourth of July festivities.

"Maybe we shouldn't have the ball game this year," Shane said. "It might look like we're not taking this murder seriously."

"I spoke to Evan Larrivee about that," Travis said. "He said he's okay with the game continuing, since the money it raises goes to the Little League program. The organization relies on that money each year."

"And if we back out, we'll never hear the end of it from the fire department," Gage said. "But we may have to shorten our practice time."

"That shouldn't hurt us," Dwight said. "Not with Shane on the mound. Everybody knows pitching wins games."

If anyone saw Shane wince, they didn't remark on it. As soon as the meeting ended, he headed for the newspaper office.

Reporter Tammy Patterson looked up from her desk as Shane approached. "Hey, there!" she said, all smiles. An energetic woman with curly brown hair and wide hazel eyes, Tammy was a familiar visitor to the sheriff's department. "I got some great shots of you pitching the other night. Want to see?"

"I would like to see the pictures you took the other night," he said. "But not the ones of me."

"Oh?" She indicated the chair beside her desk. "Have a seat and fill me in."

"I'm looking for any photos you have of the man Talia Larrivee was with," he said.

Tammy's smile vanished. "It's so horrible, what happened to her. Mr. Larrivee came in first thing this morning to drop off her obituary and to take out a big ad. He's offering a reward for information that leads to finding Talia's murderer."

"Did you speak to her Friday at the practice?" Shane asked.

Tammy shook her head as she typed on her computer keyboard. "I knew her, but we didn't run in the same circles. I saw the guy she was with, though."

"What did you think?"

She made a face. "I thought he was too old for her, and pretty rough looking, but she had a thing for bad boys—hard partiers and risk takers. I think maybe she did it to upset her dad. I mean, can you imagine? I don't guess any father wants his daughter hanging out with lowlifes, but the Larrivees are rich—high-society types."

"Talia dated ex-cons? Who?"

"Oh, she wasn't with the guy very long. I ran into them at the park last summer and she introduced me and made a point of telling me the guy had just got out of prison—like I should be impressed or something."

"Do you remember his name?"

"No. Is it important?" Her eyes widened. "Oh, wow. Do you think her ex-con ex might have come back to murder her?"

"It would be helpful if I had a name to check out."

"I honestly can't remember, but maybe one of Talia's friends will. She has a couple of women she seems pretty tight with."

"I'll ask them about him. Thanks. Now about that picture."

"Sure. Here's the file with all the shots I took that evening. Let's see what I have."

She began scrolling through the photos. She paused at one of Shane in the middle of his windup. "You've still got it," she said. "Want me to print you a copy?"

"No, thanks." He studied his form critically. He'd put on a few pounds since retiring. His leg kick wasn't as high, and he didn't have as much power. Most people probably didn't see those flaws, but they stood out to him.

Tammy scrolled through a few more photos, then stopped at one of Talia Larrivee and an older olive-skinned man with thick black hair. Tom had a dark five-o'clock shadow and a heavy brow, and he was frowning. "He doesn't look very friendly, does he?" Tammy said.

Shane studied the people around Talia and Tom. All locals—no one who might be Trey Allerton or Courtney Baker.

"Can you blow that up and crop it so it just shows him?" he asked.

"Sure." She did as he asked. "How many copies do you want?"

"Can you send the digital file to the sheriff's office?" He wrote the address on the back of one of his cards and passed it to her.

"No problem." She typed in the address and hit Send, then turned back to him. "Do you think this guy killed Talia?"

"We need to talk to him," he said.

"Well, I hope this helps." She grabbed a reporter's notebook and a pen from beside the computer. "What can you tell me about the case so far? I have the statement the sheriff sent over, but it's a little dry. There's not much detail."

"That's because we don't have much detail yet."

"Come on, Shane. Help me out here. This is a big story and all I have is that Talia's body was found yesterday up at the old Sanford Mine ruins by unnamed hikers. Mr. Larrivee told me she'd been shot in the head. And I know law enforcement are searching for three people Talia might have been with." She plucked a piece of paper from a box at the corner of her desk. "Courtney Baker, Trey Allerton and a man named Tom." She nodded to the computer screen. "I'm assuming that's Tom."

"Yes. But that's all I have for you, Tammy." He stood.

"Who were the hikers?" she asked.

"I'm pretty sure they don't want to talk about the experience."

"What about Courtney Baker? Is she related to Lauren Baker? I've seen the two of you around together a lot lately."

He sighed. "Courtney was married to Lauren's late brother. And that's all I'm going to say." He turned to leave.

"I'm going to call Lauren and ask for an interview," Tammy said.

"You do that." Maybe Lauren would appreciate the opportunity to talk about Courtney to a larger audience. He hadn't been much help to her so far. He knew she was frustrated by the lack of progress in finding her brother's widow. Maybe she even believed he didn't care. But as a law enforcement officer, he couldn't let emotion get in the way of an investigation. His training had drilled into him the importance of following procedures and being methodical. Put together a strong case and things worked out better for everyone.

He sent Lauren a text, letting her know to expect a call

from Tammy, then returned to the office to find the sheriff studying the photo of Tom. "I'll send this off to the other law enforcement offices in the state, and to the FBI," Travis said. "If we're lucky, someone will recognize him."

"How often do we get lucky like that?" Shane asked.

Travis shook his head. "Not nearly often enough."

LAUREN WAS A little nervous about talking to a reporter, but Tammy Patterson quickly put her at ease. The two met at Lauren's rental, and Tammy arrived with two iced coffees and a bag of bakery cookies. "This isn't a bribe," she said, as she handed over one of the coffees. "I didn't have time for breakfast this morning, so you get to share while we talk."

The two settled on the sofa, and Lauren showed Tammy the photograph of Courtney and Ashlyn. "Your niece is adorable," Tammy said. "And Courtney is gorgeous. People should remember if they've seen her."

"A few people have seen her with Trey Allerton, and once with Trey and Talia Larrivee and a man named Tom."

"Shane told me about Tom," Tammy said. "He stopped by the paper this morning to pick up a photo I took of Talia and Tom at ball practice the other night. That's when I made the connection between Courtney Baker and you."

"I wish I had been at that practice," Lauren said.

"So tell me about your sister-in-law," Tammy said. "What is she like?"

For the next half hour, Tammy listened and took notes while Lauren talked about Courtney's sweetness, how much she loved her late husband and her daughter, and about how Lauren believed she had been manipulated by Trey Allerton. "I understand that it's only natural for Courtney to find someone to love again. I want that for her. It would be great for her to not be alone, and for Ashlyn to have a dad. But Trey Allerton doesn't love her. He's only using her for her money."

"What about Tom?" Tammy asked. "Where does he come in?"

"I don't know. But everyone who saw him with them said Tom looked rough. Samuel Russell said he thought he was an ex-con. I guess he recognized prison tattoos or something. And now Talia has been murdered." She shuddered. "I'm just really worried about Courtney. She's the type who sees good in everyone."

"What about Shane?" Tammy asked.

The question startled her. "What do you mean?"

"What does he think has happened to Courtney?"

"He doesn't know. Or if he does, he isn't telling me."

"I've seen you with him a lot around town," Tammy said.

"He's been helping me track Courtney's movements."

"I'm a regular at the sheriff's department and I haven't seen anything about that on their list of ongoing cases," Tammy said.

"It wasn't an official investigation," Lauren admitted. "Until now. Now that she and Trey have been linked to Talia Larrivee, everyone is getting a lot more serious about looking for her."

"So Shane was helping you look for her, unofficially?" Tammy asked.

"Yes."

"He's a nice guy," Tammy said. "And a really good-looking one. And it seems like he takes his job as a deputy really serious. Not a second career I would have expected from a former Major Leaguer, but it seems to suit him."

"I never followed baseball," Lauren said.

"Maybe he likes that." Tammy bit into a cookie and chewed, looking thoughtful. "Maybe Shane is attracted to you because you accept him for who he is, not who he was."

"Oh, I don't think he's attracted to me." Even as she made the protest, her cheeks grew hot, and she remembered Shane's kiss.

Tammy laughed. "Oh, he's into you, all right. I've seen the way he looks at you."

Lauren's heart beat faster. "How does he look at me?"

"I'm no expert, but I'd say when Shane looks at you, he looks exactly like a man in love."

PRACTICE TUESDAY EVENING for their upcoming charity baseball game was meant to be a low-key affair, a brief break from the more pressing business of investigating a murder. The players had all agreed that they wouldn't invite friends and family to attend, and that they would keep it brief and businesslike.

So Shane was surprised to see Lauren on the third base sideline, talking with Adelaide. "Hello," he greeted her while waiting for practice to begin. "I didn't think you liked baseball."

"Adelaide told me I needed to be here," Lauren said.

"There's no sense sitting around that rental apartment fretting," Adelaide said. She shook her head, her earrings—were those French poodles?—jangling. "I gave her a ride here—I figure you can take her home."

He'd have to pull the office manager aside some time and let her know he didn't need her help with women. He wondered what Lauren thought of such blatant matchmaking, but a quick read of her expression revealed a pleased look. That was certainly interesting.

"Shane, we need you on the mound." Gage had agreed to serve as their player coach, and he was organizing the team for a batting drill. Shane headed for the mound.

Gage walked out to the mound a minute later. "Kerry

Swearingham, the pitcher for the firehouse team, only has one pitch," he said. "A fastball he likes to throw up and in to get guys off the plate. So give us a lot of that for now."

Shane nodded and rubbed up the ball. He could throw fastballs all night. Some of his fellow officers might even be good enough to hit one, but on game day he'd be giving the fire crew a steady diet of breaking balls and rockets. They'd be begging for the game to end.

As it was, his fellow deputies were talking trash about them by the third batter. "Come on, Shane," Dwight complained. "This is supposed to be batting practice. Give us something we can hit."

"You can hit this stuff," Shane said. "I'm not even throwing hard." It was true. His arm felt great, but he wasn't putting that much power behind these pitches. His professional teammates would have laughed him out of the dugout if he'd thrown this slow stuff to them.

Dwight ended up fouling off three pitches in a row, then it was Nate Hall's turn. The husband of Deputy Jamie Douglas, Nate was helping to fill out the team roster.

Shane glanced toward the sidelines and saw Lauren deep in conversation with a man in a sheriff's department uniform. That reserve deputy—Anderson. Wasn't he supposed to be on duty tonight?

"Are you gonna pitch or just stand there?" Gage called.

Shane forced his attention back to the game. He wound up and threw one straight down the middle.

Lauren laughed, and he looked over to see her leaning toward Anderson, who was grinning. What did the two of them find so funny?

Crack! Nate's bat connected with Shane's fastball, sending it hurtling back toward the mound.

"Shane!" someone shouted.

He started to turn, then was knocked sideways by the impact of the ball on the side of his helmet. He went down, tried to get up, then was lost to a wave of darkness.

Chapter Fifteen

Lauren didn't remember screaming. She didn't remember racing onto the field, though later people told her she had done both those things. She wasn't aware of anything until she was kneeling on the ground beside Shane's body, both hands on his chest, staring down at his very pale, very still face.

"The ball hit him on the side of the head." Gage stood over them. "He went down like a tree."

"Get that helmet off of him." The sheriff knelt beside them and reached for Shane's head.

Lauren put out a hand to stop him. "Wait," she said. "There could be injury to his neck or spine. Don't touch his head until we're sure."

Travis stared at her.

"I'm a nurse practitioner," she said. "I know what I'm talking about."

Travis nodded. "Somebody call 911," he said.

Shane moaned, and Lauren leaned over him. His heart beat strong beneath her palm and he was breathing, if a little labored. "Shane, it's Lauren," she said. "You were hit by a ball."

"You got in the way of my home run." The batter, with a female deputy beside him, hovered near. The young man shifted his gaze to Lauren. "Is he going to be all right?"

"I'm fine." Shane tried to sit up, even as Lauren pushed at his chest.

"Don't move," she commanded. "The ambulance is on the way." At least, she hoped that was true.

"Why do I need an ambulance when I have you?" Shane said. But he lay back down and closed his eyes. He was very pale, and his skin was clammy.

A list of worst-case scenarios, from fractured skull to internal bleeding, ran through Lauren's mind. He was right—they didn't need to wait for an ambulance when she had the capability of doing an initial assessment right now. "Does anyone have a flashlight I can borrow?" she asked.

"You can use mine." Chuck Anderson slipped his from his duty belt and extended it to her. Chuck had been with her on the sidelines when Shane was hit. Chuck had been telling her a funny story about a traffic stop he had made earlier in the day. The man was driving with a boa constrictor coiled around one arm because, as the man explained, "My snake likes to look out the window when we're driving around."

"Open your eyes, Shane," Lauren said.

He opened them, and she shone the light in each one, the pupils contracting as they should. "How do you feel?" she asked.

"My head hurts, and there's a rock digging into the small of my back."

"You ever get hit by a line drive when you were playing pro ball?" Gage asked.

"In the arm and chest a few times," Shane said. "Never in the head. But I saw it happen to other guys. Can I sit up now? I'm fine, really."

"Slowly," Lauren said, and took his hand.

He sat and put a hand to his head, blinking. "That really rang my bell." He took off the helmet and probed at the area around his temple. "I bet I have a beauty of a bruise there by tomorrow," he said.

The wail of an ambulance grew gradually louder. Shane groaned. "You didn't have to call the ambulance."

"Better to make sure you don't have a concussion," Travis said.

"I was wearing a helmet," Shane said. "I'm fine."

"Let them check you out, just to be sure," Lauren said.

He met her gaze, then nodded—and winced at the movement.

"Coming through!" A female paramedic pushed through the crowd around the pitcher's mound, followed by an older man. She stopped in front of Shane. "Who beaned you?" she asked.

"He's the one who threw the ball right over the plate and didn't get out of the way," the batter protested.

"You have to make sure he's okay to pitch in Sunday's game," someone at the back of the crowd called.

Lauren stood and offered a hand to the paramedic. "I'm Lauren Baker," she said. "I'm a nurse practitioner. I did a preliminary exam and his vitals are good, pupils normal, no sign of fracture or external bleeding."

"Merrily Rayford." The paramedic shook her hand. "And that's Emmett Baxter." She indicated her partner, then dropped to her knees in the dirt beside Shane. "Let's see what we've got here."

Fifteen minutes later, Merrily sat back and began packing her gear. "You check out okay, but you need to have your skull x-rayed to rule out fracture or an internal bleed. We can transport you or you can have someone else drive you."

"I'll take him." Lauren and Travis spoke at the same time.

"I'll go with Lauren," Shane said.

"The rest of you, get back out there," Gage said. "We'll work on our fielding."

A chorus of grumbling gradually receded as the others took their positions around the ballfield. Travis remained behind. "Do you need anything else?" he asked when Shane was on his feet and standing beside Lauren.

"I'm fine," Shane said. "Lauren will take good care of me."

His words, and the trust they implied, sent warmth spreading through her. Travis started to turn away, and she came out of her dreamy fog enough to say, "There is one thing, Sheriff."

Travis turned back toward them, waiting.

Lauren flushed. "Could you give us a ride to my rental? My car is there."

Shane laughed, and even the sheriff looked like he might smile. "Come on," he said. "Let's get you two out of here."

SHANE HATED HOSPITALS and tests and paperwork and being fussed over. But he put up with it, because if you were an athlete, that was what you did. Even minor injuries had to be checked out so that they didn't turn into something major. Because of that, he figured he had had most major body parts x-rayed at some point in his career that spanned from Little League to the majors.

"Looks like your helmet and your hard head saved you," the emergency room doctor pronounced two hours after Shane and Lauren's arrival at the hospital in Junction. Lauren was with him in the little exam cubicle, perched on a folding chair and studying the images of Shane's brain projected on a monitor an aid had rolled in. "You'll probably have some bruising and a headache. If anything else develops, see your regular physician." The ER doctor turned to Lauren. "You know what to look for, but I don't anticipate any problems."

"I'll keep an eye on him," she said, with a proprietary tone he thought he could get used to.

"Are you tired?" she asked when they were in her car again, headed back toward Eagle Mountain.

"I'm starving." He hadn't eaten before practice, not liking to play on a full stomach.

"What do you want to eat?" she asked.

"A cheeseburger. A really good one. And I know just the place."

He directed her to a combination bait shop, convenience store and grill by the river, where they ate cheeseburgers and fries on benches beneath leafy cottonwoods, bathed in the glow of lights strung through the branches. "I can't believe I pitched for three years to guys who were probably trying to hit me, and a fellow sheriff's deputy ends up taking me out," he said.

"How's your head?" she asked.

"I have a headache, but I don't want to talk about it."

"All right. What do you want to talk about?"

"What do you think about coming back to my place and spending the night?" Might as well come right out with it.

She blinked. "Of course. It would be a good idea to have someone with you, until you're sure you're okay."

"I'm not talking about playing nursemaid." He met and held her gaze, wanting no room for misinterpretation. "I want to know if you want to spend the night with me. In my bed. Not sleeping."

The color that flooded her cheeks was something to behold, like a suddenly blooming rose. "Oh." It was a breathy sound, like a woman might make during lovemaking. It didn't sound to him like a rejection. He took her hand. "I figure we've been dancing around the question since we kissed," he said. "So I thought I'd throw it out there."

"I don't know what to think," she said.

He stroked the back of her hand with his thumb. "Don't think. Tell me how you feel."

"All right." She stood, both hands on the table in front of her, and leaned toward him. When her lips met his, he reached for her, and she kissed him with an intensity that had him reeling as much as that line drive. When she broke the kiss, she was smiling. "Yes," she said. "Yes, I want to come with you. And spend the night. Not sleeping."

THEY RETURNED TO Shane's home, and once inside, he wrapped his arms around her and kissed her with an intensity that had every nerve buzzing with anticipation and need. "Tell me if I'm moving too fast," he said when they finally parted.

"You're not moving too fast for me." She leaned in for another kiss, which led to hands exploring each other's bodies. Clothing began to come off as they moved toward the bedroom.

She had the impression of dark furniture and comfortable surfaces as they eased onto the bed. She reached for him again and felt the lump at the side of his head where the ball had struck and for the first time remembered all that had led up to this moment. "How's your head?" she asked. "Are you feeling all right?"

"My head is fine and I'm feeling great." He began kissing along the top of her bra, tracing her cleavage with his tongue. "You feel pretty amazing, too."

"Uh-huh." It was all she could manage as he slipped off her bra and shaped his hands to her breasts, the pressure and heat of his touch magnifying every sensation.

They helped each other out of their remaining clothing and slid under the covers. They lay on their sides, facing each other, resting a moment, hands idly stroking, each taking in the other. "You're beautiful," he murmured, as he slid his hand along the curve of her hip.

"You're gorgeous." She had never been with a man who was so physically perfect, with the toned body of an athlete and the musculature of a man who spent a lot of time in the gym. "I guess being a baseball player required you to stay in shape," she said.

"It's pretty useful for a sheriff's deputy, too." He kissed the top of her shoulder as he slid his hand down, over her stomach and between her legs. She moaned with pleasure as his fingers gently traced the folds of her labia and began to stroke.

"Do you like that?" he murmured.

"Can't you tell?" She nipped at his earlobe.

He laughed, a low rumble that vibrated through her. She slid her hand down his stomach, taking her time tracing each defined ridge of his abdomen, pausing before stroking his erection, delighted by the low sigh he let out when she grasped him. "I hope you have a condom." She took it for granted that he was the kind of responsible man who would, but she'd been wrong about men before.

"Yeah. Hang on." He rolled away and opened the drawer of the bedside table and retrieved a packet. She lay back and closed her eyes, listening as he tore open the packet, breathing in the scent of cotton sheets and aroused man and some lingering memory of his aftershave. *I want to remember this moment*, she thought. *This instant before everything changes.* She hoped the changes would be good ones—she wasn't going to let worry over what might happen in the future ruin the now. She had done that too often in her life. Now was enough, and she was going to enjoy it.

Shane rolled over and reached for her again. She moved confidently with him, delighted when he urged her on top of him. "I like looking up at you," he said as she straddled him. "And I like being able to do this." He cupped her breasts, then began to stroke her nipples, sending shock-waves of sensation through her, escalating the tension within her, until she was impatient to be even closer to him.

He had already sheathed himself, and she slid onto him, wanting to savor the sensation of him filling her but driven to movement. He grasped her hips, guiding her, and they soon found a rhythm they both enjoyed. She closed her eyes, arched her back and let the sensations wash over her, his body in hers, his hands on her hips, her hands on his chest and shoulders, the taste of him when she bent to kiss him, the way his muscles contracted with each thrust, the crazy, spiraling need that drove her to move faster, sink deeper and want more.

She shuddered with the force of her orgasm, fingers digging into his shoulders, holding herself still as the de-licious sensation filled her. He waited with her, holding her a long, breathless moment, before beginning to move beneath her, driven by his own need. She opened her eyes and found him looking up at her, the wonder of the moment reflected back at her. Then they moved together again, and she felt him come beneath her, a moment of fulfillment and power that never failed to make her marvel, just a little.

Eventually, she slid off of him and lay on her side again, her head on his shoulder, his arm around her in a gesture that felt so protective and tender and right. "You're very quiet," he said after a while. "Are you okay?"

"I'm okay." She shifted so she could kiss his cheek. "I'm happy—something I haven't been for a very long time. Since Mike died, I think. Thank you for that."

"You're welcome." His arm tightened around her. "When I said what I did at the restaurant, I half expected you to tell me off for not listening to you when you said you didn't want a relationship."

"Why didn't you listen?" she asked.

"Because, while I'm sure you believed you didn't want

a relationship, I think part of you had a very different idea. And I really wanted to be with you. I had to take the risk."

"I'm glad you did."

"What changed your mind?" he asked.

"Maybe with so many bad things happening, I wanted one good thing to focus on." She reached up and touched the side of his face. "Or maybe seeing you get hit by that ball made me rethink my priorities. Or maybe it was seeing— really seeing—the way you look at me."

"How do I look?" he asked.

"Like someone I could trust," she said. Would he think she was being corny? Or be hurt that she couldn't say more? She wanted to say *Like someone I could love*, but she wasn't ready for that yet. She had used those words too lightly in the past, and they had come back to hurt her.

He smiled, and the warmth in that smile spread through her and she lay down again, not wanting him to see the sudden tears. "I'm glad you trust me," he said. "I'll do my best to never let you down."

Never was a long time, but she liked that he thought that way. Maybe one day she'd be able to make that leap, too.

THE PHONE WOKE Shane from deep slumber. Beside him, Lauren stirred. "What time is it?" she murmured.

He lifted his head to check the clock. "Seven thirty." The phone continued to ring, and it took him two tries to find it in the pocket of his pants on the floor beside the bed. The sheriff's number on the screen was like a bucket of cold water dumped over him. Awake now, he sat up on the side of the bed. "Hello?"

"We got a positive ID on that photo of Tom you got from the newspaper," Travis said. As usual, he got right to the point. "His name is Tom Chico and he's been in and out of prison for the past twenty years, for everything from armed robbery to rape."

"Any idea how he hooked up with Trey Allerton?" Shane asked.

"No, but he was living in Woodland Park when Samantha Morrison disappeared."

"That's not far from Colorado Springs," Shane said.

"Not far," Travis agreed. "I'm going to send his information to the police there and see what they come up with. Are you coming in this morning?"

"Yes, sir."

"Head's okay, then?"

"I'm fine." He still had a dull headache, but nothing a cup of strong coffee and two aspirin wouldn't cure.

"See you then," Travis said, and hung up.

Shane turned to find Lauren sitting up also, covers tucked under her arms, watching him. "Did you ever hear Courtney or Trey mention someone named Tom Chico?" he asked.

"No. Is that the Tom who was with Talia Larrivee?"

"We think so. And Mr. Russell was right—he's an ex-con." He flung back the covers. "I have to get to the office." He started to get up, then turned back to her. "Not that I wouldn't rather stay here in bed with you, but this is important."

"Of course it is," she said. "Go. I've got my car, so I can get back to my place all right."

He leaned over and kissed her. "I'll call you later."

"Let me know what you find out. I hate to think of a man with a prison record with Courtney and Ashlyn."

It wasn't the romantic goodbye he had hoped for. But Lauren wasn't with him because he was especially romantic. She had said she trusted him. He needed to work now, to live up to that trust.

Chapter Sixteen

Lauren didn't know what she thought Martin Kramer could tell her that he hadn't already told Shane and the other deputies, but she hoped if she came to see him by herself, without a gun or a lot of men in uniform around, he might trust her with details he hadn't wanted to reveal to law enforcement. If such details even existed. But she owed it to Courtney to keep searching. Shane and his fellow officers were looking for her, too, but only as she related to Talia Larrivee's murder. They were focused on finding Tom Chico, and if he wasn't with Trey and Courtney anymore, they might decide finding Courtney wasn't that important. So Wednesday after Shane left, she headed for the Full Moon Mine.

She stopped first at the trailer on the section of the Russell Ranch that Trey Allerton had leased. She parked in front of the battered structure and studied it for several minutes. The place looked even more derelict than it had on her previous visits, the grimy windows vacant, the wooden steps sagging. A gust of wind sent a dust devil dancing across the dried grass that passed for a front yard.

After a while, she got out of the car and climbed the steps, but the front door was locked. She cupped her hands around her eyes and tried to see inside, but the small glass pane in the door was so dirty she could only make out dark smudges. Nothing moved in her field of vision, and she was sure the place was unoccupied.

Back in her car, she drove on, past the Olsens' yurt. Becca Olsen, who was working in the garden behind the yurt, straightened and watched as Lauren drove past, but she gave no indication that she recognized the car or driver.

The turnoff to the mine was farther than Lauren remembered, but maybe that was only because the condition of the road forced her to slow to a crawl, guiding the car through deep ruts and around large rocks. When she finally reached the drive leading up to Kramer's shack, with its signs warning her to Keep Out! her heart was beating hard in her chest, and she almost turned back.

But no. She had come this far. She might as well talk to the old man, even if he didn't want to see her. She stopped in front of the shack and waited. Silence enveloped her, broken only by the ping of the engine cooling. Nothing moved around her, yet she had the feeling she wasn't alone.

"What do you want!"

The sudden question startled a scream from her. Kramer had emerged out of nowhere to stand beside her car, the shotgun cradled in his arms. She lowered the driver's window. "You startled me," she said, glaring at him.

He laughed. "I know a thing or two about sneaking up on people," he said. "Learned it in 'Nam." His expression grew serious again. "You're that lady cop who was here the other day with the other one, aren't you?"

"I'm not a cop," she said. "I'm just a woman who is worried about a friend. Can I get out so we can talk?"

"Move slow, and keep your hands where I can see them."

She did as he asked, leaving the keys in the ignition. "I'm not armed," she said. "I only want to know if you've seen my sister-in-law, Courtney, again. She was the pretty blonde with the little girl."

"I've had so many people traipsing through here lately I can't keep track of them all. I had to run a bunch off earlier this morning. So far, I've just been firing over their heads, but a man's got a right to defend his property."

"Who were these people?" she asked.

"I didn't bother asking for identification. I just told them to get out of here."

"Were they men or women? Young or old? How many were there?"

"Are you sure you're not a cop? You ask questions like one."

"Was a blonde woman with any of the people who trespassed on your property?" she asked, desperate for information, but not wanting to make him any angrier.

"I didn't get a good look at all of them. Maybe she was, maybe she wasn't."

Did he truly not know, or was he just being difficult?

She opened his mouth to say as much when a loud report from across the ridge startled her. She started to turn, but Kramer grabbed her arm and shoved her to the ground. "Get under the car!" he ordered. "Now!"

Another report sounded, and she realized someone was shooting at them. She scrambled under the car and lay flat. Kramer crouched beside the car and aimed over the hood. The blast of his shotgun rang in her ears, followed by a metallic thud. With growing horror, she realized a bullet had struck her car. "Why is this happening?" she shouted over the blast of Kramer's shotgun.

His answer was a stream of swearing, then he leaped up and ran from behind the car, toward the gunfire. She thought she heard the shotgun blast again, then answering shots. What if Kramer was hit? Or killed, even? Then the shooter would come after her. Could she get into the car and drive away before they reached her? She told herself she needed to get out from under the car and try, but fear paralyzed her.

While she was struggling with these thoughts, silence descended again. No gunfire, no shouting, no sound of running feet. After what seemed like a long while, Kramer returned. She didn't hear his footsteps, but she saw his boots and the legs of his overalls as he reached the car. He leaned down to look at her. "You can come out now," he said. "I think I scared them off."

Shakily, she crawled out from under the car and stood, and brushed dirt from her clothing. "Who was that?" she asked. "And why were they shooting at us?"

"I don't know who it was. I told you, I've had people up here at all hours of the day and night, harassing me."

"Have you reported this to the police?"

He snorted. "And what are they going to do about it? Anyway, there have been cop cars up and down this road all day long since they found that woman's body at the Sanford Mine. Hasn't kept this bunch from coming after me."

"But why would these people shoot at you?"

"They're trying to steal my claim. But I'm not going to let them. I'm a lot tougher than I look."

He looked pretty tough to her. "How long has this been going on?" she asked.

"Since you people were up here the other day. They've got a lot of nerve, I tell you."

"Do you think any of the people who are after you are the same men who visited you the day you saw Courtney and the dark-haired woman who was killed?"

"I already told you, I haven't got a good look at any of them. It might be the same bunch, and it might not. Seems like there are more of them. But maybe they recruited help." He took a step back. "You better go now. I've got work to do."

"Do you still have the card Deputy Ellis gave you?" she asked.

"I might have it around here somewhere."

"If you see the blonde woman, Courtney, or her little girl, Ashlyn, call the deputy. It's really important."

He shook his head. "Can't do it."

"Why not?"

"I don't have a phone. Go on now. I've wasted enough time talking."

He stood cradling the shotgun, watching as she turned her car and headed back down the driveway. Lauren spent the trip back to town replaying the events of the morning. The sudden shots, the return fire—then all was quiet again. It was surreal, but then, so much of this whole ordeal since Courtney had left Denver didn't make any sense.

ANNE-MARIE WINSTEAD JONES had spent the past week ignoring Shane's phone calls and refusing to answer the door when he stopped by her house. He finally parked around the corner from the very modern steel-and-glass townhome where she lived and waited until she stepped out the front door. She was a tall woman with a fall of thick dark hair and a thin, angular figure. "Ms. Winstead Jones, I need to speak with you," he said, intercepting her as she headed toward the bright green Mercedes GT parked in the drive.

She whipped her head around to stare at him, then picked up her pace. "I can't talk now," she said. "I have an appointment."

He deftly stepped in front of her. "You can answer a few questions now, or I will put you in my cruiser and take you to the sheriff's department and question you there," he said.

"You can't do that," she said. "I haven't done anything wrong."

"I'm investigating a woman's murder—your friend's

murder," he said. "And I need your help. If you won't voluntarily help, I can compel you to do so, though I'd rather not."

She jiggled her keys in her hand, a bright silver *A* on the fob glinting in the afternoon sun. "All right," she said after a long moment. She turned back toward the house. "You might as well come inside."

The inside of the condo matched the outside—white leather sofas, white fur rugs, chrome end tables and chairs, and everywhere a view of the mountains from the expanses of glass. Shane's first thought was that it was like living in a snow scene. In the winter it must be freezing.

Anne-Marie sank onto one of the sofas and waved toward a nearby chair. "Have a seat. What do you want to know?" She opened a drawer in the table in front of her, took a cigarette from a silver box and lit it with a crystal lighter.

"Why have you been avoiding me?" he asked.

"Why are you surprised that I don't want to talk about my best friend's death?" She folded one arm across her stomach and took a long drag on the cigarette.

"When was the last time you saw Talia Larrivee?" Shane asked.

"We had lunch last Thursday. We had lunch every Thursday. And we went shopping." She blinked rapidly, eyes shining with unshed tears.

Talia had died on Sunday. "Did you talk to her after that? Text her?"

"I texted her, but she didn't answer." She took another pull on the cigarette, her expression obscured by the sudden exhalation of smoke.

"When did you text her?" Shane asked.

She balanced the cigarette on the rim of a crystal ashtray on the coffee table and shifted to pull out a phone in a pearlescent white case. She tapped the screen with one white-tipped fingernail and scrolled. "I texted her Friday afternoon, Friday night, Saturday night and Sunday afternoon."

"Let me see." He held out his hand and she passed over the phone.

The messages started off simply enough: Pool this afternoon? I'll make margaritas.

Half an hour later: Come on in, the water is great.

Twenty minutes after that: Whassup girl? Why aren't you answering your phone?

The rest of the messages, sent over the next few days, were increasingly more agitated, varying pleas to know why Talia wasn't responding, ending with a single profane epithet. "You tried to call her, too?" Shane asked. He returned the phone.

"I tried, but it went straight to voice mail," Anne-Marie said. "At first I left messages, but she ignored those, too."

"What did you think had happened?"

She shrugged and picked up the cigarette again. "I figured she was with her new boyfriend, ignoring everyone else. He struck me as that type, you know?"

"Who was he?" Shane asked. "And what type do you mean?"

"The controlling type. The type who wants all the focus on him. She'd already blown me off a couple of times before when I wanted to go out, telling me Tom wouldn't like it." She crushed out the cigarette in the crystal dish. "I don't know who he was, really. I only met him once and I wasn't impressed."

"Tom who?"

"I never heard his last name. Talia went through a lot of men. I didn't bother getting to know most of them. I didn't want to know this one."

"Tell me about him," Shane said.

"He was almost as old as her father and he was really rough."

"What do you mean 'rough'?"

"He just..." She stared up at the ceiling, as if searching for the right words. Then she met Shane's gaze again. "You know how some young guys have this cocky attitude, all bravado and swagger? They're not really tough, but they pretend to be. Usually it's because they're so insecure. It's easy to see right through it. But with Tom it wasn't an act. Everything about him was a little crude—bad tattoos and cheap clothes." She shuddered. "He felt... dangerous. He scared me, really." She brushed a lock of hair off her forehead. "I think he scared Talia a little, too, but she liked that."

"She liked men who scared her?"

"Yeah. A little."

"So she'd dated men like Tom before?"

"Not exactly like him. But she had a boyfriend once who she told me liked to tie her up and choke her when they were having sex. It kind of freaked me out. I told her she needed to dump him right away, but she just laughed. She said she knew what she was doing. And I guess she did, because a few weeks later, he was out of the picture and she was dating some mountain climber who talked her into going skydiving with him."

"Do you know where the man who tried to choke her is now?"

"No way." She frowned. "I kept waiting for her to ditch Tom, but she didn't show any signs of losing interest in him."

"Did she mention anything Tom did that was dangerous?"

"Nothing specific." Her gaze shifted away.

"But?" he prompted. There was something, he was sure. "I asked her once what she saw in him. It was one of the times after she blew me off when I wanted the two of us to go out to a club. She said he was exciting and being with him made her feel so alive and powerful. I told her he scared me and she said I didn't need to worry about her, because she had an insurance policy if he ever stepped out of line."

"What did she mean by that?"

Anne-Marie shook her head. "She wouldn't say, but I kind of took it to mean she knew something she could use to blackmail him. Just from some other things she said. I told her that was a screwed-up way to manage a relationship, but she said that was the only kind she was good at." She looked at the drawer that held the cigarette box, as if contemplating having another.

"Tell me if you've ever seen this before." Shane took out a copy of the photograph he and Travis had found in Talia's room.

Anne-Marie took it and studied the photo of the bound woman. "This isn't Talia," she said. She handed it back to him. "I don't know who it is. What does it have to do with Talia?"

"That was found in her room after she went missing. It's a photograph of a woman who disappeared in Colorado Springs two years ago."

"Why would Talia have something like that?"

"I don't know. I was hoping you would know."

She puzzled over this, forehead creased. "Do you think she got that photograph from Tom? That that was her insurance policy?" She hugged her arms across her stomach. "Do you think that's why he killed her?"

"We don't know who killed her," Shane said.

"The minute I heard she'd been found dead, I knew he did it," she said. "If you had ever met him, you'd know it, too." Her eyes welled with tears again, and this time they spilled over, sliding down her cheeks. "Poor Talia. She was so smart about so many things, but so dumb about men. She thought danger was the same as excitement, even though I tried to tell her it wasn't."

LAUREN WAS STILL debating whether to tell Shane about her visit with Martin Kramer when he came to see her later that evening. When she answered the door, he was frowning. "What happened to your car?" he asked. "It looks like someone shot it."

"It's just cosmetic damage. I'll get it repaired when I'm back in Denver." She turned and moved into the living room, leaving him to close the door and follow.

"Who was shooting at you?" he asked. "Where were you? Why didn't you call and tell me?"

So much for keeping this from him. "I drove up to talk to Martin Kramer again," she said. "This morning. And I don't know who. The two of us were standing in front of his shack, talking, then someone started shooting at us."

"Are you all right?"

She supposed asking was a reflex, since he could clearly see she was fine. "Mr. Kramer and I are both unhurt," she said. "He shoved me under the car and started firing in the direction of the shots. I guess he scared off whoever it was."

"Did he have any idea who it was?" Shane asked.

"He said it was claim jumpers. You know he's convinced someone is trying to steal his gold mine. Though maybe there's something to that. He said various people have been harassing him since you and I were up there. At first, I thought maybe he was delusional, but I didn't imagine those gunshots."

"You shouldn't have gone up there by yourself," Shane said, as she had known he would. "You don't know anything about Kramer. He might have shot you himself."

"He didn't. In fact, he was very concerned for my

safety." She had the skinned knees to prove it, from where he had shoved her down and urged her to hide under the car. "If you want to know more, you'll need to talk to him. So, you know what I did today. What did you do?"

"I finally talked to Anne-Marie Winstead Jones."

"Who?"

"Talia Larrivee's best friend. She didn't like Talia's new boyfriend, Tom, and thinks he probably killed her. She said Talia liked dangerous men."

"And Tom Chico is dangerous," she said. "Do you really think he murdered Talia?"

"I think right now he's our prime suspect. That doesn't mean we're not going to consider all the evidence, and everyone she came in contact with, but there's a good chance he was the last person she saw. And he seems to have disappeared."

"I asked Mr. Kramer if he thought Trey and Courtney and Tom were the people who have been harassing him recently," she said. "He said he didn't know. But maybe they are. Maybe he's right and they want his gold mine. We know they've been trying to get money other ways."

"I think I need to talk to Kramer again," he said. "And Sam Russell and the Olsens."

"I don't think I realized before how much investigations involve talking to people—sometimes the same ones over and over."

"When I started the job, the sheriff told me he thought I'd be good at it, because people like me and I'm easy to talk to. I thought he'd hired me because I was in shape and did well in my classes at the academy. He told me those things were important, but every department needed someone who was good at dealing with difficult people. He thought I could be their someone."

"And are you?" she asked. "Good at dealing with difficult people?"

"Pretty much." He flashed a smile. "Charm is my secret weapon."

She moved into his arms. "I guess I'm just another victim, then."

"Never a victim." He kissed her, his hand shaped to the curve of her hip.

"You never said why you stopped by tonight," she said.

"Because I wanted to see you. I wanted to do this." He kissed her again.

"This is nice," she said. "But I feel guilty that we're not doing more to find Courtney, or to locate Talia's killer."

"I had a professor in college who said that after a hard study session you should take a break for physical activity," he said. "While your body was exercising, your mind would sort out everything you had just learned and you could figure out any remaining problems. Something to do with oxygen flow to the brain and the activity or the subconscious and some other stuff I've forgotten."

"What kind of exercise?" she asked.

"When I was in college, I played ball or ran."

"Is that what you want to do now?" She nipped his neck.

"No. I'm thinking of another kind of exercise."

She let out a whoop as he scooped her into his arms and started toward the bedroom. She thought about telling him to put her down, but only briefly. She liked the feel of his strong arms around her. He wasn't physically dangerous, like the men Talia liked to hang out with. But there was something to be said for a little emotional risk in a relationship, shaking up the status quo and trying new things.

Like getting involved with a man she had fallen for hard. One she wasn't sure she'd ever figure out how to leave.

Chapter Seventeen

Fourth of July in Eagle Mountain was equal parts nostalgia and spectacle that not even a murder investigation could dim. The local scouting troop put out flags all along the town's main street, then a parade that included everything from the high school marching band to a dozen children on bicycles proceeded from the town hall to the town park. Shane and a few of the other deputies patrolled the crowd, alert for troublemakers, but this early in the day there were none.

After the parade, the craft booths and small carnival opened. The Rotary club sold barbecue dinners and the history museum staff handed out lemonade, and Saturday ended with a dance and fireworks. The festivities continued on Sunday, with a 5K run, a church service in the park and more barbecue. Sunday afternoon, Shane and his fellow deputies convened at the ball fields for the charity baseball game, which Adelaide delighted in telling everyone "raised more money this year than ever before."

Shane had told himself this was strictly amateur stuff, that he didn't care about the outcome and it didn't matter how he performed on the mound. But once he was up there in his uniform, clutching the ball and digging the toe of his cleat against the pitching rubber, he realized it mattered a great deal. In the eyes of everyone watching, he was still a pro ballplayer, and they expected a pro performance.

He struck out the first three batters he faced, and in the bottom of the inning Gage Walker hit a double off the fire department's pitcher. Travis followed that up with a solid single, allowing Gage to score, before Nate Hall struck out and Wes Landry hit a high fly ball. Another strike-out retired the side, but the sheriff's department was up one to nothing.

Shane struck out the next two batters, but the third player to face him that inning took advantage of a fast-ball he left hanging and hit the ball over the fence. The game was tied.

"He got lucky," Gage said when they returned to the dugout and prepared for their turn to bat. "It won't happen again."

"No, it won't," Shane said. He'd been taking it easy, trying not to show off too much, but he was done with that now. These people wanted a Major League show, he'd give them one.

After a series of singles and strikeouts by the sheriff's department players, it was Shane's turn to bat. He'd never been a hitter—it wasn't what they'd recruited him for and everyone knew it. He struck out, too. Then he was back on the mound, the crowd cheering wildly. He looked into the stands and spotted a couple of people wearing replicas of his pro jersey.

Then he saw Lauren, sitting next to Adelaide, a wide smile on her face, and he felt about ten feet tall. She didn't care how he pitched or whether he won or lost the game, but suddenly he wanted nothing more than to win—for her.

The firemen weren't pro ballplayers, but they weren't pushovers, easy. Shane walked a man, then the next got a weak single. But the next six in a row went down on strikes. And so it continued. By the time the seventh—and last—inning rolled around, someone had found a piece of chalk and scrolled a line of *K*s across the bottom of the outfield scoreboard—one for every strikeout Shane had thrown.

The score was three to one when Shane took the mound in the top of the seventh. There was no talk of anyone else pitching. Such a decision would have been met with derision from the crowd, some of whom were chanting his name as he exited the dugout. "Shane! Shane! Shane! Shane!"

He felt the soreness in his arm as he threw the first pitch. Not pain, just an awareness that he had thrown a lot today, and that it had been a long time since he'd worked his muscles this hard. But he had pitched much of his career with soreness, and he knew how to deal with that.

The first batter hit two foul balls before finally striking out. He walked the next man, who was short and stocky, and hunched over the plate, shrinking the strike zone, or so it seemed to Shane. The next man struck out and the fourth batter hit a single.

Shane hit the fifth batter. He wasn't aiming for the guy, but he lost control of the ball and it thumped the man squarely on the shoulder. A groan rose from the crowd. The bases were now loaded.

"Come on, Shane!" someone yelled from the dugout. Gage, he thought.

Come on, Shane, he thought to himself, and rubbed up the ball. He tugged his hat down low and leaned toward the plate for the sign from the catcher. Not that Dwight was giving any signs. They had decided from the start that Shane would throw whatever Shane felt like throwing. Whatever the outcome of this game, it was all on him.

He wound up and threw. He winced at the sound of the ball connecting with the bat, and froze on the mound, afraid to turn around to see where the ball ended up. In the big leagues, a home run ball made a certain sound on the bat, a definitive crack like lightning striking. The metal bats they were using for this game had a different sound, loud and solid, but unreadable.

A cheer rose from the crowd and Shane forced himself to turn around. Nate stood near the outfield fence, the ball held triumphantly in his hand. Then some of the team was swarming Nate, while others gathered around Shane.

It wasn't the strikeout he would have scripted, but a fly ball was an out just the same. The sheriff's department had won the game and the cheesy trophy and bragging rights for the next year.

He searched the stands for Lauren, but she wasn't there, her seat next to Adelaide vacant. Had she left the stands to meet him at the dugout?

He pushed through the crowd and made his way to the edge of the field. Adelaide leaned over the fence and raised her voice to be heard. "Great job out there!" she called.

"Thanks! Where's Lauren?"

Adelaide shrugged and shook her head.

He told himself not to worry—she'd probably just gone to the ladies' room, or had to take a call. He focused on accepting congratulations from those around him, then posing for a team photo with the trophy.

Thirty minutes had passed by the time he made it to the parking lot, and still no sign of Lauren. No one he spoke to had seen her. Fear took up residence in his chest, making it hard to take a deep breath. He texted her number and stared at the screen, willing her to reply. Nothing.

She had disappeared. And he had to find her.

AS THE SIXTH inning drew to a close, Lauren headed to the ladies' room. She joined the line of other women, some with children in tow, and made idle conversation about the weather and the game. She had never followed any sport, and had expected to be bored today. But she had found herself caught up in the game. Watching Shane on the mound was exciting, but listening to Adelaide's running commentary about the action on the field, she had found herself captured by the drama and strategy. There was a lot more going on out there than she had imagined.

She emerged from the restroom and gazed idly across the park. Children swarmed the playscape, scrambling up the climbing wall, soaring in the swings. Then a flash of blond hair made her heart stutter in its rhythm.

A little girl in a pink dress turned to call to another child, and Lauren gasped. "Ashlyn!" In her mind, she shouted the name, but it was really only a whisper. She scanned the group of adults around the playground. A blonde woman was half-hidden by a lamppost. Was that Courtney, in those oversize black sunglasses?

Lauren ran, darting around couples and family groups. She didn't care that people stared at her as she pushed past them. She reached the play area out of breath and had to stop a moment, half doubled over from a stitch in her side. She couldn't see the little girl anymore—Ashlyn. Or the woman she was now sure was Courtney.

She moved around the play area but couldn't find them. "Are you okay?" a woman asked, a young mother with a baby in a sling.

"Did you see a little girl in a pink dress, with long blond hair?" Lauren asked. "She was just here."

"No, I haven't." The woman put one hand protectively on the child in the sling. "Is she your little girl?"

"No, my niece. Her mother was with her, but I can't find them now."

The woman relaxed a little. "There are a lot of people here today. Maybe they went into the restroom."

There was a second set of restrooms near the playground. Lauren went inside, pushing past a line of women and children. "I'm just looking for someone," she said by way of apology. She stood outside the stalls and studied the feet of the people inside. "Courtney, are you in here?" she called. "Ashlyn, it's Aunt Lauren."

No one answered. Lauren went outside and waited a few minutes, watching people as they emerged from the restroom, but Courtney and Ashlyn weren't there.

Maybe they were in the parking area. Afraid she might already have missed them, she sprinted toward the paved lot behind the play area. Every slot was full, but she didn't see a blonde woman or little girl.

She returned to the play area, thinking maybe she had overlooked them. A dozen children swarmed the playscape and the adjacent array of oversize musical instruments, but no Ashlyn. No Courtney.

She didn't know how long she had been searching when Shane found her. He was still in his baseball uniform, worry making the lines around his gold-brown eyes deeper. "Lauren, what's going on?" he asked. "I've been looking for you."

The sight of him filled her with relief. "I saw Ashlyn," she said. "She was playing, right here." She gestured to the playscape. "And Courtney, too, I think. But by the time I ran over here, they were gone. I've been looking."

He put a hand on her shoulder. "Did you try calling Courtney, to let her know you were here?"

Why hadn't she thought of that? She pulled out her phone and sent a text. I'm here by the playscape. Please let me say hello to Ashlyn.

She waited, but there was no reply. "Give her a minute," Shane said.

She looked into his eyes, afraid of the doubt she might find there. "You believe me, don't you?" she asked. "You believe I saw them?"

"Yes."

She loved him in that moment, more than she already had. How many people would have tried to persuade her that she had merely seen someone who resembled her niece and her late brother's wife? Even if Shane was silently thinking that very thing, he didn't try to tell her so, and that counted for a lot.

"It's hot out here in the sun," he said. "Let's sit down in the shade."

He steered her toward the row of benches that moments before had been filled with people, but now there was room for the two of them on the end of one bench. "Great game, Shane," someone said as they passed.

"The game!" She forced her gaze from the playground area to look at him. "I'm sorry I left before the last inning. How did it go?"

He grinned, and the expression made him look boyish. "We won."

"It was exciting," she said. "I don't think I've ever sat and watched a whole game before. Well, almost a whole game. I liked watching you pitch."

"It was tougher than I thought it would be, being out there again." He rubbed his arm.

"Is your arm hurting?" she asked.

"Just a little sore." He laughed. "I'm out of shape."

Right. He was one of the fittest people she knew. She checked her phone again. "I don't think Courtney is going to reply," she said. "For some reason she's avoiding me."

"I'm sorry." He put his hand on her back. "I know how much you'd like to see her and your niece."

She nodded and searched through the crowd on the playground and around it again. "I don't think they're coming back," she said. "I guess we'd better go."

"We can stay as long as you like," he said.

He probably wanted to take a shower and get dinner. Her stomach growled, but she didn't think she'd be able to eat. "Let's go." She stood. She'd come to Eagle Mountain thinking Courtney and Ashlyn were the most important people in her life. Maybe that wasn't so true anymore.

MONDAY MORNING THE revelry of the day before was forgotten as the deputies and sheriff convened to discuss the murder investigation. Dwight had tracked a man he thought could be Tom Chico to a campsite in the national forest, but he had left the site a week before Talia's body was found.

Shane had submitted a written report on his interview with Anne-Marie Winstead Jones on Thursday, but the sheriff had him summarize it for the group now to refresh everyone's memory. "She said Talia told her she had an insurance policy she could use if Tom stepped out of line. Anne-Marie interpreted that as something Talia could hold over Tom and threaten to blackmail him with," he said.

"Like the photograph of Samantha Morrison," Travis said.

"That was the only reason Anne-Marie could think of for Talia to have that photograph," Shane said.

"Colorado Springs hasn't gotten back to me about any possible link between Morrison and Chico," Travis said. "I'll see if I can learn anything more when I talk to them today."

"I've been checking with hotels, motels and short-term rentals in a one-hundred-mile radius of Eagle Mountain," Jamie said. "No one has rented to anyone matching the descriptions of Tom Chico, Talia Larrivee, Courtney or Ashlyn Baker, or Trey Allerton. I would have thought someone would remember Courtney and Ashlyn in particular, but no luck so far."

"Lauren thought she saw Courtney and Ashlyn yesterday, at the playground next to the ball field," Shane said. He'd been debating whether or not to mention this. While he believed Lauren had seen someone who resembled her sister-in-law and niece, she couldn't be certain of their identity. "They left before she could speak to them."

"What about Allerton or Chico?" Gage asked.

"She didn't see them. And she only glimpsed the woman and the girl, though she's pretty certain of the ID."

Travis pointed a finger at Shane. "Remind Lauren she needs to come in and give a statement about what happened at the Full Moon Mine Wednesday," he said. "I stopped by Martin Kramer's place to talk to him. His truck was there, but I couldn't find him."

"Yes, sir," Shane said. He had reported Lauren's story of someone shooting at her and Kramer, and the sheriff had ordered him and Lauren to stay away from the mine. Instead, he'd had Shane looking for unsolved crimes similar to Talia's murder in every location Chico was known to have lived. There had been plenty of cases to consider, but nothing definitive.

A tap on the door made them all fall silent. "Come in," Travis called.

Adelaide stuck her head in the door. "There's someone here to see you, Sheriff," she said. Adelaide rarely let anyone in to see Travis without an appointment. If she was interrupting a meeting to let him know he was needed, the visitor must be someone important.

"Who is it?" Travis asked.

"He says his name is Trey Allerton. He heard you've been looking for him."

Chapter Eighteen

Trey Allerton strode into the interview room at the sheriff's office with the swagger of a closing pitcher who had just won the World Series. A tall, broad-shouldered man with a handsome, boyish face, he shook hands with both Travis and Shane, then dropped into the visitor's chair, perfectly at home. "I apologize I didn't get here sooner," he said. "I just heard you wanted to speak to me."

"Thank you for coming in," Travis said. "I've asked Deputy Ellis to sit in on this interview, which I'll be recording."

Allerton nodded to Shane. "I'm not sure what I can help you with," he said. "But I'll try."

Travis settled into the chair across from Allerton, while Shane stood to one side, against the wall. He had a good view of Allerton's face from here and was between him and the door. "When was the last time you saw Talia Larrivee?" Travis asked.

Allerton frowned. "Well, let me see. It's been a while, I guess."

Travis said nothing, waiting.

"I don't think I can give you an exact date," Allerton said. "Maybe a week or ten days ago? Tom brought her around one day to see the place we're leasing from Sam Russell. That's really why I'm in the county, you know. I'm going to start a camp for underprivileged youth up there. You know, get them in the outdoors, hiking and camping, maybe riding horses, really give them a new focus in life."

"What's your relationship with Tom Chico?" Travis asked.

The frown deepened, and Allerton shook his head. "Oh, Tom is a piece of work. He was going to partner with me on the youth camp project, but a little over a week ago, we had a falling out. I realized the two of us were never going to be able to work together, so we parted ways. All perfectly amicably, though I'm sorry I wasted so much time with him."

"Why weren't you going to be able to work with him?" Travis asked.

"Tom was a little bit of a loose cannon," Allerton said. "He had a temper. And he was impatient. I tried to explain to him that a project like this, if you're going to do it right, takes time. And money. He wanted to dive right in, start building and everything, but before we could do any of that, we had to raise money. A lot of it. I've been working on that, but not fast enough for Tom."

"How did the two of you meet?" Travis asked.

Allerton rubbed his jaw. "Let me see…" He brightened. "I remember now—Courtney introduced us."

"Courtney Baker?" Shane asked.

Allerton turned to look at him. "That's her. Sweet girl. I think Tom went to her church. She said he was looking for work and I knew I'd need help with this ranch. Then he told me he had some savings he wanted to invest, and I figured why not?" He grimaced. "I guess that wasn't my best decision, though."

"Were you aware that Tom Chico had been in prison?" Travis asked.

Allerton nodded. "I found that out later, but like Courtney said, everybody deserves a second chance."

"When was the last time you saw Tom Chico?" Travis asked.

"Let me think." He sat back and crossed his ankle over one knee. "You have to realize I've been so busy, especially since Tom left, that it's hard to keep track." He tilted his head up and studied the ceiling. "I'd say it was right at a week to ten days ago. Can't be more specific than that—everything runs together. But Talia was with him. She'd been hanging around a lot lately." He chuckled. "Say what you will about Tom—I wouldn't have pegged him as a ladies' man, but Talia was crazy about him. And well, you know, she was a very good-looking woman. Rich, too. I really don't know how he did it."

"What was their relationship?" Travis asked.

"I never actually asked, but I'm pretty sure they were lovers."

"Would you say the two of them got along well?"

"Sure. Not that I saw them together that much, but she seemed really into him, and Tom liked her, too, I'm sure. I mean, she was young, rich, beautiful, and she appeared to adore him. What's not to like?"

"Where were you the last time you saw Tom Chico and Talia Larrivee together?" Travis asked.

"At the ranch. At the little trailer that's on the property. It was a dump when we first saw it, but we've fixed it up some and it will do until we get the financing to build something better."

"Who is we?"

"Me and Courtney. She's my other partner in this. The one I intend to keep. Her late husband was my best friend when I was in the army. The two of us got pretty close before he was killed in Afghanistan and we used to talk about opening a youth ranch somewhere in the Colorado mountains. Mike was killed over there, but after I got home, I visited Courtney, to pay my respects, you know. She and I really clicked. When I told her about the dream Mike and I shared, she was all for it. By then Mike had been gone two years and I think she was really lonely. And I was lonely, too. To tell you the truth, I was half in love with her before I ever met her. Mike used to talk about her all the time and I felt like I knew her."

"Where is Ms. Baker now?" Shane asked.

"Oh, she's back at the ranch. She's trying to lie low, you know, and avoid her annoying ex sister-in-law."

Shane stiffened. "What has her sister-in-law done that's annoying?" he asked.

"Oh, don't get me wrong." He sat up straighter, both feet flat on the floor. "It's great that Mike's sister is so loyal, but Courtney is a grown woman. She can look after herself and make her own decisions. Instead, Lauren thinks she has to run Courtney's life. No one wants to live like that."

"What about Ms. Baker's daughter, Ashlyn?" Shane asked.

"Sounds like you've been doing your homework," Allerton said. "Ashlyn is fine. She's with her mother."

"Back to Tom Chico," Travis said.

Allerton faced the sheriff once more. "I don't know what else I can tell you. We agreed to go our separate ways, and he and Talia left. I haven't heard a peep out of him since."

"Do you know where they were headed?" Travis asked.

"Nope."

Travis tapped a pen on his desk blotter. "Where was Chico staying?"

"I don't know that, either." Allerton leaned forward, elbows on the table, hands clasped. "Look, we were in business together, but we weren't really friends or anything. My focus has really been getting this ranch up and running."

"How much money did Chico contribute to the ranch?" Travis asked.

Allerton leaned back again. "That was a point of contention between us, too. He promised to pitch in twenty thousand dollars, but I never saw the money. He never came out and admitted he'd lied about having it, but I think that's what happened. Then he promised to get the cash, and the next thing I knew, he showed up with Talia on his arm. I think he thought he'd charm her into giving him the money. And the way she looked at him, he might have done it, too." He grinned. The look was probably meant to be boyish and charming. "Why all the questions about Talia and Tom?" he asked. "Has he done something wrong?"

"Ms. Larrivee's body was discovered several days ago in a remote area of the county," Travis said. "Mr. Chico may have been one of the last people to see her alive."

Allerton's charm deserted him, leaving him gaping and a little shrunken. "She's dead?"

"Ms. Larrivee was murdered," Travis said. "Do you have any information about that?"

Allerton held up both hands. "I don't have any information. I swear if I did, I'd tell you." He shook his head, as if trying to clear it. "Do you think Tom killed her?"

Travis didn't answer.

"Of course you think that," Allerton said. "It's why you asked me if they got along, and if I knew Tom had been in prison."

"Do you want to change anything about your earlier answers?" Travis asked.

"No. I told the truth—Tom and Talia seemed to get along great." He slumped in the chair. "But if you ask me if I think Tom *could* kill someone—maybe. I mean, he had a record, and he had a temper. If they did have a fight, maybe he knocked her around and she fell and hit her head?" He looked at the sheriff, as if for confirmation.

"Ms. Larrivee was shot," Travis said. "Did Chico own a gun?"

Allerton hesitated. "Mr. Allerton, did Tom Chico have a gun?" Travis asked again.

"I won't get in trouble, will I? I mean, ex-cons aren't supposed to have firearms, are they? And Tom did have a gun. I knew about it, but I didn't say anything because, well, because I'm smart enough not to start an argument with a man with a bad temper who has a gun."

"What kind of gun was it?" Travis asked.

"I don't know," Allerton said.

"How long were you in the army, Mr. Allerton?" Travis asked.

"Four years. And I get what you're saying. I ought to be familiar with guns, but I never saw this one out of the holster and I made a point of not looking at it too closely. I didn't want to know about it, you understand?"

"Is there anything else you can tell us about Tom Chico?" Travis asked.

"No. Except I'm sorry I ever met him."

"We'll need your contact information, in case we have more questions," Travis said.

"Sure, sure." He rattled off a phone number. "That's my mobile. There are a lot of places up here that don't have good coverage, but if I don't answer, leave a message and I'll get back to you, I promise."

"Deputy Ellis will show you out," Travis said.

Allerton didn't say anything as he and Shane walked down the hall to the front lobby. Shane thought the man beside him, shorn of his bravado and clearly shaken, was very different from the Trey Allerton they had first met.

Travis was emerging from the interview room when Shane returned. "Let's go into my office," the sheriff said.

Shane followed Travis into his office, which scarcely had room for the sheriff's desk, a bookcase and two visitors' chairs. The desk itself was neat, with only a laptop and one small stack of files, along with a photograph of Travis's wife, Lacy, mountains in the background.

"Impressions?" Travis asked as he settled behind the desk.

"He seemed genuinely shaken by the news that Talia was murdered," Shane said. "And maybe even afraid."

"Afraid of what we might find out?" Travis asked.

"Or afraid of Tom Chico. He might be thinking he's lucky he parted company with the man when he did."

"Or he could be lying about everything."

"He could," Shane agreed.

"What do you think of the story that Courtney Baker is avoiding Lauren?"

"Maybe she is. Lauren says she isn't trying to run Courtney's life, and I've never seen the two of them together to judge the relationship. But Lauren was very close to Courtney. She did Courtney's taxes and she says that Courtney is very naive and had been sheltered most of her life."

"I think she'd have to be naive to recommend Tom Chico as a business partner," Travis said.

"That was one part of Allerton's story that didn't ring true for me," Shane said. "I think he told us that because he doesn't want us to know the true circumstances of how he met Chico."

"Allerton doesn't have a record," Trey said. "As Trey Allerton or Troy Allen. But that could mean he just hasn't been caught yet. When I talk to Colorado Springs PD, I'll ask about him, too. He was stationed in the area for a little while. Maybe he and Chico met up there."

"Do you think Courtney Baker and her daughter are safe with him?" Shane asked.

"We don't have any evidence that they aren't, but it

wouldn't hurt to make sure. Why don't you swing by that trailer again and have a word with her?"

"I will." Maybe he would be able to reassure Lauren that Courtney and Ashlyn were all right and relieve a little bit of her worry.

LAUREN MADE IT a point to visit the shops nearest the sheriff's department midmorning, hoping she could catch Shane when he left the office to do whatever he was assigned to do that day. She could have called and asked him what the sheriff had to say about her sighting of Courtney and Ashlyn on Sunday, but it was always easier to talk face-to-face.

She almost didn't say anything when Shane emerged onto the sidewalk, telling herself she should be patient and wait until he was off duty that evening. Then he would probably call and tell her what she wanted to know. But just then he turned and spotted her. His smile filled her with warmth.

A few long strides brought him to her. "This is a nice surprise," he said. "What are you doing down here?"

"Hoping to see you," she said. "Sitting at home, not knowing what is going on was driving me to distraction."

"We've had some developments," he said.

"Anything you can tell me?"

"Walk with me, and we'll talk."

They headed down the sidewalk, the sparse crowd this time of day making it easy to walk side by side. He matched his stride to hers. "Trey Allerton stopped by the sheriff's department this morning," he said. "He said he heard we'd been looking for him."

She caught her breath. "Was Courtney with him?"

"No. But he assured us she and Ashlyn are fine."

She pressed her lips together to keep from saying she

didn't trust anything Allerton said. But Shane already knew that. "What else did he have to say?" she asked.

"He was very cooperative and answered all our questions."

"He can be very charming. What did he have to say about Talia?"

"He said Tom Chico brought her to see the ranch and that she was very infatuated with him. Which is in line with what her best friend said about their relationship."

"Does Trey know where Tom is now?"

"He says he and Tom went their separate ways a week to ten days ago."

"Huh. Why is that?"

"He said it was because of Tom's temper, but I think the fact that Chico didn't come up with the money he was supposed to contribute to the youth ranch project might have had more to do with their parting of the ways."

"I told you Trey is more interested in money than anything else. It's why he went after Courtney."

"He said Courtney is the one who introduced him to Tom. I'm glad I ran into you, because I wanted to ask you about that."

She stopped and faced him. "You're kidding! How would Courtney know an ex-con like Tom Chico?"

"Allerton said Tom attended her church and she was trying to help him out. Does that sound like something she would do?"

"Yes and no. I mean, Courtney does have a soft heart and she does try to help people. But she does things like babysit for a mom who has a job interview. Or she volunteers at the food pantry. She doesn't take ex-cons under her wing. And I'm positive she never mentioned anything like that to me."

"Maybe she didn't tell you because she knew it would upset you."

Maybe so. It seemed Courtney had kept other things from her, like the extent of her feelings for Trey Allerton. "I don't really care about Tom Chico," she said. "Did Trey say where Courtney and Ashlyn are?"

"He said they were waiting for him at the ranch. Supposedly, he's fixed up the trailer for the three of them to live in."

They started walking again. "I was just at the trailer on Wednesday," she said. "I stopped by on my way to see Martin Kramer. That place was in no shape to live in. And it was deserted."

She half expected him to be upset that she hadn't mentioned this until now, or to lecture her about going back out to the ranch after she had had a man pull a gun on her the last time she visited, but he didn't. "I'm going out there this afternoon to check out his story," he said. "I'm hoping to talk to Courtney."

She grabbed his arm. "Let me go with you. Please. If Courtney and Ashlyn are there, I need to see them."

He hesitated.

"What is it?" she asked, reading the distress on his face. "What's wrong?"

"Allerton said Courtney doesn't want to see you. He said she's avoiding you."

She released her hold on him. "That's a lie."

"You said when you spotted her and Ashlyn yesterday she left before you could speak to her."

"She has no reason to avoid me."

"She knows you don't approve of her relationship with Allerton. For some people, that would be enough."

She shook her head. How could she convince him that Courtney wasn't like that? The two of them had never openly argued about Allerton, and, while Lauren had tried to gently voice her concerns about Allerton, she had always acknowledged this was Courtney's decision to make.

"I only want to make sure she's safe and happy," she said. "Take me with you to the ranch. If Courtney is there, you can see for yourself that she and I still have a good relationship."

"I'm going there to question a potential witness in a murder investigation," he said. "I can't take you with me."

"Fine. I'll drive out there myself." She fished her keys from her purse. "Now."

He reached for her hand. "No."

Tears stung her eyes. "Please," she said. "Take me with you. I won't interfere with your work. But this is the whole reason I came to Eagle Mountain."

He squeezed her hand. "All right. But you need to stay in the cruiser until I'm sure it's safe."

"Of course."

They said little on the way out, but the silence wasn't uncomfortable. The low hum of the police radio provided a background for their few exchanges about the passing scenery and yesterday's game, the mundane topics providing momentary relief from the stress of this errand and everything behind it.

Shane slowed the cruiser as they neared the entrance to the Russell Ranch. "I want to stop in here a minute and see if Mr. Russell has heard or seen anything of interest," he said.

Mr. Russell was standing in front of the house when they pulled up, watching a younger man trim the branches of a large cottonwood. He walked over to them as Shane stopped the cruiser. "Hello, Deputy." He leaned down to look in the driver's window, which Shane had lowered, and nodded to Lauren. "Ma'am. What can I do for you today?"

"I wanted to check and see if you knew if anything was going on at that property you leased to Trey Allerton," Shane said.

"My hired man says they've been doing a little work

around the place," Russell said. "They hired him to do a few odd jobs for them, but I don't know a lot else. They haven't bothered me any and I try to mind my own business."

"Have you spoken to anyone from there lately?" Shane asked.

"I haven't." The furrows on the old man's weathered face deepened. "They aren't mixed up in the murder of that girl, are they?"

"We don't know," Shane said. "We'd like to talk to Tom Chico, the older man, about that. If you see him around, will you call us? Don't try to talk to him yourself."

Russell nodded. "I will. I never liked the looks of that one. I should have listened to my instincts, I guess."

The door to the ranch house opened and a young woman with a long braid of dark hair stepped onto the porch. "Dad?" she called. "Is everything all right?"

"My daughter, Willow." Russell straightened. "Everything's fine," he said. He lowered his voice and spoke to Shane. "Don't say anything to her about all this. She worries me to death about living here by myself, even though it's not like I'm ever really alone, with all the hired help and all."

The woman watched from the porch, but made no move to join them. "I'll let you go now," Shane said. "We're going to drive on out to that property. Let us know if you see Tom Chico."

"I will," Russell said. "You take care, now."

"He's such a nice man," Lauren said as they pulled onto the road again. "I hope Trey and Tom leave him alone."

"I have a feeling he knows how to take care of himself," Shane said. "Most of these ranchers do."

The area around the battered trailer on Trey Allerton's lease looked as deserted as ever. Shane pulled into the drive, then turned so the cruiser was parallel to the trailer, pointed slightly toward the exit. He left the engine running and they both stared at the old mobile home. "Is this how it looked when you were here last week?" he asked.

"Yes. And the time before that. Although when I was here last, the door was locked."

He gave her a look that said he couldn't believe she tried to go inside, but said nothing. He cut the engine but left the keys in the ignition. "I'm going to go up and knock," he said.

She watched him as he approached the door, a big man with an easy, athletic gait. He undid the snap of his holster and kept close to the trailer as he climbed the steps, then knocked hard on the front door.

Lauren was sure the trailer was empty, but after only a few seconds, the door eased open. Courtney stood in the open doorway, lovely as ever. The relief that flooded Lauren propelled her out of the car before she even registered what was happening. Shane turned and said something to her, but she was too focused on Courtney to acknowledge anything else. "Thank God you're all right," she said.

"Hello, Lauren," Courtney said. She wasn't smiling, but she didn't look angry, either. Courtney took a step back and held the door open wider. "Deputy Ellis was telling me he has a few questions. You might as well come in."

Chapter Nineteen

Shane could have berated Lauren for ignoring his order to stay in the car, but he decided to save his breath. Once inside the trailer, the two women embraced, and the affection between them seemed genuine. He had a good view of Courtney's face from where he stood by the door, and he would have said the expression reflected there was relief, as if some burden had been lifted.

At last they parted, though Lauren kept hold of Courtney's hand. Then a little blonde girl, barefoot and wearing a pink sundress, long blond curls tumbled around a cherubic face, raced into the room and launched herself at Lauren, who scooped her up, laughing. "Ashlyn, look at you!" Lauren declared. She hugged the child, then looked at Ashlyn. "I heard she'd been sick and I was worried."

Courtney looked surprised. "How did you hear that?"

"It doesn't matter. She's okay now, right?"

"Of course. It was just a little stomach virus. She's loving it here in the country." She stroked her daughter's curls as she spoke. "My little wild child."

Lauren balanced Ashlyn on one hip and looked around the table. "How long have you been living here?" she asked.

"Just a couple of nights," Courtney said. "It's only temporary, until we can build a better place to live, but I don't need anything fancy. Come on and sit down."

The two women and the girl sat on a worn plaid sofa while Shane took the only other seat in the room—a metal folding chair. "Where were you before you moved here?" Lauren asked. "Why didn't you return my calls and texts?"

"We were moving around a lot," Courtney said. "I kept meaning to answer you, but we were so busy." She shrugged. "The time never seemed right." She turned to Shane. "What did you want to ask me about, Deputy?"

Hurt shone in Lauren's eyes. Shane forced his attention away from her. He had a job he needed to do. "Trey Allerton stopped by the sheriff's department this morning to answer some questions," Shane said.

"Yes, he mentioned he was going to do that," Courtney said.

Lauren looked around the room again. Someone had cleaned the place since Shane had last seen it. "Where is Trey now?" Lauren asked.

"He had some errands to run," Courtney said. "I don't expect him for a while."

"I'd like to ask you some questions, also," Shane said. "The sheriff's department is investigating the murder of Talia Larrivee, and you may have been one of the last people to see her alive."

"Ashlyn, honey, you need to go play in your room now," Courtney said.

"But I want to stay with Aunt Lauren!"

"I'll go play with you," Lauren said. She stood. "I want to see your room."

Shane sent her a grateful look, then turned back to Courtney. She was a small woman, with delicate features, porcelain skin and very clear blue eyes. "Lauren has been very worried about you," he said, after Lauren and Ashlyn had left the room.

"I know." Courtney tucked a strand of her long blond hair behind one ear. "Maybe it's the nurse in her. She feels she has to look after people. But Ashlyn and I are fine, really."

"You don't seem shocked to hear that Talia is dead," he said.

"Murder is a horrible thing," she said. "A shocking thing. But we heard the news a couple of days ago."

"How did you hear?" Shane asked.

"Trey brought home a newspaper with the story."

So Allerton had been faking his shock in the sheriff's office. "Was Talia comfortable with Tom? Was she afraid of him?"

"I don't think she was afraid of anything." She shook her head. "I didn't really like her. Is that horrible to say about someone who is dead now? But it's the truth. I thought she was too wild and vulgar. She was always kissing Tom and draping herself over him, and at least once when they were here, I'm sure they had both been drinking. It's not the kind of behavior I want Ashlyn to see. I told Trey so and he promised to speak to them."

Laughter sounded from down the hall. Courtney looked in that direction and smiled. "Ashlyn has really missed her aunt," she said. "Thank you for bringing Lauren here today."

"Trey Allerton said you've been avoiding Lauren—that you resent the way she's interfered in your life."

Pain flickered in her blue eyes. "Trey resents what he sees as Lauren's interference. I know Lauren is just concerned for my safety."

"But you do seem to have been avoiding her. She said you saw her at the playscape yesterday and you left before she could reach you. And I have to think if you'd really wanted to return her texts or calls, you'd have found the time to do so."

She smoothed her hands down her thighs. "Sometimes

it is easier to stay away than to deal with the conflict. I'm not proud of that, but it's true."

"Conflict with Lauren?"

"And with Trey. He would rather I didn't see her."

"Is he trying to keep you from your family and friends?" Shane asked. That kind of controlling behavior could be a sign of an abusive relationship.

"Of course not," she said. "He just says—and I agree— that while we're involved in getting this project off the ground, we don't need distractions. And I know Lauren is disappointed in me. I hate that, so I guess I'm being a coward and trying to avoid confrontation, with her and with Trey." She shrugged. "It's not an ideal situation, but Ashlyn and I are fine, I promise. And when this ranch opens for the children, it will all be worth it."

"Where were you between the time you left the Ranch Motel and moving here?" he asked. She had blown off Lauren with a vague answer, but he wouldn't let her get away with that with him.

"We stayed in a rental cabin outside of Telluride for a week," she said, "then a couple of different motel rooms in Rico and Dolores. We were waiting for this place to be ready." She looked around the trailer. "I know to a lot of people this seems like a step down from where we used to live, but material things aren't important to me. Making this ranch a reality and helping those children is."

"Tell me about the ranch," Shane said. He had heard Lauren's and Allerton's versions of the story, but he was curious to know Courtney's view of the project.

"It's an idea Trey and my late husband, Mike, came up with over in Afghanistan," she said. "Planning it was a way to distract themselves from everything over there. It will be a beautiful retreat in the mountains where children from the inner city or those who have suffered trauma can come and relax and spend time in nature. We'll have horses and a pond where they can fish, trails they can hike and activities like archery and climbing. We'll have trained counsellors who can help the children. It's going to be really beautiful."

Her expression grew dreamy as she spoke, as if she was no longer seeing the dingy trailer but the camp that was to be. "It takes a lot of money to build something like that," he said.

She shrugged. "I have a lot of money. Or rather, it was Mike's money. I want to use it to create something he would be proud of."

"My understanding is much of that money is in a trust," Shane said.

She sighed. "Yes. Which makes it difficult. But Trey is working hard to get the additional funds we need."

"What is he doing to get the money?" Shane asked.

"You'd have to ask him. I'm not involved in that part of it."

"You sent a text to Lauren that upset her," Shane said. "She said it was a message for help because you referred to your late husband as Michael and yourself as Court— names you don't normally use."

Her expression clouded. "I never should have sent that message," she said. "I was upset that day."

"What were you upset about?"

She cupped her hands around her knees. "Tom was here, and he and Trey were arguing. I was afraid. But then he left and things got better."

"When did Tom leave?"

She pursed her lips. "A week ago? A little more? He and Trey had a big fight, about money, I think. Tom was supposed to contribute money to the project and he didn't."

"Was Talia Larrivee with Tom that day?"

"Yes. She was always with Tom the last week or so that he was here."

Shane took a card from his pocket and passed it to her. "If you ever need anything, anything at all, call me."

She looked at the card, then slipped it into her pocket. "That's very kind of you, but I'm sure it won't be necessary." She met his gaze with a steady look of her own. "Lauren thinks I'm fragile and naive because that's the woman Mike married. But I've been on my own for a while now—when Mike was deployed, and after he died. I've grown up a lot. I still tend to believe the best in people, but that's not the same as being ignorant of how badly they can behave." She stood. "I'm sure you have things to do, so let's go get Lauren."

Lauren and Ashlyn were seated on the floor of the first small room on the left side of the hallway, a collection of dolls with brightly colored hair spread out between them. Lauren was braiding the hair of a doll with pink hair, while Ashlyn combed the purple mane of another. "It's time for Aunt Lauren to go now," Courtney said. "You need to say goodbye."

"But I don't want her to go," Ashlyn said.

Lauren looked from Shane to Courtney, then stood. "I'll come back and play with you again soon," she said. "If that's all right with your mother."

"Of course," Courtney said. "We could even come see you."

"I hope you will come see me." Lauren put both hands on Courtney's shoulders. "You're really okay out here by yourself?" she asked.

Courtney nodded. "I'm fine. I was upset when Tom was here. I was telling Deputy Ellis that's why I sent that weird text message. But everything is fine now. I know Trey isn't your favorite person, but he and I are working hard to make this youth ranch a reality." She smiled, an expression that transformed her face from merely pretty to gorgeous. "I haven't been this excited about anything in a long time. This is going to be something that would really make Mike proud. We're going to name it after him, did I tell you that?"

Lauren shook her head. Unlike her sister-in-law, she looked stricken. She swallowed hard and forced a smile that didn't reach her eyes. "Call me if you need anything," she said. "And stay in touch."

"I will. It's hard, since cell service is so lousy up here. But I'll do my best." She patted Lauren's shoulder. "And don't worry. I really am fine."

Lauren remained silent as they returned to the car. At the road, Shane headed right. "I want to revisit the crime scene," he said. "Will you be all right waiting in the car?"

She nodded. He searched for something to say that might comfort her. "Courtney looked good. She seems to know what she's doing."

"It still worries me, her and Ashlyn up here alone with that man. And I hate that Trey has made her believe that this ranch is something Mike wanted." She drew a deep breath and sat up straighter. "But she's a grown woman. She has the right to make her own decisions. And I guess I do feel better, knowing Tom Chico isn't around anymore. At least Trey made the right decision, getting rid of him."

"They seem very serious about this ranch idea."

"Courtney is serious. I'm still suspicious of Trey, but I guess I'll just have to wait and see."

He wanted to ask her if she intended to return to Denver now that she had spoken to Courtney and seen for herself that she and Ashlyn were okay. His hands tightened on the steering wheel. He wasn't ready to hear her answer. Sure, people could have long-distance relationships, and Denver was only a six-hour drive away, but it wouldn't be the same as having her here all the time, spending every night together, as they had fallen into the habit of doing.

Yellow crime scene tape fluttered from a bush, marking

the trail up to the ruined cabin where Talia's body had been found. Shane parked the cruiser in the shade of a gnarled pinion, lowered the windows and shut off the engine. "It will take a while to hike there and back," he said.

"I'll be fine." She looked out the window. "If you didn't know what had happened up here, this would be a very peaceful spot." She glanced back at him. "Are you looking for something in particular?"

He shook his head. "I just want to see it again, and think about how it may have played out. Refresh the details in my mind." It probably wouldn't help them find Tom Chico, but he thought it might help him cement his focus on solving the crime. All of the drama with Allerton and Courtney, and even Lauren, was outside of that. He needed to think about Talia, and Tom, who was looking more and more like the murderer.

AFTER SHANE HAD disappeared from sight down the trail, Lauren gazed out at the silent landscape and tried to let the peace of the scenery fill her. She had seen Courtney and Ashlyn. They were both safe and seemingly content with the new life they had chosen. She had done what she came to Eagle Mountain to accomplish, so she should be happy.

But today had felt like another loss in the string of losses since Mike had died. It was good to see Courtney not as weighed down with grief as she had been. The youth ranch project had given her a new focus in life. She had a new strength Lauren hadn't seen before.

But there had been a new distance between her and Lauren also. Courtney had a different life now, and the two women would never be as connected as they once were. Lauren would learn to accept this, but for now she allowed herself to mourn a little.

"I did what I could, Mike," she whispered. "I looked

after her as long as she needed me to, but I think she's ready to move on." Lauren would have to move on, too.

It was warm in the car, even in the shade. She pushed open the door and let the breeze wash over her, then stood and stretched. She'd been in Eagle Mountain two weeks and hadn't ventured very far into these beautiful mountains. She should ask Shane to take her hiking. Not here, but some other trail.

Something stirred behind her and she turned, expecting to see Shane heading up the trail toward her. Instead, an older man stood beside the sheriff's department cruiser— dark haired, olive complected, with a network of black tattoos up both arms and a jagged fresh cut across his right cheek. Tom Chico.

She stood a step back. "What do you want?" she asked.

His gaze slid over her, then across the cruiser and back. Before she could react, he strode forward and seized her by the arm. "Right now, I want you."

AN HOUR AFTER leaving Lauren, Shane completed his review of the crime scene and headed back toward the trailhead at a brisk walk. He was almost to the parking area when he stopped, struck by the stillness around him. The passenger door of his cruiser stood open, and from here the vehicle appeared empty. "Lauren!" he called.

No answer.

Then he was running to the empty cruiser. "Lauren!" he called again, looking around him. Heart pounding, he looked first one way, then the other, for any sign of her. Had she slipped into the underbrush to relieve herself? Had she decided to walk back down the road to visit Courtney again?

He shook his head. The trailer where Courtney and Ashlyn lived was several miles from here. And if Lauren had gone to relieve herself, she wouldn't have gone so far that she couldn't hear him calling her.

Think! he told himself. *Think like a cop.*

He studied the area around the car, but the red gravel revealed no footprints or signs of a struggle. The surface was too hard to show the imprints of tires. Finally he gave up. He wasn't getting anywhere with this scrutiny. He tried to key the radio but was rewarded only with static. The department's repeater system was unreliable, and the county budget had yet to find funds to add more towers. He'd have to drive until he got a signal, then call for help.

He drove as fast as he dared on the rough road, sliding around turns, gravel flying up behind him. He turned in at the entrance to the Full Moon Mine. Martin Kramer was sifting through a mound of rock by his shack and looked up when Shane's cruiser skidded to a halt beside him. "I'm looking for Lauren Baker, the woman who visited you the other day, when someone fired on the two of you," Shane said, the words coming out in a rush.

"I haven't seen her," Kramer said.

"Have you seen anyone else today?" Shane asked. "Anyone at all?"

"No. For once it's been quiet around here."

"If you see Lauren, go to a neighbor's and call 911," he said. Not waiting for an answer, he left.

He went on to the trailer. Courtney came out to meet him. "Lauren is missing," he told her. "I left her in the car while I checked on the crime scene up at the Sanford Mine, and when I returned, she was gone. Have you seen her or heard from her?"

"No." Courtney shook her head, her fair skin even paler. "I don't understand. Do you think she walked away?"

"Do you think she would do that?"

"No." Another shake of the head.

"I'm worried someone took her." He got back in the cruiser. "If you see or hear from her, call me."

No one was at the Olsens' yurt. Shane called for Lauren and looked for any sign she had been there but came up empty.

At last Shane turned in at the Russell Ranch. When Willow Russell answered the front door, Shane asked, "Do you have a landline phone? Can I use it?"

"Of course." She opened the door wider to let him in.

"What's wrong?" Samuel Russell asked when Shane followed Willow into the living room. Sam sat in a recliner, a small terrier on his lap.

Shane didn't answer but dialed the sheriff's direct number. When Travis answered, Shane had to force the words out. "Lauren is missing," he said. "We were up at the crime scene. I left her alone for a few moments, and when I came back, she was gone."

He had left her and she was gone. He prayed that knowledge didn't haunt him for the rest of his life.

Tom Chico smelled like sweat and woodsmoke. The bandana he had shoved into Lauren's mouth when she started to scream tasted like dirt. She couldn't think about it or she'd gag. His fingers dug into her arm as he dragged her alongside him, hurting her. She believed he wanted to hurt her. Is this what Talia had felt in the moments before he shot her?

She pushed that thought away, too. She couldn't give in to terror. She needed to pay attention to her surroundings, to figure out where he was taking her. But nothing in this landscape looked familiar. They moved through groves of evergreen trees, over red and gray rock, with occasional glimpses of blue sky and green valleys. They climbed for a while, breathing hard in the high altitude, and once they crossed a small stream, the water red-orange from minerals in the soil. They weren't following any trail that she could discern, but he seemed to know where he was going. Whenever she could, she made a point of brushing against trees or dragging her feet in the dirt, hoping to provide a trail others could follow.

She didn't know how long they had been walking before he stopped, but she thought it was over an hour. He shoved her ahead of him into a thicket of deep brush. She tried to shield her face with her hands, but thorns raked across her, tearing her flesh and catching at her clothing.

And then she was free of the underbrush, standing in a small circular clearing with a rock firepit in the center and a green nylon dome tent erected at one side.

Tom pulled the bandana from her mouth. "Scream all you want," he said. "No one will hear you out here."

"What do you want with me?" she asked, afraid of the answer but needing to know.

"I need you to get past the cops that are looking for me." He sat on the ground in front of the tent and motioned for her to do the same. "You might as well take a load off," he said. "I imagine it will take a while for them to find us."

She looked past him at the wall of underbrush around them. Could she break through there and run back the way they came? "If you try to run, I'll shoot you," he said, and opened his jacket to show a pistol in a holster at his belt. "Better to wait."

"Wait for what?" She sat as far from him as she could get in the small clearing, her back against the trunk of a tree.

"That cop you were with and his friends will track us here eventually," he said. "Then we'll make a deal."

She wanted to keep him talking. As long as he was talking, he wasn't doing something to hurt her. "How did you get way out here?" she asked. "I never saw a car."

"I got as far as I could, then hit a rock and tore a hole in the oil pan. I shoved the wreck over a cliff so no one would spot it and I made it back here on foot." He looked around. "I like to camp, figured I would hole up here awhile, then maybe I'd run off that old miner up the road and move into his place. Then I saw you and came up with a different plan."

"What happened to Talia?" she asked. She braced herself, half expecting the question to enrage him.

"Talia did something stupid," he said, his voice as calm as if he had said that Talia had bought grapes at the grocery store. "She thought her money protected her. Sometimes it does, but not this time."

"I thought you and Trey Allerton were partners. You were going to open a youth ranch together."

"Right. It was a good cover story, anyway. Trey told me we'd make a ton of money with that scam, but he wasn't coming across with the cash, so I moved on." He shrugged. "He and that woman he's with—Courtney—are both dumb, but Trey is dangerous because he thinks he's smart."

"Trey told the sheriff that Courtney introduced the two of you—that you went to her church."

He smirked. "I've known Trey a long time. Way before she showed up. But he probably thinks that story sounds better. He's a born con artist. He's good at figuring out what people want to hear and giving it to them."

This confirmation of her worst fears about Trey made her stomach hurt. "What kind of deal are you hoping to make with the sheriff?" she asked.

"I guess we'll find out, won't we?" He grinned, a look that sent ice through her. It was the look of a man who saw her not as a person but as a commodity he could bargain with—and one he could discard without a second thought if she was no longer useful to him.

She couldn't give in to fear. Shane would be looking for her. When he got back to the cruiser and she wasn't there, he would start a search. She and Tom were on foot, just the two of them. Shane would have the whole sheriff's department—the whole town—helping to look for her.

All she had to do was stay alive long enough for him to find her.

Chapter Twenty

Shane reminded himself that as much as he wanted to charge off across the mountains in search of Lauren, floundering around with no idea of what direction to take could destroy potential evidence, and even endanger his own life or Lauren's. So he forced himself to wait the long forty-five minutes it took for Travis and Gage Walker to arrive at the trailhead.

Shane went over everything again—how he had visited the crime scene and found no new insight, then returned to the cruiser, where he had left Lauren. "The passenger door was open and she was gone," he said. "No one else was around. Lauren didn't answer my calls." The sheriff didn't ask why Shane had brought a civilian with him to question a witness, or berate him for doing so. "Let's get a search dog up here," he said. "Gage, see if Lorna Munroe from Search and Rescue is available. If we can get an idea which direction Lauren headed from here, we can focus our search better."

Other deputies arrived, and they spent the next hour combing the area immediately around the parking lot. They found an empty water bottle, a shoelace, a candy wrapper and a strip of survey ribbon—nothing connected to Lauren, but it was all dutifully catalogued. Gage returned to report that Lorna Munroe and her search dog, Daisy, were on their way.

"What do you think happened?" Gage asked, though Shane wasn't sure if the question was addressed to him or the sheriff.

"Random abductions happen," Travis said. "But given the remote location, that seems unlikely."

"Who would be hanging around a crime scene?" Gage asked.

"The murderer." Shane hadn't meant to say the word out loud, but no one reacted in shock or tried to deny the possibility. "Tom Chico has to know we're looking for him," Shane continued. "He's our chief suspect for the murder of Talia Larrivee. He may have murdered Samantha Morrison." He gritted his teeth, unable to carry the thought any further. If a man like that had Lauren…

Travis clamped a hand on his shoulder. "Do you want to go back to town?" he asked.

"No!" He didn't want to leave here until Lauren was found.

"Then get with Dwight and climb that peak over there and see if you can make out anything that will help us." He pointed to a high point a half mile away.

It was busy work. Something to keep Shane's body, if not his mind, occupied. But he appreciated it and set out with Dwight to climb the peak, where they had a view of the surrounding landscape, and realized how difficult it was to make out anything in the dense groves of trees and scattered boulders.

When they returned over an hour later, more cars filled the lot. "When Lorna and her dog return from their survey of the area, we'll start the search," Travis said. "She should be able to give us an idea of the best direction to cover. Groups of four, everyone armed and alert. No civilians this first pass, since we don't know what we're going to find.

Shane, you come with me, Dwight and Jamie. Gage, stay here to coordinate the scene."

They turned at the sound of someone approaching. A large brown dog with long legs and drooping ears burst from the woods and trotted toward them, tongue lolling. A petite middle-aged woman with short-cropped blond hair followed soon after, trailed by Deputy Wes Landry. "There's a good strong trail through there," she said, indicating a northeasterly direction. "Daisy isn't having any trouble following it. It's so good I made her turn around so we could get you. I didn't want to come up on trouble by myself."

"Are you okay leading us in, Lorna?" Travis asked. "We don't know what we're going to find here. I'll ask you to back off if there's any hint of trouble, but I can't guarantee you won't get involved if it gets ugly."

"I'm trained for this kind of thing," she said. She looked over her shoulder, in the direction she had just come. "It was a good trail. I think we can find her."

They set off, Lorna and her dog in front with the sheriff, Shane bringing up the rear. They moved quickly, the dog running ahead, then stopping to wait for them. "Can you tell if she's following one or two people?" Dwight asked.

"No way to tell," Lorna said. "She's been told to track Lauren, so she's homing in on the scent on that purse and water bottle Travis showed us. But if there's someone with her, the dog may follow that scent, too, especially if it's stronger."

"But you're sure she's still following Lauren's scent?" Travis asked.

"She's an experienced tracking dog," Lorna said. "She might lose a weak scent, but I've never known her to follow a false trail."

"Hey, I've got something here," Jamie called. They all

turned toward her, and she pointed to a bush beside the trail. "There's a thread of blue fabric here."

Shane moved in beside her and stared at the thread caught on a twig. "Lauren is wearing a shirt that color," he said.

"Flag it," Travis said. "If we need to, we can come back to it later."

They continued following the dog, in no way quiet or stealthy. Jamie dropped back to walk nearer Shane. "The sheriff must be expecting trouble, to bring us all along," she said.

"I was thinking the same thing," Shane said.

"If someone did take Lauren, it was probably only one person," she said. "We'll have the advantage in numbers."

After about an hour of walking, Daisy stopped and sat. "What's she doing?" Dwight asked.

"She's gone as far as she can go," Lorna said. She took a treat from the pouch at her waist and fed it to the dog.

Travis looked around at the thick underbrush. "Do you mean she's lost the scent?"

"She hasn't lost it," Lorna said. "This is as far as she can go." She brushed one hand across the greenery in front of them. "These wild roses are too thick for her to get through."

"I think someone has been through them." Jamie indicated a broken branch. "Not too long ago, either."

Then a woman's scream rent the air, high and long, and terrifying.

ONE MOMENT, LAUREN was seated on the ground, trying not to think about the rock digging into her backside and wondering how Tom would take it if she got up and walked around, the next he had grabbed her, jerked her to her feet and pressed a knife to her throat. "Scream!" he commanded.

Stunned, she didn't comply right away. He pressed the tip of the knife into her flesh, and startled, she yelped.

"You'll have to do better than that." He pressed the knife deeper. A hot sting, then a wet trickle down the side of her neck.

She screamed, loud and long until her throat was raw. There was a commotion on the other side of the bushes, then they split apart and Shane, followed by the sheriff and two other officers, stepped into the clearing.

The knife bit again, and Tom's arm around her tightened until she could scarcely breathe. "Don't come any closer," he said. "I swear I'll cut her."

Through a film of tears, Lauren watched Shane. She had never seen a man look so angry.

"Let her go, Tom," the sheriff said. "We'll talk about this."

"I'll do the talking," Tom said.

"I'm listening," Travis said.

"All of you, stand out here where I can see you." Tom shifted and drew the gun.

Lauren watched him out of the corners of her eyes. Her knees had turned to jelly and she fought to keep her breathing even. *You have to be strong*, she told herself. *If you have a chance to get away, you can't blow it.*

The deputies did as he asked, arranging themselves on either side of the sheriff in a line.

"Throw out your weapons. There, by the fire." Tom gestured with the gun.

Slowly, with careful movements, each officer removed his or her gun from the holster and slid it toward the firepit. Lauren tried not to look at Shane, but her gaze kept drifting back to him. Every time, she found his eyes fixed on her. That steady look comforted her, even as she worried it made him more vulnerable. What if Tom did something to hurt him and Shane didn't see the threat because he was focused on her?

"I'm going to tell you what I want, then you're going to leave here and get it for me," Tom said. "She—" he shook Lauren "—stays here until I get everything. And I mean everything."

Travis remained silent, and his face betrayed nothing, his jaw set, eyes hard.

"I want a helicopter up here, twenty thousand dollars in unmarked bills, in a backpack," Tom said. "I want the chopper to take me to Ciudad Juárez."

"Is that it?" Travis asked after a long moment of silence.

"I can make it more complicated if you like," Tom said.

"Did you kill Talia Larrivee?" Travis asked.

"I'm not answering any questions." Tom tightened his hold on Lauren again. "Get out of here now. You've got work to do."

"Let her go." Shane took a step forward. "I'll stay instead."

"The star pitcher," Tom said. "What am I going to do with you?" He shook his head. "Get out of here."

When they didn't move, he raised the pistol—not aimed at Lauren, but at Shane, an easy target standing in front of the others. Lauren's vision blurred as she imagined a bullet slamming into Shane. She screamed and doubled over. The gun fired, the report echoing around them. More shots were fired and in the chaos someone shouted for her to get down.

She didn't need the reminder. She was on her stomach, crawling toward the edge of the clearing. And then Shane was with her, his body covering hers even as the clearing around them fell silent.

"I'm okay," she reassured him. "Please tell me you're okay, too."

"I'm fine." He pulled her tight against him, against the

hard wall of his ballistics vest. She stared at him, examining his face to make sure he was telling the truth.

"He was aiming right at you," she said.

"And you threw off his aim when you ducked. It was enough time for me to dive to the ground."

She looked over his shoulder, at Tom Chico lying on the ground, blood pooling around him. "Is he dead?" she asked.

"I think so, yeah." He lifted her chin and frowned. "You're bleeding where he cut you."

She touched her hand to the sticky warmth along the side of her neck. "It's not very deep," she said. "I'll be okay." Though it might be a while before she could close her eyes and not feel the terror she had felt with that knife pressed to her throat.

Shane helped her to her feet but kept a tight hold on her as they moved toward the sheriff, who stood to one side surveying the camp. "We know he was camping out in another part of the county for a while," he said. "He must have moved here sometime after that."

"He said he busted the oil pan on his car when he hit a rock and he pushed the wrecked vehicle over a cliff," Lauren said. "He said he hiked in from there. He said something about staying here until he could run Martin Kramer off his claim, but then he saw me and came up with a different plan."

Voices rose behind them, then the underbrush parted and Gage and the rest of the force pushed in, a slight woman with a dog bringing up the rear. "I ran all the way back to the parking area," she told Travis. "I've never run so fast in my life."

The sheriff put his arm around the woman's shoulder and hugged her. "You deserve a medal, Lorna," he said. "Thanks for everything."

"Is everyone okay?" Lorna looked around the clear

ing, then her gaze rested on Tom Chico and her face lost most of its color.

"You go on back with Shane and Lauren," Travis said, turning her away. "I'll take care of things here."

No one said much of anything until they were back at the parking area. Lorna had regained her color by then and reassured them she was okay to drive herself home. She loaded the dog into her SUV and set out.

"I should take you to the hospital," Shane said.

Lauren bent and examined her neck in the side mirror of his cruiser. "I don't need a hospital," she said. "I can clean and dress this myself at home."

"I guess you could." He looked dazed still, so she put her arms around him and hugged him close. "The four of you saved my life," she said. "But I knew you'd come for me. I'm just glad you weren't hurt."

"I've never felt as terrible as I did when I had to stand there and watch him cut you," he said. "Enraged and helpless and..."

"Shhh." She pressed the tips of her fingers to her mouth. "It's okay. It's all over now."

"It's not over." He pulled back, just far enough to meet her gaze. "I would have done anything to save you in that moment. That's how much you've come to mean to me. I love you, Lauren."

Something expanded in her chest, something that felt almost too big to contain. "I love you, too," she said.

"Are you going back to Denver?" he asked. "I know your job and your home and probably your whole life is here, so it's okay if you do, as long as I can come with you."

"I think my life is here now," she said. "You're here, but so are Courtney and Ashlyn. They're the only family I have left, so I'd like to stay close, just in case they need me."

"What about your job?"

"The clinic here offered me a job, remember? And Eagle Mountain is really growing on me. I think I'm going to like it here."

"Enough to get married?" He held up a hand. "I'm not trying to rush you, but when you're ready, I'd really like us to be husband and wife."

It wasn't a grand romantic declaration or a poetic promise, but the sincerity of his plea, and his concern for her feelings, melted her heart. "Yes, I'll marry you," she said, and kissed him with all the passion the moment called for. She'd made mistakes before, falling too hard and fast. But this time, she'd gotten it right. When she'd looked into Shane's eyes in Tom Chico's camp, her heart had known this was the man for her. And she was the right woman for him.

* * * * *

COMING SOON!

We really hope you enjoyed reading this book.
If you're looking for more romance, be sure to
head to the shops when new books are
available on

Thursday 6th
January

To see which titles are coming soon, please visit
millsandboon.co.uk/nextmonth

MILLS & BOON

THE HEART OF ROMANCE

A ROMANCE FOR EVERY READER

MODERN

Prepare to be swept off your feet by sophisticated, sexy and seductive heroes, in some of the world's most glamourous and roman locations, where power and passion collide.

HISTORICAL

Escape with historical heroes from time gone by. Whether your passio for wicked Regency Rakes, muscled Vikings or rugged Highlanders, a the romance of the past.

MEDICAL

Set your pulse racing with dedicated, delectable doctors in the high-pr sure world of medicine, where emotions run high and passion, comfo love are the best medicine.

True Love

Celebrate true love with tender stories of heartfelt romance, from the rush of falling in love to the joy a new baby can bring, and a focus o emotional heart of a relationship.

Desire

Indulge in secrets and scandal, intense drama and plenty of sizzling h action with powerful and passionate heroes who have it all: wealth, st good looks…everything but the right woman.

HEROES

Experience all the excitement of a gripping thriller, with an intense mance at its heart. Resourceful, true-to-life women and strong, fearle face danger and desire - a killer combination!

To see which titles are coming soon, please visit
millsandboon.co.uk/nextmonth

LET'S TALK
Romance

For exclusive extracts, competitions
and special offers, find us online:

JOIN THE
MILLS & BOON
BOOKCLUB

* **FREE** delivery direct to your door

* **EXCLUSIVE** offers every month

* **EXCITING** rewards programme

50% OFF
YOUR FIRST
PARCEL

Join today at
Millsandboon.co.uk/Bookclub

JOIN US ON SOCIAL MEDIA!

Stay up to date with our latest releases, author news and gossip, special offers and discounts, and all the behind-the-scenes action from Mills & Boon...

 millsandboon

 millsandboonuk

 millsandboon

It might just be true love...

MILLS & BOON

Desire

Indulge in secrets and scandal, intense drama and plenty of sizzling hot action with powerful and passionate heroes who have it all: wealth, status, good looks…everything but the right woman.

MILLS & BOON
MEDICAL
Pulse-Racing Passion

Set your pulse racing with dedicated, delectable doctors in the high-pressure world of medicine, where emotions run high and passion, comfort and love are the best medicine.

MILLS & BOON
True Love
Romance from the Heart

Celebrate true love with tender stories of heartfelt romance, from the rush of falling in love to the joy a new baby can bring, and a focus on the emotional heart of a relationship.